ALSO BY DAVID RABE

FICTION

A Primitive Heart

Recital of the Dog

PLAYS

Cosmologies

The Black Monk
(based on a Chekhov story)

The Dog Problem

A Question of Mercy
(based on the diary of Richard Selzer)

Those the River Keeps

Hurlyburly

Goose and Tomtom

In the Boom Boom Room

THE VIETNAM PLAYS

Streamers

The Orphan

Sticks and Bones

The Basic Training of Pavlo Hummel

DINOSAURS
ON THE ROOF

A NOVEL

DAVID RABE

Simon & Schuster

New York   London   Toronto   Sydney

Simon & Schuster
1230 Avenue of the Americas
New York, NY 10020

First Simon & Schuster hardcover edition June 2008

SIMON & SCHUSTER and colophon are registered trademarks of Simon & Schuster, Inc.

For information about special discounts for bulk purchases, please contact Simon & Schuster Special Sales at 1-800-456-6798 or business@simonandschuster.com.

Designed by Davina Mock-Maniscalco

Manufactured in the United States of America

1   3   5   7   9   10   8   6   4   2

Library of Congress Cataloging-in-Publication Data

Rabe, David.
Dinosaurs on the roof / David Rabe.
p.   cm.
1. Older women—Fiction.   2. Rapture (Christian eschatology)—
Fiction.   3. Psychological fiction.   I. Title.
PS3568.A23D56   2008
813'.54—dc22   2008015376

ISBN-13: 978-1-4165-6405-8
ISBN-10:   1-4165-6405-5

For
my mom, Ruth.

Also
Rita, Marge, Sue,
Gladys, Louella, Eleanor,
Emma, Mayme Irma,
Lenae, Esther,
Dorrie,
Ida.

DINOSAURS
ON THE ROOF

1

As Janet crested the hill, her breath was smooth, her stride easy. Sweat streaked her brow, beading and falling. There was an unfamiliar car parked at the curb near where she lived, but she wasn't expecting anyone, and her landlords, the Luckritzes, always had relatives and friends coming and going.

Since she'd increased her distance from three to four miles today, exhaustion might have dragged at her, but the striving had turned into a gleam in her blood that pushed her to sail on. The swish of her ponytail threaded out the back of her baseball cap brushed her shoulders. Her long legs stretched and coiled, promising a future of runs, always longer, always farther. Even races. Miles of concrete flowing under her. Miles of dirt. Marathons, even. Throngs of runners in silky shorts, their lungs gasping. She would float along in a cloud of wild breathing.

A shift in the late-afternoon light turned the ragged old four-door into a shimmering green bubble. She was pretty sure it was a Chevy, and eighties. Not that she knew cars that well. And then nudging away ringlets of sweaty hair, she saw gray duct tape crisscrossing rusted scars on both the front and rear fenders and knew who was inside. Her gaze vaulted the brown siding and the shingled rooftop ahead to a fissure in the autumn colors of the tree-packed hills. Scattered houses rode the summit, and somewhere miles below, the banks of the Mississippi brought the town to an end. Across that gray slab of water rose the Wisconsin hills.

Her attempt to see into the car met only shadows thrown by a nearby oak. While telling herself to jog past, maybe gallop on into the woods, she slowed and then stalled. The window started jerking down in spasms, and the face that pushed out was that of Bernice Doorley, a lifelong friend of Janet's mother, Isabel. Caught upon the hook of the old woman's gaze, Janet felt the rewards of the run leave her. The last time she'd seen Bernice was at her mother's funeral over a year ago.

"How do," said Bernice.

"Straying a little far from home, aren't you?" Janet asked.

"Not so far. Speedometer says here I went just a little more than six miles."

"I ran about that far."

"Did you now? Look at you. All out of breath. Who you runnin' from?"

"Just running, Bernice."

"What's that called again?"

"Just 'running,' as far as I know."

"No, no, it's got some other name so it don't sound ordinary, but somehow there's more to it."

"Exercise."

"Nope."

"Jogging."

"That's the one." With a sly little smile, she pushed the door open. "Get in. Have a little rest."

Janet looked away and then back but gave no indication she would enter the car. "What brings you to my neck of the woods?"

"Lookin' for you. Isn't that clear?"

"Not really."

"Get in. I need to ask a sort of favor, and I can make it snappy."

Janet smiled but took a backward step, as if something she would be smart to avoid waited inside the car. "Listen, do you know what? We can talk, but I should take a shower. You can come up." Her attempted display of welcome made her feel like a puppet with fingers worming their way up inside her to make her act in ways she didn't mean. Why can't they just leave me alone? she thought. Bernice appeared ready to scowl, her eyes vaguely suspicious, behind the thick lenses of her glasses in clear plastic frames. "Listen," Janet explained. "What I meant was we should go inside. I need to get something to drink and jump in the shower before I catch cold."

"You want me to come inside?"

"Yeah." That was her deal, all right. Polite, compliant, and fake. A cozy little chat with Bernice was the last thing she wanted.

"Oh well, you should say what you mean, then, Janet."

"I thought I did."

"Not as far as I could tell."

Emerging into the day, Bernice made a sturdy impression, always had. Medium height and slightly overweight, she was broad across the back and hips. Her white hair was tightly curled from a recent permanent, and a white knit scarf cradled her neck. She'd even gone to the trouble of pink lipstick, eyeliner, and rouge for reasons Janet doubted had to do with her visit here. Her pleated sage green skirt and flannel jacket, hip-length and gray, seemed to have come straight from the cleaners. All dolled up for something, Bernice still looked built for lugging heavy objects, a workhorse through and through. They'd made an odd pair, her mother and Bernice. Isabel Cawley had been long-limbed and delicate, maybe even rarefied as the years went on, though there was nothing fragile about either one of them when the time came to drive a remark clear to the bone.

Bernice smiled just then, and Janet turned and looked off. The west appeared to have exploded, the aftermath radiant.

"You sure are a tall drink of water," said Bernice behind her, making it sound like a fault.

"I guess." She set off, chuckling, as if being teased were her favorite thing. It was true, though. She was like her mother, both of them angular and alluring, not model-thin, but a length boys hungered to contend with, her auburn hair a flash of genetic fire streaking away from her blond mother to her runaway father.

She led the way, circling the garage, above which her apartment extended off the house, to where she had hidden a key under a brick near the base of the stairs. As soon as Bernice rounded the corner, Janet waved and went up and let herself in. Chugging Gatorade from the fridge, she set about filling the kettle with water to boil. She was dumping Oreo cookies on a plate when Bernice strode in, set her big beige handbag on the kitchen table, and stood considering what she could see of Janet's apartment. The more or less rectangular space was divided into a kitchen and living room by copper linoleum squares in one area and reddish-brown wall-to-wall carpeting in the other.

"Help yourself," Janet told her, placing the cookies on the table. "Make yourself at home."

"You could give me a glass of milk."

"Why not?" Along with cups, saucers, and Lipton tea, she got out a half-gallon of milk, a tall glass, and then a banana for herself. "I'll be quick as I can." She left Bernice sipping, savoring, and shuffling toward the kitchen window, where the parted curtains would present the ter-raced hillside packed with neighboring homes.

A narrow hallway led to her bedroom, and by the time she arrived, her resentment at Bernice's intrusion had become complicated by a reactionary guilt. She stripped, gnawing the banana. The shower in the ad-joining bathroom filled with steam, and the water rattled on the tile, the wall, while a nagging voice yammered on about her self-centeredness—that was a good one—her standoffish temperament. It was the basic accusatory theme. Swallowing the last of the banana, she flipped the skin into the sink and shut the door. A cold heart. People liked to say she was too smart for her own good. Didn't know when to be satisfied.

Her skin reddened in blotches as the explanation for Bernice waiting in her kitchen came clear, and she understood that, counter to her first mistaken assumption, the reason Bernice was dressed to kill had every-thing to do with her visit. It was because she meant business and intended to be taken seriously once she got around to the subject of Janet's di-vorce—the way her life was a complete mess. You couldn't divorce your mother, and you couldn't divorce your father, though they could divorce each other. But you were stuck. Not that she hadn't tried, at least with her father, and with Belger, the town in which she lived. With this very moment.

Swabbing a patch of mirror out of the fog, she saw irritation in her reflected face. She knew that Bernice couldn't help but adopt the role of surrogate mom doing the good work of the dead. Most everybody thought Janet had gone off the deep end when, not long after her mother's funeral, she quit her job as an elementary-school teacher and took up the life she was now living. Which was, to the minds of many, no life. She had no job. She jogged long distances alone. Sometimes she wandered in the woods. Or maybe she drank herself into a nice high or, maybe, better yet, a nice stupor. There were periods when she read long classic novels like *Middlemarch, Bleak House,* or *The House of Mirth,* and then, somewhat mysteriously, these interests collapsed into stretches governed by tabloids, catalogs, fashion magazines, rented movies, and endless TV.

At first it had been difficult to keep people at bay, but as her solitary ambition bloomed, she saw how deeply she desired it. The friends of her childhood had turned out to be very few and not all that lasting after she went off to college. As for the relationships she'd begun while living the life of a schoolteacher, they were with busy women who had busy husbands and kids and jobs and little free time. In the beginning they all called, and she took time to explain, aware almost from the start of the way she was plotting to outmaneuver their concern. She knew how to work with their need to see themselves as good friends, while steering them back to their real interests, which were their kids, their husbands, and themselves. When the mood was right, she'd warn them to remain attentive to "the things that mattered," so they wouldn't end up divorced, like her. Last, she would mix in a few ploys about how she really needed to do what she was doing, telling them how much she was learning, and "no, she wasn't depressed," and she "missed them, too," feeling all the while like she was tightening rubber bands around her fingers, the tissue discoloring. At a certain point, sick of finding her answering machine full of messages, she pulled the plug, and the result, as the blinking red light went out, was a moment of breathtaking peace. The next day the trash collectors carried it off. If people wanted her, they could phone when she was home, and if they didn't get her, they could keep trying, or they could, as she hoped, give up.

Most did exactly that, but one or two persisted, unable to imagine how she could survive without their affection. After indulging them as long as she could stand it, she would provoke a fight. It was a tactic of last resort and usually found its opportunity around the subject of men. There were rumors about her and married men, or at least a certain married man. But she acknowledged nothing, coolly keeping gossip at bay and her frustrated friends guessing, just as she kept the lid screwed tight on certain of her other habits, such as how she dealt with stress and tedium and annoyance—how, when everything got too demanding and she really needed a time-out, she headed down to Kaiser Street. Once there, she knew how to appear lost and purposeful in just the right mix to invite one of the Crips or Bloods to approach. Working their best urban hiss, they pitched their wares, offering just about everything—crack, heroin, speed—in a half-baked code that she would politely entertain, though all she ever wanted was 'ludes and grass. Mostly, though, she kept it simple and went straight to her regular guy, Big Baby Dog. He teased her about her outmoded habits and bragged he was the only dopeman worth her time, because the rest of them were second-rate "gangsta" farmed out from Omaha or Wichita, all rejects from somewhere—Chicago, Des Moines. She figured that what he said of them was probably true of him, too—that they'd all been involved in some kind of screwup that caused them to be judged in need of training and sent to learn their trade in less competitive Belger.

Returning from her bedroom in a T-shirt and jeans, her hair wrapped in a towel and her feet bare, she found Bernice relaxing in the armchair near the apartment's largest window, which, with its teal panel curtains scooped wide, opened onto woods and sky out back. Her jacket was unbuttoned, the scarf loose. She held the empty plate on her lap. "Oreos," she sighed between chews. "Your momma loved Oreos."

"You're right about that." Janet was making sure the tags of the tea bags dangled neatly out of the mugs before adding the boiling water.

"What are you so mad about, Janet? You got a chip on your shoulder big as a house."

"Is that what you came by to talk about?"

"No."

Janet detoured for more cookies, all the while collecting her resources to tell Bernice to mind her own business. She had no idea why she was living the life she was living, and she didn't care why, because it was what she wanted, and she was going to do it until she no longer felt like doing it, and if it was weird, well, fine; and if it bothered people, well, fine. With money she'd saved from work, plus her divorce settlement and the unwanted assistance of her mother's life insurance, along with other funds Isabel had squirreled away, Janet could last at least six more months. She knew how to live even more cheaply if she had to, and if she went through every dime, it was her own fucking business. So they could all just butt out, and Bernice, as their representative, could take her platitudes and her chatty advice and stick them.

"Listen," Bernice said. "You like animals, don'tcha?"

"What?"

"I always remember that about you. When you were a little girl, even. Your momma thought you was going to be a veterinarian."

Arranging the tea on the end table beside the armchair, Janet studied Bernice, trying to see where the hell this tack would take them.

"You remember that, right?" said Bernice. "Because I have three dogs and two cats, you know."

Janet retreated to the wall. The old woman had a sentimental suck to her. The lights might as well have been dimming on everything but her strangely enchanting eyes. "It's a real mess," she said.

Janet pushed her right foot down as if to somehow move off from this moment. "Are they sick or something?"

"No, no. The dogs? No, no, they're all fine. One of the cats is old, but she still takes no sass off any of 'em. Elmira was the first one I ever had of this batch. She's got her seniority. And there's one of the dogs is old, but he's a tough one. No, no, it's the Rapture, see. That's the trouble. You heard about the Rapture?" said Bernice.

Janet decided to try a little tea, unable to imagine what Bernice was up to. "This is what, Bernice?"

"C'mon, now, you're not gonna tell me you have your head so deep in the sand, you never heard of it. It's been in the papers—it's been on the

TV. You have a TV, don't you?" She sounded annoyed, unable to see a television anywhere.

"It's in there," Janet said. "My TV." She gestured to a pine cabinet that stood against the far living room wall.

"In where?"

"The chair you're in swivels around. VHS, TV—it's all inside the cabinet."

"You got cable?"

"Yeah. Sure. Why?" Janet tightened her lips to hide how absurd the conversation was striking her.

"Look. This is no laughing matter. I feel like you're just about to break out laughing."

"I don't know why we're talking about my TV."

"We're not. It's just odd you got it locked up."

"I don't like to look at it unless I'm going to watch something."

"Fine. Good. It's your business where you keep the fool thing."

Janet struggled to hold a serious expression, while Bernice raised her hand in a vague way. Lifting her glasses to rub the bridge of her nose seemed an afterthought. "I'm talking about the Rapture, okay. This is a matter of Jesus and a bunch of special angels coming to haul some people off body and soul, all the folks who been saved. And this one load is coming out of Belger, and I am one of them going to be taken up."

Janet took a prolonged sip of tea. "Really."

"It was in the papers. It was on the TV."

"It was in the papers that you were going to be taken up?" If Bernice was nuts, the answer to this question might give Janet a way to gauge how nuts.

"No, no. That wasn't in the papers. That couldn't be in the papers, Janet. You mean like did it say, 'Bernice Doorley is being taken up'? No. It was in the papers that the Rapture is coming, and coming soon. That's what was in the papers. It's worldwide. We aren't the only ones. I'm talking about our group over at the Church of the Angels. We're not the only ones. And it's all Bible-based. This isn't one of those cults, if that's what you're thinking."

"No, no."

"What are you thinking? Not that it matters."

"Well, it matters to me, Bernice."

"That's what most people get around to saying when push comes to shove. They just get their drawers all knotted up about these cults. At least around here. But there are books you can read if you want to, at least about the idea of it. Not about how Belger fits in, but the overall notion. You know what I'm remembering about you? The way you always did have a way of diggin' in your heels. Over nothin' sometimes. Just plain stubborn."

"And I'm too smart for my own good, right? Don't know when to be satisfied."

"There's some that say that, sure."

"Well, that's not how it ever looked to me, let me tell you."

"Some of us tried to advise your momma. Just pull down your little pants and tan your hide every now and then. Take you down a peg."

"You know, I think she took that advice."

"There's worse things."

"Actually, I did read an article about that Rapture business, Bernice. This was in the Des Moines paper. And I think there was a cover story in *Time* or *Newsweek,* if I remember right."

"I don't know."

"But I didn't read any of it too carefully, because at the time I didn't know it pertained to Belger."

"Well, it pertains to some of us, anyway, and it's coming tonight."

"Tonight?"

"I'm afraid so. Which is why I'm here, as you can imagine."

"Tonight? Are you sure?"

"Of course I'm sure. That's the whole thing, because it's pretty well set I'm one of them. I'm going to be one of them saved. So you see, I'm worried about my animals."

"Is something going to happen to them?"

"Well, for Pete's sake, Janet, just use your brain for a second. I'm not certain exactly how it's going to work, but once I am taken up, they're going to be there in that house all alone."

When Janet smiled in spite of trying not to, Bernice looked disgusted by her own inability to rouse the necessary alarm. "Think for a second, will you? Who's gonna feed them? Can you answer me that? I mean, I'm just going to be sucked right up, and I'll just be gone, the Lord Jesus looking for the saved ones and dragging us right out of our living rooms, our cars. Airplanes. Buses. Some won't even know it's coming, and off they'll go. Just gone. Their seats empty. If it happened now, you would just be sittin' there, leanin' against that wallpaper with that cup of tea up to your mouth, havin' this conversation with an empty chair."

The notion of Bernice vanishing had a certain appeal. "Can I ask you something, Bernice?"

"No. Not just this second." She stood up, turned in a circle, and wiggled out of her jacket. Agitation joined with a series of charged impulses had her more confused than excited, and her ruddy, wrinkled hands smoothed the pleats on her cream-colored blouse again and again. "What about the dogs? What about the cats? Do you see? Or maybe you don't. Maybe you have no idea. It's all going to grind to a halt. I mean, the world. The whole shebang. Not tonight—I'm not saying tonight or tomorrow, even—but sometime after. And not too long, either. The timetable is a mystery, so nobody knows when, exactly. But I don't want them to go hungry in the meantime. So I'm wondering if you might feed them for me. That's what I'm wondering. If you would make sure they don't starve. Could you do that for me?"

"What about Irma? Couldn't Irma take care of all this for you?"

"Irma moved to Wisconsin. Maybe you didn't know that. All the way to Sayersville."

Bernice couldn't stop fussing with her blouse, which was chiffon, Janet noted, and closed above her breasts not by buttons but by a circular brooch. Realizing that Bernice was all dressed up this way because of what she was talking about, the Rapture, Janet took a fresh look at the newly applied clear nail polish, flawless stockings, neatly tied shoes. Bernice had even used powder to fade age spots on her cheeks and forehead. She was all set for her trip, but she seemed to have confused heaven with a night out on the town. "Sayersville's not that far," Janet said. "Just give Irma a call and—"

"Look. There's no way I can talk to her about this kind of thing. I just can't. Or anything else, for that matter. She would give me an earful. I can just hear her calling it a buncha bunk and making fun of her crazy old mother. I don't need that just now. She doesn't have a religious bone in her body. What I need is to rest assured someone will see to the animals. You know, feed 'em, walk 'em. If I just put food out, don't you know it'll all go bad in a day or so, and they won't eat it, especially Elmira, because she's such a finicky eater. Anyway, it'll all just rot and make them sick. Or they'll run out of water. And General—he's an old dog—on his last legs, you know. Why should he suffer? You see the problem."

Even with its bizarre premise, the exchange was beginning to bore Janet. "Sure," she said. She wanted an Oreo, and picking up one of the last two, she held back the impulse to say that as far as she was concerned, Bernice had more than one screw loose. "I'm just thinking this is pretty last-minute," she said and smiled.

"Why do you think I'm so stressed out? I was racking my brain—just racking it—when I remembered your mom always talkin' about how you loved animals. Talked to them. Some big collie, I remember. She even took me once to watch you and we sat in my car watching you talk to that collie. That was a sweet sight. Believe you me, I would rest a lot easier." Removing one of her earrings, she tended her earlobe where the clasp had left an imprint. "Will you?"

"I want to tell you, Bernice, I don't think it's really going to happen."

"I don't blame you for taking that attitude, I really don't, but—"

"I would just be patronizing you."

"That'll do just fine. Because I'm sure I would be thinking along those same lines if I was in your shoes. And if it doesn't happen, then you won't have to do it. But if it does, what I'm asking is simple enough, don't you think?"

A wave crawled over Janet, the sensation of unwelcome influence, as if a hypnotist were casting spells to make her let this old woman have her way. When she shook her head, the negation was mainly of certain in-comprehensible aspects of her inner life, and she said, "Sure."

"That's good of you, but I knew your momma raised you right. We were friends from the second grade on, you know." Bernice was nodding, her expression reverent. "We were soul mates, you know."

"Really?"

"Yes, we were. We often said it. But you probably don't see that as something likely, either."

"I'm not so sure I want to rule it out completely."

"Well, that's hopeful."

Some people had soul mates—they had troops of interested angels. Janet had a hypnotist devoted to making certain she obeyed other people's commands, took on their chores. "That's how I feel," she said.

"About what?"

Startled that she'd spoken, she knew better than to continue. "Nothing."

"Spit it out if it's important."

"No."

"Okay, then. Because I guess what I'd like us to do, if you're not busy right now— Do you have something to do?"

The desire in Bernice's eyes was like water rising over Janet's head. Looking for a way out, she could only wish for something she could claim as an excuse for her grudging surrender as she said, "Not a thing."

"Because what would suit me would be if you could follow me over to my house so I could show you everything, such as where the food is kept and the can opener. They all have separate bowls, okay? You could meet them, and I could give you a key to my place. That way I could just put this whole thing out of my mind. Because the way it's been going, it won't give me a second's peace."

"Okay. Sure." As she bent to the task of her socks and shoes, she sensed a change in Bernice. She found the old woman fixed on some-thing out the window, where the sunset was a fiery bruise above trees erupting from the hilltop that formed the edge of the horizon.

"Look at that," Bernice said.

"What?"

"God's face." Her tone was as saccharine and melodramatic as her gaze. "I see Him everywhere lately."

Janet studied the mixture of elm and fir trees, a pair of the tallest protruding like the prongs of a plug. "Above those two sticking out up there," she said, pointing. "Is that where you're looking?"

"He's there, Janet. Now just tie your shoes and let's go."

"Okay." She tugged the laces tight, a sputtering resentment squeezed out by the hateful willingness she felt to placate this old woman.

"I know I should have come by sooner, so we could have had more time to get everything right."

"Sure." With her eyes necessarily downcast, it seemed safe to ask, "What do you think Mom would say about all this?" She straightened impulsively, surprised that she wanted to see Bernice answer.

Bernice raised her eyebrows like she might crack a joke, but then her mood proved more sad than amused. She seemed to labor to remember Isabel accurately. "That's a tough one."

"It just occurred to me."

"I don't know. I've wondered that, but I can't say. Not for sure. One day I think one way, and on the next I got a whole different opinion. But it's all guesswork. That's the thing to keep in mind. I never had a chance to ask Isabel, because I didn't go to this particular church when she was still with us. But then I started, and now I been learning this and that, and all of a sudden this is what's happening. But I figure I'll be seeing Isabel soon." She picked up and fluffed her jacket, and with her purse under her arm, she was clearly itching to be on her way.

2

I N HER HONDA, JANET GLIDED into the growing dark where
Bernice's Chevy chugged on ahead. The narrow pavement
was bounded by houses on tilted lots packed along a decline. Animals,
Janet thought. So I'll be taking care of some animals. The notion, with a
prod from nostalgia, sent her looking out the car window, as if into the
memory of a railroad car with an autumnal countryside racing past.
What had Bernice said? Something about that big collie and the way they
spied on her as she consulted with him because he seemed so wise and
comforting down on the corner of Ambrose and Garfield. Why had they
done that? Were they worried? Or did it please them to sit and poke fun
at her foolishness? Did they have the faintest idea that because everybody
knew animals heard things people couldn't, Janet believed they knew her
thoughts? Especially that beautiful old collie. The summer she was eight
and desperately unhappy, she would lie on her belly in the grass and
chatter to him about her troubles in a rush of free association directed
toward his somber, patriarchal snout. She was sure his understanding
went beyond anything she could say, and that tenderly, wisely, he withheld comment.

Throughout the maze of her childhood, she had continued to see animals as magical beings she wanted to associate with forever—even assist
and serve. Graduating from high school with those impulses intact,
though modified and matured, she had set off by train the following fall
to begin studying to become a veterinarian at a small college in Ham-
mond, Illinois, just outside Chicago. She had long dreamed of grateful

dogs and cats, even deer, or a far-fetched elephant or bear, but from the minute she stepped aboard the train, the animals that drew her gaze were men. Seat after seat held men in work clothes, or Levi's and windbreakers, or suits and shirts with buttoned-down collars and ties snugged to the throat. She was shocked at the way her attention shifted from figure to figure with an appetite she didn't fully recognize. Of course, she'd had crushes on boys in elementary school and on through high school, where there'd been a tentative boyfriend or two, but this was different. The stubble of their beards, their meaty hands, some calloused and stained, others pale and soft, fingers as thick as broomsticks held her. Shadows folded their pants in the inky gathering of their crotches.

Within a month of her arrival on campus, she was involved in dreamy, erotic chaos with a sweet boy who attended her every whim and desire in a way that took her quickly from bliss to boredom. So she tossed in another boy, a more withheld and selfish upperclassman, Byron Link. His responses to her were mainly careless and remote, except when they were in bed, where he provided her first 'lude and where she made the unhappy discovery that his vanity and narcissism were tinder to her lust. Eventually, a sense of being shadowed by something she didn't have a clue about started to scare her. She felt on the verge of understanding a fantastic fact about herself, even as her ignorance heightened her excitement.

Neither of the boys was in her field of study, and the fading of her interest in schoolwork had a preordained quality. She resisted, studied harder, and then near the close of her second semester, she saw a beagle named Rudyard die on an operating table. The shaved fur left pinkish tissue peeled back over white bone. A series of shudders produced a halo of blood. She was surprised and realized that she had failed to fully consider the fact that the animals a vet dealt with were often in pain. Her ambition felt infantile, a fiction whose full examination made her feel vapid and thoughtless.

It wasn't long after this that Kevin Garvey, the more sensitive of the two boys, lost it with her one night in his car. He'd been going down on her when she said something—she could never remember what, they'd both been drinking, but she said it, she was sure of that. The next thing she knew, she was on the pavement outside the car, clumps of her hair ripped out, her lip split, several teeth loosened, and Kevin on top of her, his sensitivity revealed as a desperate strategy to hold back rage. He was still sobbing and slapping her. When he drove off, she got to her feet in the headlights of a car, which slowed and passed by before stopping and backing up. The elderly couple insisted on taking her to the hospital. It felt impolite to argue. A police report followed. She didn't press charges, but school authorities were notified. She and Kevin were compelled to meet jointly with a counselor, who advised them to break things off. The misery on his freckled face as he contemplated life without her gave her shameful delight. He looked panicky, as if he were being shoved into an airless environment. Life without Janet. How would he ever? She found him preposterous and had to fight not to parody his desperation. She said, "Fine, yes, all right." He groaned, and she said she thought that a complete breakup would be best. It was odd how she couldn't stop smiling at him. Individual counseling was required by the school, and it didn't take long before the counselor, a large, solemn woman named Mrs. Snell, asked her to consider the impact that her parents' divorce and her absent father might have had on her. Janet furrowed her brow in an imitation of dutiful, earnest analysis and said she hadn't thought about her father for such a long time that she couldn't remember the last time. Mrs. Snell sighed and gazed at her in a way intended to suggest gravity, along with silent warning, and then she said, "That doesn't necessarily mean what you think it does, Janet."

"Really." Janet was aware of a certain theoretical curiosity, though her primary response was smug amusement at how perfectly alone and independent she felt, which seemed to disprove every possible implication Mrs. Snell was interested in. Janet knew divorce affected people, but the way she felt sitting there seemed to prove her the exception to the rule. Not that she wasn't returned every now and then to a mood like a big room where she sat tuned in to some really bad news, but it was difficult to see how such pointless annoyances had anything to do with Kevin Garvey and her interest in his hard-on.

"You see, Janet," Mrs. Snell added somberly, with an irritating appetite to establish undeniable eye contact, "sometimes we respond to things in ways that don't look like responses at all."

"Hmmm," said Janet, wondering if maybe this woman spent too much time reading fortune cookies. But she quickly announced that she would consider these matters in a new light, since Mrs. Snell thought them important. Not that she intended to give her prick of a father another second of her precious time by surrendering to some useless long-distance voice-from-the-past disruption. She had more important things to do, like getting rid of Byron Link. He scoffed at her announcement, because she was strictly and permanently low-end, if she thought she was unplugging him, because he was a twenty-four/seven operation and had been fucking Marisa all along, and Maggie and Angela, too.

The following year she took up residence in an off-campus rooming-house. There she made do with erotic literature and self-help that proved surprisingly satisfactory. She felt sometimes that she was outsmarting a malign, arrogant force and that this force was starving without her. At times the idea boosted her arousal, moving her along, getting her off. Aiming the TV remote with her free hand, she raised the volume so that the sounds she made were interlaced with the racket of some melodrama or sitcom. Sometimes she smoked a little dope to cook her sensations, listening to Laura Branigan or Madonna, Cyndi Lauper, or that space-age, hard-hearted lead singer for Blondie. Always women, only girls, while nameless, faceless men everywhere were pining and desolate without access to her body.

By the end of her sophomore year, her incompatibility with veterinary medicine was so glaring, she left not only the program but the school. Back in Belger and living with her mother, she worked a couple of part-time jobs, one as a waitress, the other babysitting, until the idea of teaching at an elementary school occurred. If not dogs and cats, she thought, wouldn't the next best thing be kids? The following spring, off she went to Wagner College in Vida, Wisconsin, where she majored in education. She worked hard, stayed focused and out of trouble, dating boys who didn't really interest her.

She graduated early and moved in again with her mother and stayed on even after being hired by Meadow View Elementary School. She lived in a tranquil, mellow way with a sense of waiting and prelude until the day Bobby Crimmins almost crashed his Buick into her Volkswagen as they both raced for the same mall parking spot. Bobby won. In the aftermath, she harangued him about the importance of civility in the arena of mall parking, until suddenly, she found herself giggling at something he'd said. At that point the squabble turned playful and ended when he asked her out. He owned and ran a small realty company, and she surprised everyone by marrying him when he asked. Of course, that was over now. Through Bobby, divorce had slammed into her life for a second time, and it was amid the repercussions that she tasted the solitary "lifestyle," which she was now expanding. She'd kept her job and found rather quickly that it wasn't so much the teaching she loved as the hours spent with the children.

By the time she quit in the months after her mother died, she'd been at it for ten years. The cessation had been violent initially, but she'd gritted her teeth and forged ahead, as if each new day were a door she had to force open. It had not been easy, but at least chance encounters with school buses, like the one coming out of the dusk right now and rumbling past, no longer prompted outbursts of tears. Last fall she would have been forced to pull to the side of the road. She could remember steeling herself with the reminder that, when she was a teacher, her life had contained rhythmic, seasonal breaks, so her current situation could be viewed as an extended vacation. The idea was not persuasive, but her distress, contrary to its aims, convinced her that breaking from her past was necessary. As if her emotions were her enemy, she became even more determined to leave the routines that caused them. By walking away from years of habit, she hoped to look back on it all with insightful perspective.

With Bernice's house only minutes away, she started rooting through her CD case, wanting some kind of edgy diversion, and persisting until she found and popped in Alanis Morissette. One stupid thing after another, she thought, annoyed that she was going where she was going for such an absurd reason. Off to her right, the terrain spread out in a desolate expanse where a muddy slough had been drained for a development that never amounted to much. At the moment a freight train was clanking south past the lumberyard on its way to the meatpacking plant. Cows in a string of slatted cars wedged their noses into the air, the chilly light flickering over their big eyes.

Waiting near the front of her car, Bernice struck Janet as attempting a formal, maybe even gloomy, pose. Back again, Janet thought, casting a wary eye at the yellow one-story house, the paint now chipped and fading. She'd been dragged here to visit Bernice and Toby and that bundle of fun, their daughter, Irma, umpteen million times. When she was small and her dad was with them, he and Toby would get together to "shoot the shit," as Toby liked to say, the four adults collecting in the kitchen for boozy card games. Janet was handed over to Irma, who was almost seven years older and acted bored and bossed her around.

Traipsing along behind Bernice, Janet hadn't the faintest idea when she'd last spoken to Irma, but she had to wonder if she was obligated under the circumstances to call her up and let her know what was going on with her mother. The dogs were already yapping inside. It seemed unlikely that the curtains had always been gauzy and printed with daisies, as they were now, and even if they had been, how was she supposed to remember?

"Oh, now, shush," Bernice told the dogs, two floppy-eared swirls of black-and-white fur spinning around. The place had a faint animal smell, mainly dog, but cat piss, too, and cooked bacon, and good old lemon Pledge. In the distance, muttering at their intrusion, a larger black dog hobbled in their direction, his tail in a slow fidget, his rheumy eyes trying to focus. Bernice patted his old head, rousing dust, as she said something Janet didn't quite catch. One cat was sleeping on the couch, the other on the windowsill, its fat yellow torso spread like a puddle.

"I got to be careful not to get emotional," said Bernice. "But it's just a matter of doin' one darn thing you never thought you'd be doin' after another, that's the real trick to livin' your life. That's the big secret, if you ask me. Not that anybody does." She plopped her purse on the kitchen counter and hung her jacket over the back of a chair. With a nod, she marched to the cat on the sill. "Elmira, this is Janet." She patted the cat, who gazed at her tolerantly. "She's going to be takin' care of you, okay?" Bernice used a version of this ritual to introduce each pet. Ira, who had a haughty scowl, was a rich black except for the tips of his toes and the fringes of his muzzle, where white specks surrounded his pink nose. The old dog was General, a black mongrel, lean and longhaired but reminiscent of a Labrador. The other two were spaniels from the same litter, Sappy, a male, and Happy, a female. The feeding room was just off the kitchen in an alcove that existed in Janet's memory as the pantry where she had sometimes sought refuge when getting along with Irma proved too difficult. They passed a bin of gray, mildly repugnant Kitty Litter. "I change their box every two days, and the dogs, well, you gotta get them outside twice a day. Can you do that?"

"Listen, maybe this has gone far enough."

"What do you mean? What's got into you now?"

"Because you are not going to disappear, Bernice."

"Let me put it to you this way, Janet. I thought we straightened this question out."

"I agreed to go along with it."

"So go along with it."

"I'm just telling you—"

"What if I die? How about that, Janet? If I die tonight, will you take care of the animals? Let's pretend that's what we're talking about."

"It's just about as likely, Bernice. Actually, it's more likely."

"You really do have a mean streak."

She nodded, smiled, shrugged, and said, "Where do you think I picked that up?"

Bernice looked ready to scuffle, but then the resigned pucker of her lips signaled her belief that she had only one way to go. "Let's finish up here, all right? Can we do that?"

"I just don't see how it is you're so sure about it. That's all."

"Well, Hazel Vanasek took me to this preacher, if you must know. And he was talking about it. Not right away, but after a while." She settled at the kitchen table and sat rubbing the ears of one of the dogs. "I just started goin', and I enjoyed the company, and he talked about the regular things, this and that, like they all do. All in all, it was a nice bunch of people, and we got along. Better than sittin' home alone, which I did more than my share of there for a while. Sure, there were some duds, a couple of loudmouths, and one who can't help but act snooty. But over time I got more out of it than I might of thought. And then at a certain point this subject came up, and then it came up more and more often, and then he named the day and said we were all going."

"So you took his word for it? Just like that!" Janet alighted on the edge of the opposite chair.

"No, no, no, for goodness sake, no. Now, I may not be able to explain this, and I don't want you to take it wrong, but I was sitting there feeling real puzzled—I'll admit it—and some of us were whispering to see if we'd heard right, when all of a sudden I remembered how, in my surgery, I'd had this funny minute where I was off in the head, and I paid it little mind, the way you do. I'm talking about my surgery for my atrial fibrillation. It's going on three years now. Those chest pains and feeling weak day in and day out—but I am feeling good these days, in case you're wondering. It was a hard time, that time—hard—you can take my word for it, and your mom was good to me, I want to tell you. She was a good friend. And then it's less than two years later, and her heart all but explodes. There's just no telling."

"I guess not."

"Anyway, it was one heck of a thing, and not one I'd care to repeat. Because right in the middle of the surgery, I sort of woke up and I thought, Oh, my Lord, I'm gonna feel it, I'm gonna feel what they're doing, the knife and everything, and I was so scared. But when I opened my eyes, there was this man standing there, and he wasn't real, and yet I was glad to see him, and he was there just for me. He was talking to me. Nobody else—the nurses paid him no mind, because he wasn't there, as far as they knew, and I don't remember exactly what he said, but I felt a whole lot better and went back to sleep, and it crossed my mind that it was Jesus. So then the day came in Reverend Tauke's chapel when he spoke to us of what was coming, and I came to the realization that I was in that same kind of situation again. Same as the surgery. I opened my eyes and started to listen real close to Reverend Tauke, to see if I couldn't understand what he was saying. And the more I listened, the more I came to the feeling that it was all true, and that it had been Jesus in my surgery, or an angel, at the very least. I mean, it's real hard to explain, and I know it sounds crazy. But if you think about it, a person would have to say that's what the Bible is. Chapter and verse, page after page, one crazy thing after another. This one, that one, who's got the most screws loose? Moses? Abraham? You tell me. So why should it be any different now?"

Janet stood and said, "Can I have a drink of water?" At the sink quickly, she started the faucet running, her finger under the flow.

"There's Diet 7UP in the fridge, if you want it."

"This is fine. Listen, do you know what I think. People are born, and they're born in one country or another, in one city and one religion or another, or maybe no religion. But into this family with whatever it consists of—or doesn't consist of—and all this is what determines their upbringing, their formative years—religion, economics, which all feeds into and influences their genetic makeup, which they're born with, right—so it's a given. It is what it is, propensities and all, and so each person ends up a certain way as a result. And they live accordingly, and what they want is on that basis. The basis of who they are or think they are. Even though almost everyone is a lot more alike than they think—what they want—what people everywhere want, and yet it appears to be different if you go person by person. Because it's somehow their own, and they're one of a kind, as far as they know." She paused to enjoy a long, cold drink of water.

"Okay."

"That's what I think. And so you're going along with this group for your own reasons."

"Do you know what? I think maybe you're gettin' too smart for me with all that. It may be true, I don't know, but off the top of my head, it sounds pretty narrow."

"Smart but narrow?"

"I'm no genius, but I don't see how it fits with what I said. Does it?"

Janet chuckled in a way that felt rude and led her to decide to give up on whatever it was she was doing. "Well, you can think about it."

"I hope you're not tryin' to change my mind, Janet."

"No, I just thought I'd say something."

"Because I'm not looking to have that happen any more than I'm looking to change your mind about anything. Everybody knows you been acting real odd—that you been havin' a hard time, but—"

"Is that right? That's what everybody knows?"

"Nobody knows what to make of you, though."

"Maybe they should just stop trying."

"The truth is, I'd like to hear your side of it myself, if there was a way you could explain so the average person could understand. And I guess I'd have to be less pressed for time. Things just don't matter the way they used to. I don't mean they don't matter at all, but I'm leavin', and I don't even know if I'll be wearin' my clothes. As you probably noticed, or maybe you didn't—I got kinda dressy, because that's the kind of question I can't stop worrying myself sick about."

"You do look pretty snazzy."

"I guess, but it's foolish, because how's it gonna matter in heaven?"

"I have no idea." Janet sank back into thoughts that left her feeling like a child darting into a strange room only to wish she hadn't been so confident she knew where she was going.

"'Course you don't," Bernice said, then went on to explain that the cats' bowls were on the top shelf, so the dogs couldn't get at them to steal the food. "Which is exactly what you would do if you could," she informed Sappy, who trailed them. "Now, there's a whole rigamarole to this, Janet. You ought to jot it down."

"Jot what down?"

"So you get it right." From a shelf near the refrigerator, she produced a notepad with a pen attached by a white string, and with Janet scribbling, she went through the names again. "Okay, so I'd say first thing to do is walk them. You can find the leashes just here." She gestured to a colorful collection of nylon straps dangling on the pantry wall. "You get that done, you feed them a certain way." She glanced at Janet, frowning at the fact that the pen was idle. "You'll regret not taking notes. You mark my word."

"Sorry, sorry."

"The cats twice a day, and they each get half a can. There's six varieties, and I try to give 'em both the same each day. That way there's no jealousy. But make it different day to day. Because they get fussy. Now, if you run out and need to buy more, there's a check signed and ready to go for three hundred dollars." Bernice unveiled a sealed blue envelope beneath a basket of onions. "You want my perishables. Not much. Some apples in the fridge."

"No, thanks."

"Just look through and help yourself. There's milk, too. Ice cream. I figure Irma will come around fairly quick. Or you can contact her once I'm gone. I'm hoping she'll take the place over and find it in her heart to take the animals on. Or if you want them, you can have them."

Janet was more impassive than entertained by the relief she felt at knowing she had no choice. Still, an odd little giggle preceded her answer. "My landlord doesn't allow pets."

"Not even cats?"

"No."

Bernice could only shake her head at such wickedness. "The dogs get some kibble from that bucket, and there's more in the bag there. You got to keep it high up on the shelf like it is, and it's hell to lift, but they bust into it if you don't keep it out of their reach. Food, food, food. Happy and Sappy get half a cup and then half a can of the canned twice a day. They'll gobble it down like there's no tomorrow. But General's another matter. Him you got to cater to because he's on his last legs, so I figure fine with me. You give a whole can twice a day. These here." She patted an orderly array stacked on the second shelf. "If he sticks his nose up, which is something he's doing more lately, well, there's these special ones of stuff it's a rarity for him to get a taste of, like kangaroo. Vet says it should tempt him." The labeling on this batch was vaguely institutional. "Don't use them unless you have to, because they go for a pretty penny. There's times he'll say 'no thank you' even to them, and that's when you resort to hot dogs and cheese. Or there's frozen turkey burgers in there. I'll go so far as give him one if I have to. Boil the dogs, fry the burgers. The other thing is, you got to get one of each of these pills down him in the morning." She held out a white plastic bottle. "They're these steroids to stimulate his appetite and then the Rimadyl for his arthritis." Here she rattled an orange prescription vial. "I wrap 'em up in cheese. You try slipping them into his regular food, he'll just pick 'em out. But the cheese he gobbles. And you got to give him time to eat and keep the other dogs away. I usually put him in the bathroom—let him take as long as he wants. And like I said, walk them first thing you come in. That'd be my advice. Just out in the yard. I tole you about the leashes. And I'd appreciate it if you picked up the poop. So the yard don't look like trash lives here. There's a pooper-scooper right out beside the front steps. Just take a look when you go. Now, I went pretty fast, so do you think I should go over it again?"

"Well, some," Janet said. "Not all, but some."

"Okay. Which parts?"

It took another twenty minutes before Bernice was satisfied, and they stood by the door with Janet tearing her scribbles from the notebook. She'd written little, but she folded the pages and deposited them in the breast pocket of her denim jacket, as if they were of the utmost value. Closing the snap, she thought how she was agreeing to this insanity only because the crazy old bat would be there in the morning to handle it all.

With a somewhat ceremonial air, Bernice was preparing to reach into her handbag, which struck Janet at this second as not simply big but bizarrely oversize, with a thick brass clasp. "Don't want to forget these." The two house keys flashed, coming together with a clink. "Back door, front door," she said, indicating the B printed with permanent marker on the fat part of one key, then the F on the other. She seemed to sort through a series of emotions that brought little satisfaction and didn't quite end as she handed the keys over, and rummaged in her bag to dig out a small bottle of Tylenol. "For my arthritis," she said, fiddling with the tamper-resistant lid. "Not as bad as some I've seen—they can hardly take a step. So I'm lucky. But I have to make do with Tylenol. There's this other good one, naproxen, Hazel takes, but I can't because of the one I take for my heart." She caught two of the white oblong pills in her palm and headed for the sink. "Come around some morning—then I really go to town. This one, that one—three, four, five of the little devils." She sipped and swallowed. "You know the thing that gets me in all this is how I will miss out on taking care of General. I'd like to see him through to the end, but it's not my call, as far as I can tell." With the pills washed down, she rinsed the glass and gave Janet a naughty smile. "And the other thing I'd like to be here for is to see how things turn out on some of my stories. *The Guiding Light* and *General Hospital*. You watch them any?"

"No, I don't."

"Your mom loved them. But it's just as well you don't get started on the fool things. That'd be my advice. I'm just goin' to put them out of my mind, since I'll be hightailing it out of here soon enough. Though I was hoping to see that nasty one get what's comin' to her on *The Guiding Light*. She's a terrible person. No two ways about it."

"Right," said Janet, tossing the keys and catching them.

"Be careful with them now. Put 'em in your purse. Where's your purse?"

"It's out in the car."

"Put them where you can find them, Janet. You mark my words."

"I will. So what time do you suggest I come by in the morning?"

"Well, I can promise that if you get here much after ten, you'll be picking poop off the rug."

"Gotcha," she said, turning to go. It was night, the sun down, the sky a quilted haze. She was partway down the walk when a playful, impish impulse too strong to ignore stopped her. She called, "Wait!" far too loudly because Bernice was still framed in the doorway, wrapping her shoulders in a shawl against the chill.

"What now?" Bernice said.

"You know what? I just thought of something, Bernice. What if I'm going, too?"

"Where?"

"Well, with you."

"You mean with Jesus?"

"Now, that would be a problem, wouldn't it?"

"What has got into you? I suppose you can't help yourself, or you figure you can't, anyway. But you don't have to be contrary every chance you get, Janet. You're not goin'."

"You said some people don't have any idea about it, and they're just grabbed up. That's what you said."

"You're not goin', Janet."

"I could be one of those who doesn't know about it."

"I don't think so."

"Why?"

"I just don't is why. That's why. Now get in the car and go on home. I'll put in a good word for you with Jesus."

"Right," said Janet, moving to her car.

"All you need to worry about is keeping on my good side. Just do what you promised. I wish I could've managed to give you a little more warning, but I think you're gonna be up to it."

3

AFTER A QUICK STOP AT a McDonald's, Janet ate her burger and fries on the road, while evening advanced. She was drawing hard on the straw for the last of her Coke and nearing the crest above her home, where she knew for a split second that Bernice would be waiting once again in some weird continuation of her ability to mess with Janet's day. When in fact there was a vehicle under the streetlight, her satisfaction felt slightly paranormal. However, the red Lexus bathed in the arc of artificial glow prompted little mystery. There would be no duct tape on this coddled machine—just Wayne Miller waiting inside. By the time she parked and strode over, he had rolled down the window and arranged his chin on his bare forearm, his dark hair, keen eyes, and dimpled grin framed in the opening.

"Wayne," she said.

"Yes, it is."

She could smell the vodka and orange juice he liked to drink. He nodded in her direction, letting his eyes flit up to hers, where they took some kind of measurement. His hand passed through his hair to signal that, in case she had any doubts, he was undergoing a lot of emotion. The radio played a faint sea swell of sound, all pure background. He had the dial fixed, as he always did, to KDBQ, where the listening was easy, the songs generated out of a perpetual 1970s estuary.

"I wish you could have arrived just a couple a minutes ago," he told her. "Then you could have heard that song they were playing. It was killer."

She had little doubt the lethal tune she'd missed was something by James Taylor. Wayne had been told once too often that he bore a resemblance to the young James Taylor, so he was always finding significance in the haphazard appearance of a James Taylor song. She felt like pointing out the idiocy of this habit, but she had other things on her mind. "I thought we had an agreement, Wayne."

"I know what we agreed to. But I was under duress. You put me under duress."

"I thought I could count on you, but I guess I should have known better."

"I have to talk to you, Janet. That's why I came by like this, even though I knew you'd be angry."

She let her glance strike him with a hint of intrigue, as if she were drawn to him, and then spoke matter-of-factly. "I don't want to be standing out here like this in public. Anybody could drive by. We're just making a spectacle of ourselves. I'm going to go inside."

"But you know we have to talk."

"I'm going inside."

"I'm sorry I came by, but I couldn't hold back."

"Just move your car around the corner and then come in, and we can talk for five minutes."

"Oh. Okay." His eyes betrayed complete surprise, followed quickly by every happy calculation he really should have done better to hide.

"Five minutes to talk. But that's all. Just to talk. You hear me, Wayne?"

"Yes, I do."

She really did want to get out of there before being spotted by her landlords. With its back entrance and distance from the Luckritz bedrooms, her apartment offered useful privacy. "Okay, then," she said.

His nod was a shade excessive, his effort to appear cooperative and earnest turning him into a ten-year-old hoping to look manly. "Okay."

As she headed around the garage, she knew he was decoding her offer to see him behind closed doors as an invitation to fuck, and her own point of view on the question was hardly definitive. He'd looked gleaming and hazardous sitting there. There was no getting around seeing him as an opportunity that, if properly used, could wipe away the bullshit residue of her day. Just because she'd told Wayne once that she was done with him didn't mean she couldn't tell him again. She was ripe for a little craziness, just as she had been when she first got tangled up with him, even though he was married. Or maybe because he was married. Because they were both married. Things with Bobby had started off fine. The intensity of his courtship had surprised her, as if it were a game she didn't have to take seriously because she hadn't agreed to play. His abundant desire, his flowers and cards, his conquest and monopoly of her answering machine with snippets and monologues, sometimes witty, sometimes impassioned, left her feeling buoyant with a sense of dissolving alternatives, so that after a few short weeks, there he was in her bed, in her bathroom, in her kitchen, and it was only a matter of months before they were married.

And though she could never be certain, she suspected that the uncanny procedure that would reverse foreground and background over the next three years began precisely as they said "I do" and kissed. Nevertheless, it had seemed out of the blue the first time Bobby's appeal was shoved from view, his flaws exposed, if only briefly. When they reappeared a short time later, only then to once again vanish, they were even more grating. In this way, they struck and fled countless times and at a quickening pace until finally, she was unable to argue any longer that he was more than this snide, repulsive loudmouth she couldn't recall inviting in. It was as if she'd been released from a spell when, night after night, she lay in a delirium of sleepless distress. What had she been thinking? He sold real estate. He bartered, exaggerated, lied. Suddenly, repulsed by his shortcomings, she could no longer ignore his tiny bald spot, thickening waist, and worst of all, the unbearable, unnameable vice hidden in his sour morning breath.

School was her refuge, and she went off each day trying to believe that things would change. The fourth-grade classroom brought daily satisfactions, the faces and energy fixated on her, hands poking the air in hope of her attention. It was while chatting at a citywide education conference with Wayne Miller, who was a history teacher and junior varsity football coach at Belger Central, the high school, that she started joking about the "semi-sadistic pleasure" she took in the sight of the kids squirming wordlessly for her to pick them, groaning because they thought they had the answer. Something in him paused and suggested that she consider the ring of that phrase. He tilted, eyeing her from an angle that forced the notion to hang between them. His glance was all innuendo and playful suggestion. She tried to look away, managed a partial pivot, but then returned, encountering him even more directly. He smiled to let her see that he was confident he knew her better than she knew herself. The smile angered her, but it didn't keep her out of his car that night, the passenger seat falling out from under her, as he loomed, pushing her down. With the first touch of his lips, she didn't know what she felt, and she thought, Well, that was nothing much. Then his lips opened, and the surge racing through her was as much panic as anything else. With his tongue, he stirred cravings she had banned as useless, even harmful. The hunger flooded back, the shame thrusting her fingers into his hair. She wanted to hurt him. He knocked her hands loose. Zippers, buttons, belts, the whole deal. She groaned and said, "No, no," and then he groaned, sounding like the children when they thought they had the answer. The next time they fucked in a motel, then a different motel, the apartment of a friend of his, a field—actually, a playground in the dark, starting on a swing, but ending in the grass, the shadow of the chains swaying over them, the swing itself squeaking. The available beds were many and could be repeated, and with each succeeding encounter, the galling stupidity of her marriage to Bobby became harder to bear.

A year went by before Wayne's wife found Janet's underwear wedged between the backrest and the seat cushion of his car, and her explosion declared Wayne's marriage over. Janet saw the moment as an opportunity to trash her own. Bobby had traveled to Waterloo for a convention, and she called him and made the receptionist drag him out of a presentation to tell him what was going on and that she wanted a divorce. He said he wouldn't stand for it. His resistance struck her as haughty. She shrieked that he had no choice. He said he didn't want to talk about it just then, but she better understand that as far as he was concerned, he always had a choice, and in this case especially, because it was his marriage they were talking about and he was a player in his own goddamn marriage, and also, and furthermore, he needed to know her goddamn reasons for even thinking such a thing, let alone saying it. She'd already told him about Wayne, but she threw him into the mix again. Bobby's response was to assert that, as much as he hated hearing about some other man, it wasn't enough. "Okay," she told him, "because you're fat and bald and full of shit."

"Oh," he said. "Well, I see. In that case, no problem. Thank you very much. That's just fine by me." He hung up, surprising her. She took the edge off the surprise with some Jack Daniel's, then sat down in their kitchen to study her surprise, which somehow shouldn't have existed. Now, what exactly had she expected after saying that? Her best answer was that she had no idea, and the taste of folly trailing that thought was hard to ignore. All of a sudden she sort of missed Bobby. He wasn't really fat, and he wasn't completely full of shit. Then came the next and biggest surprise. Wayne didn't want his marriage to end. He negotiated, begged, bartered, lied, charmed, and who knew what else to get back with his wife.

Janet hung tough, though, didn't give an inch. She hadn't wanted anything permanent with him anyway. But she did want something permanent with Bobby, which was to be rid of him. She was taking the leap, and fuck having a safety net. She moved out, knowing she was leaving many of her legal rights behind, packing her clothes and whatever else felt uniquely hers. She could not wait for the four-year fiasco of their so-called marriage to end. A difficult few days at her mother's place were followed by a week in a motel, and then she found her apartment.

The first night Wayne appeared at her door, she let him in, and when he kept appearing before, after, and during her divorce proceedings, she kept letting him in. The legal wrangling ended when she abruptly agreed to a settlement against her lawyer's advice. By then she'd traveled a long ways toward understanding that her current arrangement with Wayne was not merely acceptable but desirable, this jerk who phoned at unexpected hours and then raced up with his cock already a bulge in his pants, like some kind of burglar or prowler.

Which was more or less what he seemed at the moment as she stood in her kitchen, listening to his footfalls on the outside stairs. She closed her eyes and tried to imagine that it wasn't Wayne but a complete stranger. This other person, this other body wanting to walk into the dimness and walk right to her, like she'd dreamed him up, just undressing and smiling and humping and then leaving when he was done. All without a word, maybe. All in the dark and without a clear look at him. Hearing herself laugh derailed her thoughts, but the aura of intrigue had magnified around the figure knocking at her door, pushing his way in to find her sitting in that big old armchair. She didn't speak, telling herself that whoever this was, she didn't know him, didn't want him, had left the door unlocked by accident.

"Hey," he said, in a sound mostly suggestive breath, barely a word.

She still didn't respond. He loomed in the doorway, a shape ringed by the reach of the streetlight. He slowly draped his windbreaker over a kitchen chair. She did nothing as he took hold of her and moved her back to the armchair, and she said nothing until he had all her clothes off except for her underpants, and then she said, "You think you can just walk in here and do this, don't you?"

"I'm doing it," he said.

"Yeah, I guess you are. I give you that." She lifted her hips to help him, fixing her fingers in his hair with a ferocity that wanted to tear out clumps. "Look out," she said, "you asshole."

He smiled and produced a nub of marijuana from somewhere. He lit up and took a toke and passed it over. She was grateful because she'd run out. As she inhaled, he worked his mouth on her neck and shoulders. When she pulled him down, he was saying, "Baby, baby, baby." He'd started saying it when his hands, roaming under her T-shirt, first touched her belly, and then her bra with her breasts sweetly inside, and he'd kept saying it for a while, maybe stopping for this or that, but he was back to it now, his lips pausing near her lips to manage this rhythmic word, his incantation of whatever. Fucking. Romance. James Taylor. She went into a kind of state then, opening up to something that Wayne could not possibly provide or arrange for or be, though he participated while grunting from somewhere inside it. Then she remembered the collie, and her face felt pressed against the wire between them as she peered at him past blades of grass and rambled on about her secrets, while he watched her with interested, caring eyes. In a burst of wordless feeling, she longed for something more, and spiraling against Wayne, she demanded it of him, and he wasn't up to it, but he was what she had. He was behind her now, and in her, his belly curved over her butt and back, his hands on her nipples, and she covered his grasp with her own and worked his fingers like they were her own and he was delicious, or something was, a kind of promise turning into a rush of promises whose momentum drew her on. A shape flickered through her consciousness that she realized was aerial and had a wingspan as broad as that of a commercial aircraft.

Waking up felt sudden, but she didn't know if it was or wasn't. She felt catapulted from a dream she couldn't remember at all. Wayne was snoring, and she had to go to the bathroom, so it could have been him or her bladder that had roused her. Somewhere along the line, they'd reeled from wherever they'd started to her bed, where they'd finished, and then she'd gone out like a light, and so, apparently, had he.

She left him stealthily. He was a lean sprawl of pale skin on the white sheets, his chest bare, his right arm flung over his brow like he was thinking about a difficult question. To see him there gave her a bad feeling. Though he wouldn't be there long. The digital clock on her bedside table was shifting its greenish numerals from 1:32 to 1:33 with a faint pulsation. She stood watching for the next number, determined to see it arrive, even though she had to pee. The night her mother died, she'd been with Wayne. Isabel had gone to the movies with a few friends, and in the parking lot afterward, as they minced along chattering, her mother suddenly, wordlessly swooned. They'd called for help, and an ambulance came to take her to Koopman Hospital, where the doctors could do nothing. It had been a massive heart attack. Bernice had been there, and after they all drove to the hospital, she'd tried to alert Janet, phoning and phoning. But of course there was no way to reach Janet because she was clamped to

Wayne on that shoddy little bed in the Night Lite Motel west of town, moonlight pawing the windows, while the air conditioner battled the sweltering August night, the blinds sprung, the cracked glass patched with clear packing tape. The phone in her apartment must have rung and rung, but Janet, lost in her struggle to drink in every drop of pleasure possible from fucking her married man, was nowhere to be found. She wanted to blame Wayne when she found out all that had happened, but instead, or perhaps fueled by that blame merging with her guilt, she clung to him. With everything disappearing, her mom carried off, her dad long gone, her marriage finished, and the scary, violent impulse to quit her job closing in, the thought of jettisoning Wayne was more than she could handle. He wasn't around much anyway, wanting little to do with her beyond fucking, which was fine with her. The elimination of brain and being he sometimes brought was, as far as she knew, about all she hoped for.

But then a few months back—it was late July and hot and sticky with August looming—he'd called, wanting to come by. She was surprised to realize she wanted him to mention that the first anniversary of her mother's death was nearing, but he didn't say word one on the subject. And listening to him talk, she watched a kind of tawdry haze spread over their proposed rendezvous that night, or any night, for that matter, a neon glow of vulgar, shameful loneliness. She told him no. She said it several times. But he insisted, showing up at her door, where she told him she was done with him. It was over. His needy squint turned inward and then appeared to take note of a faraway object. He looked kind of relieved, leaving, and he'd stayed away until tonight.

Back from the bathroom, she climbed into bed, where the silvery wink of Wayne's watchband made her regret having been so carried away earlier that she hadn't slipped it off his wrist the way she liked to, so he'd be naked from tip to toe. If it was going to screech at her, as it had on four other occasions when the alarm went off after they'd stayed together into the early morning, she wished it were somewhere else—on the floor or bedside table. Just like she wished that at least once she had challenged him, if only teasingly, with her belief that the alarm was set so he would meet the deadline he and his wife had agreed on. Janet was sure they'd redefined faithfulness in their marriage as Wayne getting home by a certain hour, no matter where he'd been. No questions asked.

After a few minutes, when the silence dragged on except for his demure little bouts of snoring, she settled onto her back, her thoughts random and skittering until they came upon Bernice. She smiled, then felt annoyed at Bernice's intrusions and demands, along with her own compliance. It didn't take long before she was amused again, then surprisingly worried, as she pictured crazy old Bernice in her living room, waiting for whatever she thought was coming, the moon in the window, a freight train clanking by, a storm of angels on the horizon, like the ones painted on the ceiling of a church.

4

Bernice wiped herself daintily, trying, as she always did, to use as little toilet paper as possible. Threads of misery darted through her finger joints, and a catch in her shoulder made her stop, though she wasn't quite finished. She sighed, feeling plenty fed up, but also a little wistful that this might be the last time she did this. The night was quiet around her. It was hard to know how her body would fare after all the hoopla and show coming up. But the likelihood was it would be gone, or changed so much from what it had been, it might as well be gone. Probably not a lot of peeing in heaven, even with all the bodies raised up. But bodies, still. Could there be all this plumbing and flushing in that big high place? She felt a shade squeamish, like having these kinds of ideas was disrespectful to Jesus. Well, I'll just have to wait and see, she told herself, and the thought guided her eyes to the window high in the wall, as if the thing she sought might appear. But the angle didn't give her much of a view, and the blind was pulled partway down, so she had to imagine the night beyond.

My last pee, she thought. She looked at her hands resting on her pale thighs opened by the way she was situated on the toilet. Regret was like stirred-up dust falling inside her. Lord, she thought. Nostalgia was one reckless fool, the way it could take any old thing and tack on a bunch of claims more suitable to a precious heirloom. My last pee. This second time, the idea forced her to let out a bit of a snort at how funny it was. But she stayed sitting and waiting to pee some more. She knew she still might, because even though the urge had been strong enough to force her out of bed, she'd had to sit there real patient, breathing to relax, knowing she best not get all tensed up. So it was sensible to let a minute or two pass and give things a chance. It was her body, all right, and in a lot of ways she could boss it around, but there were times and places where it had a mind of its own. After a while, though, she was standing and flushing without even deciding she'd had enough. Well, I guess that's that, she thought.

Happy and Sappy were outside the door. Not General. He didn't trouble himself with all that much these days. The other two were breathy shadows eager for her to show the way they should all go in the dark. She knew the layout like the back of her hand, but with her glasses off, she might as well have been on the prowl inside a cloud. Her fingers floated to the hallway switch, where they hesitated, as she worried that it was foolhardy to spotlight her whereabouts. She had the sense that there was somebody in her house, an intruder who had lost track of her, so why make herself conspicuous. No need to ask for trouble. It had been the same when she got up to go. She'd been laying there for a while, wondering if she should fight to keep awake. Was it okay to put on a nightgown? Every sound had made her nervous, whether it came from the street, from one of the animals, from something passing high overhead that might not be an airplane. The heating unit went on and off. The walls groaned. And then she must have been dozing, because the urge to pee had opened her eyes. Beyond that she hadn't been able to move a muscle, all but paralyzed by the notion of rising and walking, for fear of coming to the attention of a presence she sensed lurking nearby. She wondered if it was Jesus, or one of the angels, though it could be something just plain scary loose in the night. Whatever it was, she saw no reason to stand out in a crowd. But then the pee started leaking, and she didn't have a second to lose.

Now she was tiptoeing, like a scared little mouse, until she made certain the bulky shape in front of her was the bed. Her heart was racing, and she prayed it would slow. Given her problems, she didn't want to drop dead before Jesus got there. For the umpteenth time, she reminded herself that she knew better and knew it was all a matter of God's grace and glory. She lay back, praying for help, and wondering all over again if she should put on her nightgown and get comfortable. She'd rolled her stockings down to her ankles but still wore her Depends. Somehow she just wasn't ready to give up looking presentable after taking forever to decide on her outfit. She'd considered every possible skirt and dress she owned, all the while feeling drawn to her baby-blue pantsuit. When she posed, holding it up in front of her, the image in her vanity mirror had been a sharp reminder of how much she liked the way she looked in it, and how comfortable she felt wearing it. But what bothered her and won out in the long run was her fear that it might not be respectful. Not formal enough, not serious. She wanted to be proper, and knew it was foolish to be making a big deal out of her clothes, but there was no way around the feeling that she was expecting important company. The most important ever, angels and the Lord, so how could she not want to look suitable, in spite of the fact that finding certainty about what might be suitable for such an occasion was about as likely as pushing back the hands of time. But at least things were simple in the shoe department, where her orthopedic lace-ups didn't have a single competitor.

Happy and Sappy were watching, and she wondered what they would make of this whole crazy fuss when it happened. And the cats, too. She tried to imagine being Elmira zonked out and then this angel flies into the house. Or maybe more than one. Were they going to come through the roof? In the windows? Would they open the windows? Break the glass? Cut open the roof? Just elbow the beams and shingles aside like somebody barging through a curtain? And would they seem the least bit unusual to a cat? Maybe even these gigantic birds? What did a cat think, anyway? Or a dog? They sure seemed to care about things.

She sat up. "Elmira," she said, "where are you?" She put on her glasses and strained to find the cat whose shape emerged on a footstool beneath the window turned hazy by the streetlight. Bernice was stroking the blanket the way she might Elmira's fur. Just then Ira sprang onto the bed. Suddenly, Bernice didn't like being unable to see General, who was off in the other room. In spite of the risks of what might wait in the dark, she went to him, and in spite of her aches and pains and his protests, she dragged his bed into the hall outside her bedroom door, where she could keep an eye on him. Happy and Sappy got all stirred up by such strange goings-on, while General staggered behind her, annoyed and confused. He prowled his bed in circles, searching for the special spot he'd lost when she disturbed him. Everybody and everything was so damn particular. Poor old General, driven by dissatisfaction, either found what he was after or gave up, because he flopped abruptly, his haunches dragging the rest of him down with a grunt. Happy and Sappy were stalking her bed, their peace of mind disrupted by the nervous way Bernice was acting. Happy looked up, her big ears tensing and relaxing. She wasn't alarmed but seemed to be asking if anything was required of her. No, thought Bernice. Not at the moment. What a group. What a menagerie.

She lifted her Bible from the bedside table and turned on her reading lamp. The light made her nervous but also gave her hope that she might find something soothing. She thought a psalm might be what she wanted, if only she could find the right one. Maybe if she— At the jangle of the telephone, she nearly jumped out of her skin. Happy and Sappy bounded onto the bed, Sappy landing with all his weight on her ankle. "Watch where you're goin'. I'm not some rock here," she scolded, jerking her foot free. Ira scanned them all from a regal perspective that in no way meant he was alarmed, but he certainly did not like having his sleep disturbed. Bernice was so confused, she stood and threw on the ceiling lights, as if seeing would help her know what to do. The commotion had General up, his cocked ears searching like those gigantic radar machines you saw in movies trying to pluck answers from the air, even though he couldn't hear a thing anymore. And the phone kept ringing. Lord, Bernice thought, hastily returning the room to darkness. Now what? Aside from the ordinary questions about a call at this hour, she had to cope with this tomfoolery in her head, where it was angels on the line, and this was her wake-up call. Or the second she responded, Reverend Tauke would announce that it was all going to start. Or he would tell her she'd been dropped from the list, or the whole thing had been called off and he was sitting in the living room of the parsonage, working his way through his list of contact numbers, like the host of a canceled party. By now General had come partway into her room, and when she met his eyes, their intent was as clear as if he'd shouted at her: What the hell is going on?

Feeling rebuked and driven by the memory of other phone calls in other nights, almost all of them bringing bad news—illness or accident and death—what choice did she have but to answer. Utterly put upon by everything and everybody, dogs, cats, Reverend Tauke, even God and His angels, she let loose a resentful snort. "Hello."

"Bernice, it's Janet," said the voice on the other end. "Listen, I'm sorry to wake you."

"Janet." Bernice gave the name a turn, like it belonged to somebody she couldn't remember ever having heard of. Good Lord, she thought.

"I thought you might be awake. How's everything going?"

"Fine, Janet. What are you doing? You scared me half to death."

"Sorry. I have to tell you something."

"How do you mean?"

"That's why I'm calling."

"You're not going to back out on me, are you? I sure hope not. What are you doing up, anyway? You're sure there's nothing wrong."

"No, no, no. Well, sort of."

"You can't back out now. We're all so worked up over here, you have no idea. You're about all we got to count on."

"I'm not backing out, Bernice. But it wouldn't matter if I was. I had a dream. Just now—it woke me up. It was a vision. Like in your surgery."

"That wasn't no dream. Not in that surgery."

"Sure it was. I mean, it was like a dream."

"What are you talking about? I woke up. That's what happened to me. In the middle of surgery. Scariest thing I ever went through. You can imagine. There they are. These people with their knives and whatnot, and you wake up. Just imagine."

"Right."

"So that wasn't a dream. I never called it a dream because I never would have. I thought I might die of pure fright until the vision came along. I told you that."

"Right."

"It was then and there—that split second, the whole thing turned around. I just wasn't scared anymore."

"Right, right."

It sounded to Bernice like Janet was stumbling from word to word. Just having all kinds of trouble, like her thoughts were awkward objects it was hard to work with. "Okay, then, Janet. What are you calling about? I don't see what that is as of yet."

"What I mean is, I was dreaming. So it was different than your surgery in one way, but like it in this other way."

"Okay, but what way?"

"I just woke up. I was asleep and dreaming, only the way I was dreaming was very different than any other dream I ever had."

"How?"

"The way it felt. It didn't feel like a dream."

"How did it feel?"

"What do you mean?"

"I'm trying to get at how it was different from other dreams you had."

"It reminded me of what you said. Remember you said that in your surgery, it was like a dream, only different. I thought of that same idea. There was an angel, and he was as big as a Boeing 707, and he wanted to tell me something. At first I didn't want to talk to him, but he was very insistent. I tried not to hear him, but somehow I had to. I just had to."

"Okay," said Bernice. "I'm with you."

"So what it turned out to be was that he had come to tell me something, but it wasn't for me. It was for you, because you weren't going. Even if it happens. Even if everybody else goes. That you shouldn't go. And I should tell you. There were still things for you to do here. On earth. Lots of things."

"What'd he look like?"

"What do you mean? He was big. You know. Wings. An angel. Kind of gleaming eyes and a wingspan that— well, it was as wide as on a commercial aircraft."

Poor kid, Bernice thought. Just a misfit from start to finish. She couldn't get anything right. Ever since she was little and lying in the grass, staring at that old penned-up collie, her expression all mushy, like she was falling in love. Just went off the track, giving up on Bobby Crimmins when he was as sweet as a chocolate chip cookie, at least as far as Bernice could tell, based mainly on what Isabel said and kept on saying even after the divorce. Well, especially after the divorce. Now, that was a crazy business—Isabel and Bobby carrying on in the way they did once Bobby and Janet got divorced. You'da thought they might just start something up, not that it was possible. Though the way things went these days, you never could tell. That kinda funny business sure happened often enough on her soaps. If they'da been on *The Guiding Light* or *General Hospital,* or if Isabel had been younger, there might've been hell to pay. And now Janet was up there in that little apartment doing nothing, from what people said, except running around in more ways than one. This guy or that guy, but especially that one, Wayne what's-his-name. And then actually running all over the countryside, working up a sweat and ending up where she started. And now this phone call.

Bernice couldn't tell if the right thing to do was to humor Janet, or give her a dose of the truth. The animals had settled a bit. Happy and Sappy were grooming each other at the foot of the bed. It never failed to give Bernice a sweet twinge to see them licking away at each other. Right now it was Sappy, with his face stuck up like nothing could be better than to have Happy slurping along his snout. General had flopped in the hall, and Ira was nestling his nose deeper into the curve of his own belly.

Bernice didn't know how long she'd gone without hearing a word Janet said. The poor kid was talking a blue streak, and Bernice was fishing around for a clear sense of what to do, when she blurted out, "This was a dream tonight. You just woke up from it. That's your point?"

"Yes."

"Wait a minute, wait a minute. I think we have to look at this thing some other way. Let me help you out. My guess is this angel—if he was an angel—was talking to you."

"He was definitely an angel. And he was talking to me—that's what I'm saying. But the information was for you."

Something struck Bernice odd just then. She'd noticed it earlier but had failed to focus on it the way she should have. "Why are you whispering?"

"Well," Janet said, "it's late."

"I don't see how that would matter to you one way or the other. Last time I looked, you lived alone. That's my thought. So speak up. Who you going to bother?"

The silence was rich with hints like little fires lighting a path for Bernice to follow. Pretty soon she was going to get a look at something, and it'd be fun to see it.

"It doesn't matter. Why does it matter?" Janet said at last. "It's just the way I'm talking."

"Except I can hardly hear you."

"You seem to be doing just fine."

"I gotta tell you, it's a strain. Talk up."

"Just listen."

"What?" Bernice said. "I didn't quite catch that."

"Oh, Bernice, don't act stupid."

"Unless you're not alone. Is that it, you got company, Janet? If so, say so, and I'll stop badgering you on this front, but if you don't, would you just please have a little consideration for a—"

"You're not going, Bernice. When they go. If they go."

Lord, she's a stubborn little thing, Bernice thought. "Janet," she said, "let's keep in mind that you are the one saying this. You see my point. This is just according to you."

"Actually, it's according to the angel."

"In your dream."

"I guess."

"What'd he do, come to the wrong house? Don't he know where I live? You'd think if he had this kind of news for me, the least he could do is locate the right street address and give the message face-to-face."

"You would think that, sure. I just hope you don't expect me to explain the angel's behavior to you. I'm new to this, you know. You're the experienced one."

"I think that's the whole thing in a nutshell. How are you going to know anything about what he meant or didn't?"

"I'm not talking about that."

"You sure are."

"I mean his meaning. No. I don't want to get involved in that. In anything to do with his meaning. What he—"

"Well, that's what you're doing, whether you want to or not, because what you said not more than a second ago, unless I misunderstood—I mean, if we just backpedal—"

"No, no. I'm just talking about what he said. The actual words. The sentence and what he—"

"Okay, okay. And what he said, as far as you're trying to tell me, is that I'm not going."

"That's more or less the way he put it."

"Can I point out something, Janet? I think I have to. He's in your dream, and you're the one not going. You're asleep, and you woke up and you— I appreciate your troubling yourself for me, but Reverend Tauke has spoken on this matter. As if he knew this kind of mix-up might crop up and cause some kind of trouble, so he—"

"Bernice! Wait!" Her whisper was hoarse, like she wanted to shout but didn't dare. "Here's where I'm stuck. Because what sense would that make, since we both know I'm not going?"

"That's right. That's what I'm—"

"I don't need some angel to tell me."

"If you'd just let me get my two cents' worth in, that's what I'm saying. It wasn't a real angel, but just a dream. You had a dream with an angel in it. That's where I'd put my money. Given everything that's been going on and our discussion this afternoon, you misunderstood. You're just confused."

In the silence, she could almost see Janet seated somewhere in her apartment, some man tangled in the nearby sheets. Probably that Wayne what's-his-name from up at school. What was his name? She knew it, and it troubled her that she couldn't come up with it.

"You know what, Bernice? I guess I thought I ought to give you a heads-up, you know. Just in case."

"Okay. So you did." On the other hand, Bernice wondered, why would she be bothering to call me if she has some man in her bed?

"What is going on over there? Anything?" Janet asked.

"It's quiet, more or less. But it could all happen in a flash, I would guess. So let's try and remember, the night is young."

"So it is. So it is, Bernice. Okay, enough's enough. I'll come by about ten. See you then."

The mockery was hard to miss, and though the smart thing was to pay it no mind, just let it pass, Bernice found herself saying, "I'm taking note of that dig. Don't think I'm not, Janet."

"What dig?"

"Like you don't know. You just can't help but be a snot every now and then, can you?"

"I guess not."

"That'd be my assessment."

"Okay, then, let's call it a night."

"Sure. Good night."

"Good night."

Bernice put the phone down and sat in the dark. All the animals were peaceful, except for General, whom she could hear off slurping and gulping at his water bowl. A terrible thirst preyed on him these days. Partly, it was from the steroids he took to stimulate his appetite, but no matter what the cause, he sounded desperate lapping on and on, and she felt that she should stop him, because it didn't seem good for him to drink so much. She'd have dog piss to clean up in the morning. Or somebody would. His bladder was a real trial. Almost worse than her own. She wondered if maybe she should lock him up in the bathroom the way she'd done a while back when she'd covered a hospital bed pad with a blanket for him to sleep on, and then she would throw the whole mess in the washer each morning. But he was too pitiful, moaning and sopping and so distraught over his inability to get away from what he'd done. She couldn't keep it up.

He'd stopped now, and she pictured him wandering around confused about why his bed wasn't where it belonged. She'd have to go help him if he didn't remember soon. But he came trekking into the hall, his front legs almost crossing, his stiff hind legs stabbing clumsily, as if he could only hope the floor was still there. He put himself down carefully. The plaid cover was removable and could be washed if he peed on it, along with the bed itself, though cramming that big thing into the washer was a chore.

They were all quiet, each animal a clump of inky fur and constant breath. She exhaled, hoping to join them, trying to match their easy rhythm. Her ears were sore from the clasps of the earrings, and though she regretted not keeping them on till the big event, she had to remove them to her bedside table. Same with the brooch.

When she lay back, the troublesome bulge under her turned out to be her Bible. She enfolded it in her arms, drawing the Good Book close, rumpling her blouse for sure. After all the care she'd taken, now she was sleeping in her clothes. But she was at the end of her rope. Just a little shut-eye. Forty winks. And maybe she'd never wake up. Maybe she'd just be gone. No more worries about anything.

With her eyes closed, she saw faint shapes, the resting bodies of her pets that seemed to float around her, while their names bobbed about in her head—General, Happy, Ira, Elmira, Sappy—each comforting and friendly on its own, and hinting, as they trailed one after the other, at some unknown childhood song.

5

WHAT A LOAD OF BULLSHIT, thought Janet. She tucked her feet under her butt in the armchair, resisting the urge to slam the phone down. First she'd racked her brain to come up with some sort of scheme to help Bernice, and after finally hitting upon this lie about angels and sleep and whatever, she had to figure out whether or not it was right to make the call. So she'd made the call, trying to coddle the crazy old bitch, and ended up lectured and feeling idiotic. On the verge of picking the phone back up to inform Bernice she could feed her own damn animals, she realized that Wayne was staring at her.

"What're you doing?" he asked.

Embarrassed that he might have eavesdropped, she tugged down on the hem of the oversize T-shirt she'd put on before making the call. He padded around the hall corner into the kitchen for a drink from the tap, and she explained, keeping close to the truth but exaggerating certain phrases to make Bernice sound ridiculous. With an apple plucked from the fridge, he ambled off and she followed until he flopped back into bed. She hovered in the doorway, tilting against the sill. Getting a laugh out of Wayne could stop him from asking too many questions. At the same time, mocking Bernice had lowered the level of her irritation.

"I heard of that," he said.

"Have you, now?"

"Hasn't everybody?"

"Actually, I doubt it. There's nothing everybody has heard of."

"Wanna bet she doesn't go?" He took a big bite of apple, chewed, and chuckled. "She'll be there feeding her own animals and making up some sorry-assed excuse."

"That would be my bet."

"So why the hell are you calling her?"

"I'm just indulging her."

"But why are you calling her?"

"I'm indulging her, I told you."

"I don't get it."

"Well, I've done my best to explain it."

"Okay, then, come on here and indulge me. We don't have all that much time together, and you're over there calling up this old biddy. Not the best use of our time, I don't think."

"Probably not."

"C'mon, now. C'mon, let me indulge you."

"You were sleeping." Unmoving, she hoped she appeared reluctant, even while enjoying the dimples that came and went as he spoke in the half-light sneaking through the blinds. "I woke up, you know. I got restless."

"You should have woke me up. I'm like a dog. You poke me, I'm ready to go." He loved to play the simple soul, a bit of a shitkicker, which was his background, since he'd grown up on a farm, but most of the enduring traits were a willed pose, and they both knew it. Still, it was fun to pretend he didn't teach high school but was just some country boy.

"I was worried about Bernice, and what I got for my trouble was she scolds me like a child."

"Isn't that the way of it. No good deed goes unpunished. And all the while I'm right here. You know what I wish? I wish you'd just leaned over and gave me a kiss while I was still sleeping."

"Yeah?"

"That's right."

She was warming to him, and it was perfectly agreeable the way his eyes shone as he watched her attraction to him grow. She floated across, letting it seem his words drew her, and maybe they did.

"Just like I was Sleeping Beauty," he said, and set the last of the apple down.

"So that'd make me the Prince."

"Yes, it would. And you know what I would like more than anything?" He took her hand to his thigh and slid it to his cock. "See, you could do this to wake me up. That'd be one way."

"I think the Prince kisses his beauty."

"That'd even be better." He put his lips to hers, loitering, like maybe this little sweetness was all he needed and he couldn't believe his luck. He retreated, but barely, so his eyes were vague dark spheres, and he looked kind of bashful and sneaky, the apple sweet on his mouth. "I'd give anything if you'd do that. Wake me up with a kiss. Wake me up with your mouth on my cock. Just pull me up from a dream, and wake me up, and there you are."

"We could pretend you're sleeping now," she said as she nudged along his chest toward his belly, and thought, What the hell am I doing? But momentum had its effects, among them a certain sense of irresistibility, which she recognized as his desire combining with her more or less automatic interest in what he wanted.

He sank back, saying, "I am feeling drowsy." The startling screech of his wristwatch alarm was like a nasty stranger stomping into the room. He fumbled to shut it up. Though nothing definite went through her mind, her foggy interest in him was shoved aside by short-lived amazement that left her embarrassed. He smiled, opening his arms like a playful drunk. " 'I'm a steamroller, baby,' " he sang, doing a fairly decent imitation of James Taylor with his voice and the way he stuck his head straight forward. " 'And I'm bound to roll you over. I'm a cement mixer, baby, and I'm—' "

"You're a landfill is what you are," she said.

"What I am is yours to do with as you want."

"Didn't your wife just call?"

"Of course not. What?"

"I'm talking about your watch."

"Listen, now. Let's not let reality creep into this sweet moment. It's been way too long since we had time enough and—"

"Hey, Wayne," she said, "the alarm has sounded."

"Okay, okay." His voice rose and fell, close to singing. "I know."

"So rise and shine. Time to go."

"No, no, no." He sort of hummed the words, as if he were background to her lead in some kind of duet.

"Gotta meet that deadline."

"C'mon, now." He rode the words to get close to her, entwining her wrists in his big hands.

That he thought he could work his way back to the situation minutes ago, when she was inches from sucking his cock, infuriated her. But the anger was risky. The intensity dragged her toward some twisted juncture where going down on him might seem vengeful and necessary, her fury perverted. She pulled hard, freeing her hands, as if escape were only a matter of getting out of his grasp. She was going to dig a ditch between them, fill it with fire. "The point I'm trying to make, Wayne, is get out."

"Let's go back. Just back up. Forget about the goddamn stupid watch. It shouldn't have happened. I promise it will never—"

"I told you before, dammit, I asked you before—you should not come around here."

"I can't stay away. It won't work."

"It'll work if you do it. It will work just fine if you stay the fuck away."

"We tried it. Look where we are."

"Well, we're going to try it again."

"What for, honey? It makes no sense to do it if it doesn't work."

"So we can practice. This wasn't supposed to happen."

"But it had to. You know it had to."

"Why did it have to, Wayne? Because of some power between us. Some allure, some compelling hypnotic bullshit." Oh, right, she thought, the hypnotist. He had to be in on this one for sure. "Abracadabra! Wayne!"

"What?"

"Abra-fucking-cadabra! I think if you think that, all you're doing is thinking about your hard-on."

He barely moved yet communicated hurt disbelief. "Well, sure. What's wrong with that?" He took a second to absorb the aftershock, at last locating a perspective that made him almost shout, "I'll tell you what! Nothing. Except that you just try to belittle us, the way we feel together, the way—"

"Keep your voice down!"

"You're getting me all worked up because you don't seem capable of anything more than belittling everything we—"

"Fine. Great. If that's what I'm doing—whatever I'm doing—fine." She saw his eyes flitting, like those of a kid cheating on a test, as he peeked at his watch. It was a strain not to scream at him, but she substituted her palm slamming into her forehead, like a cartoon character getting a big idea. "Listen to me. It's over. Whatever it is, it has to end. It's over."

"I don't agree. I think we have to air this thing out. Ventilate it—give it a chance to breathe."

The way he spoke, matching her hush, made her leery that, while they might keep from rousing her landlord, their conspiratorial whisper was drawing them together the way it would if they shared an underlying goal. "No," she told him. "We just have to stop. Stop talking about it and stop doing it."

"Okay, all right," he said, and scanned the room wearily.

She figured he was looking for his clothes while trying to appear beaten into submission by her arguments. But she guessed the truth was he'd run out of time, and if he didn't get a move on, the shit would hit the fan at home. "So you've come to your senses," she said. "Attaboy." As his confusion mounted, she realized he'd completely forgotten getting out of his clothes in the other room. The chance to make him late stirred a vengeful image of him racing across town that was erased by her wish to be alone. "The other room, Wayne! Remember. The chair!"

He threw his hands up as if he could not believe how unfair she was being. "So let me ask you one question. If this isn't what's supposed to happen, what is supposed to happen?"

"You're supposed to go."

He shook his head, his dismay leading him to locate his red cotton briefs balled up on the floor. "When people talk about how something is 'supposed to' happen, it just means other people want it. It means it isn't what you want or I want. And there are a lot of goddamned 'supposed to's in this world. Too damn many."

"So get out."

"Didn't you hear me?" He sat to tug on his briefs.

"Every word. And in this case, Wayne, it's what I want. I want it."

"All right." He stood and stomped from the room. "I need to get home, anyway."

"Yes, you do." She was right with him. "You have some kind of an arrangement, don't you—you and the Mrs.?"

"Me and Sally? No, no. We just let things be."

"When is it, Wayne? When's the deadline? When is it still acceptable for you to come sneaking in?"

"I just told you. We just let—"

"Bullshit."

"We don't need that kind of conventional crap."

"So why set the alarm?"

"I have my own rules." All at once, reaching for his pants on the floor, he cracked up. "Anyway, she's a heavy sleeper."

"Now you're going to laugh about it?"

"I don't know. I guess. You tickle me."

That almost got her going, and she had to tighten her lips to keep from joining him. He always had that ability, the way things flowed over him like he was a rock in the rapids and whatever passed by was just fine.

"I have three kids, you know, I can't walk out on them. I can't turn into some deadbeat dad just to suit you."

"Wayne," she said. "Not now."

"What?" He gave her a flash of doe-eyed, offended innocence meant to explain that if she felt goaded or humiliated, it had nothing to do with him, because he was simply stating facts.

"I don't mean to scare you, but maybe you ought to think about why you said that. A moment of self-examination, okay? You think you could handle that, Wayne?"

"Sure. But what's the big deal? You know I have kids."

"That's right. I've seen you all at the mall. You and her and them—the family and the family man—so why tell me?"

"You're telling me to get out. Why do you think you have to say that?"

"Because I want you to get out."

He laughed again. "Okay. If that's what you want." Carefully, stuffing in the tail of his unbuttoned shirt, he said, "Not that you know what you want."

"Tell me how to make it any goddamn clearer, Wayne."

"I think you could make it clearer if you knew what it was. If you knew what you wanted. But it would still be bullshit, clear or not." He buckled his belt and stepped into one shoe, then bent to pick up the other. "I love you. You know that. I love you, honey, but you have to want to see me, too, or it's just too hard. It's just too hard."

"What are you talking about?"

"I can't keep doing this."

"I don't want you to keep doing it. That's what I'm telling you, you fucking idiot." Now she was laughing, and the pang she felt marked how she would miss him and mostly, she would miss his enviable knack of living untroubled by the fact that he made so little sense.

"You don't know what you're telling me," he said. "That's why it keeps changing around."

He brushed past, his hands snatching at her to move her aside, and his touch launched a sensation that almost won her back, a nip of desire eager to take her over. But he didn't seem to notice, or to feel it himself. As he faced her, he was intent on nothing more than making his point. "You're nuts," he said. "You're like talking to a child. But I love you."

"You know why you like James Taylor so much, is because you are just like him. New words every now and then. Sort of. But it's always the same old tune."

He gazed at her, and she could see him fighting to keep a straight face, but his higher principles forbade even mild amusement at any slander against James Taylor. It felt like the last thing that could possibly occur when his maroon windbreaker rose from the chair and the door slammed shut behind him.

She stood very still. Then she started for the bedroom window to make certain he went. If she needed a reason to peek past the shut venetian blinds, that was it. The Lexus sneaked up from its hiding place beyond the corner, and then, as he was about to creep by, the engine revved and he shot under the streetlight. Even muffled by the walls, the roar shocked the quiet street. His taillights climbed to the tip of the hillside, where they vanished. Nothing moved across the landscape other than black clouds above the rows of orderly houses, as if the night were preparing something angry and offended, because of how she had just acted and what she had done, sending him away.

She went to the back door and bolted it shut, and in the immediate silence after the click, it was as if a precious plate had tumbled and she was waiting for the crash. Both her anger and her groundless misgiving felt darkly prescient. She needed a drink and poured an inch of Jack Daniel's and took it with a turn of her wrist. But it did nothing to stop the festering impression that Wayne was out there telling his buddies what she had done, and they were all laughing to hide their rage as they drank and teased him, turning into a mob.

She could not keep away from the back door, the parted curtains uncovering the descent of the stairs to the point where vision was defeated. Not that Wayne and his buddies were the only lowlifes who might come calling. Just last month cops had busted a meth lab maybe a quarter of a mile into those trees, and meth dealers and addicts were totally random in their deranged cravings, and though she had no use for that crap, Ed Suther and Karl Rupp had graduated from high school with her, and they were both dealers and users. Any time he got half a chance, Rupp gave her a sort of unhinged, you-know-you-want-to-fuck-me stare. And as long as she was charting lunacy, she shouldn't skip the homicidal time bomb holed up in some normal enough home in a neighborhood just like hers. There he was, pacing in circles to hold back the mayhem he longed to release in order to express himself beyond what he had so far managed with his buffed car, his manicured lawns.

Closing her fingers on the doorknob, she pulled hard, proving that the bolt would hold, and her success bought a giddy, full-blown moment of self-mockery, which she fully deserved, because her behavior was becoming ridiculous.

Back in bed, she arranged one of the pillows alongside her, then tugged the sheet and blanket over her shoulders. Enclosing the compliant pillow in her arms, she nestled in yearning for sleep, while the strange sense of absence she hoped to keep at bay filled the room.

6

Bernice was at the kitchen table, eating ice cream. Having parceled out two scoops of her favorite, Blue Bunny pistachio almond, into a bowl, she was determined to make every spoonful last, just the way she used to with her brother Hank, sitting on the curb in front of the corner grocery store on a summer night, watching the cars go by, licking away at the tasty trickles running down the cone so not a drop could go to waste, and feeling like they'd struck it rich with the cold sweetness melting in their mouths.

She had dozed after talking to Janet until a weird scraping followed by a shriek had startled her awake, fearful that the roof was shredding like the plaster and lumber were no more than tissue paper in the monstrous fingers of an angel. Her dry mouth and tongue had felt packed with sand, her heart stuck between beats, though her pale bedroom ceiling remained. She might have relaxed had not Happy and Sappy chosen that second to bound up onto her bed. They'd shaken themselves excitedly and attended her like little soldiers ready for whatever duty might come. Finally getting her glasses on, she'd wanted to scold them but had been too happy to see them. The bedroom windows were pretty much the way she'd left them—the mild chill in the room entering through the one she'd nudged open for fresh air at bedtime. As she'd moved to close things up, the shriek had come again, and she'd recognized the brakes of a big truck crossing the connector to one of the warehouses. The puzzle of the scraping had continued to nag her until she'd heard General scrabbling about in the kitchen. His toenails, probably in need of trimming, had been grinding on the hardwood floor. He'd been circling his empty water bowl, so she'd given him a refill and compared the wall clock to her watch, and both had been a little past four.

Sure enough, she'd needed to pee again, and it had seemed an adventure and sort of unusual when she had to poo. She'd come out of the bathroom feeling oddly successful and free, like a child skipping school, and surprisingly wide awake, putting the lights on without giving it a second thought. Probably Janet's phone call, and all that hullabaloo, had changed things around, making the way she'd been on pins and needles seem pointless. Plus she'd had some sleep. Of course, she'd come out of it looking to find the world near its end. But maybe she was just getting used to that kind of thing, and that was the simple fact of the matter, because all at once she'd realized she was hungry. Standing there giving her little house the once-over, she'd made her mind up to have a midnight snack and to make it ice cream. Knowing that the smart thing would be to protect her blouse from any possible mess, she'd hurried to her bedroom, where she'd pulled on her turquoise sweatshirt embroidered with hearts and doggies. As long as she was there, she'd grabbed the brooch and earrings so they'd be handy in case she needed to put them on in a rush.

The kitchen had flashed with pristine sharpness and dazzle the instant the lights switched on. The silver trim of the refrigerator drawers had shared a winking glitter with the pink of the Tupperware, the green of the celery, the blazing red of half a tomato in a baggie, the escaping cool a lovely breeze.

So there she sat, scooping out her second helping of pistachio almond from the pint carton, which was likely to end up licked clean, because she did love her ice cream. A question that had come to her a few minutes ago, and which she couldn't recall this second, had started her thinking there wouldn't be a lot different about this night if she was waiting to die instead of waiting for what she was waiting for. She'd recoiled, not wanting to get morbid, trying to push the notion away, but it was like a rainstorm that had caught her out-of-doors, and wherever she turned, there it was. She glanced at her brooch and earrings neatly placed and within easy reach on the tabletop. More than half of her Blue Bunny pint remained as she returned it to the freezer. Except if she was dying, she thought, she would probably be sick and suffering and not eating ice cream. Unless she was going to be murdered. She could be eating ice cream then. Or if she dropped over of a heart attack, which would probably be what happened when her number came up—then she might be sitting like this, eating ice cream. But, of course, she couldn't know ahead of time that she was going to be murdered or drop over, and so she wouldn't be waiting. Though if she was someone who was going to be executed, she would know, and she could be eating ice cream. In fact the odds were high that she would be eating ice cream. If she was on death row, and the day, the hour, the method were all known, she would have picked out her last meal. Ice cream, for sure. But then she would be a murderer or worse. Whatever might be worse. There was some kind of label for it—a special kind of murderer. She couldn't come up with the category but knew it existed, because they used it on Court TV. "Monster. Brute. Sociopath." That was one that got said a lot. But she wasn't any kind of murderer and would never be.

The main point, though, was that what she was dealing with was so brand-new it had never happened before. It was a one-of-a-kind sort of thing, and so hard to think about because, when you got right down to it, it was hard to know what it was. Mainly because it was untried. First time out of the chute. Dying, she guessed, might be like looking into a darkness full of unknown things and bad feelings for sure, this hole, or some kind of back alley a person was wandering down or lost in. Or like a long walk in the dark woods, the way her cousin Miriam had died sixty years ago, running away from home, but making it only as far as a ditch she couldn't see on such a moonless night. So in she went headfirst like a varmint into a trap set just for her, and when she hit, she broke her neck. But tonight what Bernice was waiting for wasn't dark and wasn't a hole, but rather, this embrace from on high. The coming of these rescuing angels with big arms and hands and wings of blazing light, and what the hell was she talking about and thinking about, anyway?

She struggled up and hurried to the refrigerator for more ice cream.

It looked like she was starting to wonder about things she shouldn't—she was starting to doubt, just like Reverend Tauke had warned her she might, warned them all they probably would, and she was glad for that, because she could feel how her state of mind was pigheaded and not ready to give an inch as she sat back down and took a big bite. She was beginning to question whether she believed one hundred percent the way she was supposed to that the Rapture was coming to bear her off, and did she even want to? And did she have a choice? She wished she could stop these thoughts, or at least hide them from sight, but they were like ants in the cupboard now, just pouring in.

She should get her Bible, she knew, not that she felt sharp enough to handle a complete sentence, let alone a whole scripture. The sugar had her brain in an uproar, and her eyesight was hazy even with her glasses on at this late hour.

Wanting to dull the sting of her irreverent thoughts, along with the feeling of being not only sinful but washed up, she was helpless to keep her mind from melting into the dreamy sweetness soaking her tongue when she heard a weird, sensual cry. The ice cream wasn't enough to draw that kind of a moan from her, and besides, the source was behind her. She turned, and there was Sappy on his back, writhing and kicking the air with delight, his head back, his shoulders and fanny squirming in opposite directions, and all the while this drunken happiness sang out of him. Happy was seated formally, watching with interest, while Bernice felt dumbstruck and privileged, almost, as if she were witnessing a natural wonder—Sappy twisting and moaning, his feet up in the air—and the way she felt brought back gazing off at the Grand Canyon when they'd gone there, her and Toby, pulling off to the side, the two of them putting coins in the mounted binoculars and sighing and declaring their appreciation of the craggy streaks of color and glare, just letting it pour over them, this crazy rock pile and miles of dazzle, like they were looking into an explosion. It had been something, all right, and they'd tried out this or that word to take hold of what they were feeling about the unusualness everywhere around them, and the weird sensation that they were pioneers in an unexplored world, when the simple truth was everybody pretty much knew about it and millions had seen it, and they were only now finding it for themselves. But that was the fun of it, when you got right down to it, because they were there together, and if they'd never seen it before, it was somehow like nobody ever had. Isabel was with them, and Edgar, too, neither of them showing a hint of trouble or unhappiness. She could see her own dear husband, Toby, and the thoughtful way he read the brochures on glaciers and geology and recited the details he found, like it mattered what he understood or didn't. Like there was something big and important at stake, something that needed to be proved, such as the fact that he was smart. Not all that long ago, really, and he was sturdy and happy, and as far as anybody would have judged, even the best doctor in the world, just the picture of health. Of course, the cancer might not have been in him then, though it also could have been, sneaky thing that it was. Years went by before it made itself known, and then it just ran wild. She wished she hadn't been so hard on Janet before. The poor kid.

"Bernice," she said, condemning her sharp tongue the way she would the fault of a thickheaded stranger. "When are you going to learn?" Just had to have the upper hand all the time, barking away at Isabel's poor orphaned child. Of course, she couldn't get along with her own daughter, so why wouldn't she snap Janet's head off? She sighed, considering the way things with Irma seemed so hopeless. How'd that ever come to be? Couldn't even ask a favor. Had to go to Janet. One thing for certain, it was a sorry state of affairs. And now all this picking at Janet. Had to chew her out because of a phone call intended to help. Even if it did seem meddlesome. Still, she knew better. Knew things about Janet that ought to have made her bend a little. What about all that? It shocked her, this idea, this sudden question. What about all the things she knew? Because there had to be some important things mixed in with all the ordinary, plain, everyday details, didn't there? Maybe even stuff nobody besides her knew, when they ought to.

For example, wasn't it right to ask if Janet Cawley knew what her father did and said on the day he left forever? Did she remember how he gave her a pat on the head and said she looked prettier than a girl ought to dare? Then he'd walked up to Isabel and planted a kiss on her cheek. Bernice might as well have been there, the way she could picture just how he took the grocery list for the things he intended to pick up on his way home from work that evening and then went out the door. In the first days after he didn't show up, when it was still anybody's guess what had happened and so possible to think anything at all, Isabel had more or less gone crazy, and in her craziness, she spelled out every detail of that last precious morning. She was like a detective on a cop show who had lost her mind, telling Bernice over and over, sorting out every move Edgar made, every word he said. The trouble was, the clues from that morning were pretty much the details from every morning. And then during maybe the hundredth telling, she added that maybe he had been a little odd. Maybe she had noticed something but not known to pay attention. Maybe he was a pinch too cheerful. But still, it was out of the blue, as far as any sane person could have known. After the first wave of worry, and the calls to the neighbors and his friends and the people he worked with, a deeper alarm set in. The police were called, and they sat in the kitchen asking questions, so the last morning was rerun a few more times. There were even trips to the morgue to look at unclaimed bodies of unknown men. And when one of them seemed a lot like Edgar, Isabel almost said it was him. She had confided this fact to Bernice later on, explaining how she'd wanted to make it all stop. Of course, she wouldn't have gotten away with it. Or maybe she would have. Maybe if she'd had a closed casket so nobody got to walk up to say, "Hey, that's not Edgar." Her pride and hopes and everything she had believed about her marriage might have been saved, though it felt reckless, as if saying he was dead and buried would seal her fate. And what about the people waiting for this stranger? They'd never know how he ended up dead in the backyard of a house for sale, where no one lived, stripped of all his jewelry and his billfold gone. What was he doing there? Who knew? And maybe at that very second, as she was about to tell the lie, those people who knew the dead man and who were worried about him, maybe they were on their way to the morgue, traveling a narrow dirt road from some little town nearby, or a farm they owned and worked, and by the time they got there, Isabel's lie would have stolen him from the ranks of unclaimed dead men, and they'd never see him, never know. And so when push finally came to shove, she hadn't been able to do it, she told Bernice, confessing in the end. It just wasn't fair. And, anyway, it was already pretty clear how the whole thing was going to turn out. He wasn't coming back, and lying wouldn't change a thing.

It was right in the midst of that moment, or one that came along pretty quickly behind it, that Isabel more or less sank from sight. Bernice had never seen anything quite like it in anyone she knew personally. It was like this cloud came up around her very best friend, this smoke like Bernice could remember from the fire at the Tomlinsons' house, and the fire department came and the flames were bursting higher and higher and Mrs. Tomlinson was in the attic window screaming and waving at everyone, and Bernice was just a little girl in her father's arms, but she could see Mrs. Tomlinson waving and screaming but not jumping out the window, like everyone was shouting at her to do, and then the smoke wiped her away as the firemen in their big black coats were sinking through the flames leaping out of the downstairs windows and devouring the wall where the house was nothing like a house anymore, but more like what you saw looking in the window of the furnace in her grandpa's basement. Isabel vanished just like that, though, unlike Mrs. Tomlinson— who was never seen again except as a spooky sack of bone and cinders that Bernice overheard her parents describe as too small to ever have been a person, let alone Mrs. Tomlinson, who'd been big and fat—Isabel returned. But changed. She was someone Bernice thought she knew as well as the palm of her own hand, but when Isabel reappeared from wherever she had gone, she had left part of herself behind, the way old clothes are stowed in boxes tied with clothesline and stuck in a basement corner. Today, from watching television and all those kinds of shows that brought things up out of the shadows, well, anybody would know to say about Isabel that she was depressed. That she was having a bout with clinical depression. Nowadays you could hardly turn on the television or a radio talk show without running into some kind of report or confession by a famous actor or newscaster, describing their battle with this kind of problem. But back then all you could do was think, Get a grip. Or you could maybe offer some slogans and promising song lyrics. Bernice had in fact gone over one afternoon with a bottle of Mogen David wine—a big bottle, and she got herself soused, and Isabel got soused, too. Bernice could remember spouting things like "Time heals all wounds." And "It's always darkest before the dawn." Which, if somebody were to ask her right this second, she'd have to say was not exactly true. Sometimes it was darkest in the middle of the night. And there were wounds—she had a few—that lasted as long as you did. Not that a thing had to be true for a person to say it. For goodness sake, if things had to be ironclad facts in order to get spoken, the world would be a quiet place. She knew that now for sure, and probably had known it back then. Advice just had to be encouraging, like pushing a car stuck in the snow. You just pushed. The afternoon had a lot of ups and downs, and it sort of whirled along until it got to a point where the two of them were singing "Look for the Silver Lining" and "Side by Side" and "On the Sunny Side of the Street." After they'd sung and drunk the bottle empty, they'd collapsed on the couch eating Velveeta cheese and rye crackers until Isabel started to weep and pound the arm of the couch and Bernice puked. It was right about then that Janet came home from school and found them. Isabel said she had a stomachache and it hurt so bad she was crying, and Bernice had one, too, and so she had thrown up. Janet studied them with a serious, worried expression that showed a world of concern and disappointment and more than a smidgen of disbelief, and then she went over to her little wooden desk in the corner of the living room and she got out her books and started doing her homework.

With her ice cream bowl empty now, the spoon loose in her fingers, Bernice wondered how much Janet remembered from all that and what she'd made of whatever she did remember. She'd been such a little thing. Although when they plopped Bernice onto her father's shoulders that night so she could get a good look at Mrs. Tomlinson, she'd been a lot younger than little Janet was when her dad ran off and she wandered home from school and stepped into her living room to find one of them drunk, the other puking. No wonder she started huddling up in the grass with big collie dogs and sharing her heart. Her daddy had disappeared, and her momma was more or less gone, too. Altered beyond recognition by hocus-pocus like body snatchers were on the prowl and she was their main target. There had been a lot of movies about that back then, with people getting removed from their bodies, and the bodies looking normal unless you peered right into their eyes. What was the name of that one? It was about Mars. They were from Mars. The body-invading people who weren't people but alien monsters pretending to be people. Isabel had been a lot like that, normal as far as the surface but spooky if you took a good look. And all during this same period, and without giving anybody a heads-up, or even a hint, she was getting ready to change again in another, even more drastic way. Not so drastic as this last one outside the movie theater, though, because after that, she was just gone. Over a year now since the funeral. It just didn't seem possible. But if you got right down to it, and why not give it a try, what was the difference between Isabel disappearing for the last time and what Bernice was waiting for tonight? So there she was, sort of back where she'd started. On death row. But how was it any different, really, except maybe in the fact that for Isabel, the angels were invisible. Or maybe not. Who knew what Isabel saw? Except that whatever Isabel saw, it didn't bear on tonight, because the idea for Bernice was that she was saved, and she wasn't going to die but would go flying off. That was the difference she had to bear in mind, and it was a big difference, the only trouble being the way she didn't feel saved.

She had to stop for a second and look around like someone might be eavesdropping on the inside of her head, where her thoughts felt like they were sneaking around, whispering to each other. Well, I hope Isabel is saved, too, she went on in a more public way, because then Isabel would be waiting and their old friendship could be rekindled, the old times regained. She wondered if that was part of what being saved made a person feel. Who knew? Maybe it was like most of what a person had to put up with in this life—one day one thing, and something else the next. What she did know, though, was that she felt restless, along with wanting a little more ice cream.

Lord, she thought, hear me, okay? I am yours. Come and take me.

She hoped that the Lord, if He was listening, found her more convincing than she found herself. Though she knew from Reverend Tauke that she didn't have to feel any one way or believe in everything one hundred percent for every second of every day. In fact she shouldn't even try to, or hope to, because she probably couldn't do it and would make a mess of it, being a sinner. Being flawed. Being mortal. She sure knew a lot of dead people. Just tonight they'd all come sailing through her head one after another. Like Mrs. Tomlinson. Hadn't thought of her for a long time. And Toby, dear Toby. Well, he was a regular in her thoughts every few minutes, whether he belonged to the subject or not. She might be wondering if she needed new shoes and there he'd be, or watching TV and he'd seem to be in the show somehow, or making a grocery list and he'd be wanting cheese or milk or popcorn. And then there'd been her cousin Miriam. Tonight she'd seemed to want to nudge Bernice for a second or two with a reminder of her long-lost spirit, that long-ago life so short. Poor Miriam with her blazing green eyes getting mad over a trifle nobody back at the house she'd run from had the slightest notion about. But Bernice knew about that—how some little thing could sting you through and through, the way whatever had stung her and Irma until it left them these feuding strangers drawing lines in the sand like pigheaded little kids. Over what? Some totally dumb thing, whatever it was. Some remark Grandpa Demming had made a long time ago, and it had cut Irma to the quick and stuck in her like a fishhook she couldn't pull out. What was it Grandpa had said? He could be rough. No argument there. And so when Bernice didn't take her side, Irma pulled the door shut and locked it from the inside, and that was that. Every time one of them brought it up, they had another fight. Irma just might as well have absconded, like Miriam turning fugitive with her hurt feelings, never thinking for one second that the way she was running into the woods was the way she was going to spend her last moments on earth. Same with Isabel. Just going to the movies.

She wished Irma would telephone right this second. That the ringing would all but explode and it would be Irma, but that wasn't going to happen, because she was too much of a spoiled brat. Too busy to bother.

She'd probably come around when it was over, though, looking to see what was in it for her, looking for Bernice's last will and testament when everybody realized she was gone. How would that work? she wondered. No body to be found and pronounced dead. Not that it was her problem. Irma would find that little box of keepsakes Bernice had put away, with the ring from her mother and the old pocket watch for Alex John that had belonged to her mom's dad, Grandpa Thill. Not that it was something that would ever interest Alex John, or any other kid these days with their computers and earphones clamped on their ears. But all that would come later, when Bernice was long gone and people were wondering what had happened to her. But for tonight she was alone, and that was pretty much the way she was going to stay. Just her with her dogs and of course all these dead folks as far as the eye could see, and they were around now, a lot of them, or at least they might be, watching her, waiting. Her mom would be, anyway, if she could be. She'd always been kind of quiet and faint even when she was alive. Dead folks sticking their heads down from the heavens, poking through the clouds, like an upside down field of dandelions, the gray dusty kind that kids could blow away with a puff. And some of them people she didn't even know personally, like movie stars she'd had a crush on, or admired, or rooted for, as they lived through those stories, because you did that with them, squeezing tight the arms of the chair where you sat in the dark, the projector firing this hose of light onto the big white screen, where they were brighter than Mrs. Tomlinson in her burning window, so it was natural that she missed them, too. Everybody did. Like Clark Gable and Cary Grant and that sweet little old man, and that other one, he'd never been as famous as Gable or Grant or Cooper or Wayne, but you felt that he was down-to-earth so a person could count on him, because he had a way about him. Actually, it was Isabel who felt that way. It was Isabel who had the crush on Dana Andrews, though Bernice remembered him.

And hadn't it in fact been at a Dana Andrews movie when that first dreary stretch ended for Isabel? Bernice was pretty sure it was. She saw the two of them outside the old Orpheum Theater with the Buzzy Bee Café across the street and Isabel grinning ear to ear. It had been this movie with Dana Andrews and all these other ones flying these big airplanes dropping bombs down through the air crowded with black explosions. Bombers raining down bombs. Somebody shouting, "Bombs away!" And Isabel stood there like the cat that ate the canary, and the cloud around her faded, and she started to almost yell when she talked. Or was it the following day? It could have been the next day, but it had to do with the way Isabel had loved Dana Andrews, of that there was no doubt. It seemed she had discovered somehow—maybe from all the bombs booming and sending up fire—that the way out of those shadows covering her up was to get loud and noisy, and so she got into this mode of crazy excitement, like she was at a party and she was a little tipsy. It was a newfangled approach to making do, like a fancy dress she happened to find that she would just put on and wear whether it fit or not. Instantly, or maybe overnight, she was the complete opposite of what she had been, high-spirited and cheerful instead of gloomy and downcast. But she was still inside something, maybe not a fog anymore, maybe more like a bauble, and she could see out and you could see in, but a person didn't feel exactly connected to what she was pointing out and all keyed up about, talking a mile a minute, just jumping for joy. She was like one of those fireworks rising up and filling the sky with noise and color, and you watched and went "Uhhhh" and "Ahhhh," but something in the way she whistled and popped reminded you of real bombs and the harm they could do if you got too close or were careless around them, though there was no arguing that being down in the dumps was better. Still, every now and then Bernice couldn't help but take offense, like Isabel was somebody wearing brazen clothes at a funeral. And most of the time it was something going on between Isabel and Janet that brought this feeling on.

She'd watched Janet struggle to get used to her semi-silent, more or less sleepwalking mom, and then out of the blue, the poor kid was face-to-face with this joker, this life of the party for whom every little thing was a cause for long, drawn-out laughter, until one day she asked, "Momma, what are you doing?"

"Starting my new life. The longest journey starts with a single step."

Bernice could remember thinking that sounded like a smart enough way to put it. So maybe Isabel did know what she was up to. But Janet looked stricken, even a little ill, and she said, "Momma, no. You can't say that."

"I sure can. I just did."

They were in the kitchen of the apartment Isabel had moved them into after being forced to sell the house, which was mostly mortgaged—oh, what a sad sight that was, the two of them trying not to look back as they drove off and Bernice and Toby followed, giving moral support—so there they were in the kitchen, Isabel and Bernice drinking coffee with cream and sugar and smoking cigarettes—that was still going on, everybody lighting up and hacking away, and in her case headed for heart problems. Edgar had been gone close to a year, and Janet, who was around eight, was eating cereal, probably Cheerios out of a pink plastic bowl with milk and a chopped-up banana. "But they will arrest you."

"Who?"

"The government."

"Don't be silly. The government doesn't care what I say."

"But Momma, for goodness sake, you're talking like Mao Tse-tung."

"Did he say that?"

"Yes, he did."

"I don't care who said it; it's my motto. Who is he?"

"He's a Communist."

"Who?"

"Mao Tse-tung."

"And he said that—what I just said?"

"Yes."

"Well, then he was one very smart Communist."

"Don't say that, Momma. He does all these mean terrible things, and he has these mean terrible police called Red Guards who hurt everyone—they take them and—"

"Janet! Nobody cares what we're saying here! So just put a lid on it."

"But they do."

"Who?"

"You know."

"Is it these mean police who are in China you're worried about?"

"No. Not them."

"Because we don't have to worry about anybody in China. We can just drop a bomb on them."

"It's not them."

"Where'd you get wind of this? I hope they're not teaching you this kind of baloney at school."

"No."

"Where then? You tell me where."

"Miss Tross read a newspaper story."

"Oh, she did, did she. That's what I thought. What for?"

"I don't know."

"She's got no business causing this kind of trouble. I've got a good mind to call her up and tell her to stick to reading, writing, and 'rithmetic."

"Don't do that, Momma."

"I think I'd like to give her a piece of my mind. Look how worked up you are."

"Just don't call her up."

"Why? Are you afraid of her, too?"

"No. It's them. The ones who are here. Those ones. They listen in. They tap on your telephones and put bugs in your houses."

"Pardon me?" said Isabel, zeroing in on her daughter with a look that said she had the goods on her at last.

"There's tapping noises on our telephones sometimes, Momma, and it's maybe them."

"Well, get a load of this one, will you, Bernice?"

Isabel had fired Bernice a sardonic gleam so willful and confident, Bernice felt its power with a slap of such vivid sensation right there where she sat in her kitchen that she turned to search for Isabel close by. She saw the window, the curtains furled like the arms of a gown, and through them the familiar streetlight, and then she was back with Janet marching up to her mother as she had long ago to whisper, "Momma, Momma, he was talking about taking over the world. That was his journey—first taking over China and then the whole world with his communism and throwing God out. That was where he was going with his first step."

"Well, that's no concern of mine, because what he—"

"You can't say that. That's crazy to say that and think you can get away with—"

"Is that what you think? You're so important they're all listening in on you? The police and the FBI and the president probably, too?"

"I hate you, I hate you."

"Shush, now, Janet. That's enough," Isabel said, rolling her eyes at Bernice. "Is she right? About this Chinaman?"

"I've heard of him," Bernice allowed.

"I am right! I'm telling you, Momma, I'm—"

"Janet! I think I'm asking Bernice, if you don't mind—if you could just put a plug in it for a second!"

"Mrs. Doorley, please tell her I'm right," Janet begged.

"I said I'd heard of him, Janet. And he don't amount to so much anymore. I think he's even dead."

"Oh, he is not! How can you be so stupid? The both of you."

"We have other concerns," Isabel told her. "Things that take up our time, concerns you know nothing about, and you won't until you get to—"

"But they're stupid. You're stupid. It's all stupid."

"Well, listen to you now, will you?" Isabel's long arm snaked out, the hooked fingers tapping the air with her cigarette inches from Janet's face. "Do you want me to dump that bowl of Cheerios on top of your pretty little head, talking to me like that, is that what you think you want? Because I will."

"You're going to get us put in jail."

"Don't get so damn dramatic. I'm talking about my life and my journey, and it don't have anything to do with his communism, for goodness sake, or any other kind of politics. That's nothing to do with my journey. We're not in the same ballpark, him and me. I don't know the man, and I don't want to know him."

Bernice could remember Janet's face. Or maybe it was Mrs. Tomlinson's. But whoever she was remembering, their eyes were bulging, and they struck Bernice as going wildly, hopelessly out of control with this panicky rush. If she was honest—and why not be at a moment like this—Bernice knew that she didn't have a real memory of her thoughts back then. She felt as if she did, but she probably didn't. On the other hand, she was sure she knew what she was thinking now, and maybe her current thoughts were exactly the same as what had gone on way back when, only she didn't know it. Could never know for sure. Poor Janet. She'd looked like something heavy had dropped on her foot. Or somebody had taken her by the scruff of the neck and was holding her underwater. Because she didn't know what was going on. Couldn't catch up. Isabel's moody unhappiness, her multiple personalities, Janet's whole world turned upside down, her daddy disappearing, the divorce that was in the works, world communism—the whole kit and caboodle—it was all being dumped on top of her by her mother's brand-new, energetic, smiley determination to get back on track. Janet might as well have wandered into the path of some real Communist who couldn't care less about anybody's journey but his own. He was taking his first step, and if his big boot came down on top of some little girl's head, that was fine by him. So Isabel was just stomping right over any notion or feeling Janet might have come to. Or tried to come to. Or was wondering about. Isabel was skilled at discarding things, which she'd proved by discarding herself for a time, and so now anything that did not fit in with her new outlook was headed for the scrap heap. Janet had gaped at her mother like somebody looking at an X-ray of something terrible that should not be there. It should not be anywhere. And Bernice could remember Isabel—this she was sure she had right—Isabel hooting and throwing her hands skyward, as if celebrating some newfound delight which was this crazy, hopeless look in her daughter's eyes, wreathed in cigarette smoke.

Janet started blubbering, big gulps of air and stringy snot coming out of her like somebody was giving her a good whipping right there at the table.

Later on, probably that same night—though it could have been a few days later, but there was no doubt it was in the same general time period, and no doubt Janet was near enough to overhear every word Isabel and Bernice were saying, and no doubt Janet was listening, even though her head was bowed over her homework at that little desk, but she wasn't contemplating the Revolutionary War, or the Civil War, or Christopher Columbus, or any such thing, as Isabel talked on and on with unnecessary volume about her point of view and her "needs," as she called them. The gist of her spiel was that she'd been on her own for a while now, and she was beginning to see the value of life without Edgar. It was a matter of "Goodbye and good riddance," and Janet had better come around to that same way of thinking, because it was the right way, the best way, the only way. She raised her left hand, making a show of the fact that her wedding band had disappeared. And if Janet didn't hop on the bandwagon—if she couldn't or wouldn't, if she wanted to hang on to the heartbreak—she would have to carry on down that road all by her lonesome, because Isabel was not holding herself back for anybody or anything at this point. Certainly not for Janet, who was probably the reason the man was gone in the first place.

Bernice thought Janet might faint. What could she do or think? What could she make of such goings-on except that the world was a madhouse with not a soul to trust? Betrayal at every breath, that was what her mother was telling her to expect, along with delivering the scathing news that she was a fool who had misunderstood every second of her life up to this minute.

It was the one and only time Bernice could remember ever wanting to give Isabel a good smack right in the mouth. Just haul off and let her know what for. They'd known each other pretty much all their lives, but for a second Bernice could remember thinking, I can't be friends with this woman. I really can't. But of course she hadn't followed through. She spoke up but didn't lay into Isabel with the scolding she deserved. She said enough to cause a tiff between them, but not so much they couldn't make up. Bernice just didn't have the nerve for more. There was too much between them, starting with the way they'd met walking to grade school in the morning from the same direction and cutting across that empty lot between the Frey's and Windor's. They'd attended Benjamin Franklin

High School, worked at JCPenney's, two peas in a pod, maids of honor at each other's weddings, as close as sisters. Through thick and thin. Runaway husband. Dying husband. Dead husband. Parents in nursing and— Well, you name it.

But no more. Because a person could look high and low for Isabel now, drive around to all the spots where she'd been and ought to still be, but there'd be only strangers waiting behind every door—in the apartment where she'd been a child and the house she'd owned later on with Edgar, the apartment she'd ended up in—nothing but strangers.

Well, sure, there was a gravestone. That marker with her name on it, and that could be found. But it didn't amount to much when you got right down to it, not everything it was cracked up to be. You could go there, stand there, sure, think some things, try to remember, but it wasn't like having a friend. It couldn't compare to picking her up in your car to go to the mall, shooting the breeze the whole way. You might say some things as you stood there, but it wasn't like real talking, even on the phone, or having a good time together watching TV. It always felt sort of fitting to get ready to go, like planning a real visit, the promise of contact, but then you got there and saw the stone and the grass and the hundred other stones nearby, and farther off hundreds and hundreds more, and part of your brain traveled away without you even meaning for it to happen and barely noticing at first, but off it went to the stones all over that cemetery, hundreds and hundreds more, well, it had to be thousands, and that led on to a sense of all the graveyards in Belger and then all the other towns in Iowa, the Midwest, even, and before you could stop it, the whole darn country, and all this without meaning to, just thinking and hardly paying attention, but next thing you knew, you were looking over all the dead and buried people in the whole world, and then history wanted in, and time and countries that didn't even exist anymore, and you had the whole thing falling through your brain, all these centuries of cemeteries like a snowstorm of markers in the zillions, and so this one you were walking up to, or had already reached, well, it wasn't much. Isabel had just sort of wobbled, walking along after the movie that night with Bernice and Edna Mackey and Betsy Redenbacker. She'd complained about the heat and wished she was back inside the air-conditioned theater. Somebody—Edna, if Bernice remembered right—reminded them of a funny thing in the movie, and they all laughed, so Isabel was laughing one minute and wobbling the next. Sort of sat down. Her knees buckled and she went down fast. Yelped with the jolt when she hit so hard and out of control, and then she lay down on her side, and she turned her back to them the way you do when you're embarrassed. Not a word.

They shouted at each other and ran around, calling 911 on the pay phone in the theater lobby, and the ambulance came pretty fast, but they could have taken all day, stopped for a snack, because by the time they screeched up, there was nothing for them to do except haul her away. Bernice and Betsy had managed to move Isabel enough to get a look. First they'd said her name, asked her what she was doing, and then they bent down to her nervously, like she was dangerous—up to no good and trying to trick them, like a spider or snake ready to bite. Bernice could remember the crazy feeling that Isabel might harm her, that Isabel wanted to harm them all, badly, as they turned her over, all three of them yelling, Betsy and Bernice doing the actual touching. They were dripping sweat, the bunch of them, dark blotches showing through their clothes. It took only one quick look to bring confusion bursting out of them, and helplessness. Oh my God. What happened? I don't believe it, oh my heavens, no. Because while the rest of them were pouring perspiration, Isabel's brow was cool and her eyes utterly empty, leaving no doubt the deal was done. Bernice sat down next to her, moving carefully and slowly, and then she took Isabel's fingers in her own. She said a prayer and commanded herself to peer directly into Isabel's eyes, which weren't anyone's eyes anymore. They were foggy and dull, turned in an instant into cheap jewelry filled with glop. Maybe the color remained and the pupils had shape, but they beat light back, sending it off without letting anything in.

"She's dead," Bernice said looking up, like what she was saying meant something they all understood.

The noisy splatter of liquid hitting wood and calling her from her thoughts was the sound of General pissing in the corner. She knew it before she spied him in the murk with his leg half cocked. "You damn fool," she said.

The cloud that had consumed Isabel when her husband ran off had swooped back that last night in a similar but far more hard-hearted form. It was a surprise for sure, no arguing with it. And so Isabel Cawley, from start to finish, the whole bag of tricks, was put away in a box like the clothes in the basement.

Carrying a large towel, Bernice had to hike her skirt up, her creaky old knees giving out a click or two and hurting more as she got down to the floor than when she was actually on all fours swabbing away. She used round, thoroughgoing strokes and fretted that she was going to crawl into some part of the pee. "You're spoiled, you know," she told General, who was slouching toward his bed. She labored a second or two more. "Well, I know, you're right," she said, like she was General talking back. "But it's your fault." She nodded and, uncertain which of them she was, tacked on "Thank you very much."

After washing her hands, she landed back at the table, feeling exhausted. But it wasn't from General. No, not hardly. He was the least of what this night had put her through.

The ice cream bowl was empty except for dribs and drabs, and she lifted it close so she could lick it clean. That was one good thing about living with animals—you could eat any way you wanted. Pistachio almond ice cream was odd, when you got right down to it. Not like when there'd been only vanilla and chocolate and you thought yourself lucky to have them. When had she had her first taste of pistachio almond, she wondered, and felt that if she waited, the exact minute would separate from all the other minutes that had made up her life to this point, and come to her.

Happy and Sappy were seated at a polite distance, studying her patiently, optimistically. She stopped and lowered the bowl to the floor, and they started nosing in with polite regard for each other. Ira sailed up onto the table, his belly humming, and Bernice patted him.

Pressure swam through her head as she stood, so she faltered, wondering how long she'd been up. The digital clock on the microwave read 4:33, and the Timex on her wrist was just about the same, maybe 4:30. Lord, she thought. A regular night owl. Up to the wee hours. And beginning to pay the price. Her hand trembled as she opened the refrigerator and got out the half-gallon of milk. She poured first into the empty ice cream bowl and then into four fresh bowls brought from the cabinet for all the animals to drink. General lay close by. Frustrated by his deafness, he had begun positioning himself in ways that allowed him to keep a close eye on whatever went on so he wouldn't miss out. She placed his bowl so he could reach it easily.

With everyone slurping away, she removed her sweatshirt, doubled it over the back of a chair, and headed toward her bedroom, all of a sudden so done in that she ached from head to toe. Halfway tipsy and a little dizzy, she didn't know that her course had changed until she was approaching the haze of a living room window, and she filled with uneasy curiosity and suspense about the state of the world beyond her walls.

The dark was heavy in the sky and heavier near the ground. Streetlights dotted the distant connector, where the support poles were unseen, the bulbs appearing to hang from the sky, sending up halos. A lone truck crossed the wasteland that not so long ago had been a slough, a muddy backwater home to frogs and snakes and sunfish and crappies. There'd been a long neck of land she used to walk out onto, coming down from the road with her grandpa Thill to go fishing for sunfish, him rambling on the way he liked to about what he'd done when he was her age, or this one or that one he'd run with back then—he loved telling stories about "the olden days." The farther they went out, the more the ground narrowed beneath them, and with the brackish surface widespread on both sides, Bernice could squint and almost believe she was walking on water. But now it was just this flat desolate industrial center like some half-baked desert, all the water gone and not too much industry, and no sunfish, that was for sure, and no grandpa, either.

In spite of all the big plans, the whole thing had pretty much been a bust, because the establishments that made the move were few and far between, such as Kandem Lumberyard, and that electrical place with the red trim and some nice lamps, even if they were pricey, a few warehouses, and Madigan Auto Parts. The Madigan twins had been in grade school with Isabel and Bernice, but in high school there was only one of them left, Mary Madigan, looking very strange all by herself, almost less than a person, sort of cut in half and squeezed dry after Carrie drowned in the river.

Dawn was gathering behind the black overhead, sending blades of light out before its advance, their force multiplying behind the inky canopy like it was some kind of metallic shield, and it was being hammered on from the other side by giants with gigantic hammers beating on the darkness, and cracks were beginning to show, splinters and gouges in a spreading web of light.

It was all she could do to get herself down the hall to the bedroom and then across the last few feet to the bed before she just fell, with sleep crawling all over her, impatient and demanding, while she labored to get out of her shoes and then her Depends. She just had to. Didn't she deserve a little comfort? And she would still look presentable if the angels came.

Sleep seemed to growl, pushing her down, tired and fed up with waiting. She sighed and gave in.

7

WAYNE JUST THOUGHT HE COULD show up with any kind of half-baked sorry-assed story and then do what he wanted and go. That was Wayne, all right. Coming and going. Janet smiled, seeing him at the instant of release, his face straining with disbelief at how good he felt but also with a childish complaint because he had thought there would be more in it for him. In spite of the fact that he was fun, in spite of the fact that he fucked okay, worked at it, had a certain feel for her, she couldn't let this thing with him start back up. Actually, he fucked better than okay sometimes. Those were the times when he was selfish and clamoring after what he wanted, oblivious to anything but his own sensations, so he pushed her around and turned her whichever way suited him, facedown, faceup, because he was just sex then. But tonight he'd been thoughtful, like he was trying to make up for something, render some kind of an apology with the way he touched her. He was so busy demonstrating that he could be considerate that he never really got around to taking over and forgetting who the hell she was, so she could forget who the hell she was, because all she wanted from him was for him to—to what? What was it? She was trying to see into the coy feeling that was backing away into hiding. Hadn't she wanted to do what she'd done? Send him packing?

She sat up, then flopped back in her empty, tangled bed, grinding her teeth. Because the maddening, irritating thing of it was that she hadn't really sent him away. He'd left because it was time to go. Which left Janet the one who had been tossed aside.

A glance at the window showed a glow moving past gaps in the shut blinds, fragmentary swimming shapes indicating wind. She went over to look out and the vista was all restlessness, a horizon fabricated of vapors, nearby trees, sky, and distant bluffs, the nearly full moon slipping out from craggy banks.

Wayne must be arriving home just about now, she figured. She saw him skulking through one room or another, removing his shoes, Mr. Stealth, Mr. Clever, then his pants, stealing into their bedroom, maybe peeking in first, then easing onto the bed and, if his wife didn't stir, inching his way under the covers. Or would he need to wash up first in the bathroom off their bedroom? More likely, he would use one farther away. One belonging to the kids. The little kids in their beds, two boys in one room, the girl in another. Because of them, he would never leave his wife. Never walk out and move in with Janet. Because of the goddamn kids.

A spear went through her, pure yearning. What should she do? What would it take? To break up his home! To get Wayne away from his wife! Knowing so viscerally and absolutely what she wanted left her shaken by a craving as single-minded as lust, and bewildered by her failure to see it before now. She had to have Wayne, had to envelop and possess him, doing whatever was needed from this minute of clarity on, until she drew him away from his wife, and they were together, the two of them, so they could—

It was preposterous. An elastic band stretched beyond its capacity, the concept snapped and stung her. It was as humiliating as a slap in the face or an enemy finding out some embarrassing truth about her. She had no idea what she wanted, but it wasn't Wayne. And yet the way she could not stop thinking about him and replaying the earlier parts of the night made her feel disgusted with herself. For letting him go. But first of all for letting him in, and taking him to bed, and sure, for fucking him. But ending up like this was even more revolting.

She was in the kitchen pouring Jack Daniel's into a sturdy glass. All right, she thought, tilting her head back to take in the warmth of the whiskey. Pouring another, she made her way back to bed, where she closed her eyes to better attend to the heat that was the liquor's first and best quality. The tentative but unmistakable knock at the door startled her, and she sat stock-still, recalling the faint rattle that she'd heard and ignored just seconds before. Alertly, she examined the silence in which footsteps descended the stairs outside.

Hurrying to her bedroom, she peeked beneath the blind and thought she saw the front of Wayne's Lexus just beyond the curve of the corner. A fragment of fender glossed with streetlight was barely visible, given her awkward vantage. It looked like he was standing beside it, peering up, or was she mistaking a shadow for a person? Her lights were all out. She couldn't see any expression, but something in the posture struck a note of reckless abandon. When he bolted from view within a cluster of trees, he was traveling at an angle that would bring him to the stairs that rose to her apartment. She waited, then went down the hall to the kitchen, where she heard him moving stealthily on the small porch on the other side of her door. He was probably trying to figure out how quiet he had to be in order to keep from waking her landlord or any of his family. Given these signs of premeditation, it seemed safe to think Wayne wasn't totally plastered, even though he'd probably done some more drinking.

Then the door scraped and shuddered, but the locks held. Seconds later, a repetition made her realize he was trying to force his way in with some kind of slow-motion pressure. She imagined him leaning there just behind that thin sheet of wood, his shoulder and heft urging surrender. Then he said something that could have been her name. He sighed, almost moaning, and said it again, though this time she wasn't positive he had called her, and so she inched closer warily, her lungs tight and shallow, until he grunted faintly, and the door rattled in protest against whatever he was doing. She thought she heard him sigh, and then there was more scratching that made no sense, unless he was picking the lock. But it lacked focus, like he was using his nails, like he had little claws scuffling at her door. C'mon, Wayne, she thought. Do it. Rear back and crash. You want in, put your shoulder to it. She crouched, spellbound by the silence into which her instinct rushed to tell her she knew he was out there calculating the risks of breaking in.

But an enigmatic noise made her think he was leaving. The way it all faded seemed to take him down the stairs. Seconds later, he drove off. She hurried to the bedroom window. If he wanted in, why hadn't he been more forceful? And why was he back, anyway? Why hadn't he gone home? Or had he gone home and that was why he was back? He and his wife had a fight, so he came scurrying back to Janet. And now, because she hadn't flung the door wide open for him, he was running away in some adolescent snit that would hand him over to the nearest bar and more to drink. Maybe even some other woman. Fine with me, she thought, just as her phone rang.

She rose from where she was seated on the floor by the window and went for a touch more Jack Daniel's. The bite of the liquor would energize her first words to him when she answered—if she answered. She pictured him at the Exxon a few blocks away, tapping his fist against the glass of the phone booth. When the ringing stopped, she stole over, and of course, only the dial tone awaited her. She hung up slowly, and then almost without thinking, though with clear and decisive movement, she unplugged the jack. Let it ring all it wanted, she was done for the night.

Needing to drag the covers up against the chill, she found the dark mixing with her anxiety in an edgy, volatile concoction. She was brimming with annoyed curiosity, a prowling resentment. She sipped the last of her drink, but the promise of calm was hopelessly overpowered by her obsession to know right this second whether or not the phone was ringing. Whether Wayne was trying to get to her. Whether anyone was trying to get to her. But especially Wayne. Because the ringing could be constant, but she would never know it.

Fed up and trying to be amused by her own capriciousness, she reconnected the phone and was almost back in bed when she heard him bumbling about on the stairs. But after a few seconds, she began to doubt he was there. Peeking out onto the street failed to reveal his car. But then whispering at the door, followed by a clatter along the wall, brought her hurrying back, wondering if he was stretched out over the banister in some acrobatic attempt to peer in the nearest kitchen window or, if it was open, climb in. But it was locked and veiled by curtains. He'd probably done some more drinking. Maybe had a bottle in the car. She could hear grunting and imagined a rock climber straining out over the dark. Then she heard her name as he said it several times, sort of whining and not managing complete words. The sad plaintive tone made her think of an animal, which made her think of Bernice. She could not keep from giggling, even though she pressed her palms against her mouth and bent her head toward the floor. Wayne sounded like one of Bernice's animals wanting something. Like that Rapture nonsense had come to pass, and the animals, having been left behind, were begging to go along into whatever they made of that weird dimension that had swept through their house. She tilted her glass to her lips but received only a slight dribble and fumes.

Thumping on the stairs worried her that Wayne, fleeing for some reason, had fallen. Maybe he'd heard her making fun of him and had gotten embarrassed or annoyed. She tried to read the silence, and then a car moving quietly off suggested his whereabouts. When she looked out, the street was empty.

Now what? she thought. Well, she could have another drink, which was what she was doing when the phone started ringing again, and she started laughing. Something was very funny. She didn't answer, imagining him pounding his fist in frustration in a phone booth somewhere as the room fell silent. But not for long. Three, four, five times it came at her, as if he were shouting. It was a pattern that repeated—the ringing, the stopping, the starting—about every five minutes for a while. Then the intervals grew longer, becoming more like fifteen minutes. It was all winding down. Him, the night, his desire, his willpower. She could feel his weariness in the lengthening silences. She could hear the way he was giving up.

At the window, she took another drink and admitted that she was a little drunk, peering out and feeling that she was higher than two stories. Not just high from drinking, and not just on the second floor, but high up in the clouds and looking down on the life she had left behind. As if she were an old woman flying, as if she were Bernice. Giggles came in a burst, and it seemed she belonged to a crowd roaring at the antics of a clown.

She fixed another whiskey—"One last pop for the road"—and sank between the sheets. She dreaded the state of mind circling her and promising to take her over if she didn't get to sleep. Her interior rant had the temperament of a haughty, dismissive stranger, and she shifted to her side. She prayed she wouldn't have to resort to that melatonin crap she had somewhere. Her supply of 'ludes was gone, as was all her grass. That taste Wayne had shared had whetted her appetite, and she was definitely in need of relief, a time-out after this daylong barrage of bullshit. She should have picked up something on her way back from Bernice's. It would have been easy. There was a point halfway where it was only a few short blocks over to Kaiser Street and Big Baby Dog's place.

She flopped to her other side, like that might help her slip her anxiety. She should have left well enough alone with Wayne instead of picking a fight and getting all worked up. She'd been feeling fine, having fun, and then she just tore into him. The alarm had gone off, sure, but all things considered, so what?

Even though the booze had, if anything, increased her agitation, she was climbing out of bed for one more drink when she heard him at the door again. Hesitating only to collect her balance, she raced to the kitchen. The locks flew open, and she jerked the door wide.

Moonlight washed the peeling gray of the stairway in eerie white, while the steps and railing fell away into shadow. She had expected to find him right there on the landing, a sad little boy looking needy. But the stairway was empty. Had he fled when he heard her crossing from the bedroom? Changed his mind? What? Maybe he was embarrassed about letting his crazy coming and going expose his hunger to see her. Or maybe he thought it would be cute to play some kind of a game and hide and then jump out, making her scream. She hoped he wasn't about to scare the shit out of her.

"Wayne," she whispered. "This has gone on long enough." She started down the steps. "What do you think you're doing?" Midway, she slowed, scanning left and right, and when she reached the bottom, the grainy pavement was cold on her bare feet. "Wayne?" Wind delivered traffic sounds from Teale Boulevard on the other side of the hills. Dry leaves rattled and the air was frosty.

The front of the house offered no evidence of him. The only cars nearby were her Honda at the curb and her landlord's Dodge Durango in the driveway. A pickup, an SUV, three or four sedans occupied other driveways or sat along the street. Flaring lights drew her attention to a small home notched into a tier above the houses bounding the street. Illumination puffed into the dark, accommodating somebody who worked an early shift. Or maybe, like her, they simply couldn't sleep.

It was hard to understand how Wayne could have gotten away so quickly. The moon, though shrouded, was forceful enough to drown the streetlight in a barren lunar glow, while she stood alone in her undies and T-shirt, folding her arms over her breasts to ward off the cold. Beginning to shiver, she was sick of Wayne and his games, and of herself for playing along, as she hurried home, scampering up the stairs, where the door was closed. She knew it was locked before she touched the knob, but disbelief insisted that she tug repeatedly. "Oh, no." She felt so goddamn stupid. A fucking idiot child locked out of her own house. "Dammit," she said. Had the wind forced it shut? It must have. "Dammit," she hissed, frustration making her dig her fingers into her hair. What the hell was she going to do? She didn't dare make too much noise trying to get in, or she'd wake the Luckritzes. Maybe even have them calling the cops. Not that there was much she could try. Struggling out to one of the windows was pointless, even if possible. She had locked them all, idiot that she was.

Starting down as if following a clear plan, she reversed and sat on the top step. Her landlord, Mr. Luckritz, went to work early, and once he was gone, she could contact his wife, Eileen. Make up some harebrained explanation. People got locked out all the time. She tried the door once more, and this time the knob felt icy. As she resumed her perch, a bitter gust cut through her, and she hugged herself tighter.

Half a dozen leaves gave up their hold in an overhead scramble of branches, each a drifting blotch, while one swam from the others to graze her forearm. Deep within massive clouds, the moon seemed to sink farther. She feared the temperature might drop drastically. It might even fall below freezing. Was she going to just sit there and turn into a block of ice?

She went down the steps all the way to the bottom, then scampered back up. What a stupid, crazy thing to have done. Seated and hunched forward, tugging her T-shirt over her knees and as far down over her shins as it would go, she wrapped her arms around her legs, and then, along with the wintry air, dread of another kind blew into her thoughts. What if she was stuck out here because of a trick? What if her racing heart was right, and she was realizing too late that some degenerate had drawn her into a trap by luring her out and now he was rushing up to grab her? What if it had never been Wayne at her door? But she'd seen him, hadn't she? Or had she only imagined it was him? Those phone calls might have been Wayne for a while and then somebody else. Or some crank all along. Some phantom shape in a dim location devoid of identifying traits, his back turned, head hunkered into rounded shoulders. That fucking Karl Rupp and his ossified, you-know-you-want-to-fuck-me stare. What about him? Burglars, rapists. Those goddamn Crips and Bloods knew her first name, and she could have let her last name slip. A phone book would give them her address. There was always one of them trying to reel her in. Every now and then Big Baby Dog would train those earnest bloodshot eyes of his on her and tell her to go on now and use her ATM card, so she'd have all the money she needed to party. He'd help her. She might have been reckless.

She rubbed her palms over her bare arms. She had no choice but to wake up somebody in the Luckritz household. Vowing to face the music, preparing some kind of speech, maybe a joke, or maybe just tears, she started around to the front door. And there was her car.

When the door opened, she all but jumped inside, squealing with surprise. Her enormous relief brought a sense of triumphant escape, as if something inconceivable had occurred and far more than her neighborhood had been left behind. Pushing the buttons to lock the doors, and checking them one after the other, her sense of shelter strengthened, as if she were sealed up in a metal and glass bubble, like a space capsule to protect her in a dangerous environment. She looked out and found that the night had been tamed, every threat defused and returned to normal.

After a while, she climbed into the backseat, figuring to stretch out

and try to sleep a little, and to her amazement, she looked down at the
tattered brown army blanket and the raggedy towels she'd used to protect
the upholstery when she'd hauled her broken air conditioner to the
dump. They were neatly piled on the floor. In a mood of favor and privilege, she rolled two of the towels into a pillow. One more remained to
spread over her chest. She tucked the blanket snugly from head to toe
and instantly felt sleep was possible. Not even Wayne would think to look
for her here. With her eyes open, she rested, and with her eyes closed, she
sighed, her thoughts flitting about as if on errands of their own, and she
watched contentedly as they danced and swam from tomorrow to yesterday and then on to this and that until the old collie appeared and she remembered the grass outside his pen. With her nose almost touching his
snout, she had told him about her father and what might have happened.
Like maybe he'd been the victim of an alien abduction. Or a Mob hit. Or
maybe he'd fallen at the hands of a serial killer. Such things did occur, she
reminded the tolerant old dog. While he thoughtfully attended her, she
described the whirling lights of a spaceship run by creepy little men in
green suits. She told how her dad must have offended crooks with his
honesty and so he had been stuffed into the trunk of a black car with
tinted windows by thugs in dark suits. Or, drugged and dragged into
some basement, he had been hacked to pieces by a chubby neighbor in
spectacles.

All this was long past. Still, she wanted to whisper more into his big
shaggy ears. Sleep was close, and soon it would bear her away to an even
more fantastical explanation. Somewhere there was one. Somewhere it
waited. Just drive off into the countryside. She saw a meadow crowded
with weeds, dandelions, some thistles, sure, some ragweed, milkweed,
sure, and sumac, lots of sumac, maybe a fallen tree, the limbs sticking up.
It wouldn't be so hard. Not really. Not at all. She saw herself arriving at a
refuge like she used to believe existed for her and that dog she'd wanted
so badly to rescue, who never got out of his pen. Sure, she thought, just
find some secluded place. Some out-of-the-way spot. Bring some booze
and the right CDs. What would they be? No James Taylor. No, no. Who
should it be, though, really? Ani DiFranco, maybe. Sarah McLachlan. No

Doubt—that gangly blonde. Alanis Morissette for sure, for sure. Run a length of garden hose up from the exhaust pipe into the window. Cram the hose in tight, tape it tight, then feed it up into the window, already rolled down an inch with rags stuffed in to fill the gap around the hose. Nothing to it. Turn on the engine. Turn on the CD. What would it be? Which singer? Use duct tape. Bring tape. The hose. CDs. A full tank of gas. She was in a twilight of near sleep, a jabbering reverie trailing along and taking her toward bottomless slumber, and yet she hadn't reached that mindless site, nor was she in any way awake, and so she was nowhere. Just listening to the lyrics, the voice and the melody, and feeling entranced. Just hear the music. Sure. Okay. Turn on the engine. Have a big drink. Nothing to it. Just on the verge, the wonderful verge. Moving to it.

8

BERNICE FIGURED THE TIME HAD come to pay the piper. She was going to have to open her eyes and start making do with the facts. First of all, the sun was up, and second of all, she'd slept late, because her alarm clock read just past 7:30. But the big fact, the main fact was that she was still there. Still in her apartment, still in her bed. The roof was intact, windows, the whole rigmarole. It might as well have been just another day. In fact, she thought, it more or less *was* just another day, and she wanted some coffee. Had to pee and get her old bones moving. She reached for her glasses on the bedside table. That brought the room into focus, Happy and Sappy on the floor nearby with their jaws resting on their crossed paws like some fool had posed them. At the foot of the bed, Ira rose alertly, studying Bernice, and then Elmira startled her, springing from the windowsill to stalk a light beam flickering along the baseboard.

Headed for the bathroom in her fluffy house slippers, she almost tripped on General's empty bed clogging the hallway. She remembered last seeing him in the kitchen but found him sprawled in the living room on the spot that his bed usually occupied, as if to remind her where he belonged. His pose on the hard floor was so perfectly motionless that she worried he was dead. However, getting close, she saw his chest inflate ever so slightly. She touched his brow, and he shuddered, turning to her in annoyance.

"It's okay," she said, backing away. "Just checking."

He stayed on her, demanding or declaring something, the light in his eyes glittery, like there was some bright idea flying around inside him. Bernice made a quick stop in the kitchen to turn on the teakettle, and though she feared she might start to dribble, she dragged General's bed back out where he wanted it before racing to the bathroom. But she didn't make it without wetting the floor a little.

Her clothes were rumpled and clingy, her skirt twisted, the back of her blouse loose. Regretting the removal of her Depends last night, she glanced out the door at her trail of piss. The disgust she felt turned her arrangement on the toilet into a kind of squat, like she planned to run the instant she was done, which was pretty much what happened.

In the bedroom, she took yesterday's dirty old pair up from the floor and stuffed them into the plastic garbage bag inside the special lidded trash can in the corner where she kept the smelly old things until she had a chance to get them outside on Monday, which was garbage pickup day. Exactly six remained in the box on the floor of the closet, so she tugged on a fresh set.

With a roll of paper towels clamped under her arm, she hauled a kitchen chair to the mess she'd made in the living room. "How stupid can you get?" she asked, and pressed her palms into the seat for support as she got down to business. At least she'd hit the floor and not the rug. "I guess they don't call it a second childhood for nothing," she said, patting away. Happy and Sappy sauntered up, intrigued by her presence at their level. They sniffed the urine, not for the first time, she was sure, and licked her ear and cheek. Turning to avoid Happy's tongue, she was face-to-face with Sappy. His big curious eyes filled with acceptance. "You'd think I would be housebroke after all these years, wouldn't you," she confided.

Waiting for water to boil, she filled a glass from the tap and laid out her pills, one each of purple and pink, and then two Tylenol. She was due for the bone-loss one but thought she'd take it later because it upset her stomach. Or maybe take it never. That'd be one side benefit of flyin' off to heaven. Her eyes kept darting to the brooch and earrings on the table, because lying there in broad daylight the way they were, after having been left out all night, seemed to threaten them with harm or theft, and she vowed to wear them or put them away where they belonged.

Once the shrill of the whistle drew her to the stove, she got out her tin of vanilla-flavored instant coffee and the skim milk. She had no idea what she was supposed to do. Call Reverend Tauke? She wasn't sure that would be right, and she didn't have the nerve even if it was. Hazel Vanasek was the one to get ahold of. But it was pretty careless of Hazel not to have called her. If Hazel had a considerate bone in her body, she would have picked up the phone by now. After all, it was Hazel got her into this thing. That dang Hazel, she thought, and her arms frosted over in goose bumps because Hazel might be gone. Hazel might have been taken up. They all might have been taken up except for Bernice, who was left behind for one reason or another, sitting in her kitchen sipping coffee just like that pushy Janet had warned her. The notion sent her to the window, where the day revealed an ordinary enough sun, clouds, and the connector occupied by sparse traffic in both directions. Opening the front door, she saw nothing that a person could call unusual, except the way the temperature seemed to have warmed up a bit. What she needed to do was turn on the radio, maybe the TV along with it. See if there was anything on the news. People disappearing and all. That ought to have all those reporters making a fuss.

She found music on the local radio station, and after a few minutes, the only interruption was a commercial for Westcot Dry Cleaners. Same with the TV, though the programming was network and the commercial for Sears. Did that mean nobody went? Or could it be the whole deal was being kept secret? Some kind of cover-up. Lord, she thought, wondering what she should do.

Well, there were the dishes from last night. The kitchen looked like she'd had company and broken out dessert for half a dozen guests. It was fun to remember the six of them gathered there last night. We had a good time, she thought, and now they were working their way to her again, looking for breakfast. Dogs. Cats. Morning. They loved to eat. But who didn't? With the dishes and liquid detergent in the sink, the tap slow to heat up, she had time to consider calling Janet. But she wasn't ready to deal with a bunch of backtalk just yet. Because that was what she'd get. A lot of smug, know-it-all, I-told-you-so remarks.

Plucking a dish from the mass of bubbles, Bernice applied the sponge, and the phone rang. She ran right to it but stopped, worrying that it was Janet wanting to get out of coming over. Or who knew. Some early-bird telemarketers. She wished she had one of those answering machines so she could listen in to who it was if they started talking. Maybe it was Hazel. Or Reverend Tauke. Except he'd never call. The bottom line was she didn't care to answer especially if it was him, and that thought made her feel sinful and squeamish. She had no choice about being saved. If she was saved, she was saved. It was like somebody else grabbed up the phone, but she was the one who said, "Hello."

"Bernice. This is Hazel."

"It's about time you gave me a call. So I guess you're still here."

"Yes, I am."

"Me, too."

"Reverend Tauke says we have to remember that the day is twenty-four hours. That a day goes midnight to midnight. And, of course, he's right. So it could happen at any second all day, right up to midnight tonight, when this day is over and done with."

"I don't get it."

"What?"

"That's what he said?" Bernice turned off the faucet and started drying her hands on a dish towel so she could get to her coffee, figuring a burst of caffeine might sharpen her up. "Midnight and— What was that?"

"Don't ask me to explain it, but it wasn't just last night that it could happen—it could happen all day today, up to midnight tonight, when this day is over. And he said we can come over to see him if we want to. A lot of people are going over."

"Over where? The church? The parsonage?"

"Don't you want to see him? I do. I'd like to go see him. He wants us all to come over. I think he thinks we all probably want to see each other."

"Can I ask you something?" Bernice took a gulp of coffee, because she really needed help. "I don't quite get this. Did he ever say anything about midnight before? At some earlier point, I mean, and I missed it. Wasn't the thing he kept saying that last night was the time? That's what I remember."

"He's very upset with himself, Bernice. He said he misread the information he was getting."

"He misread it in what way?"

"That's what he said."

"How much of it?"

"This is the information he was getting that was telling him what to say to us." Hazel sounded as breathless and full of herself as some cocky newscaster breaking the big story. "You know, how it came over him."

"Right. I figured that was what you were talking about." Bernice knew she ought to just calm down and enjoy her coffee, which had cooled but was still tasty. Still, she couldn't help how she felt. It wasn't right, the way he'd had them up chasing their tails all night.

"Can you imagine how easy it would be to get something like that wrong?"

"I guess."

"What's there to guess about?"

"It just seems to me he was very particular, so I'm just wishing he would have left things a little unclear, if that's what they were."

"You're very disappointed, aren't you."

"What?"

"I can hear it in your voice."

"No."

"I can hear it, Bernice. And I don't think you're listening to me. Because he's apologizing. That's what he's saying—he got it wrong. Think how big that is of a man like him to admit he made a mistake."

"I guess."

"You know I'm right. He told us it was last night, because he took certain information to mean 'night.'" Hazel pronounced the word like it might have a lot of possibilities but she knew the only one worth a lick. "Something in the way it was sent to him made him feel it was a matter of night, and so he said it was going to be last night, but what he believes now is it was the AM—the dark AM, or after—past midnight and before the next midnight. Because once he thought back and looked at his notes and tried to remember exactly how it came to him, he remembered that the way it was when it came and the way he talked about it was—well—" When she stopped, the silence left Bernice at the mercy of this carping, mulish voice inside her that didn't pause even when Hazel finished up by saying, "Anyway, he had to realize he had misstepped. It could have been last night after midnight, but it could also be anytime today or tonight before midnight."

"I still don't get it," Bernice told her.

"That's why we should get out there. I'm trying to explain it, but I don't know enough. He's got to be the one. But it was a lesson in humility for him, he said, and he was feeling very contrite. That was the word he used. 'I feel so contrite,' he said."

"I don't know."

"What don't you know?"

"Maybe he just shot his mouth off—like anybody might—just barkin' up the wrong tree." Bernice sounded scornful, all right, and feeling it was maybe uncalled for, and knowing Hazel would find it offensive, she tacked on "I know I shouldn't talk that way."

"You certainly should not. Why can't you just give the poor man the benefit of the doubt? He made a mistake. People do, you know."

"Yes, they do."

"So I'd get off my high horse if I were you."

"Where were you when he told all this to you?" Bernice climbed out of her chair and went back to the dishes.

"Home. My place. I called him."

"I thought about doin' that." With the phone clamped between her ear and a raised shoulder, Bernice got back to work.

"Is that water running? What are you doing?"

"Couple dishes."

"You want to go over when you're done? To Reverend Tauke's? Let's go over. I'm goin' over."

"I didn't get a lot of sleep last night. I'm feelin' kind of frazzled."

"It was exciting, wasn't it? Waiting like that!"

"Being up all night I'm tired, that's for sure." The last of the bowls came clean with a few swirls of the sponge and one more rinse. The windows above the sink were filled with brightness.

"I'm going over. Let's go over."

"Is it an all-day affair or what?"

"You mean at his place? I guess. He didn't set a time or anything. Should I come pick you up?"

"Now? No, I got a few things to do first."

"I think we ought to get over there. I think he needs us to let him know it's okay he made a mistake. How quick can you be ready?"

"I just woke up."

"So what do you need, fifteen-twenty minutes?"

"Hazel, I just woke up. It takes me more than fifteen minutes to put my shoes on."

"How long do you need?"

"That's what I'm saying. Maybe you should just go ahead on your own, and I can—"

"I'd rather wait for you."

"Fine, but you sound like you're itchin' to go."

"It was just so thrilling last night; I'm still worked up. What could be more exciting than talking to Reverend Tauke about how he made a mistake, and almost at the same time—well, at the same time—getting ready to meet Jesus? It's like we're in the Bible. You know the way Jesus would say a parable but nobody would get it, not even the disciples? That's what I keep thinking. We are living in the Bible right now. You and me. What is it you have to do before you can go over?"

"Things. You know. Morning things that have to be done." Bernice let the sink drain and switched on the burner under the teakettle for more coffee.

"Like what?"

"You know what I'm talking about."

"No, I don't."

"Morning things—I do them every morning. You must do them, too."

"Sure."

"That's what I mean. I'm not saying it's anything earth-shattering. I can't even say what it is right off, but you know the kinds of things I'm talking about. They have to be done."

"Maybe I could help you."

"Listen, I think you should go over on your own, and I could meet you there. I got my own car."

"How soon can you be ready?"

"I don't know."

"What do you have to do?"

"Hazel, didn't I just say I don't know? I haven't even started in on figuring them out, but I know they're there. Because they're there every morning." She spooned the sweet-smelling coffee into the cup stealthily, feeling like she was doing something Hazel shouldn't know about.

"I just think it would be more fun if we went together."

Ira bawled at his empty bowl. "Well, one is feed the animals," said Bernice. "That's one of the things. Off the top of my head." Elmira joined Ira, the two of them circling and sniffing.

"I thought Janet Crimmins was doin' all that for you."

"She is. She's coming by to do it. And she's not Crimmins anymore. She's divorced, you know. So she's back to Cawley. Janet Cawley."

"Can't they wait till she gets here? When's she comin'?"

"Why should they? I'm here, so I'll do it."

"You spoil them animals."

"Well, they count on me."

"Then why on earth did you ever pick a bad apple like her to take care of them? I hate to tell you, but if we'd all gone off last night and they were stuck having to depend on the likes of her, they'da gone hungry."

Sappy let out a scolding squeal, while Happy posed politely, as if to offset the bad behavior of her brother.

"She's got time yet, Hazel. She'll get here."

"But she won't. I'd bet my bottom dollar. Even if she is Isabel's daughter, she's an odd duck, Bernice, and you know it. What's going on with her up there all alone and no job?"

"She says she's fine."

"Sure she says she's fine. What else is she going to say? But I don't think we can take her word for it. Not when there's people seen her running all over that part of town, this wild look in her eye. Sometimes in these little shorts at night."

"There's a lot of girls do that, Hazel."

"No, there's not. There's some. And they're all younger and maybe on a high school team of some sort. My niece Kristen did that because she was on the cross country team."

"Sometimes older girls run to lose weight or—"

"She doesn't need to lose any weight. I hope that's not why she's doing it."

"No."

"Because she's a beanpole. Did she say that was why?"

"No."

"Because you know what that would mean. Eating disorder of some kind in spades. She's skin and bones."

"She didn't say it."

"She's thirty-five if she's a day, isn't she? Do you know? How old is she?"

"I don't know, exactly. Right around thirty-five."

"I think she's that and then some."

"She's thirty-six at most." Elmira bounced onto the table and crouched to lick up milk Bernice had spilled mixing her fresh coffee. They were all in an uproar except General, though the truth of the matter was she didn't have a clue about General. The way he was sprawled, she couldn't see if his eyes were open or closed, let alone get a fix on his mood. "Listen. Hazel."

"What?"

"If we're going to get over to Reverend Tauke's, I really need to get after these chores here, don't you think? Once I get my bearings, I'll call you back."

"Okay. Because I just think it'd be better if we went together."

"But if you get restless and need to go on over, I want you to feel free to—"

"I'm going to wait for you. You can't be all that long doin' whatever it is."

"Well, then, let me get going."

"Okay. But Bernice—you know these things I was just saying about Janet Cawley. As far as I can tell, I'm quoting you on a lot of them. Like about her running all over the place and living alone and acting funny. One way or another, I think they are things you said to me."

"I could have, I guess."

"No, no, don't guess. Give me a real answer."

"I'm giving you a real answer, which is it's likely I said things along those lines at some point, okay?"

"Or is my memory way off base, because it could be."

"No, I said them."

"So why are you arguing with me?"

"I don't know."

"Did you just lose track for a second?"

"No. It was more like I just didn't like the sound of them coming out of your mouth. Something didn't seem right. I may have said them, but I'm not sure I believe them."

"Then why say them?"

"I wish I knew."

"I'm not sure I'm following your drift on that one, Bernice."

"That's all right. Listen, I'll call you."

Bernice hung up and hustled to the pantry for kibble and cans of food, then went around gathering the bowls. When the cats, snaking between her ankles, almost tripped her, she begged, "Will you just give me a minute, if it's not too much trouble?" Their coaxing got worse, their backs humped to remind her of how hungry they were as she put their bowls up high and got Happy and Sappy settled at their regular spot on the kitchen floor. General could be thought to be sitting, as long as she skipped the way his torso was tilted like he was top-heavy, his stiff fore-legs bracing him, and his eyes funny-looking.

Wrapping Rimadyl and steroid pills in cheese and carrying his bowl, she started for the bathroom, where she intended to lock him away, so the other two couldn't rob him. "C'mon, now. You know where you eat." When he failed to follow, she called, "General!" She stomped her foot. "Let's go! I got more to do than coddle you."

He took several obedient steps but then stumbled sideways, as if hit by a violent wind, his hindquarters so out of kilter that try as he might, he couldn't keep his rump from dragging him over. He hit hard, and Happy and Sappy glanced up from eating. General squealed, fighting to get upright, and Happy grew attentive. Like a drunk, General reeled to his left until he slammed down again.

Clutching his bowl, she gaped. General was a stray she'd taken in, so his age was uncertain, but based on a vet's early estimate, he must be pushing fifteen at least. Happy was approaching General with an inter-ested expression, her neck lowering. Bernice followed. She placed the bowl in front of General. Happy sniffed the old dog's right front paw and then his shoulder in an exploratory manner.

"C'mon, now, eat a little for me," Bernice said as she pulled over a chair so she could sit and pet him. Sappy had shifted and was licking away at Happy's empty bowl while General studied his food glumly. She closed her fingers on his ear, massaging, as if she might waken his appe-tite, one pleasure leading to another. "C'mon, now." She'd owned or known a lot of dogs, going back to when she was a kid, and she knew the inability to walk was often the beginning of the end. General raised his eyes to her. Distant and lonely, he called to her from behind some weird affliction like a fireworks display falling through his brain.

9

J ANET COULDN'T REMEMBER WHAT HAD caused the trouble, but it involved a hat. The urge to go somewhere in order to pinpoint the damage nearly got her moving, but she didn't have good directions. She'd done something to cause grief. And yet she was mainly a witness positioned at an ever increasing distance. There she was, looking through a window onto a storm of bending branches and flying rain, as she awoke in her car, peering after the evaporating dream.

She straightened and sat stiffly. A black Ford station wagon sailed up the hill. Mr. Wilbur came out of his stucco home across the way and scurried in untied sneakers down to the curb for his newspaper. A slamming door made Janet duck, knowing the sound announced her landlord, Fritz Luckritz, heading for work. She stayed low until the engine of his departing car faded away. Just then Eileen Luckritz came out. A frazzled woman in house slippers, she held a fistful of aqua terry-cloth robe shut at her throat as she herded her two children into the morning. The school bus was already close. Boxy and perilous, it groaned to a standstill. The bus's stop sign swiveled into the street, and Janet felt a faint sad twinge because she would not be waiting at the other end to teach Andy and Sarah Luckritz and the two additional girls and the boy trudging dutifully aboard with their overstuffed book bags.

Eileen was already fleeing up the walk. Not wanting to attract attention while the bus idled, Janet feared Eileen would get away before she could signal. At last the bus huffed into motion. "Eileen. It's me. Here. In my car. Hi." She was halfway out, her bare feet on the pavement.

Wheeling around, Eileen was startled, but not for long, her puzzlement shoved aside by a show of exaggerated surprise. "Janet, you're in your underpants."

In her frenzy, she'd let the blanket fall into a tangle at her feet. "I know, I know. Don't ask."

Eileen ogled the interior of the car. "Don't ask what?" On her tiptoes, she performed in the far-fetched style of a children's game. "Is it that you don't want me asking why you are in your car in your underpants, Janet?" As if someone had to be hiding in the car, Eileen gawked into every nook and cranny. "Did something bad happen somewhere and you had to leave in a hurry?"

"No, no. I just got locked out of my apartment."

"But what were you doing driving home in your underpants? You must be freezing."

"No, no, that's not what happened. I didn't drive home, I was home." Having given up on the blanket, she was working to secure the larger of the towels around her waist. "I came out to get something from the car, and I got locked out. Could you just get me your extra key? I need a shower and a cup of coffee. I'm late for a favor I have to do for somebody."

"Okey dokey," Eileen said, sounding a warning even as she appeared to comply. Janet sat in the open door until Eileen returned in a dress she must have pulled on over her head, mussing her hair. "Here," she said, giving Janet the robe along with the key. "Get home and get dressed, and then when you bring the key back, so I have it the next time you need it, you can tell me the whole story. Okay? Deal?"

"I just told you the whole story. That's all the story there is. And I don't need the robe." Handing it back, she started off. "Thanks so much."

The ridicule in Eileen's extra-loud throat-clearing was like a hook in Janet's back, letting her know she better put on the brakes. Eileen waved aside the fluff of Janet's claims. "C'mon, now."

"There isn't any story, Eileen. Honest."

"Well, I have one to tell you, then. About when I had to go to the kitchen in the night and I saw a man outside—and luckily, before I called 911 or woke up Fritz, I realized this man was coming down your stairs, and then he said your name and looked up at your window."

Janet nodded and said, "Oh," in a way that mostly had to do with a powerful wish that she was still asleep.

"I might have called 911 anyway, but then he drove off. Maybe you should put this on just for a second." Eileen advanced with the robe. "Your lips look a little blue."

Janet accepted the robe less out of a need to keep warm than from an instinct that it would be smart to go along with whatever Eileen wanted. "I hope I didn't disturb the kids. I sure hope Fritz didn't lose any sleep."

"Oh, don't worry about him." Eileen expanded the concept of Fritz's unimportance with a shrug Janet didn't buy for one second. "But this fella last night. He was shadowy and hard to see, but there was enough of him to know he was cute. But scary still. You know the train of thought. Strange man. Night. I'm half asleep. And who says prowlers can't be good-looking? There was that Ted Bundy, right? But then just about the time my heart's about to jump through my skin, he says your name and starts around toward the front of the house. I saw him drive off." Her widening eyes made clear she was having fun even if Janet wasn't.

"My feet are freezing."

"C'mon down quick as you can. We'll have some coffee." Eileen clapped her hands as if she'd just won a big prize.

"Okay," Janet said. But once she was up in her apartment, she flopped at the kitchen table, pinching the little bones in her toes, rubbing numb skin. Her thoughts were far from clear. Tempted by the warmth she knew waited in Jack Daniel's, she went instead to the shower and started the hot water flowing. After hastily rigging her coffeemaker with Medaglia D'Oro from the fridge, she stepped under the pounding spray. Crispness and vigor dissolved the chill and the crud left from sleeping in her god-damn car and screwing Wayne. But her thoughts remained unaffected, grubbily swirling with an undercurrent the soap could not reach any more than it could wipe away the ache in the backs of her eyes.

She wanted that coffee and sat in her own white corduroy robe tied tight to drink it and wait for the caffeine to work. Now she had to deal with Eileen. And for sure she still had her Bernice problem. She was supposed to be over there by ten. On the other hand, maybe she could handle Bernice by phoning, because once the old biddy answered, it would be established that, having failed to blast off, she was available to feed her own animals, and Janet could take a nap, then maybe go for a run, catch a movie. Pouring a second cup, she thought, I've got to get in a run. Enough with the booze. I need some 'ludes.

When she decided to check the news, it annoyed her that she could not escape an expectation of actual reports about people disappearing. Advancing the dial, she awaited word of cars with no drivers. Beds empty. Houses inexplicably uninhabited. Yeah, right, she thought. A police report of a man running up and down her stairs was more likely. Along with alarmed accounts of this scantily clad chick holed up in her car.

The glowing band produced a newscaster who informed her there'd been a break-in at a local gas station. A small fire in a warehouse. An earthquake in Turkey that left thousands homeless or dead. In an African nation she'd never heard of, hundreds had died in gun battles following a failed coup. When a jolly jingle cut in to sell cars, it was safe to conclude that the day was ordinary even in its calamities.

Dialing Bernice's number brought a busy signal. But at least that proved she was there. Up, alive, and bothering somebody else. The weatherman was proclaiming Indian summer, a warming trend over the next five-day forecast with highs in the upper sixties and lows in the mid- to high forties. She liked the idea and wondered how she might take advantage of the good weather. Hitting redial got her the busy signal again, while the weatherman warned of a cold front headed their way by Wednesday of next week, so they better enjoy the beautiful weather while they could. Today would be perfect, with a likely high of 68 and a low of 45. The record high for this day, October 16, 1997, was a balmy 83 degrees way back in 1954. To find the low, they would—

When her phone rang, and she realized that the reason Bernice's line had been busy was because Bernice had been trying to call her. "Hello, there," she said.

"C'mon, what are you doing?" It was Eileen. "Get a move on, will you?"

"I'm just getting ready. I told you, I have to do this favor for somebody."

"What favor?"

"It's just something I have to do."

"Well, c'mon, then. Shake a leg."

"Okay, but I'm starving. I'm going to have to—"

"I'll whip you up some eggs. How do you like them—scrambled? Sunny side?"

"I don't want to put you to any trouble."

"Nothing to it. I got some Jimmy Dean sausages. You'll never want to leave. See you in a few."

Janet replaced the handset and then leaned on it as if she might pioneer a crushing new method of hanging up that would fuse the apparatus irrevocably. All these goddamn people. It felt like blackmail, the way she was expected to trot on down and bare her soul for Eileen's entertainment all because Eileen was her landlord, somebody capable of seeing to it that she was put out on the street. And how could she possibly dish out enough dirt about Wayne to satisfy Eileen without making herself sound like a home-wrecking slut?

So now her morning was going to be taken over by blathering with Eileen and then racing off to suit Bernice. Unless Bernice was home, as she certainly seemed to be. If Janet wanted to skip at least that part of this barrage of obnoxious obligations, what she had to do was verify that Bernice was still on the planet. In other words, she had to talk to Bernice. Besides producing a cringe that led to a groan of self-ridicule, the idea sent her to the cabinet for a swallow of Jack Daniel's. She started with a little one, and then, after dialing Bernice's number, she paced back for a nice healthy gulp as she listened to the ongoing busy signal. Wasn't that proof enough?

Ready to climb into some clothes, she decided the hell with it, what she needed was a run. With her shorts and jogging bra on, she sat to tie her Reeboks, and under the barely conscious influence of duty and diligence, she hit redial and slowly woke to the knowledge that what she was hearing now was the buzzing version of the phone ringing in Bernice's home. She waited as it persisted, and waited more, mild anxiety contending with resentment for the right to dictate her mood. She hung up, tried again, and got the same result.

Hoping to negate the urge to rush right over, she reminded herself that only minutes ago the line had been busy. But she was already switching to a clean pair of jeans. She pulled a sweater on over her T-shirt. The clock on the dresser read 9:22. With her denim jacket in hand and her purse slung over her shoulder, she set out for the door but detoured to the bathroom to squirt toothpaste into her mouth. About to spit out the antiseptic glop, she was struck by the shimmer of her face, and as if confronting someone in the mirror who hassled her constantly, mistrusting her every decision, she said, "Oh, go fuck yourself."

Eileen's doorbell managed only a halfhearted ping, but the door sprang open. "I thought you'd decided to ditch me."

"Sorry."

Eileen had spruced up, fixing her hair, a light touch of makeup and an upgraded housedress. The Mr. Coffee carafe was full to the brim, the kitchen table set with mugs and everything coffee needed, along with grape jelly and margarine.

"I really have to run," Janet said as Eileen started to pour.

"You'll just have to talk fast. Okay?"

"Okay."

"You need your coffee, right? At least I know I do." Eileen spun to the stove, where she tipped a frying pan toward a plate. "Now that I've had a minute or two, I realize maybe you don't want to talk about any of this as much as I might." Grinning, she placed sausage and heaped eggs in front of Janet. "So feel free to tell me to mind my own business, but the mystery man—it was Wayne Miller, wasn't it."

Hearing her own voice say "Mmm-hmmm" without any hesitation startled Janet.

Eileen nodded. "I thought it was him."

"Well, it was."

"I was pretty sure. He looked all worked up about something."

"I guess he was." The next surprise was a lighthearted impulse to say whatever the hell came into her head. The point was to amuse Eileen, while keeping in mind that nothing could alter the bottomless fraud between them.

Stirring sugar into her coffee, Eileen had Janet in her sights, but she grew tentative, as if she'd spotted something unexpected. "I'll put the muffins in, okay, and you just chow down."

"But you're warned—it's eat and run."

"He's still married, right?"

"Wayne? Yes. I think he is. He sure is. I would say he is." Janet's delivery presented each phrase as fundamentally distinct from the others, though she wasn't the one to make the nuances clear.

"I know they had some trouble. Do you know her? Sally. I don't really, though I met her at some function, and I worked with her aunt part-time at the school cafeteria. That's Mildred Lumke." When Janet let the silence linger, Eileen wondered, "How many kids do they have?"

"Three, I think. Or is it four?" She chewed a moment, then gazed into the coffee she was about to sample. "No, it's three."

"You sound a little mixed up on the subject."

"You can say that again."

Settling opposite Janet, Eileen said, "Well, I guess you're in the stew, then, huh?"

"Oh, I don't know. He's a little on the useless side, if you ask me, and I guess you have. Fun sometimes, sure. But now he won't leave me alone."

"You don't want him coming by?"

"Not really."

"Did you tell him?"

"As far as I'm concerned, I sure did."

"He don't listen, I guess. He was a pretty wild teenager, as I remember."

"English might as well be a foreign language unless what you're saying suits him. That's Wayne, okay?"

"So he's been coming by here a lot, would you say?"

Censure waited inside the twist Eileen had given the phrase "a lot," and Janet knew enough to dodge it. "No, no. I wouldn't say a lot. Not at all."

"Here, I mean. Coming by here. Because that's not something I'd be crazy about my kids getting too familiar with."

"Of course not. I won't say never. But not often. We were getting together elsewhere. You know what I mean."

"Sure. Motels and such."

"Yeah. He had a friend's apartment sometimes. Because I didn't want him coming here, for a lot of reasons."

"I would guess not. It's your place and all, but still. He is a cute one, though."

The way Eileen's interest kept being replaced by judgment or vicarious enjoyment of the titillating details warned Janet that more was going on than met the eye. "I have the feeling you knew something before last night."

"What? About him? Well, there's always talk."

"See, that's what I was afraid of. My reputation and like that."

"The thing is—a lot of people knew he was involved in that business that led to your divorce. It wasn't on the six o'clock news, but it wasn't a secret."

"That's exactly what I mean." She stared at the chunk of sausage speared on the end of her fork for a thoughtful moment, to heighten the sense of sincerity she knew Eileen would love. "Because, I mean, I got to where I had to call it off. A person gets caught up in things, you know, and then they know better. But that's not good enough for him."

"So you're saying—if I'm hearing you right—it sounds like you're saying that Wayne Miller is stalking you."

"I never thought of it that way."

"Well, maybe you should."

Worried that drying her hair hastily had left her looking a little on the wild side, Janet tried to curl the sides to stay behind her ears. "I guess, technically speaking, he is."

"What are you going to do about it?"

"I don't think there's anything to do, or that needs to be done. It's not anything to worry about, I don't think. He's just sort of stuck. But I'll tell you who I am worried about, and that's Bernice Doorley."

"Bernice Doorley? What's she got to do with it?"

"Nothing. No, no, this is something else." Janet had no idea what possessed her to toss Bernice into the mix with Wayne, except they both had aggravated her recently. "Bernice is nutty in her own right. She's got her own issues." Janet chewed away at the sausage. "Nothing to do with Wayne, except they're both operating without a valid license." The toaster popped, but Eileen was too engaged to notice. "I think the muffins are ready."

"Oh, right. Sure. Thanks."

Janet used the moment to search her delight in mocking Bernice, but not to slow or stop it. "She's sort of stalking me, too. Bernice, I mean. At least she was parked outside the house waiting for me the other day. You know, all those animals she has, well, what she expects is that she's going to be taken off in the Rapture. You know what I mean, right?"

"Bernice Doorley?"

"Right."

"Bernice Doorley thinks she's going off in the Rapture?"

"Right. You got it." Janet offered arched eyebrows along with a conspiratorial grin. "She says it was in the papers." Increasingly, it excited her to present this ridiculous version of Bernice. "But I sure didn't see those headlines. 'Bernice Doorley Is Going to Heaven.'"

"Me, neither. I think I missed the paper that day. But did she actually say that?"

Sensing that a little hesitation might strengthen her tactic, Janet took a sip and sat back. "That she was going? Or that it was in the papers?"

"Either one."

"Well, there's more than her involved—I know that. Local people, I mean. But the problem for her is all her animals. That's where I come in."

"Does Irma know?"

"Does she know what?"

"Well, any of it. Because her mother acting that way—thinking that way—would not sit well with her."

"In fact, I think Irma not knowing is partly what brings me into the picture." Another, even more annoying wave of insecurity about her appearance started Janet fiddling with her hair again.

"You know, they haven't been getting along. Irma and Bernice. It's a sad state of affairs."

"I gathered that."

"There's weeks go by they don't say a word. Don't bother to pick up the phone, either one of them. It's not right."

"That's the impression I have. I asked her about Irma helping out, but—"

"What'd she say? Probably 'Forget about it.'"

"Well, you know. That would have to be the gist of it, even though she actually didn't say all that much. Just enough for me to form a pretty clear picture of trouble between them if I filled in a blank or two."

"You're right on the money. Me and Irma went to high school together. Graduated same year. We stayed close for a while, then went our separate ways, but we reconnected a couple of years ago. Bumped into each other at that new Chinese restaurant, and it was like no time had passed at all." Eileen's pause demanded that her recovered friendship with Irma be viewed as out of the ordinary. "I don't think a week goes by that we don't have something to say to each other."

"I didn't know you two were friends."

"Of course you did. She's been here for dinner. You've seen her—seen her car. She parks right out front."

"I'm sure, but I just—"

"We asked you in for a cup of coffee that one time. You sat a good twenty minutes."

"Oh, sure. What am I thinking? Her and the little boy."

"Alex John. But not her husband, John—he was working nights. Well, we're close again. Me and Irma. Very close." This time the nod Eileen offered declared her forthcoming information noteworthy because she'd gotten it straight from the horse's mouth. "It's been hard for some time now. There's days Irma wants to make it up, and other days when she just knows she'd be better off forgetting the whole thing. Just forget she ever had a mother. I think mainly Irma's just hurt bad, and she wants to mend fences, but she loses hope because it doesn't seem possible. I couldn't be that way with my mom, I know. But I'm wondering if maybe Bernice is getting a little funny, after what you're telling me. And maybe that's what's going on. Senile, you know."

"I don't know."

"She's got to be seventy if she's a day."

"My mom was seventy." She was trying to just go along with Eileen, keep things on an even keel.

"It comes on people in different ways. At different times. Different symptoms. There's no telling. But any time past sixty, they're at risk. How'd she seem to you?"

"I have to say, she seemed okay in that way. She came up here and found me, spelled things out about what she wanted, like I was saying. Very direct. Very clear."

"Okay, but what are we to think that proves if we take into account what she was here for? Just think what she wanted."

"I guess a person could see something in that. But it's not like she's alone in this thing. This Rapture thing. Unless maybe there's a whole boatload up there, and none of them are hooked up right."

"Well, they find each other, you know. Crazy people. They have a knack for it. So I'd have to say that's expected."

"There's a minister at the helm. Reverend something. It's all local people, and there's a church. I mean, they get together at a church. So that gives it a legitimate sound when she talks about it. On the other hand, of course everything I'm telling you, every word, is according to Bernice."

Eileen wasn't listening. A few seconds back something had called to her, a weighty distraction that only now let her return, looking suspicious. "You said 'Reverend'? I'm wondering Reverend who? Did she say?"

"She used a name, but I'm not sure what it was."

"Was it Marshall?"

"I don't think so. You mean was it a Reverend Marshall?"

"Yes."

"I'd have to say no."

"I bet it's Reverend Clarkson. It's got to be Reverend Clarkson."

"I'm not sure I'd even recognize the name if I heard it. But that doesn't sound right."

"I went to his service a few times, and I came to the conclusion he was running on empty. I went back—wanted to be fair—but things as that man saw them didn't offer much I cared to consider on a regular basis. Craziest sermons, I swear. I bet it was him. Andrew Clarkson."

"I don't think so."

"There's another one I know of you cannot trust any further than you could throw him. Cantillion? Does that sound right?"

"I just don't remember."

"Burgmeyer?"

"You know, I have to go." The clock on the microwave read 10:02. Standing, Janet downed the last of her coffee to show she couldn't bear to waste a drop. "I promised I'd check in on the animals and feed them if she was gone."

"Well, you don't think she's going to be gone, do you?"

"She's not answering her phone."

"She's probably out, Janet. I mean, you don't really think she could be gone in that Rapture way."

"No, no."

"So why go over?"

"I just think I should."

"I see that's what you think, but I'm asking why? That's the part I can't make out."

"I told her I would. You know. I said so."

"But why do you want to waste your time when she probably fed the animals already and then went out to do something else? Went shopping. Or she's got a doctor's appointment. You get to be her age, you always have a doctor's appointment."

Janet had reached the door. "Well, I promised. You know."

Rising from her chair, Eileen mimed recoil as if Janet's remark had been a heavy object thrown against her. She added a melodramatic gasp and capped off the whole trick by jutting her head forward. "You promised?"

"Yeah."

"Janet."

"What?"

"You're a funny one."

She supposed she was. Not exactly entertaining, but comical in ways that were not a regular occurrence in Eileen's kitchen. And while the teasing was playful and friendly, it hid a scornful verdict, and ferreting out its full measure, Janet felt privileged. Eileen's disapproval identified her as a kind of dissident fully prepared to endure the ridicule of those around her, until she at last escaped them. A funny one.

Waving goodbye, she went out the door, and the phrase traveled with her, bubbling about. But maybe she was more. Not just a funny one, but—the Funny One.

Behind the wheel, something in the motion of her fingers on the key brought a prickly feeling of enchantment. The engine rumbled, vibrations buzzing her butt, and the sensations of a dream attempted to reach out to her. A car that looked exactly like her car was filling with fog, then rising skyward. Weightless, it climbed like a helium balloon. Was that the way it went? A steady stream of wisps murmured around her, the insinuations of a dream. If it was a dream. The interior grew cloudy. Or did it turn into a cloud, delicate as an eggshell with her inside, gliding to an unknown, inhospitable altitude. And it was effortless. There was nothing to it, as if the Funny One were lighter than air. The Funny One was voyaging off. Wacky, she thought, sailing over the ridgeline.

She didn't know how she'd gotten to an intersection, where the traffic light was turning green. A bronze sedan slowed in front of her, its left signal indicating that it was about to change lanes. She shifted to squeeze past on the right, and the driver cut into her path. She stomped the brake and squealed away from the blur that loomed and vanished up a driveway. She sliced into and out of the opposing lane. The guy in the sedan hit his horn, and she caught a snatch of bleached yellow hair, a baseball cap on backward.

Right, she thought. You asshole, you should have the whole fucking road to yourself. Except that I have very important tasks that need my immediate goddamn attention. So there she was, taking a corner and facing the fact that kowtowing to Bernice by heading over to handle this bullshit had almost gotten her killed. She expected to laugh, the brimming sensation promising at least the pleasure of irony, but what she let out was a growl. "Goddamn bullshit!" She squeezed the steering wheel and rocked in her seat. "Fucking bullshit! Bullshit! What the hell am I doing? What?" She slammed her palm on the wheel. "Somebody answer me!"

A mix of shame and uselessness told her that someone who considered her absurd had his eye on her. The road had widened into a four-lane, making the outdated Oldsmobile traveling alongside her the likely source. She saw a straw hat, and under it an elderly man hunched as if he feared his car might behave uncontrollably. In the passenger seat, a white-haired woman was out like a light, her eyes shut, her head lolling.

"This is the Funny One speaking here," Janet said, "and I'm asking!" She felt like she was winding down. "Any answer will do." She felt like she was no longer alone, or even driving, but off somewhere confiding in a friend. Who it was, exactly, she didn't know. But she could feel affection, and she awaited a response, listening closely, as though there really was someone riding with her. All right, she thought after a while. She was the Funny One, and the Funny One was driving and talking to herself. She turned a corner, smiling. She'd get over to Bernice's place and straighten things out and then come home and maybe take a nap before getting out for a run, depending on how she felt. Or she might run before she napped, if she wanted. Or something unexpected might come along. There was a weightless, fluttery quality to her mood that made ideas hard to pursue, her plans and decisions unraveling even as she shaped them. But she kept trying to follow the threads, while hoping not to notice, or at least to find amusing, their disjointed number and the way they disappeared before arriving anywhere.

10

GENERAL HADN'T EATEN A BITE, and he kept falling over. He'd even puked a little of that sickening yellow stuff, that bile. It took the wind out of her when he tumbled again and she had to stand there watching how he no sooner hit the floor than he started scrambling on those frail legs. He was dancing along like the floor was wavy, his scared eyes wanting help. She called his name and said, "Good boy," to reassure him this wasn't some punishment come his way because he'd done something bad. He banged into the wall, where he yelped and dropped. This time he seemed to give up a little.

It was a low blow that made her feel empty. Of course this wasn't the first time she'd worried the end was near. Every morning, or whenever she came back from an errand or even just left a room and found him sprawled, she half expected he might be dead. His sleep took him so deep that she often had to poke him. But he always startled awake, his head sweeping up to find her. In the dirty trick of dog years, he was anywhere from ninety-eight to a hundred and five. Good God.

But he was back at it. Haunches shivering, his hind legs levered his backside up, while his forelegs stayed folded so he was sort of kneeling when his feet skidded out from under him. He hit, grunting, his eyes on Bernice.

"It's okay," she said. "You take it easy now." She stroked his dusty, worn-out coat. His bones bumped her palm, as did the knobby tumors sown all over him. They'd all been tested and judged benign, but who knew? "Good boy," she said. "Yes, you are."

Elmira was curled on the couch, while Ira was in the sun on the windowsill, their interest in General nonexistent. But Sappy and Happy were intrigued. Bernice wasn't sure if they were concerned or just jealous of all the attention General was getting. Sappy nudged her, insinuating his snout under the hand that was petting General. "Really," she said. "C'mon, now. General needs this. Don't be so selfish, okay?" Happy licked her fingers and then sat down, while Sappy gazed at her as if realizing that she was gorgeous. Bernice snorted, unable to keep from grinning back. She squeezed his ear and bopped him lightly on the head. General had calmed. She looked directly into his eyes and said, "Stay, General. You stay."

Returning with a hot dog and a freshly filled water bowl, she let him lap a little. General had always snapped at food, and his failing eyesight made it likely he would nip her, so she fed him the meat in chunks placed on her palm. The eager way he swallowed and looked for more struck her as encouraging. He was back at the water bowl, slurping and wobbling, when she called the vet's office. She explained she had an emergency. "It's General. He can't walk."

"Not at all?"

"Well, some. But he's falling down. I need to come in, okay?"

"How quickly can you get here, Mrs. Doorley? Doctor Hoffenbach will see you as soon as you arrive."

"I'll be there before ten."

"Try not to worry."

The Old Red Barn Animal Hospital was a good twelve miles out of town. Several vets were nearer, but Bernice didn't let the inconvenience hold her back. She'd come to trust Dr. Hoffenbach. He'd tended her pets for a decade or more, so they'd been through thick and thin. A few years back he'd scared her something awful when he'd asked her to join him in an examining room where they could talk privately. His tone had made her so nervous, she didn't really hear as he explained how his conscience demanded that he give her a ten percent discount because of all the pets she owned. She was so busy preparing for the worst that he was just this haze talking. But then the meaning came through, and she had to look away because she didn't want to embarrass herself, acting like a big baby.

Sappy and Happy needed to be walked. And of course that damn Janet hadn't shown. Reluctant to do their business on the lawn, both dogs ended up dropping turds just off the curb in the street, where Bernice couldn't let them lay. As she hurried back to the front steps for the pooper-scooper, she heard the phone ringing. She caught the dogs and raced into the house but the phone went silent. "Couldn't hang on for another second, could you?" she snarled, as if to scare the ringing into starting back up. Nagged and hounded from every angle, she was doing the best she knew how. The last of the turds was halfway onto the metal pan when the phone came chasing after her again. She worked the scooper to drop the poop onto her own lawn, which she hated doing, but she had to get in there and answer. This time the darn thing went quiet before she even reached the steps. Still she stomped over, dialing angrily. When Hazel answered, Bernice said, "Did you just call?"

"What? No. Did somebody call you?"

"Yes."

"Who?"

"I don't know. I didn't answer."

"Well, why not, for heaven's sake?"

"I mean, I tried to answer, but— Listen, Hazel, I don't have time to explain, but I think you better head on over to Reverend Tauke's on your own. Maybe I can meet you there later, but I have to go out to the vet's because one of the dogs is sick."

"What do you mean?"

"One of the dogs is sick. He's sick. Now I want to get going, okay? And I think you should, too."

"But I told you, I don't want to do it alone."

"I know that."

"That's not how I want to go."

"Okay. But I don't know what I can do about that. You can wait if you want, I guess, and I'll do my best to—"

"How long?"

"What?"

"How long will you be?"

"I don't know. It's out of the way where I go, twelve miles or so one way, and then I'll—"

"Twelve miles? Why go so far?"

"That's where it is. That's where I go, and they said they would squeeze me in, but I really have no way to judge how long it will all—"

"I wish I'd known. I just turned down a ride from Jean Hines. She wanted me to go with her, but I said I had to wait for you."

"Well, you didn't have to do that."

"You know very well we said we were going to go together."

"It would have been okay."

"But if I just went off, you might have been mad or had your feelings hurt. How was I supposed to know? You should have called me."

"That's what I'm doing."

"I don't want to sit around here all day. We'll miss everything. How long will you be?"

"I don't know how long. Didn't I just say that? I think what I'll do is I'll call you after I get there. I might have some idea then."

"Which dog is it?"

"Why?"

"I don't know."

"General."

"Which one's he?"

"The old one, the black one."

"What's wrong with him?"

"I think he's dying."

"Oh, goodness. Is that what the vet says?"

"Hazel, that's what I'm trying to do is go find out what he says! If I could get off the phone."

"I'm sorry. I'm so worked up after all that last night."

Bernice knew she should let it pass, but Hazel's phrasing left her feeling she'd missed out on something. "All what last night?"

"Waiting."

"Oh, okay."

But just as she'd feared, she'd revved Hazel up, and on she went. "You know. Waiting, waiting! That's why I want to get over and see Reverend Tauke, because I'm hoping he'll tell us something. And sure, I can go alone, but last night it came over me that of all the people in my life—at least of those still alive—you were the one I was going to miss the most. And even though I knew we'd all be together up there in glory, there was something about being done with Belger and our lives here in Iowa that made me know how much our friendship meant to me."

"Oh," said Bernice. This was so far out in left field that her mind emptied except for the guilty need to say something nice back. More than anything else, she was embarrassed, because she'd never felt anything like that about Hazel. Nor had it ever crossed her mind that she had a place so high up in Hazel's affections. There were people Bernice missed, and some were women, like Isabel, for one, and her mom's sister, Aunt Clara, who'd been like a queen when Bernice was small, and her own mom, for sure, and Irma, who was so very distant, though still alive. But would she miss Hazel? It was a question that made her sad, whatever the answer. "I didn't know that, Hazel."

"Me, neither, until last night. You and Isabel were always so close, you know."

"Yeah." Bernice wasn't sure what that had to do with the price of apples, and was hoping Hazel might give her a little more to go by when her roving glance caught General with his head on his paws, his eyes feverish. "I gotta go."

"Call me later."

"Okay," Bernice said, and hung up before either one of them could get in another word.

Wanting her car as close to the house as possible, she pulled into her neighbor's driveway. With the back passenger door left open, she hurried inside, reminding herself to make sure her shoes were tied good and tight, because the last thing she needed was to trip. Using a trick she'd learned from Dr. Hoffenbach when Pumpkin, her yellow Lab, got sick a decade ago, she looped a bath towel under General's belly. With one end clutched in each hand, she got him going. The two steps down to the grass were just about more than she could handle. She had to waddle along to support him from behind, puffing and grunting, her arms ready to come out of their sockets. She couldn't help it. She had to take a break. The towel went slack, and General plopped onto his side. Her pulses throbbed, and her heart felt ready to burst from having to support all the fuss counting on it, her breath going in and out, her blood going every which way in all those veins inside her so she could think and walk and stand there worrying about General. Suddenly, she saw the two of them dead on the lawn. She was belly up, with her eyes turned into fogged-up mirrors like Isabel's that night, while General lay silently beside her. All because she was trying to do everything without any help. It was too much for one person. She was getting what she deserved for not knowing better than to count on Janet Cawley. Where the hell was she? If things had gone the way they were supposed to last night, there'd be dog shit all over the house. In a couple of days, the litter boxes would overflow so they'd all be shitting and peeing anywhere they could find a spot, like hobos, the bunch of them starving because Janet Cawley couldn't be bothered to keep her word.

When she figured the time had come to try a few more steps, General grumbled, but did his best to go along with her lunacy. By the time they reached the car, her fingers were cramping, her arms shaking, as she raised up his front end, and with him scrambling, heaved. He landed, muttering like a cranky old man. Probably wanted nothing more than to curl up under a bush and get the whole thing over with.

But at least they were on their way, and she went straight for the shortcut she liked that took her twisting down a number of back roads. Some people—Hazel was one—said it was just somebody's half-baked idea of a shortcut that didn't do a thing except put wear on your tires from so much winding around. But Bernice had driven both ways one afternoon, proving it was shorter by three tenths. And on a day like today, when speed mattered, it felt like she got to the interstate in no time flat.

What lay ahead was blazing concrete that seemed to go on forever, disappearing off through Iowa, maybe all the way to California. She'd taken trips, but only because Toby liked them. She settled into the slow lane, planning to stay. The whole world of fools in their sedans and mobile homes, their SUVs and pickup trucks, could go right on rushing to the ends of the earth, just as long as they left her out of it. And those eighteen-wheelers most of all, they were the worst, or this fiery red monstrosity roaring up on her left in a storm that tried to gobble her up. But she was having none of it. She was going where she was going, and that was all there was to it. When the shoulder got a little too close, she had to correct, and just then the sign for the animal hospital jumped up on her right, big and bright and hard to miss, maybe six foot tall with the name in bold print under the cutout figures of this cat and dog with birds roosting on their shoulders, and all their natural color, and all looking down on her like they knew how hard she was working to get General some help.

It was no easy matter, lugging him out onto the gravel of the parking lot. He groaned, human-sounding and sad. All of a sudden the front door slammed, and someone came running toward her. "What are you doing, Mrs. Doorley?" It was Susie, one of the assistants. "Go on inside and have a seat. I'll see he gets in. There's more than enough commotion around here without you hurting yourself and making more."

Bernice didn't see that she was causing any commotion beyond what was necessary, but Susie was nice most of the time. Inside, the first person she saw was a teenage girl in the corner with a yapping puppy on a leash. Probably skipping school. Politely separated by some empty chairs, a heavyset woman huddled over a big tabby cat asleep on her lap. The hound dog sprawled on the floor belonged to a bearded fella in bib overalls. At the counter, a middle-aged pair looked tense. Probably late middle age, to be exact, most likely some sort of early retirement, or how else could they both be there at this time of day? Could have been her and Toby, with a little luck. Behind them a pair of greyhounds squirmed, tangling their leashes. As she approached to report her arrival, Bernice thought she'd be considerate and said, "Careful, there, you don't trip."

The woman swiveled with an ornery, walleyed stare that advised Bernice to mind her own business, while the man was letting the receptionist know where he stood in no uncertain terms. "It's just too much. You see that."

"We know you're here, Mrs. Doorley," the receptionist told her without lifting her eyes from the paperwork that had the three of them tied in knots.

Lord, thought Bernice. They had the heat on way too high. The place was boiling. Struggling out of her jacket, she vowed not to complain, but she wasn't going to let them ignore General, either. "I'm sorry, but somebody said—whoever I spoke to on the phone—well, they—"

"That was me. We spoke." Now the receptionist straightened, and her name was Lisa, Bernice recalled, and she could see Lisa deciding it just might be worth her while to disregard the billing problem long enough to show who was boss. "I'm afraid we had some changes. There was an accident on the Verner farm. Dr. Hoffenbach had to run over there, so we're backed up. But Dr. Manders will be with you as soon as possible."

Dr. Manders? She didn't want Dr. Manders, who was little more than a child, and a woman to boot. "Dr. Hoffenbach's gone? I was told he'd be here."

"He was, but like I said, he had to go on a farm call." Looking past Bernice, Lisa said, "Hello, General."

Susie was easing General onto the floor. "Mrs. Doorley, you must've just about bust a gut doing this on your own." She searched out an empty chair. "Don't you have somebody who could help you out?"

"I did, but they let me down." She joined Susie, the both of them looking to take a load off. Bernice felt she deserved a little sympathy, and it struck her that she might prompt some by saying gloomily, "Janet Cawley. She was supposed to come by."

Susie smiled. "Don't know her."

Bernice had half a mind to walk out, and might have if she could have thought of where to go. Dr. Manders was fine for run-of-the-mill stuff, but not worth a hill of beans in something like this.

"Pretty spiffy blouse you got on there, Mrs. Doorley. Something special going on?"

Lord, Bernice thought. She'd forgotten all about being so gussied up. Here she sat in the best outfit she owned with no idea how to explain it, but she sure didn't want people thinking she was putting on airs. She smiled and gestured pointlessly.

Susie placed her palms on her thighs, as if dealing with General had left her so worn out, she doubted she could make it to her feet without extra leverage. "Well, back to the salt mines."

"Did something happen over at the Verner farm?" she asked, hoping a little show of interest in Susie's other duties would show that, no matter how Bernice might be dressed, she was down to earth.

"Oh yeah," said Susie. "It was that Hopkins boy, Butch—he got drunk and ran his pickup into the Verner fence. The cows took off. So, Butch, who don't have a dime's worth of sense, starts trying to flee the scene, but he loses control and smacks into one of the cows. Broke his own nose and got stuck in a ditch for good. So there's all kinds of medical help wanted over there." She patted General's head before standing. "Poor old guy's having trouble, huh?"

"Yeah. I'm worried."

"Well, he's old," Susie said, walking away.

That was a cold, completely uncalled-for remark, and it got Bernice close to snapping at Susie. She knew better, though, even if the snippy little thing deserved it. What she had to do was count to ten. What she needed to do was occupy her mind. She could at least take a second to fold her flannel jacket nicely, instead of holding it all bunched up. She thought about the Hopkins boy and all the trouble he was in with skidding tires and crazed cows. Then she reached for a *People* magazine in a nearby pile, thinking the pictures of this or that movie star might distract her, along with the story of one or another of their romances and how it was ending or starting up, or maybe some other kind of difficulty they were facing. The shiny faces sailed by at parties and award shindigs, their white smiles haunted by poor old General, who was so sick and scared. *We might have to put General down.* That was the kind of fake, infuriating phrase they'd probably use. And right then and there, it seemed to her that it ought to be General she was reading about in the pages of *People* magazine, his sad story unfolding, a photograph of his paw stuck out and this big needle getting closer. She would probably have to let them do it. She couldn't lug him around like this. Maybe she'd say a little prayer. Just for the comfort of it, so she'd know what was the right thing to do and have the strength for it.

She was unprepared when her prayers veered off, leaving ease behind and carrying her down some back road, until she arrived where Reverend Tauke stood waiting in his dark suit, and she realized she'd forgotten all about him. It didn't seem possible. It was hard to believe but still true that she'd forgotten about last night and all that didn't happen. She winced guiltily fearing that he was mad and that she'd cost herself everything by losing track, because it could still happen. Maybe this instant, or in the next one, right here and now, before she finished another breath, these invisible arms sweeping her out of her chair and into their winged and singing whirlwind.

11

Janet arrived at Bernice's, planning to get in and out quickly, but was brought up short by an unanticipated desire. She wanted her entrance to create the impression that the events of last night had turned out exactly as she had expected. Which she firmly believed was the case, since the whole thing was nuts. And yet to walk in without some idea of Bernice's status made her feel vulnerable, as if the entire situation were an elaborate trick to embarrass her.

She slipped up to a living room window, where the glass was a smear in the high morning sun, her reflection planted amid the daisies printed on the curtains. Then a fragment of rug surfaced with a yellow cat walking over it. She was forming her hands into a tunnel of shade to manufacture focus when she heard an automobile behind her. A shiny, maybe even fresh-from-the-showroom plum-colored Toyota sat aimed in the wrong direction so the driver's side faced Janet. She didn't recognize the car but knew it didn't belong to Bernice. And with this thought came the awareness that the old duct-taped Chevy was nowhere to be seen. Just then the door of the Toyota opened on Hazel Vanasek, her wide-set eyes alarmed.

Janet waved hello, and as if she'd fired a gun to start a race, Hazel lunged to get out, her thick feet just about exploding the navy pumps restraining them. She sprang over the curb, stuffing her car keys into her purse and shouting to Janet, who was only yards away. "Is she all right?"

"What?"

"Bernice! Bernice! Is she all right?"

"I think so. I mean, I didn't see anything wrong. But I couldn't see in. What's wrong?"

"Why were you looking in the window?"

"I was trying to see her."

"But you didn't?"

"No. Just the cat. One of the cats walking."

"Because I got to tell you, you scared the bejeezus out of me, peeking in like that. I thought something terrible must have come to pass."

"Sorry."

"What in God's name were you doing, if you think you can tell me?"

"I was trying to see in and see if she was all right."

"Why wouldn't she be all right?"

"I'm sorry I gave you a start, Hazel."

Hazel was fleshy, her body adrift in bulges shoving around the fake red suede jacket belted and zippered and swelling at her hips. "There's enough going on without you piling on needless worry." Her stride was almost bowlegged, the broad planes of her face surrounding her rimless glasses freckled and flushed, her once red hair dyed to a coppery tint and styled with bangs. "I don't think she's in there, anyway."

Janet glanced at the house. All the windows were shimmering veils. Suddenly, the dogs inside sounded a wild alarm. She knocked, then rang the bell. "Where is she if she's not here?"

"I told you she's gone, and you should know she fed them," Hazel said. "They had their breakfast."

"How do you know?" It made Janet uneasy to feel the lock respond to the turn of the key in her hand, as if she hadn't been invited.

"She told me how you were supposed to be there to help her but you weren't doing it."

"I was supposed to get here by ten."

"Well, it's twenty after, the way I tell time."

"So I'm a little late."

"You don't have to explain yourself to me."

Then shut up, Janet thought. The spaniels took their rowdy fit to another level as they tried to hold their ground. "Hush now," she said. "We met." Plucking the note with the info from her jacket, she said, "C'mon, Happy. Hey there, Sappy." Their ears lifted in giddy recognition, and when she offered each an open palm, they licked hopefully. "See how they like hearing their names?"

"How come they got such stupid names?"

Janet crossed to the pantry. "I'll give 'em a treat to keep 'em calm."

"Well, just keep in mind there's no need to feed 'em again," she said, following alongside.

More than what Hazel said, it was her tone that reshuffled Janet's perspective so that a fading thought came back into prominence. "Wait a minute. You talked to her?"

"Sure did. A couple times."

"And she was all right?"

"Pretty much."

"So what is all this with you showing up the way you did and carrying on about, 'How is she? How is she?'"

"Why are you asking about that? It was you peeping in that window gimme such a shock. You coulda been a criminal up to no good."

"Okay, okay. But you kept it up. After you knew who I was and you jumped out of the car like the house was on fire. It was obvious you knew who I was, but it was like you were trying to get my goat or something."

"Get your goat? Me getting out of the car?"

"Yes."

"I don't have time for the likes of that. Getting your goat. Good Lord." Hazel plunked her purse, which was navy, like her shoes, on the countertop and turned on the tap water. "I drove up into a situation here that set me off, and sad to say, it's just my nature that once I'm set off runnin' in a certain direction—it don't matter which way or if there's any sense to it—well, there's a certain amount I'm gonna travel before I know to slow down and stop."

"So have we gone far enough now?"

"I'm getting sick of it, I can tell you that." Hazel swiped her finger under the water and, satisfied that it was cold enough, filled a plastic tumbler. "Bernice and me been friends over fifty years, you know. We keep track of each other."

One of the cats swirled around Janet's ankles. The puff and purr of the torso exhaled an air of entitlement, but Janet wasn't interested. She was savoring Hazel's blue eye shadow, the red lipstick matched to her nail polish, the overall sense of foiled enthusiasm in her poor old countenance. Unzipping her jacket as if she needed freedom to enjoy the water she was about to drink, Hazel unveiled a khaki blazer with large gold buttons over a matching khaki skirt. Janet had to double-check but then was sure that Hazel's dangle earrings were almost identical to the blazer's buttons. Hazel and Bernice were a pair, all right, ready for their trip in their Sunday best, like corpses at a wake. She could almost hear them consulting about what to wear. "So, Hazel, I guess we can move along to more important matters, then."

"Suit yourself."

Janet snorted. "Wouldn't that be an unexpected treat."

"What kind of a remark is that, I'd like to know."

Shoving her foot to dislodge the cat from her ankles, Janet succeeded in making the animal whine. Instantly, she was face-to-face with an impulse that reminded her for the millionth time how her ambition to become a vet had been folly, because what she wanted was to kick the stupid creature square in its annoying oblong head. "What did it sound like?"

"Like something hard to see the point of," Hazel said. "Is there one?" Her fingers patted the scoop-necked mustard-gold blouse peeking out from the blazer, then moved on to several of the fake pearls on a single strand around her neck, like she was worried they had gone off somewhere or maybe simply gone unnoticed.

What Janet wanted was to teach this obnoxious cat a little something about life, because it really shouldn't be so certain the world existed to satisfy its wishes. "So I don't have to feed them," she said.

"Nope."

"I'm still going to give these two something. Want a cookie?" she sang to the spaniels, and they scampered to her, gazing up worshipfully.

"Look at them fools," said Hazel.

"I guess they know the word 'cookie.' "

As if continuing to converse with her, the dog she thought was Happy wagged her tail while the other one groaned, drool spilling over his bottom lip.

"That's just plain pathetic," said Hazel, and took off her jacket.

Janet couldn't help but delight in the ecstasy of the spaniels at this chance to gobble dry chunks from her palm. Reaching for more bone-shaped tidbits, she smiled at her devotees and, out of the corner of her eye, saw Hazel shimmy and shake, as if giving her plumpness a chance to rearrange its layers. "Anyway, Hazel," she said, "when you say Bernice is gone, what exactly do you mean? That's what I'd like to know."

"I mean she's gone."

"But do you mean gone in any special way, or maybe—"

"She's at the vet's?"

Janet held steady, opting for repetition. "She's at the vet's."

"I think so."

Watching Hazel nod, Janet felt once again that she was at risk of falling victim to a prank. "I'm trying to get at something, okay, Hazel? Bernice had to tell me what was supposed to happen last night."

"I figured."

"So it didn't happen, and she's at the vet's is what you're telling me?"

"That's where she said she hadda go."

"Did she say why?"

"One of the dogs—the old one. She thinks he's going to die."

"Oh, no. Really?" Janet looked at her list. "General. The old one is General. The black one."

"If you say so."

"He's the old one."

"Well, she said he was old."

"And he's not here. He was here last evening." They both looked around, as if General might have gone unnoticed, while Janet folded the note with heightened care. "I figured it would all turn out this way. Not that she would end up at the vet's—but that even if she wasn't here, it just meant she'd gone somewhere ordinary and not that the Rapture business had actually happened. Because I tried to call earlier and got a busy signal, so I figured she was here."

"That was probably me she was on with. We talked quite a spell."

"Around eight or eight fifteen. Maybe eight thirty?"

"I was trying to get her to go somewhere with me, but she couldn't."

"So I guess that's that. I'm done."

Hazel leaned forward to dramatize her disagreement. "I wouldn't go that far."

"Well, sure—with helping her. She fed the dogs and cats. And the other thing didn't happen."

"You're jumping the gun. You got brakes, give 'em a tap. It didn't happen last night, but the likelihood is it's going to happen later today is what we think."

"That's not what Bernice said."

"Probably not. Last night was the way it was looking, and nobody thought any different after what Reverend Tauke told us. He said it. So we all said it. But it's comin' later. I mean, it just goes to show you."

Janet wheeled into the pantry for several more dog treats. Alertly, Happy and Sappy pranced up, and she crouched, breaking the fake little bones into pieces. "Look, Hazel, I want to say this, okay?"

"What?"

"This. You don't really believe this crap."

"What crap? What are you calling crap?"

"This Rapture crap and you're all going."

"Okay, now. Let's not get started on that one. And you might just keep a civil tongue in your mouth."

"And you might just make some sense."

"That suits me fine."

"I mean, it's an idea and all that, Hazel. So sure, it's in books and movies, and in that sense you believe it. In a way that— What's the right way to say this? In a fictional sense. Like a fairy tale. In a fairy-tale sense. Okay?"

"It's no fairy tale to me, I can tell you that."

"Well, what would you call it?"

"I'd call it the Bible, that's what I'd call it. I'd call it the word of God."

"There's nothing in the Bible about you and Bernice going. Or are you saying there is?"

"Don't be stupid. Of course not. But we are part of Reverend Tauke's congregation. And he was told we were going."

"By who?"

"Who do you think?"

"I don't know. God?"

"It's his mission. He's a devoted man."

"Fine. I'm sure he is, but—"

"Maybe we shouldn't talk about this. I don't feel right just—"

"Wait, wait. I'm not saying you don't believe it, but that it's a matter of belief in a theoretical sense. That kind of thing. But beyond that you can't—not in a way that it's real. That it's going to happen. To you. For sure."

"I think you're getting out of your depth. I'd have to say the way you put things makes you sound ignorant."

Janet flung open the refrigerator and pulled out a Diet 7UP. "So it could still happen? It was supposed to and it didn't, but it still could. That's your idea."

"Yes, it is. That'd be one way of putting it."

"When?"

"When what? When is it going to happen?"

"Right."

"Your job is to feed the animals, if you want to be of use."

"But that is what you're telling me. Your point is that it didn't happen, but it still could?"

"Nobody asked you for anything but feeding the animals. Don't concern yourself with the rest of it."

"But I'd like to have some idea. Is it this week? This month?"

"No, no." Hazel looked worried, and she ricocheted around the tiny kitchen until she bounced out and landed in the recliner, where she sat and started rocking.

"Sometime this year? Next year?"

Hazel shook her head, her eyes reduced to a hostile squint. "Okay, now. There was a mix-up about the time frame. He had the idea right, Reverend Tauke did, but he didn't look at it right. That happens with people."

"You know what? Fine." She took a long fizzy gulp. "Let me be honest. I'm thinking about my own life. I have things to do, you know—my own things. So I'm just wondering how long I'll be tied up if I go along with these shenanigans. I mean, if it doesn't happen today, are you all going to start saying that it's going to happen tomorrow?"

"Nobody said anything about tomorrow that I know of."

"As of yet."

"You're the only one talking about tomorrow."

"I'm just trying to understand how far my obligation goes in this thing." Janet burped. "Sorry."

"I think you're doing a little more than that."

"Like what?" She flopped onto the davenport and sat guzzling more of her drink.

"I think we both know."

"I'm sorry, but I don't. I haven't the faintest."

"Snide!"

"What?"

"The proof is in the pudding, so don't pretend otherwise. And I've had just about enough of it."

"I'm being snide?"

"I think I'd rather not get into it."

"Why not?"

"Look at you. Just itching for a fight. I think I'd rather go on outside." She rose, brushing the front of her blazer, as if arguing with Janet had scattered crumbs all over her. "No, sir, I don't think I'll stay here to be in-sulted by the likes of you, Janet Cawley."

"How have I insulted you? I'm the one in the dark. I'm the one every-body thinks they can keep in the dark."

Hazel marched back into the kitchen to retrieve her purse and jacket, and once she had them, she puffed up. "These animals are your responsibility. I don't want you trying to use this conversation to shirk your duties with Bernice. That's between the two of you. Just be sure and lock up when you leave, and then you can get on with this business of yours you're so all fired up about that you can't spare a minute. Whatever it is you think you do these days. Not that anybody knows. What is it, anyway?"

"What?"

"Your business. What do you think you're doing with your life? People wonder, you know. They can't help it. They see things. Things are noticed. A lot of people loved your mother."

"I thought you wanted to leave."

"Well, thank you for reminding me. At least you're good for somethin'." She strolled off but faltered short of the door, looking crestfallen, her shoulders drooping. The gaze she finally showed Janet was such a concoction of mawkish reproach and regret, it was hard to take seriously. "This is not how I want to be spending my last hours. You can scoff if you want, but when Jesus comes to find me, this kind of petty squabble won't set me in the right light. I don't like talkin' about doubt and that kind of thing. You go right ahead, but I don't care to. I can't say I never had any, because there's no getting around the facts. But if the Lord comes looking, I gotta be worth finding." She looked haggard, like an old soldier determined to get back to her duties, which at the moment consisted of pushing the door open. But it could close on its own.

Janet stood and stepped forward. The outside world was narrowly displayed in green, gray, and blue—grass, pavement, and sky. She was surprised by a sense of regret. But wasn't enough enough? Why should she feel bad?

A moist fluttering on her hand drew her to one of the spaniels sniffing out a pulverized cookie locked in her fist. Her fingers fell open, and she squatted, allowing him to lick away while his partner waited patiently. Or was it her partner? Caught by their optimism, Janet felt she was peering into a wealth of trust. Or else perfect fucking stupidity. "Okay," she said, grabbing a treat for the dog who waited, and then she was out the door.

The Toyota's engine was barely a whisper, the exhaust spilling fumes in a spiral. Hazel sat frowning over the instrument panel as if processing a complex set of readings she had to complete before she got going. Janet pressed her hand to the window, then scratched with her nails, and Hazel responded by ignoring her. About to shout, Janet saw that the door wasn't fully secured, so she tugged the breach wider. "Is something wrong?"

"Watch yourself."

"Is there a problem?"

"I don't think you're the one to ask that question."

"I mean with the car."

"Car's fine."

"The way you were checking everything."

"I just check things. I check before I go. And then I go. Don't start insulting my car."

"No, no. Far from it. It's a beauty. Brand-new, looks like?"

"Almost."

"I noticed when you drove up. I thought, Look at that. What a nice car."

"It's pretty handy, let me tell you. Not even broke in."

"What's the mileage?"

"Under two thousand. Nineteen hundred and something." Hazel eyed the odometer. "Nineteen hundred and twenty-eight miles and some tenths. Point four. My nephew bought it for me. You remember him. Francis Reynolds. He's my sister Glenda's boy."

"He bought you this car, Hazel?"

"Yes, he did."

"He was a year ahead of me. Or was it— No, no, Francis was two years ahead of me in high school, so I knew him, but not all that well."

"He's in Des Moines now. Three little ones. Just had a third in August. Middle of the night. August twelfth. They called me first thing in the morning. I'm talking about five AM. That kind of morning. Glenda's been dead a while now, so I'm a substitute. I know. And that's fine with me—I'm happy to have the chance. Except maybe not so happy at that hour. I jumped, and the funniest thing was the way I sat there like a dumbbell. It was goofy how I didn't know what that ringing belonged to.

But then it came to me, I guess, because I picked it up, and they started talking. It took me a bit to get over being so mixed up, I have to say, but they were doing all the talking. Francis was. All girls, he's got. Oldest is seven. So that's seven, four, and a newborn. They're under the gun, as you can imagine. It's a load. And she's working part-time. Don't ask me why. That man's a wonderful provider. Wonderful. Not that there's ever too much money coming in. She has these computer skills and wants to keep up with things, she says. Emily Frommolt. Cute as a button. No two ways about that. And good-hearted once you get through this front she thinks she has to put up. Glenda loved her. She's kind of shy if you get right down to it, and there's some find her off-putting till they get to know her. Her and Glenda had a couple of go-tos early on. The fur flew. When I met Emily, I'd have to say I could see how she could rub you wrong. But they got past all that, and Glenda came to love her. She was awful good when Glenda got sick. Anyway, she's from Des Moines, Emily is, so that's where they are."

"I was wondering, because 'Emily Frommolt' didn't ring a bell."

"There's Frommolts around here, but if they're connected, it's not close. Her people are Des Moines and thereabouts. Now you know how I'd love to see that little one, don't you. As you may know, I never had any of my own. But that's just my little tragedy. It wasn't in the cards. Glenda had three, so Francis has a brother and a sister, but he's the one took to me. I don't know what it is about babies. Some people say it's the fresh smell. Now, I wouldn't argue that's not part of it, and I have no idea what the rest of it is. I just know it's powerful, the way I want to see her. Abigail. Isn't that the sweetest little name? But I don't know when it's likely I'll get to lay eyes on her. What with the distance and all, I'm here, and they're all the way there. So he wanted me to have a nice car."

"That was really thoughtful."

"I just about passed out when they drove it up—these men from the dealership—and they told me it was mine. They put the title in my hands. Just handed it over, and then the phone started ringing and it was Francis explaining how he wanted to do it for me. You coulda knocked me over with a feather. I had to sit down. As you can imagine. I was bawling. We're blood, sure, but good Lord. A car. And a brand-new Camry, like I wouldn't have been thrilled with something smaller. I still can't get over it. I'm pretty much on my own around here, so it's a miracle as far as groceries and whatnot."

"That's what everybody says. It gives you some independence."

"It's true, too. Not that I can drive out to Des Moines or anything like that. Not that Francis expects that."

"He'll get here with that baby first chance he gets."

"Sure."

"He always seemed that way to me in school. I didn't know him well, him being older, but it was how he struck me. Considerate."

"It's true. He really is." Hazel laid her hands on the curve of the dashboard in a grateful caress. "I ran out of gas the other day. That's what I was checking when you come out. Missed the little red warning light and everything. Just didn't notice. Sat there by the side of the road just feeling so stupid and lost. Sobbing like a big baby. It was a mystery to me what had happened. Until people stopped. Nice man and his wife. They weren't all that much younger than me, and nicely dressed. Him especially. And of course he just had to have a little fun at my expense. You know, me endin' up like that. Being so dumb. Couldn't just help me out. Had to tease me. But I didn't begrudge him. You get to be his age, a good joke starts looking scarce as hen's teeth. Let him laugh if it makes him feel better. At least he stopped." She sought Janet out then, persisting until she had eye contact, as if answering a challenge. "I know Francis is thinking about getting here and bringing that baby, the first opportunity comes his way. He knows how much it would mean. But with school started back up, the two older ones going every day, and him using up all his vacation time at the birth—I just don't see it happening. I thought about driving out there, I really did. But then, like I said, I ran out of gas, and something about that little episode shut the door. Made me feel so bad about myself. That I could end up sittin' on the side of the road like that. Well, it just filled me up with doubt. Actin' too big for my britches. Especially with my diabetes and all. It can make you funny in the head. And it's a terrible long jaunt, as anybody'd tell you. Gotta cross the whole state.

Be the same for him trying to come here with that whole gang he's got now for only a weekend. I was thinking I could take the bus. And I could, I guess. They'd be happy to have me, and Emily could use the help, that's for sure. Just go for a week. That's probably what I should do."

Hazel smiled, and Janet could see the trip unfolding behind her dreaming eyes, but then she started. She gave Janet an embarrassed glance, tugging the zipper on her jacket up an inch or so, as if a wintry forecast had sounded inside her.

Janet knew what had happened and knew not to comment but could not resist trying to see what Hazel must be imagining, namely angels, or some saintly figure in the sky, reminding her that the end was near. Janet beheld the dazzle of the day, clear and blue and dappled with fluffs of cloud. "Indian summer," she said.

"Hmmmmm."

"The weather. It's beautiful."

The confusion in Hazel's stare worsened, as if she was becoming more and more unsure what exactly hovered around her. She lifted her glasses and rubbed her eyes before turning blearily to Janet. "There's a cold spell comin' is what they're sayin'. So I guess we better enjoy it while we got it."

"You know, Hazel, I came out to apologize. That's why I ran to catch up before you took off."

"Oh," said Hazel, still unfocused.

"We just got off on the wrong foot."

"It happens."

"Yes, it does."

"Happens to the best of us is my experience."

"I just didn't feel right about it. There was no reason for it." Surprised by warmth, and willing to let it deepen between them, if that was its inclination, Janet saw making a little joke as the perfect next step. "On the other hand, there's probably a reason or two one of us could have come up with, if you know what I mean."

"Do you love Jesus?"

Janet blinked, hoping to hide her astonishment. "Well," she said. Did she dare answer the question? While she wondered, her head started shaking in a gesture she knew arose from her predicament but that she feared could be mistaken for a negative reply.

"Because I do. I really do," said Hazel. "And it makes me feel good."

"Good."

"It is good."

Janet wanted to at least quiet her head and deliver an encouraging smile. But to her amazement, she went further, saying, "There've been times, I'm sure."

"Times when . . . what?" Hazel looked painfully puzzled.

"When I did."

"When you loved Him, you mean?"

Janet nodded. "Yes."

"Well, spit it out, then," Hazel commanded. "Just get it off your chest. We're on the downslide. You know. It's a coal chute to hell, this world. And you're on your way down into that basement if you don't get right with the Lord. Straight into the furnace."

For a second Janet saw flames, but the heat she felt was embarrassment, a flush of hurt and outrage that she had been dumb enough to trust Hazel. The old woman's laugh was not amused but condescending. Would she never learn? Finding something silly in Janet had lifted Hazel's spirits, but it left her looking unkind. She peered right past Janet into space where there was no one, but she seemed to see a true and valued friend offering blessings and private advice, which left her at peace. "Do you know the truth, Janet? I come out here with my dander up and ready to go racin' off like I was gonna show you. Those kinda thoughts. When the truth is, I need to wait here. Bernice told me she would call me when she got back from the vet's, so I was home waiting, but I was too antsy. It's a terrible feeling, antsy. So it wasn't long before I was in my car, on my way over here, planning to sit and wait, and that way I'd have that much of a head start on things when she got back. So you see now what I'm gettin' at? There's not much point in me drivin' off when I'd just have to sit somewhere nearby, watching till you left before I drove back and parked again. Because it's important I'm here when she gets back. That way we can scoot on over to Reverend Tauke's, because it's a pretty good jaunt over to the old Tiedeman place, and we don't have a second to lose. You know that Tiedeman bunch had that big farm for years?"

"Oh, that little church."

"You know it?"

"Seen it. You know, passing by."

"Well, that's Reverend Tauke's place. And it's a darn sweet little chapel, if I do say so myself."

"I wondered about it—you know, driving by.' "

Hazel seemed to have a quick, wary thought that scrunched up her mouth, but it went unspoken. "Anyway, like I said, I'll just wait for Bernice so we can go, because there are things he's got to tell us that we need to hear."

"So I guess I'm still on with the animals, right? I mean, I have to come back and feed them at dinnertime."

"I thought we'd settled that one."

"Just trying to be sure."

Hazel examined the palm of her hand as if uncovering a puzzling bit of news. "It'd be a big help if you fed them animals, Janet. You know how Bernice frets. It'd go a long way to putting her mind at ease, knowing that was taken care of."

"Sure. No problem. And you know, Hazel—you don't have to sit out here in the car. You could wait inside."

"I think not. This'll be fine. That way you can lock up and be on your way, knowing you left things right." Hazel dipped toward Janet, and then pulled backward, twisting sideways to haul her feet into the car, before the wide-open door swung shut.

The moment was disorienting and oddly painful, as if the door had slammed on Janet's fingers. Somewhere in the midst of their chat, she had hunkered down on the grass with her chin on her knees encircled in the hoop of her arms.

Her first few steps were aimless, but then she picked up speed on her way back to the house. Suddenly, the bright spread of morning was a grim landscape she wanted to get out of. Happy and Sappy sprang at her arrival, as if she'd been gone for decades. They licked her hand and danced, and she pushed at one and said, "Not now." But they insisted, standing on their hind legs to fondle and prod her. "I said stop it! Get off me!" She repelled them. One fell away and paused to consider. The other jumped back with a wail. "No! Just do as you're told!" When the worry in the creature's eyes was replaced by an earnest attempt to understand, Janet's chest let loose with a strange noise of her own, and salt and spit and sobbing burst out of her.

She scurried around the little house, handing out more cookies and checking the water bowls. One was nearly empty. Another needed to be refilled because the contents looked slimy. She labored to the sink, tears and garbage gushing out. Filth and bile because she'd trusted Hazel. Because she'd let Hazel scold and lecture her. All this slobber and snot coming from having a car door closed in her face by some old Jesus freak who couldn't help being preachy and insulting. Mucus and resentment because she'd let Bernice boss her around, because she hadn't given Wayne a piece of her mind, phlegm and disgust at listening to that fucking idiot Hazel go on and on about Francis, Francis, Francis. Fucking Francis, whom she couldn't remember beyond a chubby adolescent smudge in a school hall.

Clearly, her agitation intrigued the cats; their eyes traced her every move as she found and distributed their treats. The dogs, having given up on pursuit, observed from a careful distance, one sitting, the other flopped on its belly, their mood uneasy.

Back in the kitchen, she waited with her hands on either side of the sink to prop her up. "You idiot," she said, and then she spat, turning on the faucet to flush the yellow glob away. "You fucking waste of time." She monitored the air she was taking in, alert to the possibility that the end of this fit could be the start of an even wilder tumult. "Goddammit, enough!" She blew her nose. "Just more crap."

A gulp of air was followed by water splashed in her face and water in a glass to drink. It was coming to an end, and she marked her progress by drawing paper towels from their spool and then surrendering to a bitter, scoffing growl. Foretold in the sound was her release from a lengthy period of servitude spent tending a ridiculous, insufferable person whom she was sick of and whom she knew to be herself. "Okay," she said, inhaling, as if to capture enough air to last a lifetime.

Her course across the lawn was on a diagonal aimed directly for her Honda on the far side of the road. A quick farewell wave in Hazel's direction was all she intended, but Hazel was sprawled like a sunbather at the beach, the front seat of her car tilted back. Janet heard music, a chorus of male and female voices full of yearning leaking into the morning air from the radio, or more likely, a state-of-the-art CD player, thanks to the wonderful Francis. Hazel rose slightly to take a bite from a candy bar, her head swaying dreamily. The doors were shut, the engine a low grumble. Exhaust fumes snaked skyward. It was when Hazel reached for an open container of orange juice on the dashboard that she noticed Janet and smiled. Janet waved and mouthed, "Bye," pivoting to go. The words "Lord" and "Jesus" followed her, riding the pious voices sustained by simpleminded drumbeats and synthesizer chords innate to love songs on easy-listening radio. But then the voices transformed, enlarging their hopes and claims, the drums booming with militant ardor rising from Hazel's shiny car.

12

W HEN THE HAND FELL ON Bernice's shoulder, she squinted
up into an angry smile.

"Did you hear me?" Susie said.

Realizing her name must have been called without her hearing, she
said, "No. Sort of."

"You can go in now."

Susie did the hard work of helping General down the hall into the
second of three examining rooms, where Bernice expected to find Dr.
Manders waiting. But they struggled into an empty room, and before she
could complain, Susie took off, shutting the door. Alone with the medici-
nal smell that fed the fear that had her heartsick already, she hung her
jacket over the back of the chair and sat, feeling neglected while General
napped at her feet. In spite of her best effort, she got hotter under the collar and more gloomy with each passing second, and it was a good ten
minutes' worth of those kinds of seconds before the very important Dr.
Manders could be bothered to come in the door.

"Hello, Mrs. Doorley. General's not feeling so well, I hear."

"No, he's not, and he could have died waiting." Bernice figured she
was making a mistake, but she'd had enough.

Dr. Manders shied away from Bernice and her remark. She carried a
clipboard and was done up to look cute in a bookish way, though her
wire-framed glasses only made her look affected. "Things are a little cha-
otic for us at the moment," she said, smiling. "But the reason for the delay
was explained to you."

"To me, sure. But what about General? How's he supposed to know?"

Dr. Manders nodded as if this was a perfectly sensible conversation they were having. Mid-thirties, she had a slight figure, long dark hair, and a tolerant smile. "Well, let's not keep him waiting any longer." After a glance at the clipboard, she focused on General, who lay crookedly, his chin listing off his paws. "So tell me what's going on."

"Well, he can't walk right. He falls over."

"You're saying that he actually falls over."

"Yes, I am. Because that's what he does."

"When did this start?"

"The first that I know of was this morning."

"About what time?"

"First thing. Right away. Early."

"What about eating? Did he eat?"

"No. And he loves his food. That's one of the things about him, he's old, but he's still got a big appetite. But today not a bite except for some hot dog. But you should know he'd have to be dead and buried not to eat hot dog."

"Have you noticed anything unusual about his eyes?"

"His eyes? What about them?"

"Anything odd. Unusual."

"Well, he seems scared."

"Would you say his eyes are sort of—let's use the word 'sparking'?"

"Sparking? I don't know." The word and its use in a question about General gave Bernice the sense that Dr. Manders saw her as a source of valuable clues, and she set about sorting through the jumble of the morning. "I'm trying to think how that would look. 'Sparking.'"

"It's just a way of saying it."

"I remember one point when he seemed almost feverish."

"I see. And when he falls, how does it happen?"

"I'm not sure I know what you mean. He can't walk."

"What I'm asking is does it seem he's collapsing because his legs are weak—that his hips are giving out? Or is it more like he's dizzy?"

"I don't think there's much doubt he's dizzy. He staggers around, and then over he goes."

Bernice appreciated the rapid scribbling by Dr. Manders that followed this exchange. It wasn't the first note jotted down, but here the pen was flying.

"And when he falls," Dr. Manders wondered, "is there a pattern? What I mean is, does he fall one way consistently—to his left all the time, or his right, or is it both sides?"

"I'm not sure I noticed. If I had to guess, I would guess it's to his right. But I can't say for sure. Is it important? It probably is."

Dr. Manders turned to place the clipboard on the table against the wall. Something had changed, sending her mood off in a direction Bernice couldn't read, and the mystery made her nervous. "I need to examine him now. I'll have to weigh him and draw some blood."

General was so clumsy that arranging him on the flat metal scale was a chore even with both of them working at it and him doing his best to cooperate. When Dr. Manders inserted the thermometer into his rectum, he was unable to stifle a halfhearted growl, but he wasn't threatening anybody, just kind of complaining, and who could blame him.

"That's not very comfortable, is it, old fella," Dr. Manders said soothingly.

Bernice nodded as if she'd been spoken to. She was grateful for the way Dr. Manders was behaving now, and when their eyes met accidentally, she felt a strong chord of sisterhood.

"I think I'll draw the blood here rather than make him go into the back. If that's all right."

"Whatever you think."

"It's a precaution to test his liver function and certain other factors."

She called instructions over the intercom and then got interested in General's ears. The furry triangles sagged over her fingers as she shined her little light into his head. When Susie arrived carrying a syringe and some vials, Bernice retreated to a chair in the corner.

The needle slid into his fur, and General stared at Susie and then off into space, as if what was leaking out of him was the last of his faith in people. Susie patted him on the head. "He's a tough old boy," she said, and walked off with his blood.

Dr. Manders spoke while contemplating her clipboard. "We see a lot of this in old dogs. It's called old-dog vestibular syndrome. They get on in years, and ear infections bring on this kind of problem in the connections between the inner/middle ear and the brain, causing ataxia."

"I'm not sure I'm following this as well as I should. How bad off is he?"

"I'm going to prescribe an antibiotic and prednisone."

"Okay." Bernice checked with General as if he might have a deeper grasp of things, but he was staring at the door.

"Most dogs respond well to these medications. Antibiotic, anti-inflammatory. Sometimes in a day or so."

"And then what?"

"I expect him to be back to normal fairly soon."

Bernice's heart gave a joyful little skip, even though she didn't believe she could have heard right. "Is that what you're saying? Antibiotics can fix it?"

"Yes. Most of the time it's—"

"But he's not eating normal. I told you. That's not right, now, is it?" She scolded herself for clinging to the negative. Some grim sense worn into her like a brand didn't want Dr. Manders sugarcoating things, or rushing, or losing interest. "I want the truth, okay?"

"Of course. The tests I'm running on his blood are to guarantee there's nothing else going on. But I'm confident this is the problem. With no sense of balance, he's dizzy, so he's nauseated. It's like you—if you're dizzy and nauseated, I bet you don't want to eat all that much, do you?"

"I sure don't."

"And that funny look in his eyes is because for him, it's like the room is spinning. What he's feeling is that everything is going around and around. It's as if somebody has him by the hind legs and they're whirling him twenty-four hours a day."

"Oh, poor General." Bernice could just about feel the sickening, out-of-control sensations.

"I'm surprised you never ran into this before with your dogs."

"Don't think I have. None that I know of." But she was already wondering if she had—maybe that was what had been wrong with her pa's dog. A little arthritic, old Red had started staggering and falling. Her pa had said he was done for, then taken him out in the yard and put the .22 rifle to the back of his head.

Eager to comfort General, Bernice all but jumped from her chair. It was a surprise to find her feet had fallen asleep, while her head was filling with a vague white absence. Somebody was sliding sandpaper slowly through her brain, and the air was nothing but fizz and bubbles. She reached out, hoping something would be there and maybe it would be the wall, and something was. People were saying things. One voice, the loudest and most annoyed, resembled her own, while another was calling sweetly, "Mrs. Doorley." Every so often a tan shimmer showed up and went away like a shorted-out lightbulb, and then it became a painted flat surface beside a calendar with dates and a picture of kittens in flowers hanging on the wall of the examining room. "Whoa," she said. "Now I'm getting it, too—that old-dog whatever."

"Are you all right?"

"Pretty much. Almost. Whoa."

"Sit down. I have you." And she did, tiny Dr. Manders, solid as a rock. "You almost fell over."

"I sure did. But I think sitting is what did it, so maybe I'll stand. I was half holding my breath all that while, you know. Worrying. Lemme take a second."

"Are you sure?"

Bernice nodded, though she was still unsteady and drifting far from any certainty except for being glad that scary little episode hadn't lasted much longer. Dr. Manders was tilted like a dog asking a question, and Bernice wanted to say something reassuring but thought it might be a good idea to take several big breaths first. "Maybe I will just sit a second," she said, hoping for the chair. When she felt it under her, she saw what a good idea getting off her feet was. Along with letting her gather her wits and gumption, it would give her a chance to show her cooperative side and make clear how she thought that Dr. Manders was smart as a whip, because she had been right in the first place.

"Can you rest this afternoon, Mrs. Doorley? You and General both ought to take it easy, if you can."

"That sounds good to me, after all this carrying on we been through. Okay, General?" She nudged him with her foot but thought she wouldn't bend to pat him just yet. "He'll go for a nap, I bet." When his wandering gaze found her, he seemed filled with wide-ranging skepticism. Pinwheels of light swam in the murk of his eyes. "How long will he be in this whirling room of his?"

"It shouldn't last. I'm going to start his medication with an injection. You can pick up a prescription at the desk and continue in the morning. One of each. All right? The directions are on the bottles."

Bernice was slightly distracted, trying to plan tomorrow morning in her mind so she would do it right, all her pills, and his, and now two more for General. It was one more thing she would have to take care of. If push came to shove, she could make a list.

"You'll probably find him getting better in a day or so, and back to normal before a week."

Bernice said, "Good," and instantly felt terrible, because it wasn't going to be another thing for her to take care of—it was another thing she'd have to count on that damn Janet to handle. What a mess. It was all too much, and her head wavered with the weight of it.

"Is something wrong, Mrs. Doorley?"

"What?"

"How are you feeling? Are you okay?"

Bernice looked around. The room was stable, and the floor, too, the walls and calendar steady. She stood up, nodding to convey her recovery. "Okay," she said, and then, convinced the room's decorations had to reflect Dr. Manders's personal taste, she added, "That's a pretty calendar."

Dr. Manders smiled. "Thank you. Why don't you take care of things up front, and I'll get someone to help General."

Dr. Manders slipped out the side door, and after giving General a pat, Bernice did as she was told. She expected the worst from sassy Lisa, but the bill was handled as if something magical had turned paperwork into Lisa's favorite pastime. The sack of prescriptions she handed over came with a cheerful flourish. "Good news, I hear."

"Yes, it is, Lisa. Really good news." Bernice wondered if maybe the poor woman's bad mood before had been completely due to that pair giving her a hard time about every last penny.

Susie appeared with General in tow, and all the assistants behind the desk, along with the other pet owners waiting their turn, even a nurse who stepped out from the back—they all watched appreciatively, as if General's leaving was a wonderful thing to see.

"Beautiful day, isn't it?" said Susie, blinking up at the sun. "I'll take a whole month of days just like this one. But we better enjoy it. I hear there's a cold front coming in."

"That's what I hear, too, but it ain't here yet." Bernice made a show out of the fact that she carried her jacket rather than wore it as they crossed in the clean sharp air.

"There you go, Mrs. Doorley. That's showing them who's boss."

Susie smiled her farewell, and it occurred to Bernice that after the rough day they'd all had here, what with hurt cows and smashed cars and that troublemaker Butch Hopkins, General getting his hopeful diagnosis had given them a boost—been just what they needed, uplifting their spirits and making it all seem worthwhile.

On the feeder road to the interstate, she saw Dr. Hoffenbach returning. His van was coated in mud so thick it could have passed for camouflage. She hurried to form an okay sign, because he was the last person on earth she wanted to miss out on the good cheer she and General were spreading. What Hazel had said about losing Bernice after they were all gone was true, Bernice realized, for her about Dr. Hoffenbach, and the proof was the nip of heartache she felt when she sought him behind her, but he was not to be found. It was doubtful he'd understood her gesture, but she was sure they would tell him at the office.

Entering the interstate, she was shocked by the traffic, everybody and his brother pouring on right when it would make things hard for her. The late-morning sun had her blinking, the pavement like a greasy skillet ready to catch fire. And she had seven or eight miles before she could get off the crazy thing. Vehicles of every size and shape were stampeding around, like they all thought they owned the road. She squinted and bent forward, then worked the visor to blunt the dazzle. That helped some, and she made another mile or so with nasty blurs of color whirring past while she hugged the shoulder, making full use of the slow lane. A change in the angle of the sun put the glare back into her eyes. She was fiddling with the visor again when General made a squashed, miserable yelp in the backseat, like his head was under a blanket.

"Hey now," she said, and he squealed at her. "Okay, okay." He barked once, a single, exasperated demand, before surrendering to an avalanche of alarmed yips and squeaks, and she knew he had to pee. Probably had to poo, too. Because with everything going on this morning, she'd neglected to walk him. Needing to get a sense of his desperation, she tried the rearview mirror, but the oval couldn't find him no matter how she aimed it. She was leery of turning around, and yet had to try with him carrying on like he was. A twinge in her neck caught her up short, as she glimpsed him fighting to stand. He'd rather explode than go in the car, but what else could he do? With his spark-filled eyes and frantic cries, he looked ready to blow a fuse. "General!" she shouted. "Hang on!"

When she turned back, something was wrong. The white lines were crooked. "What kinda goings-on's this?" she muttered. Somebody had the lanes all slanting in this crazy way from her left to her right, leaving her completely baffled. They'd even managed to shove her out of the slow lane. Somehow it had gotten behind her and way over to her right alongside the shoulder. Only then did it occur to her that the lines were crooked and disturbing because she was drifting. In fact, she was almost sideways and about to wander into the fast lane.

She veered sharply, maybe too sharply. Instantly, red paint drenched the rear window, covering her mirror, where this gigantic hybrid kind of truck-car-bus jumped at her honking and flashing its lights. Again she lurched, helplessly shutting her eyes. Grabbed and squeezed and dragged and once again sideways, she was headed in the other direction. General was howling, the seat belt was sawing her in half, and she had a split-second notion that poor General was a hound from hell, which was not a thought she had a spare second to scoff at. About to smack into the guardrail, she was straining like a pilot in a movie about an out-of-control airplane. Machinery under the floorboard groaned and sent shudders into her feet, and that red monstrosity screamed past with its horn blaring, as if the driver believed that for lack of a gun, he would kill her with honking. However, she was still there, alive and steering, as he shot into the hubbub ahead. Fine with her if he wanted to lay on his horn till he got sick and tired of it. The rude loudmouth was flying from view like a stone down a well, and she bade him good riddance, because he had scared the dickens out of her.

Checking her mirror, she saw pavement flowing away in her wake with a dozen or so cars arranged in an orderly fashion, which told her she must be pretty much straight. Though it did strike her as a little odd the way all those vehicles seemed to be matching her speed and keeping their distance. Not that she could worry about it with General thrashing and wailing. A Bonneville cruised up on her left, and the distinguished gentleman in a beautiful gray suit behind the wheel, along with his equally distinguished passenger in a blue suit, stared at her as if she were a deeply personal disappointment when she didn't even know them.

General was pushing against the back of her seat, almost hurling his full weight, and he had her so overwrought, she thought she might pee herself. "Okay, okay," she said, thankful she'd replaced her Depends. It was getting to be more than she could handle, especially now, because an exit was rushing up on her right, and she thought she ought to take it, even though her speed was nowhere near sensible. She jerked the wheel hard, throwing up stones and dust and sending General across the backseat like he was water dumped from a bucket.

The Exxon station with a mini-mall directly ahead was overrun by cars at the pumps and people sauntering in and out, some of them stopping to gawk at this old jalopy barreling off the highway and coming straight at them. Given how she was already the center of attention, Bernice could see that this was not the place to squeal up and let her dog start shitting and pissing.

Maybe a hundred yards ahead was a cornfield, a thick tawny expanse running along for acres. Soon the stalks were blurring into rows of whipping russet splashed with faded green. All she wanted was enough shoulder to get off safely. General was at such a hopeless pitch, she wondered if she could get away with stopping right where she was, throwing on her emergency blinkers and doing what had to be done. In her confusion, she was toeing the brake when a gap appeared, and she discovered what turned out to be a lane forged into the corn. It was maybe a tractor's width—one of those alleys a farmer cuts so he can move his big machinery around. Certain General couldn't last, she slowed, then took the plunge, the Chevy's bottom scraping as she nosed her way in and bounced to a stop.

General was raising the roof. "No, no, no!" she told him. Climbing out and slamming the door before he could follow, she shocked him into momentary silence, while she was surprised to feel shy and ill at ease, because she was trespassing where nothing belonged to her and no one wanted her. The corridor was plenty wide, but the privacy and solitude made her feel she was in a strange, uncivilized part of the world, as if she had ended up deep in the wilderness. Poor General was pleading, while she took a second to drape her jacket, which she'd carried from the car for no good reason, over some sturdy-looking corn. She knew General would come flying out, so she called his name sternly, to remind him who was boss, as she opened the door. He hurtled into her, pushing his paws into her belly, where he seemed to stall midair. Bouncing backward until the rough ground tripped her, she slammed down on her keister, ass over appetite, and General crash-landed next to her, grunting, the towel tangled around a rear leg. He shook his head, his eyes finding her with a woeful look that somehow managed to hold out hope for guidance. She could feel the dirt coming coldly through her clothing, and she felt chilled and wet. Flat on her back, she couldn't help but note how the billowing stalks were like small trees topped by sickle-shaped leaves against the blue sky. But that was about all the time she had for sightseeing, because General was whining and scrabbling. "What a pair," she said. "Good Lord, General. I'm trying to fix this mess, you know."

It was like somebody kept getting in her way as she battled onto her hands and knees, then strained and grunted to get her feet available for an attempt to rise. At the count of three, she did her best to push upright and stay there, tottering sideways. General lay on his side raving. He was pitiful, but she was winded and gasping so badly it scared her. "Now, now. Now, now," she said to calm him. She shook and brushed off her jacket, buying another few seconds before putting it on. The towel was tangled under him, and she found she was adjusting and fixing it long before she was ready. She heaved to get him standing and aimed down the shadowy lane. The pressure she couldn't help exerting on his gut was liable to squeeze the shit and piss right out of him, but it was a risk she had to take. Waddling along, her arms sore, a stitch in her side, she kept picturing crap spewing all over her shoes. The air had a bite to it, the leaves chattering hoarsely. When he started fighting to take up his peeing position, she figured they were pretty much in the middle of nowhere. His bark was a frazzled declaration that he couldn't take another second of her insanity. Cocking his leg, he started to fall, and she hung on, mincing her feet out of the line of fire, dreading splatter on her shoes and stockings. The pee sputtered, then shot out in a wide stream, and she was reminded of Toby when he'd been sick and wetting the bed. They'd put a catheter in him, and he'd ripped the damn thing loose, and this miserable soup of blood and piss had come out all over the sheets.

Just then two birds zoomed close, black as sin and big. Their boldness was frightful. They came again, rushing headlong at her until the last possible second, when they flapped and lifted. Crows, she saw, dive-bombing her and about to take her eyes out, because they thought she was there to steal their corn.

The stench, thick and piercing, made her recoil, her nostrils trying to shut. General had squatted, and now he was close to collapsing into the shit he'd put down between her shoes. She jerked at him, disregarding the stress she was inflicting, and marched him a good ten yards from the mess and stink before she stopped and he sat. His glance bemoaned his confusion over who she had become or why he had ever trusted her. But then he seemed to find a tolerable explanation, or maybe he recalled some other pointless ordeal she'd put him through. He inched his front legs forward until he lay on his belly, and from there he rolled to his side.

In the quiet, she heard traffic on the interstate. She reached behind her to touch her fanny. She could feel crud, like an accidental poo on her skirt, and her fingers came away stained a light brown. General wheezed, and she thought he might snore, his chest rising and falling calmly while she still panted, and the sound of cars and voices blew in from the mini-mall. It wasn't far, and people must be crowding in and out, buying gas and coffee and chips. Shifting shapes whispered around her, the crowns of stalks bowing and pulling away. She brushed at a tickling sensation on her ear, and for no reason she could say, the gesture urged her to go walking on. And she wanted to do it. Just walking. Fluctuations in the light narrowed and dimmed the path, but not her excitement, though it seemed to belong to a child whose hopes were new, and that could hardly be her. No, she hadn't been that for a long time. But if she were—if she were a kid standing here—she would do it, just stroll off down that trail. No need to care where it went. Her and her dog. A kid and her pup. Just the two of them. A couple of spring chickens setting off into the future. Where would it take them?

She nodded solemnly and said, "Not hardly." She felt like chuckling but didn't, thinking, Second childhood, I guess. "No need to guess," she said. "Comes with the territory." Okay, all right, you betcha. Now, she knew very well she was the one doing the thinking and talking, and the listening, too, but those few ideas had cried out to be spoken aloud, and she'd let them. She was old, so she was entitled to be a little goofy if she felt like it, especially when she had just been scared silly by the walls of that examining room disappearing and General turning ashen, like he was a dog of dust blowing away at her feet and she was at death's door. Dr. Manders had shouted, "Mrs. Doorley!" so loud it had made Bernice want to see Dr. Manders. She remembered feeling like a lost child about to ride the wrong bus out of the station, when somebody kind and thoughtful and named Dr. Manders had pointed out the mistake. Bernice shook her head, wondering if she was remembering what had actually happened. Maybe there were parts to fainting a person couldn't take in when they were actually fainting. Too scared, maybe. Because it had scared the living daylights out of her.

General slept at her feet. Her fingers were stiffening, though it wasn't all that cold. Time to get back to the car. But she didn't budge, stuffing her hands into her jacket pockets and peering into the densely uncountable stalks, some only a foot away. She plucked a faded ear, imagining the bright green it would have possessed only weeks ago, the hairlike oily plumes. She fingered the leaves curiously, as if she hadn't shucked and cooked thousands, starting as a kid and ending up with the two she'd boiled last week. The shape in her palm felt unfamiliar and interesting, and she brought it closer. Noting how the rusty kernels blended in rows with yellow stragglers, she heard a thump, followed by a kind of hissing crackle and then a louder thump. She looked and saw the walls of stalks. The noise was coming toward her. She listened for an engine. Not a picker, but maybe a tractor and that thing they used to chop the fields when the season was over. Now she was going to have to cope with some cranky old farmer scolding her for being on his land. Certain he would call her a thief, she tossed the ear aside. Her backward glance ran to her car, which struck her as somebody else's vehicle jammed there to block her way out. The racket was rhythmic and closing in swiftly. She imagined farmers with shotguns, some old fart and his crotchety son, the stalks splintering before their angry advance. But wouldn't there have to be a posse of them to make this much of a ruckus? And then she heard a sigh, or something like a sigh, only larger, the intake of enormous lungs getting ready to do something, maybe even preparing to speak.

General was on his feet. Deaf as a post, he'd picked up some scent that demanded he pay attention. She tried to see into his spinning eyes, and in those same seconds knew that it wasn't farmers. At a point where all her questions had failed to find answers, intuition was whispering that it knew what was coming. That it had known all along, and she had, too. Because it was going to happen, just as Reverend Tauke had forewarned.

General peered off nervously and pressed against her leg. The way the corn had intrigued her should have told her. The birds had flown close, and she should have known. The crazy way she'd arrived here was a dead giveaway. What else did she need? Because what was all that if not signs of otherworldly things?

Are you nuts? she asked herself, demanding an answer. And yet even as she scoffed, she could hear Reverend Tauke pleading the way he did in sermons sometimes that she understand. Nutty or not, signs were all over the place, and now for the first time, she was seeing them for what they were. She was seeing them as signs. The field shivered with a blustery force blowing the crackle and thump straight at her. She hoped that she was ready and prayed that if she was right and this was it, somebody would come and find General after she whooshed off. Squinting into the rattling, shaking smudge of stalks and shadows, she fearfully awaited the onrushing angels, and she saw a deer. And then another. Two for an instant, then a third. They sailed through the corn like hurtling snatches of earth. Some stalks parted, others crumpled. She could hear their hooves and hear their panting, and the first two burst into the path where she stood, a pair of does immediately pivoting away. General let out a groan as a third landed almost on top of him. Raw and gangling, this one seemed to Bernice like a wild teenage boy, and when he caught sight of Bernice so close, he gaped in pure animal surprise. She saw his muscles gather. Delicate limbs exploded and sent him after the others. The first two were some twenty yards away, the white of their tails tracing each leap, and the third strained to follow their fading clatter. Then all at once and somehow unexpectedly, they were gone.

She was listening to the traffic on the highway, the voices at the mini-mall. General sat with his head high, his ears poised. Knowing he couldn't chase them, he appeared content to study the bent and broken stalks quivering where they'd disappeared.

A woman or young boy laughed. Somewhere on the highway, air brakes on a tractor-trailer fired a violent cry. The quiet field was unprepared for the cold that came in a blast, as if winter resented this warm weather and wanted to pummel everything and everybody right now. A popping sound blew in. It took her a second to realize she didn't know what it was or where it had come from. By this time, the pop-pop-popping came again, and in the repetition, she heard a rifle. She scanned the crumpled corn marking where the deer had run. Wanting to find the direction from which gunfire was sailing in, she turned in a circle. Pop, pop, pop. But this time it didn't seem to be in the same place. She searched, going in one direction and then another, and all she saw was corn. She bowed her head, putting everything she had into helping her ears get a fix. It seemed the deer might have run toward the guns. She looked to General, half thinking he might help, the way he always had. But he either lacked interest or heard nothing or was feeling dizzy, because he was settling onto his belly as if he expected they would be there a long time, so he better get comfortable.

Decaying corn hemmed her in while high white clouds were shredding into a chain of dissolving wisps, leaving sky. The wind kept changing. The traffic was louder.

13

T HE CHANCE TO GO FOR a run was there if she wanted it. Or maybe she would take a nap first. Whatever she wanted. Janet was trying to concentrate on the fact that after the corner of Windsor and Camp Belloch, the snarled traffic would lighten, and she would get home quickly. Or maybe just a nap and forget about running today, but whatever she did, she should probably stop along the way to pick up the duct tape and hose. Oh, right. She nodded, feeling the prickly summons of the forgotten errand. I'd better do that one. Can't skip that one, or there'll be hell to pay.

She supposed it was Hanrahan's Hardware, with its billboard-sized burst of a sign drifting away on her right, that had reminded her. Already past the driveway, she was being hauled farther off by the ongoing traffic. The really weird thing about the errand was the way she couldn't remember who she was doing it for. But she shouldn't be surprised, considering the way she was at everybody's beck and call these days, taking orders from Bernice and even Hazel.

She used a Sunoco station to turn around and maneuvered her way back until, across from Hanrahan's, she waited for a break in the traffic, stalling everybody behind her. At least two of the items could be found inside, the roll of two-inch duct tape and a length of garden hose. Not the CDs, though. She'd have to find them somewhere else. Bernice was always using duct tape on her car, so the tape was probably hers. But it made no sense that Janet was buying CDs for Bernice or Hazel. Though it was true that Hazel had been listening to CDs. Could this be something

Wayne had asked her to do and she was still doing it? It was the kind of thing that happened. You walked into a room and couldn't remember what you'd come in to do or what you were looking for. But then you usually did. It popped into your mind once you stopped trying.

A dry cleaning van had halted, leaving room for her to cross, the driver waving for her to hurry, and she darted into Hanrahan's lot. As soon as she remembered who had asked her to run the errand, or if they showed up wanting their items, she wouldn't have to dash around to find them. She could say, *Okay, here they are!*

A clerk arranging snow shovels near the front broke from his project to ask if she needed help. "Not at the moment, thanks." In the garden section, some hoses hung in circles off pegs on the wall. Others were stacked on the floor. But she seemed to know nothing about the right style or even the necessary length. Some were green, others black. Did color matter? She felt peculiar standing there, embarrassed by her ignorance, feeling dreamy and charmed by the household objects everywhere. Paint cans stood in rows, each bearing a swatch of color. Was someone playing a trick on her? Or maybe it was more like a game, and in the game she had pulled into the lot where she left her car and walked until she stood here, thinking that six feet of hose might be too little. Twelve might be too much. What had Eileen called her? A Silly One? No, that wasn't it. She was a Funny One. And ten feet of black hose would have to do. She didn't think she needed a nozzle or end attachment, and told the clerk, whom she couldn't remember summoning, but there he was. He nodded, repeated her specifications, and strode off, promising he'd have the hose ready at the counter.

"Sure," she said, watching him go down the aisle, where another young man studied a rack of hammers.

"What's up?" the clerk said.

"Hey," the young man responded. "What're you doing?"

"What's it look like? Nothing. Working, man. You know."

"I need a new hammer or else at least a handle."

He patted the sweat-stained tool belt he wore slung off one hip, his palm settling on the blue-gray hammerhead. Gazing up at the elevated display gave him a studious quality, as if he were contemplating art in a museum. His forearms and boot tops were splattered with white paint. "Hey," he said, sagging his hip to bump his buddy. The bounce brought him around toward Janet. Or maybe he was turning intentionally, having sensed her attention. He found her, and she felt his core gather somehow. His substance grew poised. A hidden part of him was very attentive, and she felt it waiting inside him for her to affect it, to stir it. Let's fuck, she thought. His blue eyes narrowed in a show of surprise and recognition, as if he wanted her to know he could read minds and he'd just had a look at hers. He was squinting and half smiling, and when he wheeled back to his friend, he confided something.

She didn't want to be there for the next development. She passed a barrier of plumbing paraphernalia and was soon scanning brushes and paint cans, tiers of rollers. Hammers. Saws. And finally, tape. Scotch and black electrical, plastic in diverse colors, and, of course, duct tape. As her hand extended to make a choice, she wondered if gray was what she'd been asked to supply.

"Yo, now, look what's in my way. Got her hand on her sassy hip like she's sassy. You see what I mean. Is that what you do now? You walk up into this store and you get stuck somewhere like this?"

It was Big Baby Dog in oversize black pants and a maroon long-sleeved T-shirt drooping out from under the orange hooded sweatshirt that was the last sagging layer over his bulk. He had a ball cap on, the New York Knicks logo and bill angled out over his left ear.

"Hey," she said.

"You had that kind of mood about you. You see what I mean."

She nodded. Half a dozen gold chains burdened his wide neck. Rings crowded every finger. Both ears and one nostril were decked out with studs and rings. The top of his head didn't reach her nose, but there was enough meat on him to make three of her.

"Just looking to buy some tape," she said.

"Me, too. What kind you after?"

She shrugged, plucking a roll of gray and turning to go.

"Yo," he said. "I was thinkin' I'd get that one."

Her gaze bounced off the bitter sparkle he fixed on her. Waiting to be understood, he expected to be obeyed. His voice was a purring growl. "That's my roll of tape. That's the one I'm buyin'. Give it to me. I ain't playin'." His big hand grew bigger, and she surrendered what he wanted. "You can get yourself a different one. You see what I mean. Check it out."

She faced the display, stretching for a replacement, this time black.

"You been off somewhere, Judy?"

"What?"

He spent a few seconds thinking over a troubling matter that made him suspicious, as if he'd been running and she'd tripped him. "Is that your name? It don't sound right. You see what I mean. If I'm wrong here, I don't want to stay wrong. You see what I mean."

She could have tossed off anything, and yet she gave him, "Janet."

"I'm just playin'. You see what I mean, Janet. I ain't askin' you to step out. We ain't in no situation. You know I'm playin', don't you!"

"You said you weren't playin'."

"Well, I got to say things, don't I? You see what I mean. Most of the time that's my way. It's just words. You see what I mean. That's part of it. Part of the playin'. I need my enjoyment. You see what I mean. I'm still down where I do what I do, and I am doin' it. You know that."

"Of course, sure."

"You got to know that. What do you need?"

"Nothing right now."

"You got to need something. I know you do. Sure you do. You see what I mean."

"I have to go," she said. "I'm late, okay?"

"Me, too. Everybody's flyin' around like there ain't enough days in the week. Monday, Tuesday. What's next? You see what I mean. We all got to go somewhere. I am on my way and just here. At this in-between place. But just tell me what you need."

"Nothing right now, okay?"

"I don't know if it's okay or not."

A figure came around the corner behind Big Baby Dog. Shiny and lanky, he glowered from high over Big Baby Dog's shoulder, as if he wanted to make certain Janet noted the contrast between his smooth-skinned, regal blackness and the way Big Baby Dog was pockmarked and faded. He was tall and long in the same exaggerated way Big Baby Dog was thick and squat. His blue running suit had silver piping, and he was draped in chains and riddled with piercings, but on him the effect was turned stylish by some inherent elegance.

"This is Mr. Bats. He come down from Chicago. You see what I mean. I don't think you know him."

"No," she said.

"You can say hello."

"Sure, but I really need to go now. Really."

"You can still say hello."

"Hello."

"His name is Mr. Bats."

"That ain't my real name." Mr. Bats had a disappointingly thin voice. He carried two hip-length black leather jackets, one of which, she figured, belonged to Big Baby Dog.

"We are here to buy lumber." Big Baby Dog grinned. "We're building shelves and all that for our new forty-five-inch rear-projection TV. You see what I mean. Got home theater surround sound."

"That'll be fun for you."

"You got you some truth right there, Janet."

"Next time you're down," Mr. Bats said, "you can watch a movie with us."

"Sure she can. Have some ice cream."

"We got porno sometimes," said Mr. Bats. "You like porno?" He glanced at Big Baby Dog, and then they both watched Janet.

"Everybody likes porno," said Big Baby Dog.

"Maybe she don't. Do you? Do you like porno?"

She shrugged and smiled, nodding and wavering from side to side, launching as many mixed messages as she could possibly send. She hoped to get away without a word.

"We got other kinds, too," Mr. Bats offered, looking sincere and sounding thoughtful. "Rent anything. Sometimes even them old ones."

"Black-and-white."

She was turning away when Mr. Bats said, "Black-and-white's the best. Same with ice cream, the best a man can eat is vanilla that's got chocolate inside."

She waved goodbye without looking back. Behind her, they erupted in gagging, sputtering barks meant to represent enjoyment but sounding enraged. They stomped around as if fun paid its biggest dividends when it resembled beating the crap out of somebody.

The clerk at the front register was leaning close to a big-bellied customer who wore a carpenter's belt loaded with tools, and they were a very interested pair as she approached. The clerk nodded to the shelving beyond which Mr. Bats and Big Baby Dog were still rampaging.

"Good Lord," said the clerk. He was middle-aged, and the checkerboard pattern of his short-sleeved shirt tightened across his broad back as he placed her hose on the counter. "What's goin' on back there?"

His buddy edged in. "They're bad apples, you know."

"Were they harassing you?" The clerk somehow demanded that his question dictate silence until, with a nod to his companion, he went on. "Art took a peek, and he saw what was goin' on."

"It looked like you were talking to them. Did you want to talk to them?"

"They asked me some questions is all."

"What about?" On the lookout for anything sinister, Art narrowed his eyes.

"Well, it was over there by the tape. And so it was about tape."

The clerk leaned close. "You don't know them, but they just start talking?"

"No, I don't know them."

"You don't know about the tape, do you? What could they ask you?"

"It didn't amount to much, you know."

"You're not a clerk." Art seemed to believe he was making a crucial point.

"No." Determined to give them as little as possible, she smiled and tucked a stray hair behind her ear. Faint perspiration moistened her armpits.

"If they want to ask about the tape, they ought to ask store personnel."

"I guess. But I was there."

"They're bad apples." Art's big hands settled on either side of his belly like it was an object he was preparing to move. His nod invited her to share his knowledge, and she wanted to reject the bond he'd assumed between them, but instead she yielded, meeting his gaze so he could peer into her. "Drugs," he told her. "The both of them."

"What'd they want to know about tape?" said the clerk.

"It was color. Just about color—the colors—and I don't know. It didn't make much sense."

"How could it with them two?"

The clerk had turned away to punch codes and numbers into the cash register. "Seventeen-twelve," he said, looking up. "Cash or charge?"

"Cash," she said, and put down a twenty.

He made change quickly, then lifted the hose, which he had secured with a plastic tie. "You need any help getting that out to the car?'"

"No, thanks."

"I'm runnin', too," said Art, stepping ahead to hold the door for her.

"Thanks."

His smile declared that conclusions regarding her, or, for that matter, anything at all, didn't interest him much. Following along, he seemed to have lost track of their entire conversation. He nodded a friendly farewell and hurried toward a pickup truck that said Weber Construction on the door. The first clerk she'd dealt with rested against a rear fender, smoking alongside the other young man, the one she'd looked at, the one with paint on his boots.

She wanted out of there fast. But then she floated over the dim interior of the trunk. The silhouette of the lid touched the tape and hose. Just as her need for them had reached out to her earlier, their purpose, along with the person behind their purchase, felt identifiable, as if opening the trunk were the key and all she needed to do was wait. But the intimation of someone racing up behind her spun her so quickly the idea never had a chance to develop. She was squinting into a blinding reflection off the window of a parked car and then into the face of the paint-splattered, sandy-haired young guy in his boots and tool belt who needed only a few more strides to reach her. Here it comes, she thought, getting ready for whatever line of bullshit he would throw, knowing full well she had only herself to blame after that hard fuck-me stare she'd given inside.

"Hi," he said.

She nodded. "Hi."

His hands were pressed together, and as he advanced toward her, making an impression of vigor, they parted with a suggestion of reticence, even apology. "I'm Robbie Oberhoffer, Miss Cawley. You taught me in the fourth grade! It was— I don't know. Back a ways."

Could it be? She blinked, took a step back as if inches might give her the needed perspective. "Robbie?"

"Oberhoffer. Do you remember me?"

"Of course."

"Do you? Great. It must be ten years ago, or close."

"At least." And then she saw the nine-year-old in a lingering afterimage right in front of her.

"How's everything?"

"Good. And you?"

"Good. Okay." He shrugged, only to have his ease brushed aside by uncertainty. He seemed to believe he'd broken something he wasn't sure how to fix.

"Working for Weber, I see," she said, determined to sound upbeat. "I hear they're good to work for." She had no idea what she was talking about—knew nothing about Weber Construction.

He glanced in the direction of the truck and then raised both hands to the top of his head. "Well, I was off in college at Grinnell, but then we had some trouble at home, and the money ran short. So I dropped out."

"Oh. I didn't know that."

"Yeah."

"I mean about college, even. That you were going to begin with."

"It was only a couple weeks. I'm going back. Probably have to work this whole year and save up and then get back."

"Great. You should."

"I want to. I was getting the hang of it, I think. No, I'm going back. Anyway, I just wanted to say hello. We ran into each other back there." He flung a hand toward the store.

She followed his gesture, wanting to reassure him that she remembered, but uncertain how much to acknowledge. "Right."

"Anyway, I just wanted to say hi."

"I'm glad you did. And go back to school. Don't give up on it."

"No, I won't. I will not. Things got a little ragged at home. My dad died."

"Oh, no."

"Yeah, he did. And I have younger brothers. Two of them. I mean, they're in high school. But one's only a freshman. Dad had been helping me with tuition and all, but that was the end of that."

"That's really too bad. I'm so sorry."

"I know."

"Was he sick? I mean, did you have any kind of warning?"

"No, no, no." This time his shrug carried a strong philosophical conviction that he expected every ounce of information he might find useful to remain hidden for a long time.

"I'm trying to think if I ever met him."

"You must have. Teacher conference or like that."

His desire that she remember had an urgency she was quick to satisfy. "I'm sure I did."

"Lawrence. He was Lawrence Oberhoffer."

"Of course. That's right."

"Do you remember?"

Not at all certain, she knew the value of nodding.

"He was my height exactly. Thicker. Not fat. Thicker."

"Yes, yes."

He smiled with relief and then ran into a thought that, failing to remove the smile, infused it with irony. "The way it went was— I mean, believe it or not, he was out in the backyard tossing a football around with my brother, Edward, who plays high school varsity—and Edward threw a long pass, and Dad, you know, running to catch it, going all out, like victory and defeat hung in the balance, well, he tripped on this little stump and just went headlong into this other tree still standing. He'd cut the first one down himself, but forgot. Knocked himself out. Had a concussion nobody knew about, and that night when he fell asleep, he went into a coma because nobody knew he had a concussion. So in the middle of the coma, he has a stroke. It's just this avalanche of misfortune. I don't understand it, you know. Misfortune after misfortune. Mom called me. I left school and drove home. We're all sitting around the bed. It's a day or two like that. Sitting and praying. But he never wakes up. I was there alone with him. It was the middle of the night. I prayed a lot that night. Had a hard time quitting. But eventually, I started to do a little homework. Trying to keep up. I guess I dozed off, because all of a sudden everybody was red alert. Nurses storming the place and yelling at each other, and I'm like— What? What? What? And that was it. It was over. Crazy, huh?"

Her wish to speak could not bring to mind a word that didn't feel worthless. She watched him glance at the boot he had cocked backward, the hard toe tapping the concrete. "Lord," she said, "the things that happen to people."

"Boy, you got that one on the nose."

"Really." She tried to mark the moment as valuable and unique between them in a way he could see.

"I can tell you, I've had just about enough of it, too. If nobody minds, I could use a break."

He was grinning, and she was afraid to let her gaze climb to his eyes. Instead, she slipped inward, leaving behind a faint distraction for him to wonder about. Belonging to her very first class, Robbie Oberhoffer had been maybe four feet tall, with roundish cheeks and a sturdy presence. Somewhere in this solid-seeming young man, who was taller than she by several inches, that boy was yet to fully dissolve. "I lost my mom not long ago," she said.

"Yeah? Wow."

"Heart attack. Of course, she was older. Your dad was what? Fifty?"

"Just forty-seven."

"Mom was seventy."

"That's older, sure. But still. Were you with her?"

"No. She was with some friends."

"I'm sorry to hear that. I had no idea."

"Of course not. How could you?"

"I could have, but I didn't. What I mean is, I hope I didn't stir things up for you."

"No, no. Don't think twice about it. I'm glad you came over. It was a while ago with my mom."

"Good," he said, and then he grimaced. His upper body drew back, his hand waving to erase what he'd said. "I don't mean good that—you know—I shouldn't have said 'good.' "

"It's fine," she said. "I know what you meant."

"I just wanted to say hi."

"You were right to. Really." She took the chance now, or it happened before she could prevent it, and checked out his eyes, which were wide open and full of a simple, friendly accessibility. "Well," she said. "You're a big boy now, Robbie."

"Sort of." He laughed, then wheeled to go, reading her last words as a way of saying goodbye. "Great weather we're having, huh?"

"Beautiful. Let's hope it lasts."

"Can't last too long." He smiled. The pickup truck gave a terse little beep. In the driver's seat, big-bellied Art had the engine running, and Robbie set off at a jog. After a few strides, he reversed so he was skipping backward when he called, "I remember your class. I remember specific days sometimes."

She watched him swing up into the rear bed and drop so his back rested against the cab. Sensing he was about to glance at her, she canceled the possibility by acting interested in her car as the truck sped off behind her. She felt so lonely. So fucking lonely. Or maybe she just knew it suddenly.

She slammed down the trunk lid and stalked around to get behind the wheel. Motion flooded her as she shot from the parking lot. She was driving blindly around a slow curve when she went headlong into a moody, waiting emptiness. Alone in her car, she was even more solitary inside a deepening, mesmerizing wasteland.

She journeyed along, steering, braking, keeping safely in her lane, but it was like sleepwalking, following behind whatever traveled in front of her—sedan or wagon or pickup. She would hang with one for a mile or so, and another for a turn or two. Sometimes people wondered what was happening to them, or who they were becoming, and they declared that they were not themselves. I'm not myself today, they said. I'm not myself right now. She could have been one of them. "I'm not myself," she said. "I'm just not feeling like myself today." So who was she? Robbie Oberhoffer had offered her a chance to contact the little boy he had once been. Was she doing the same now with herself? Trying to detect, hoping to touch. Something not fully departed.

As she cruised off an old paved road onto a stretch of rutted dirt, the wheels jolted and kicked, bouncing her around. But after a few yards, it was nice. She was beyond the city limits. She was roaming untended landscape on a shrinking path. Sumac and shrubs crowded her, rattling the fenders, groping the door, and she wondered if it was time to turn back.

But then she came to a clearing and slowed to a stop near a narrow channel of brightly rippling water. She could hear the current muttering in the shallows. Beyond the tall grass, the opposite embankment rose steeply to a line of white birch, while the shore where she sat tapered to the water's edge. The channel flowed from hidden backwater, widening here, as it fed into the river. She could see the Mississippi through a screen of branches, the full span concealed, but there, plunging south below the Wisconsin hills.

She felt happy to have come here. She felt delivered, cared for, considered. Rolling down the window to feel the wind, she could see moving leaves, swaying branches, and she realized she felt unexpectedly loved. It was as if this moment had been scheduled for ages by people who knew her intimately—by Mom, who was dead, and Dad, who was probably dead, and might as well be, even if he wasn't, because he'd been declared dead. How she had hated that moment, hated that declaration. But the plan for her had begun long before that. It had begun way back at the instant they saw each other for the first time. How difficult it was to believe that there had ever been such a moment. She'd heard them describe it, and yet it was impossible that such an event had really happened to them in the same way that things happened to her. The first dance they danced. Their first touch, first embrace, first everything. And they scared her because they knew so much that she didn't. She had lain on the floor at their feet, or half asleep on the couch, while their pleasure in each other washed over her as they told the story of how they met and who they were before they put on their shirts and shoes and girdles and dresses and went to that dance hall to become Mom and Dad. Hearing their voices back then, she had been far from their minds, maybe the last thing on their minds, slight and forgotten, but just as real as she was now in her car, having driven to this place by the murmuring river where the leaves let go one at a time.

For a single overwhelming instant, she felt that her dad had not gone missing, that there had been no divorce, that her mother had not declared him dead without giving him a chance to be there to explain, casting him from their lives as if he were a ghost to be chased from life itself, because "abandoning" them, he deserved to be "abandoned." He deserved to be declared dead.

How strange, she thought, to have come here.

14

I F ANYBODY HAD BOTHERED TO ask Bernice about the last thing she wanted to come home to, she would've said it was Hazel Vanasek in that brand-new Toyota of hers, parked so she all but blocked the front door. But there she was. Apparently, Bernice wasn't to be allowed into her own home without getting an earful. Probably scolded for being away too long. Or else forced to hear all over again about the wonderful Toyota and the even more wonderful nephew. Brag, brag, brag till the cows came home. But not today. No, sir, she wasn't running scared just because Hazel thought she owned the place.

She pulled up close and climbed out, good and ready to set things straight. She would get over to Reverend Tauke's as fast as she could, and she wasn't going to stand for a lot of badgering, and she would get her point through Hazel's thick skull if she had to use a hammer.

But Hazel wasn't moving. Bernice put a flat palm against the glass. In spite of the music playing and the motor running, Hazel was sound asleep. Now, would you look at that? With her head back and her mouth open, she was a slack-mouthed goner. Bernice was not only surprised but let down, because she'd been looking forward to giving Hazel a piece of her mind. The music was the kind that normally got people clapping their hands, all worked up and inspired, but not Hazel. She was zonked. It was that one bunch of singers, most of them black people Reverend Tauke liked from that other reverend on TV—what was his name? Big, smiley, roly-poly fella. So maybe six months ago, Reverend Tauke had ordered all these tapes and CDs that he sold to the congregation at a price he claimed was not a penny over cost. Bernice had felt duty-bound to check things out by watching the show and comparing prices. She'd felt a little funny suspecting Reverend Tauke, but you couldn't be too careful. Thinking anybody was above the almighty dollar was a sure way to end up cheated. It didn't matter all his talking about God. Money could get inside most people and drag them off the straight and narrow. So she started her little investigation and felt a terrible burden was lifted when things came out on the up-and-up. Down to the penny, taking into account shipping and handling. And the music was fine. More than pleasant, to her way of thinking. So she bought a copy, and even if she didn't go overboard like a lot of people, she played it plenty of evenings eating alone with her animals. The way she saw it, there was a time and a place for those kinds of uplifting tunes that got you feeling better than you should half the time, and the other half you were ready to blubber with missing something.

When the breeze shoved a whiff of exhaust fumes at her, she shook her head. Hazel's snazzy Toyota might not be a gas-guzzler like Bernice's big old Chevy, but that didn't make it sensible to burn fuel going nowhere. Might as well put matches to dollar bills and watch them go up in smoke.

Still, there was an opportunity here if Bernice could get into the house without being seen. She might sneak in a little nap of her own. It was sure what she wanted, because she was wiped out. A chance to flop— even if only for half an hour.

It added suspense to see General staring at her out the window, and she would have bet dollars to doughnuts he knew what was going on, the way he stayed quiet. After positioning the towel, the two of them getting the hang of it through practice, she couldn't help but think he halfway expected this was the way he would get around from now on, her waddling along behind him everywhere he went. "Don't get too used to this," she told him. "This is a one-time thing."

When the dogs started yapping, she had to leave General and get the door open to tell them, "Shush!" They quieted but ran out to help. "Get back in there! C'mon! Hush now!" Once she had everybody inside, she paused, a criminal sneaking off from her crime, because she was being extremely inconsiderate. Hazel was a reddish sprawl inside the Toyota under its halo of fumes. But after all she'd been through at the vet's and in that cornfield, Bernice had a hunch she was suffering from one of those adrenaline rushes like they talked about on TV sometimes. They left you wrung out. No wonder she was limp as a wet dishrag and all of a sudden famished. She took off for the kitchen with Happy and Sappy trundling along. There was bread and Velveeta cheese, and she slapped it together with mayonnaise and lettuce. Grabbing a Diet 7UP, she turned around to the startling sight of her home ablaze in cleanliness and order, every speck gushing with welcoming sunshine in the windows. It was like her little house was boasting, as if it felt underappreciated, as if she'd hurt its feelings coming in without paying the slightest bit of attention. She sighed and thought General looked thankful, too. He lapped away at his water bowl and coped with his whirling room by taking sideways steps. They had battled their way back where they belonged, was how she looked at things. The cats approached, their spines arched to invite her touch. "I'm glad to see you, too."

But as she settled at the kitchen table to enjoy her sandwich, she saw her brooch and earrings and realized they were still sitting where she'd seen them this morning. She'd left them out all night and then, instead of putting them away like she knew she should, she'd forgotten all about them again. It made her sick to think she could be so neglectful, like those earrings given by Toby on their thirtieth wedding anniversary, and the brooch, a fiftieth birthday gift from Isabel, were worthless, run-of-the-mill trinkets. She picked them up, and red-hot bile sprang in a bitter burp from her gut to her throat. She didn't think she'd be able to swallow her last mouthful of sandwich. And then she did, belching and gasping, but nothing soothed her throat or kept more of the nasty stuff from coming up. It scared her, like she was about to puke. Dr. Manders had told her to rest. Doctor's orders, she thought, reaching the sink, where she splashed tap water all over her brow and cheeks, slopping it up and down her front before filling a plastic cup and taking a long drink. Please, Lord, she thought, aiming for her bed. I got to hit the hay.

Tile flowed beneath her, and she saw her blouse wet in the front and dog hair all over the sage green of her skirt, which she knew was muddy on the fanny. The red and white sailboat on the brown hall throw rug reminded her of the day Toby had flung it down proudly, like it was fur off some wild animal he'd shot and skinned, instead of a sale item from Rhomberg's Department Store. Finally, she saw her feet on the rosy fluff of the shag in her bedroom, where she had to fight for air, her heart jumbled and fluttery, so she worried she hadn't taken her medications, even though she knew she had, and she was thinking, I could die like this. Never knowing what hit me. So it's just the end. Over and out. Them darn angels knocking me silly before they made their move. She would be helpless as a scared child in the hands of brutes as big as buildings with no interest whatsoever in what she might or might not want. No mercy. They wouldn't give a hoot. She could protest all she wanted. Dig in her heels. Kick up a fuss. Just doing their duty like military fools.

She concentrated on placing the brooch and earrings on the bedside table before starting to pry off her shoes, poking the toe of one into the heel of the other. But she had been too conscientious tying the bows that morning on her orthodontic sneakers. They weren't coming off. She strained and thought, No, orthodontic was teeth. But she ought to get her poor feet out anyway, or she'd wake up to the misery of scrunched toes and bunions aching like they had teeth and were eating her when she wasn't even dead. Like whatever ate you once you were dead. Once you were in the grave and things came to eat you. Roaches and other underground things. Worms or bugs. It was just horrible to think about. My arm, she thought. My poor little fingers. My hands. Teeth appeared, chomping and snapping away to empty her shoes. Teeth in beetles and worms and snakes, even. It was a good thing you were dead when that bunch got hold of you. That was about the only good thing a person could say about being dead. But it still didn't strike her as right. Rats. Rats were in on it, too, if they got a chance. It didn't strike her as fair. Even for an old lady. A poor old body as worn down and dried up as hers. Because it wasn't fair. Eaten up by the likes of maggots and grubs. And larva. Larva had something to do with it. And children singing all the while. Little children with teasing, mocking voices because they thought they were safe because they were young and green and so they didn't have to worry because it was all far away and it wasn't even real. But it was real and it wasn't far away. Not ever. It was right there, somewhere in the evening coming up from the ground as the sun went down into the nighttime, and up it climbed, like this big snake swallowing the light in sooty coils rising out of the dirt and out of the hills while those little teasing voices sang, *The worms crawl in, the worms crawl out, the worms play pinochle on your snout.* She'd done that, too, when she was small. Sung like that when she was a kid and didn't know any better. She could hear her own voice amid the taunting harmonies, the innocent foolishness. The tears that crept up from inside her to overflow in droplets trailing down her cheeks seemed to be caused by the pain in her poor feet, her overblown swollen feet still puffing up more and more, these impractical, unhandy feet on the ends of her legs, as big as clown shoes.

For a while she was quiet. She glimpsed something. It looked like her plans for tomorrow, these shapes waiting in a row, while off in the opposite direction her past was arranged in another row, though it was all breaking apart, her memories like hunks of ice falling off a bigger hunk of ice, and her plans, too, all groaning and tumbling into the sea. A nature show on TV, that's what it was. Icebergs into the waves. It was enough to make her feel scared, hearing her life groaning and seeing it crumble. It felt like she was going to pieces, and maybe she was, but the pieces were connected somehow, like beads on a necklace or islands in a chain. And she was on one of the islands, or maybe she was on all of them. And so, knowing where she was, it was okay to sleep, because now she knew where to go to look for and find Bernice. Just as she knew that the pressures nudging against her were friendly and furry, making it safe to pay no attention. Safe to wallow and snooze. Safe to surrender. Safe to let her weary bones rest.

Even though they were beginning to bang at the walls. Even though they were thrashing and battering and kicking to crack open the ceiling. Even though they were roaring to get in. Even though they were stomping with their big feet right over her head. Raising high and slamming down their gigantic legs to hammer open the ceiling. Even though there were dinosaurs on the roof. It wasn't angels. They were not feathered. They had wings but no plumes. They were coated in scales full of angles. Not angels but angles with razor-sharp edges. They were gigantic dragons with big heads and jaws full of knives. And they were coming through, their hideous feet pushing aside beams and shingles and plaster, chopping and hewing and smiting everything to get in and grab and shake her.

"What?" she said to Hazel's face as it burst through the mess.

"Why didn't you wake me? Now look what happened." Hazel was right on top of her, jabbing pointy fingers into her shoulder.

"Let go of me, Hazel!"

"I will not."

"I swear! Get off me!"

"You gotta wake up."

"I'm warning you, I will give you a good one, you don't cut this out." Bernice reared back her right fist.

"Okay," Hazel said, and she straightened. "But you were sleeping."

"Well, I ain't anymore."

"We were both sleeping. I couldn't believe it. We're going to miss everything. Didn't you see me out there?"

"Where?"

"In front of your house. You had to."

"Well, sure."

"This copper woke me up. Or I swear I'd still be out there."

"What copper?"

"Pulled up in his squad car. Rapped on my window. Scared the bejeezus out of me."

"There was a copper here?"

"He woke me up, I just told you. Right outside."

"Why'd he do that?"

"He said I looked suspicious. He thought I was dead." They studied each other for a moment. "He come banging on my window."

"When was this?"

"Not five minutes ago. That's what I'm telling you."

"Is he gone?"

"I don't know. I sure hope so."

Bernice stood on stiffened knees, and in spite of shocks up and down her spine, she staggered to a front window. The street looked okay to her, the pavement shining normally, the neighboring houses peaceful, her car along with Hazel's parked nicely, though both were facing in the wrong direction.

"Did he say anything about the way we're parked?"

"Yes, he did. He didn't like it."

"I don't see him."

"He drove off toward downtown. But he could still be around, I guess."

"Why would he do that?"

"I don't know."

"That'd be a good one. Stake us out."

"He wasn't staking anybody out, Bernice. He was just on patrol. Like they're supposed to. He come around the block. He saw me sitting there aimed the wrong way, and then he come around again, and he had a funny feeling. He started to worry. He started thinking maybe he ought to be concerned. He started thinking maybe—"

"Hazel! Just cut it out!" She felt like everything about Hazel was an attack, the look in her eye, the sound of her voice, every word out of her mouth. It was because she'd jumped up from a sound sleep and needed coffee or something. Maybe a minute's peace. "You don't know what the man was thinking, so don't try and tell me you do. I wasn't born yesterday."

"Well, excuse me, but if you don't mind, what I'm trying to share here is his personal comments. We had a little chat. It's my guess that once he saw how riled up he got me, he thought he better talk me down. So he took the time to explain himself, how the second time he drove around the block, it struck him suddenly that I might be dead. It come to him that might be why the engine was running. I was dead. Or I could die from the engine running and a leak of those deadly fumes coming up through the floorboards."

"I gotta have some coffee or something." Bernice shuffled into the kitchen with Hazel staying right on her heels.

"Carbon monoxide, you know. It sneaks up through the floorboards. Nobody even knows," Hazel said, sounding like she was telling a ghost story. "That happens."

"I guess."

"What's there to guess about? Don't you remember the Knothe brothers and what happened to them? The way they were listening to that ball game—it's the Cubs and somebody, and they got the engine running to keep the battery from wearing down, and it was a little chilly, if I remember right, so they want some heat. And so that was the way that went until the car ran out of gas and shut off, but they were long dead, the two of them sitting in the front seat like statues. That's what Margie Furlong told me. She saw them. Did you know them?"

"It was the Cardinals."

"What was?"

"The other team. One brother loved the Cubs, and the other one loved the Cardinals."

"That's right. There was a lot of talk about that."

"Nobody knew why. Why'd he love the Cardinals? Never spent a day in St. Louis in his life."

They were bustling about, Bernice putting the teakettle on, while Hazel banged around in the cabinet for mugs like the place was her own. "People thought they had some kind of bet," she said, "and the game was close, and that led them to lose track."

"I knew the older one. Vern," Bernice told her. "He lived awhile in Chicago, so he got involved with the Cubs, and he just kept up with them after he moved back here."

"I didn't know that one well, Vern, but I sure—"

"You knew his wife, right? She was the oldest of the Krumpe girls—a year behind us at school?" Hazel nodded, but the look in her eye said she was off in the clouds, a million miles away. "I knew Vern from him and Toby being in the same bowling league," Bernice continued. "Nice friendly fella. Always gave me a big hello if I saw him on the street. But the other brother, the younger one. He was an oddball. Gotta like the Cardinals."

"He's the one I knew better, even though he was younger. I had such a crush on him once."

"What do you mean by that?"

"This was in high school."

Hazel was dumping spoonfuls of instant coffee into both mugs, almost twice what Bernice used normally, but she let it go, figuring a good jolt might suit her. "Did I know that?"

"That I had a crush? Maybe. Maybe not. It didn't amount to much. I mean, outside of myself. But I can tell you, I was mad for him. Pretty much went off my rocker."

"You would. That's just like you—goin' head over heels over the likes of that one." Bernice glared at the teakettle, like it was deliberately refusing to boil. "Big mystery man, right. Wasn't that the way most people thought about him? Everything's a mystery. Stupid if you ask me."

"Horace."

"Right. Horace Knothe. Big mystery man."

"He said he was named after a famous poet."

"Why'd he say that?"

"Because he was named after a famous poet, I guess. I liked him."

Bernice stretched her hand out in a gesture intended to get Hazel to step aside. "I gotta go to the bathroom."

"So why tell me?"

They were jammed into the narrow space between the stove and the table, where Bernice felt trapped by Hazel in her khaki outfit with its fancy gold buttons, shoulder pads squaring her off like she wasn't wide enough. "Because I'd like you to get out of the way, if you could manage to move."

Hazel appeared to find the solution to their predicament beyond her. "I don't know why you have to jump down my throat."

"I gotta pee." That was just about all the justification she thought she needed. The urge had arrived with such force, she didn't know what was worse, Hazel acting like stepping aside was this big inconvenience, or knowing she didn't have a spare second unless she wanted to end up changing her Depends again. Since it looked like her only hope was to shove her way past, that's what she did, and not exactly gentle about it, either.

"You're in a foul mood, Bernice. Why not just admit it? You gotta even start picking on poor Horace Knothe. And him dead and gone all these years."

"He was an odd duck, Hazel."

"Let the poor man rest. What'd he ever do to you?"

"You asked for my opinion, and that's it," Bernice said, and slipped into the bathroom, shutting the door firmly.

"I don't know what you expect from a person," Hazel called. "Maybe I came in overly excited. I was probably way too pushy. I can see that, but I woke up to such a fright—think about that, why don't you."

Growing faint before becoming loud once more, Hazel's voice depicted her going to the kitchen and back, probably to shut off the teakettle while Bernice wrestled with her clothes. Peeing again, she thought, and chuckled, though she would have been hard-pressed to say what was funny.

"This big policeman looking in my window. I got so tongue-tied I could hardly get my name out right. He wants to see my license and registration and all that, like he'd pulled me over for speeding. Which only happened twice in my whole life. And I didn't like it either time."

"I think he was showing off."

"Showing off?"

"Sure."

"I don't see that."

"Sure. Acting all high and mighty about you sitting in your car." Bernice yawned and gave her head a nasty shake, like that might get her brain back on the job.

"I don't see that at all."

"Don't you think there might have been some real criminal goings-on somewhere in town that maybe needed his attention?"

"How would I know?"

"But no—he's gotta come around here scaring you half to death. That's hardly the job the city pays him to do."

"What are you talking about?"

"Scaring you! How many times do I have to say it?"

"Well, I scared him."

"You scared me, too, Hazel. Jumping on me like that in the middle of a sound sleep. And you wonder why I'm cranky."

"I'm sorry. But I was just so worried we're going to miss everything. What are you doing in there, anyway?"

"I'm peeing. If that's all right with you."

"You sure are taking your time. How's your bladder? Is your bladder all right? Maybe you have an infection."

"My bladder's fine. Except it's old." The urge to poo was creeping up on her, one dilapidated body part whispering to another, so she might as well stay put and give things a chance.

"I couldn't believe you didn't wake me up. That's what set me off." Hazel had a tone that made her apology sound accusatory. "You walked right past me. I can't fathom it."

"I wanted to let you rest."

"How could you think that after all we talked about this morning about how important it was to get over to Reverend Tauke's? You shoulda known sleep was the last thing I wanted."

Since her bowels appeared fickle, Bernice wiped and pulled her Depends up and her skirt down. "That's asking me to know an awful lot based on not very much, Hazel." She was unprepared for the shock of her appearance in the mirror. Her hair stuck out on both sides like somebody invisible had hold of it. To top it off, her lipstick was smudged, and her breath in her cupped palm was worse than General's.

Hazel tapped on the door. "How much longer are you going to be?"

"Just hold your horses," Bernice said, sniffing her armpits. The problem was, a person got used to her own BO.

"Anyway, we're wasting time." Hazel banged the door good this time. "Bernice. C'mon. I gotta pee, too."

Because the sound of running water would betray that she was finished, Bernice postponed washing up. She stood there, giving her urine the once-over. It looked sort of pale. "Hazel, I'm telling you, you gotta get off my back and give me a moment's rest." On the other hand, she wasn't going to be a prisoner in her own bathroom. Sprinkling a sweetened dust of Cashmere Bouquet on various body parts as best she could with her clothes still on, she called, "You hear me out there?"

"Yes, I hear you. I'm right outside the door waiting my turn to get in, for Pete's sake."

"Let's leave Pete out of it."

"What?"

"Let's leave Pete out of it!" Cashmere Bouquet was her ace in the hole, the way it pretty much dared BO to try and make trouble. She flushed and opened the spigot over her hands. "I have more going on than I can handle, but I still have to figure out what needs to be done. I barely had a wink of sleep." She shook her fingers to get them drying and went to shut the water off only to have the knob spin with no effect. "Even if I did sleep, I doubt I got any rest." Something was loose, a washer or screw. Was she going to have to call a plumber? she worried, just as the freewheeling knob caught and the water went off. "I'll be out in a minute," she said, and reached for the mouthwash.

"Promises, promises."

"There's things to do. Responsibilities." All crumpled and creased, her blouse didn't appear to have a respectable inch, and trying to spruce up her skirt by patting and smoothing was useless. She looked like she'd gotten dressed out of a hamper of dirty laundry. Every bit of elastic or fabric touching her was gummy and clinging. She opened the door and stepped out. "It's all yours."

Hazel was jiggling and jumping around. "It's about time."

Suddenly aware of her half-strangled feet, Bernice winced. It felt as if her shoes had shrunk and were driving pins into her bunions. Still, as she started for her bedroom, she managed to say, "I can't just go racing off. I got animals to think of. They're living things, in case you forgot."

The bathroom door opened just enough for Hazel to stick her head out. "Janet Cawley's all set to take care of things on that front."

"What?"

"She's coming back to feed them tonight. Their dinner," Hazel announced, and disappeared.

Bernice stared at the door. "How do you know?"

"I saw to it for you, Bernice."

With the torment in her feet building, Bernice tried to use the wall for support. "You saw her? She was here?"

"Yes, I did, and she asked if all that was still on her plate, and I took it upon myself to speak up for what I knew you would want. We actually spent a couple nice minutes together."

Bernice raised one foot and then the other. "Doing what?"

"I'd have to say she was more on top of the situation than I expected. Where'd you get this toilet paper?"

"What?"

"In here. Was it expensive? It's a funny brand."

"No, it's just generic."

"I think I might have been wrong about her," Hazel called, and Bernice wanted to hear more, but her need to get her shoes off catapulted her down the hall to her bed, where she heard Hazel going on from the other side of several walls. "Or halfway wrong, because it'd be stretching the truth to say she wasn't acting peculiar when I pulled up. She was peeping in your windows, Bernice."

With only one shoe off, Bernice needed to take five. Flabby rolls of belly fat had jabbed into her until the strain left her winded, like she was failing some Olympic event that demanded years of training. Meanwhile, the foot she had liberated sank onto its mate, grinding the instep to unleash delicious sensations that begged her to stay put, which she did, refusing to give up until the pleas from her other foot became heartbreaking. She dove for the remaining shoe, and her feet sought each other out like old friends, the best of lost sisters delivering relief to her arches, gratification to her instep and toes. Her eyelids fell, and she sank away, her feet like a couple of lusty soap-opera lovers who couldn't get enough of each other.

"What in God's name are you doing?" said Hazel.

Bernice knew better than to open her eyes but did anyway. Hazel stood in the doorway. "I don't believe what I'm seeing, Bernice!"

"What?"

"You've got your shoes off! I thought we were getting ready to go." She sounded heartsick and betrayed. "I come out of the bathroom, and you're sitting there barefoot."

"Well, I took my shoes off." She grabbed one and determinedly tugged the heel wider.

"I can't turn my back for five seconds."

"Quit bugging me."

"You're like a two-year-old. I'm starting to feel like I'm gonna have to use dynamite to blast you out of here."

"I took my shoes off, Hazel. Let's not lose track of how that's the thing you're having this conniption about. I slept in my shoes. My feet were killing me."

"Don't let's get started on that one."

"Why not? It's true."

"Because I'm the one that got left outside in my car sound asleep is why not. That's why not. And as sure as God made little green apples, I had my clothes on. I had my shoes on. But do you hear me complaining?"

"Of course not. You're too busy bossing people around."

"Not everything goes our way, Bernice."

"You can say that again." Abruptly, Bernice stood and kicked off the shoe she'd gotten partway on. "I need a shower. I need some clean clothes."

"Now you're talking about a shower?"

"And don't you make a federal case out of it!"

"All right, all right. But whatever you're going to do, hurry up."

"Hazel! How about this? I don't want to hurry up. I am sick and tired of hurrying up. If you're rarin' to go so bad—go!"

"Oh, don't start that again."

"We have two cars. I'll have my nice relaxing shower and come when I can."

"You're going to be the death of me, I swear. I don't know why you're acting this way!"

"No, you don't. Because you're not the one who had to cope with your dog nearly dying on you this morning, are you? No, you're not. That's me. And you're not the one had to go drivin' on some crazy road with all these people honking and giving you nasty looks. I don't think that was you. You didn't come this close to crashing your car—" Her thumb and forefinger squeezed air until the tips shook. She was weeping and back on the bed. When had she started that kind of foolishness? Just blubbering away. "This close," she said, fighting to get the words out so they sounded like more than bubbles and wheezes. "And runnin' around this cornfield with deer nearly trampling me and hunters and guns. They were shooting, Hazel. They were shooting."

"What are you talking about?"

"My morning."

"I thought you went to the vet's."

"I did."

"What's all this other business, then?"

Bernice wanted to put her hands over her eyes but didn't have the gumption. She was stuck just sitting there downcast over the rose-colored rug. "General had to pee. So what was I supposed to do? He was goin' crazy, poor old guy. The corn was so tall. It all happened fast. These deer runnin'. All these gunshots. But I don't think they knew which way to go. I didn't know what they were at first—they could have been anything. But they were just these confused deer."

"Goodness. Where was all this?"

One more gulp forced her to pluck Kleenex from the bedside table. "I'm just not used to all this, you know."

Hazel was fighting her own set of weepy squeaks. "I'm upset, too, Bernice. I'm in a dither, too." Her lower lip fluttered. "Now you got me going." She sounded peeved, like her tears were an injustice. She nudged past Bernice to grab a fistful of Kleenex, then jumped back to the foot of the bed, where she cast what Bernice feared was a judgmental eye over the bedroom. Clothing on the floor, a half-full coffee mug left on the vanity beside balled-up tissues stained with makeup. The hamper was overflowing, and out of nowhere—though it must have been there all along—the inescapable stench of dirty Depends in the corner trash. Bernice waited for Hazel to sniff disapprovingly. But nothing happened except Hazel took a ragged breath and dabbed Kleenex at her eyes.

Seconds passed, and Bernice couldn't help but take in the way they were just sitting there side by side sniffling and cleaning snot out of their noses, neither daring to say another word. "This is stupid," said Bernice.

"Well, you started it."

Bernice laughed but found she was way too upset to enjoy it.

"You should take that shower if you really want to, Bernice."

"I had it in me to brain you, Hazel. If there'd been a frying pan handy, look out."

"Murder."

"Then the coppers would have really been all over this place."

Hazel folded her hands in her lap. The dismayed shake of her head seemed to say that she knew her failings well. "All this waiting and hoping for Jesus. It's a tough one. I just know I'll feel so much better when we get out to Reverend Tauke's. I want to stop worryin' that I'll miss out. If I'm supposed to be part of things, I want to be there and have the right info and guidelines. I just don't understand it the way Reverend Tauke does. I was a wreck last night. What was it going to be like, you know, Jesus and all those angels? How could they possibly notice me? I took it all for granted before and thought I knew—I mean that I really knew—but I really don't. Do you?"

"Nope."

Withdrawing her glasses, Hazel dabbed at her eyes and met Bernice with a naked, blank expression. "I'd lost all track of Horace Knothe by the time they found him sitting in that car. But it still hit me hard to hear that he was dead. Like the way he loved the St. Louis Cardinals and nobody could say why. I felt like he knew things most people didn't. He never called me after that one date we had. That was it. Not that it was a one-sided affair, because it wasn't. Now, I can't prove that it wasn't, but he did tell that friend of his, Artie Widrig, something along similar lines about me, and then Artie told me years later when he was drunk one night at somebody's house. This get-together. It was outside. Barbecue and whatnot. He thought it was funny. Artie, I mean. Horace was dead and buried by this point. You know who I mean, Artie Widrig, the one who fell and broke both his legs working construction on that high-rise parking garage in—I think it was Moline—and then later he crashed his car into a tree and ended up paralyzed. He was a drunk, I guess. I don't know why he chose to tell me about Horace at that late date. But he had a high old time doin' it, let me tell you. I'da liked to slap that smirk off his face, because he was havin' the time of his life lettin' me know how I'd missed out. But he had a mean streak. People said so, and I don't think he liked me. I waited for Horace to call after that one date. I was sure he would. I'm talking about at first. When it was fresh. When it mattered. Anyway, he didn't. Or I missed it. So I just don't want to miss out on anything more." The care with which she replaced her glasses announced how badly she wanted to see as well as hear Bernice from this point on. "I'd like to pray now. The two of us. See if we can pray for guidance and help so we stop being so hard on each other. Okay?"

"Okay," said Bernice.

"I admit I was wrong coming in here the way I did. But I felt like you were sabotaging us ever getting to Reverand Tauke's, and I guess I over-reacted."

Bernice folded her right arm across her belly, making a little table for her left elbow. As her chin sank into her palm, she said, "I can see why."

"Can you?"

She had to deal with some confusion and disagreement, none of it willing to vanish completely. "I really can."

Hazel grunted, like understanding had just smacked into her, and Bernice felt similarly, as if a large book had been shut. Hazel bowed her head and closed her eyes. Bernice placed her hands on her lap, her lowering eyelids blotting out the room.

"Dear Lord, we're asking," Hazel prayed, "Bernice and I are asking for your help today. For your gentle help so we can get through this in a better way. Dear Lord, we know our lives are in your hands one way or the other. We love you, Lord, so just help us be nicer to each other. In your name. In Jesus' name. Amen."

"Amen."

Bernice was in no rush to depart that darkness, where it seemed piety and grace had a chance. But then she was looking at Hazel, who said, "You should probably go ahead with that shower like you want."

"Okay."

The ringing phone might as well have been somebody screaming. Hazel yelped, and reflex shot Bernice toward the bedside table, but she put the brakes on just in time. "I'm going to ignore it. No, no. I'll just jump in the shower."

"But what if it's him?"

"Who?"

"Reverend Tauke. I think you should answer."

About to grab her pink flannel robe from its closet hook, she said, "Reverend Tauke has never called me in his life."

"I'll answer. You don't have to."

"No."

"Why?"

"Because it's my phone, and I don't want to talk to anybody."

"I'll say you're not here. But I just have this gut feeling it's him. How many rings is that? I wish we'd counted. It must be important! He might have news."

"You're not going to stop, are you?" Hazel was flushed and wide-eyed, a teakettle building steam. Bernice faced the towels stacked in her hallway closet and felt she was tossing away something utterly useless as she said, "Oh, go ahead."

"Hello?" Hazel answered behind her. "Oh. Hello." When Hazel's voice shuddered, Bernice stopped in her tracks and turned. Hazel had a finger to her lips for silence. She grimaced and shook her head, but Bernice wasn't interested in any stupid pantomime.

"Just tell me who it is!"

"Irma," Hazel whispered. "It's Irma."

"Irma?"

Hazel winced to reprimand Bernice for speaking so loudly. As if the cat wasn't already out of the bag, she pressed the handset against her belly, pretending to smother the trouble she'd started.

"What does she want?"

"I don't know. She's your daughter."

Ready to jump down Hazel's throat, Bernice was even more enraged at herself. How had she let this happen? She tramped over and took the phone. "Hello."

"Hi, Mom."

"Hello."

"Hi. How's everything? What's going on?"

"This is quite a surprise, Irma."

"What is?"

"I'm thinking about the fact that you called me, that you're calling me. That's a surprise."

"I guess."

"I can vouch for it."

"Okay," said Irma, and she coughed before going on. "I guess you're not about to let things ride for even a little, are you. Just throw down the gauntlet first second."

"Well, I'm just wondering what's the occasion?"

"Okay, okay."

"I can't even remember the last time."

"I should have called, Mom. It's not easy."

"Picking up the phone, you mean. No, no, that's a hard one, all right."

"Do you see that? I mean, think for one second about how you'd feel if you called me, and before you got two words out, I was digging at you and picking the way you are at me. Before I even got two words out. You don't know what's been going on in my life!"

"Now, that's a fact. Though I might if you called once in a while."

"Good Lord. I mean, you don't know if John's holding down a job, or if little Alex John is sick or something, or doing well in school. Or if I'm okay. Are we making ends meet?"

"So, are you?"

"Yes! But there could be problems. Or illness. There could be."

"Is there?"

"I mean, you haven't been exactly ringing my phone off the wall, Mom. You could pick up the phone every now and then. It wouldn't kill you. You could be the one who, you know—who initiates. It goes both ways, the telephone."

"So why did you call, Irma?"

"Could we have lunch tomorrow, maybe?"

The question sounded fake and prepackaged, every word part of some front Irma was putting on that forced Bernice to say, "Wait a minute. Wait one minute."

"What for?"

"This is us you're asking about? Me and you?"

"Yes."

"What's going on?"

"Could we do that?"

"What's going on, Irma? Something is going on. There's no need to bother with all that kind of—whatever it is. Double-talk. I mean, lunch. Out of the blue. Don't be a phony."

"You are brutal! Do you know that? Brutal! Okay, I'm just a little worried. We can forget lunch. But I heard something. Something about you. It worried me. Eileen Luckritz, you know, she rents that little apartment to Janet Cawley, and we're still friends. Eileen and me. We reconnected a while back."

"Right."

"So I heard something. That you were involved in something."

"I see. Right."

"From Eileen. Who got it from Janet."

Bernice gave Hazel, who was sheepish and nervous, an unforgiving look and said, "Do you know, Irma, actually, I have to go. Hazel's here. Hazel Vanasek. And we were about to head off and do something."

"What?"

"Oh, it wouldn't interest you. It's just our kind of thing."

"Could we talk about this, Mom?"

"No need."

"Well, I think there is."

"Let me assure you on this score. Because I know what you're referring to, and people get other people's business mixed up all the time, as you well know. Nine times out of ten. And you can bet that's what happened here. This one says something to that one, and she blabs to the next one, and that one's got to get on the phone to somebody else, and before you know it, they're all in a tizzy—they got everything wrong, and we're on the phone like this, talking and talking."

Hazel was slinking into the hall as if separation would nullify whatever involvement the mention of her name had alleged. Bernice wanted to order her back, but Irma was asking, "When are you going to be home from whatever you and Hazel are doing?"

"Why?"

"So we can talk!"

"How about in the next day or so, I give you a call?"

"Maybe tonight. What about tonight?"

"I'm not sure I can."

"Of course you can. Why couldn't you? I mean, you can, Mother. If you want to."

"Irma! Listen to me! I don't know what you think you're doing. But I can tell you I don't want you sticking your busy little nose into my business. You don't speak to me for months on end, and now you're going to call up like you care! I don't think so! And all because of whatever this is you think you heard! I don't think so! Are you following this? Because I can tell you for a fact that if you weren't worried last week or the week before or the week before that one or the one before that, then you got nothing to worry about now!"

"You're awful."

"It takes two, just remember that."

"A fucking bitch!"

"I'm going to hang up now."

"A nasty, nasty, mean, hard-hearted, just heartless goddamn stupid—"

"I'm going to hang up now."

"What is wrong with you?"

"It takes one to know one, Irma. Keep that where you can see it. It takes one to—"

"That sharp tongue of yours, Mom, it's so hateful."

"Here's an idea—you could have one of those little magnets made up. They hang on the refrigerator so a person can see them several times a day without having to go to the trouble of thinking or looking things up, and yours could read, 'It takes one to—'"

The clatter of plastic stopped her. After several clanks and gasps, a slight electronic pop brought silence. Deep inside the racket, she could see Irma slamming the phone down in one mismatched hang-up after another. Trembling and fit to be tied, even a touch light-headed, Bernice wanted to be careful with her next move. She hoped to appear calm, neatening the doily under the phone she had replaced. Turning to Hazel, who watched warily from the hall, she offered a counterfeit smile as she said, "Anyway."

"Goodness." Hazel playacted relief to show how lucky they were to have survived. "What was that all about?"

"I think we should go."

"Oh. Okay."

Bernice scanned the room, feeling there was somebody close by she had to consult, and she would find them in a second, and it wasn't Hazel. It was Toby, and she had to settle for the silver framed close-up on her dresser, his big nose and deep-set eyes under that peaked cap she could never convince him was too old-fashioned to wear because he believed it made him look dapper. She saw again how she'd been right about the cap, especially given the shirt he had buttoned up to the neck. The wide blue and green bands from top to bottom looked like tire tracks from some car that had run him over. Not that her opinion of his shirt mattered just now, because in spite of knowing better, in spite of knowing she needed a helping hand, he was very disappointed in her because of how she'd just flown off the handle at their daughter. They both knew better, but for all the good it did them, they might as well have not bothered knowing a darn thing.

Bernice could feel Hazel's eyes on her as she moved to the bed for her shoes. "Bernice, this don't feel right. You know you don't want to show up out there lookin' like you don't care to look presentable. And you have to feel yucky. Don't you feel yucky?"

Bernice raised her arms and took an unhappy sniff of her armpits. Odors of all kinds seeped from every nook and cranny in her ramshackle old body. Anticipating the chapel and everybody packed tight and her as ripe as some bum off the street, she said, "I'll hurry."

"You bet your boots you will," said Hazel.

15

J ANET COUNTED ON A GOOD run to energize her. It always
worked. Just yesterday she'd flown over this first section, but
already the mild upgrade felt torturous. Her thighs ached. Unnaturally
heavy, each stride ended with a thud that begged her to quit. Maybe she
should have eaten something or taken the nap she'd considered, instead
of darting in and jumping into her gear. The gradual but relentless steep-
ening of the climb felt designed to grind her to a halt.

If only she could get to the top, she would be rewarded with the start
of a long decline, but lifting her gaze from the blur of the sidewalk, she
was dismayed. It seemed miles yet. Her hair flopped around, an aggravating nuisance, tickling her cheeks and falling into her eyes. Annoyed that
she'd failed to bring a cap, she didn't even notice the curb until her right
foot landed clumsily. Impact knifed into her hip. Something pinged in
her spine. Her legs were so pliant, she staggered and believed she was
about to go down hard in the street. Her resistance brought the opposite
curb too quickly, and her overdone lunge felt drunken.

When she peeked, the summit was closer. At least she wasn't in some
surreal haze where her destination retreated at a pace demonically
matched to her advance. She vowed to pound on until this first frustrat-
ing phase was behind her and her second wind could kick in.

But the next time she checked, her goal seemed impossibly distant.
She was panting like she belonged in a sickbed. The road appeared to end
at the crest, as if at a cliff, and emerging into view from the other side was
a sleek silver car with an unnerving familiarity that it took her some sec-

onds to grasp. It was Bobby Crimmins. Her ex-husband was headed toward her in the still-brand-new-looking Mercury Grand Marquis that
he'd purchased right after their divorce, calling it his "just reward," his
"celebration of freedom." In the first months after she'd left him, she'd
had to stomach accounts of how "cute" he was, how "brave," as he soft-
ened his animosity shrewdly, through a self-deprecating tactic that excused his most vindictive remark as mischievous charm. But she knew
the truth. He was thin-skinned and spiteful and armed to the teeth with
toxicity held back by cunning, camouflaged by wit and primed for her as
he bided his time. And who could blame him? After all, she'd seen him
naked and said no, thank you. Slept under his hammering snores and billowing dreams and said no, thank you.

But what if his reason for driving here had nothing to do with her? He
did work in real estate, after all. A neighboring house could be up for sale.
He might have a friend in the area. On the other hand, she had to be ready,
just in case. A juicy comment from some mutual acquaintance could have
sent him to see for himself how fucked up her life had become.

Deciding to create a casual, energetic impression until he drove by, if
he drove by, she fought to pick up her pace. The car was slowing and
drifting to the curb. He must have seen her. Could she just run by without appearing weirdly oblivious or intimidated? Indecision reduced her
to a walk, and she worked to catch her breath, because the thought of
him coming upon her gasping made her feel vulnerable. Unless it was
something else entirely. Unless he was still hooked on her, still in love
with her, and that was why he was here. She swept back her hair and wondered if it could have been him outside her apartment last night. In the
strangeness of that memory, Bobby crept up her stairs. Bobby peeked
through her curtains.

An elderly man was tilting across the front seat of Bobby's car to look
out the lowering passenger-side window. He wore a gray sweater over a
collared blue shirt with a blue bow tie. Where's Bobby? she wanted to ask,
but wariness advised her to wait. Meanwhile the man waved a sheet of
paper in a friendly way. "Here's the thing. I must have missed my turn. Or
maybe not. Maybe I didn't come to it yet."

He appealed to her instantly. She liked everything about him, especially the fact that he wasn't Bobby. "It happens all the time," she told him. "There's a lot of funny little streets up here."

"I wanted to turn on Rabbit Hollow, which I did, I think, and then onto Cominsky, which is this one. But where's Sullivan?" He fluttered his notes in a vaudevillian spoof of futility.

"Sullivan?" she said, as if street names gave her singular delight.

"Yes. Sullivan." Just like that, he looked glad to be lost now that he'd found her.

"Well, it's not your fault. Whoever gave you directions sent you down Cominsky when you should have gone a block more to High Grove. Sullivan runs off High Grove. But it doesn't run through."

"Oh. Okay. So I go back and then over." He lacked the flexibility to scan behind him, but he made a good try. "I see. Thanks." He waved and took off, scooting in and out of a driveway, gathering speed to the peak, where he went right.

She didn't immediately absorb that he was gone. Something lingered, a demand for her attention, and then hateful Bobby came sweeping back. Shouldn't that be his real name? Fat Snide Balding Hateful Bobby Crimmins. What a prick! In the last days they'd spent together, she'd felt a pull toward reconciliation that she rebuffed by calling him names, by mocking him, even though she should have known better. He was not a snake to poke carelessly. Prime among his early triumphs had been his discovery that satirizing mutual acquaintances could get her giggling crazily. He zeroed in on a deep well of contempt she barely knew she possessed. At times he left her doubled up, begging for relief, which made him do more, unable to resist the pleasure of bringing her to giddy tears, along with the blow job he knew would be his reward after he performed for her, his adoring audience of one. Under her appreciation, his skills flourished, his barbs teaching his dangers, along with his number one rule, which was that while he might mock the world, only a fool would mock him.

She sat on the curb, her long legs folded, knees sticking up on either side of her bowed head, eyes on the gutter, where twigs, grass, and debris stared up from the mud. She poked a shard of glass, a dingy gum wrapper.

Following their breakup, he had skipped around town, explaining that he was "fine—just picking up the pieces." If the moment felt receptive, he would throw his hands high to thank heaven for rescuing him from that cold fish Janet Cawley. "Oh Lord, protect those poor fourth-graders!" Some friends urged her to retaliate against his bullshit quips dispensed in bars and restaurants like he was a campaigning politician, Bobby Crimmins running for small-minded prick. The problem for her wasn't so much what he said as the fact that she didn't care. All she wanted was to be rid of him. Her friends grew frustrated. How could she let him get away with it? After a while, their nagging became annoying, and she asked them to back off. Gradually, Bobby took over the entire space once occupied by their coupledom. And she hadn't cared about that, either. He could have them all if they were that shallow, that hopelessly stupid.

She wasn't going to run another step, she saw. Not today. It was a dismal realization made as she stood up. It hadn't been Bobby's car, but it had delivered him anyway, entangling her in his endless oppressive, suffocating vengeance. She aimed for home, and her feet appeared almost severed from her body as they flopped in and out of her downcast vision. If she had really wanted to end the pain of running uphill, she should have done this a lot sooner, simply given up.

She wasn't sure when she'd foundered, but she was down on the curb again with another three hundred yards, at least, before she was home. She felt chewed up and half swallowed. Some Jack Daniel's would lift her out of this funk. She imagined the heat flowing to her mouth from the lip of the bottle, then on to a place deep inside her, and that was enough to convince her to move.

But she'd barely gotten clear of the ground when anger tore her intention to tatters, and she was sagging backward until she lay flat across the sidewalk, her gaze filling with sky. Clouds ruffled the glare like furrows in snow, and the surrounding color went from sapphire to turquoise to teal and on to other gradations expanding over vast, inhuman distances with a sense of ghostly, terrifying fluidity and depth. Because in the end, Bobby had found a way to insinuate his malice past her indifference to all that he said against her. He'd worked until he got to her, until he got under her skin. When his gossip and lies failed, when nothing he tried seemed to matter to her, he thrashed around pointlessly and then made his move on her mother. And Isabel responded. Isabel welcomed what he did. Enjoyed it. Had the time of her life, and Janet, watching in disbelief, had known she was looking into a poison-filled cup she did not dare drink, and yet she had to know the taste.

She shut her eyes and felt that something gauzy had been ripped off an open wound. If the sky scared her, it was really time to get up and go home. But her mind could not move from under the blue emptiness streaming into her head, where it hung like the eye of a giant, beyond the reach of speculation. She was transfixed by waves of information delivered in shadowy insinuations she could not unravel. There were things that she knew, some philosophical, others scientific that she considered facts accepted by everyone. They were certainties. Verities. Of course the vastness of the universe was intimidating. Everybody knew that. Zillions of stars in the void hurling down corridors of light that made them visible but did not make them real, because the light proved only their possibility. They didn't have to exist out there any longer. It could be merely light left over, because they were—if they were—so far beyond anybody's grasp or measurement, no matter how smart or expert or—Well, okay, she knew that. And she knew they consisted of chemicals and minerals, just as she did. People were made of the same stuff as stars. Could that be true? It didn't seem that it could be. But she'd read it somewhere and felt confident about her memory. She could even see the paperback page. And if it was true of everyone, then it was true of her—of her blood and skin, her heart, lungs, liver, etc., all busily doing whatever they did—she had studied them, at least in dogs and cats—and the truth was they performed, these organs, stoically, indifferently, while at the very top of this pumping, sloshing hubbub in a sack, at the very crown sat her brain teeming with pictures and words electrically transmitted, and these were her thoughts, which she was inside right this second, remembering Bobby, remembering her mom. And afraid of the sky. She knew enough to smile, though her sense of humor wasn't working the way it was supposed to. She really had to get home. She was stretched out in the middle of the sidewalk. If Bobby drove past, he'd see that she was a complete mess. Wasn't that a good enough reason to get up?

Her hands adjusted, positioning to help her rise, but then she thought, Not really. Because Bobby wasn't coming. It had been some old stranger before, and it wasn't going to be Bobby ever.

She opened her eyes. The sky remained dotted with widespread clouds. Was it beautiful? Was it vast? Was it scary? As she tried to articulate what she saw, words confessed a diminishing faith in their ability to render precise, dependable relations between themselves and the things they ought to depict. Like the clouds, words were adrift and no longer valuable, not even as approximations, because—

The noise, a smack like the crack of a whip, jerked her into a sitting position. From atop a concrete stoop attached to a small brick one-story home, a woman looked across the lawn at Janet. "What's going on there? You got some kind of problem down there?"

"What?"

"Maybe you ought to let me know what's going on. Did you take a spill? Are you all right?" Holding a broom, the woman stood in a flower-print housedress under a white apron.

"No, no."

"Do you need some kind of help?"

"What? I'm sorry. No. Nothing's wrong."

"I thought you just said you weren't all right."

"No, I didn't."

"I beg to differ. I asked you, and you said, 'No, no.'"

"I was just saying, 'No, no,' I didn't fall down or anything."

"You been sitting out there on my curbing for quite some time. I thought maybe something happened."

"I was just sitting." It had probably been the screen door slamming that startled her. "I live right down the road."

"You live around here? Where?"

"Just down there a ways. At the Luckritzes'. I didn't mean to disturb you."

"You're not a Luckritz."

The woman's suspicion made Janet feel she needed to give a detailed explanation. "No," she said. "They have that apartment above the garage."

"You board down there, is that it?"

"Yes."

"Because you're not a Luckritz."

"No. I rent."

"It isn't something I see every day. Somebody sitting there like that on my curbing. A grown-up, anyway. Kids, sure, they do anything these days, but you were there quite a while. I thought maybe you were hurt or sick or lost or something."

"No. I'm okay." Janet brushed bits of debris off her sweatpants. "You might have seen me running. I run along here sometimes."

The woman squinted, sorting data she wasn't all that happy to have on hand. "Is that you?" She seemed to find Janet at the other end of a long dim tunnel.

"Again, I apologize if I upset you."

"No, no. Take more than that to upset me."

"Anyway. I apologize."

"Accepted." Satisfied enough to shrug, the woman said, "Beautiful day, isn't it?"

"I hear it's not going to last, though. Cold front headed our way."

"That's what I hear. Well, enjoy it while you can."

Janet nodded and walked backward, watching the woman flail away with her broom, raising a brown mist that swirled to the level of her knees, then a single brown leaf that wobbled and fell.

Beautiful day, Janet thought. Enjoy it while you can. Cold front on its way. Not going to last. She went straight up the stairs to her apartment, and in to the kitchen cabinet where the Jack Daniel's waited. After grabbing a quick swallow from the bottle and rinsing a cloudy glass, she poured a healthy splash. The level had dipped below the label, a discovery that made her uneasy, and she scanned the room as if somebody might have been stealing her whiskey.

The shower sputtered and came on freezing, and she jumped clear.

Her insides were fragile, as if coated in frost, the water a downpour of stones. Frantically, she fiddled with the handles. Her interior wanted more of the warmth the whiskey had offered but failed to sustain. She had the temperature as close to scalding as she could bear when she re-entered, turning her back to the spray. With the heat a facsimile of ardor, her hands fell to her thighs. She brushed the fuzz between and then stroked gently, coaxing. But she was remote, her actions robotic, and she stopped and stood there under the flood.

Trailing a towel she intended to wrap around herself, she wandered to bed. The long heave of her arm pulled up the comforter. She wanted to sleep, or at least shut her eyes, but her thoughts danced on, following the old man in Bobby's car and then finding Bobby, this time across from her mother in some murky depiction that could have been dinner at a corner table under a skylight with the moon above in the form of a huge silver wave. Had they really done that? Yes. At the Rivertop Castle, the restaurant everybody thought the finest within a hundred-mile drive and that Bobby declared one of the finest in the world. That was the kind of hyped-up bull he specialized in. He had an assortment of such pretentious catch-phrases, which he'd utilized on Janet, so it was safe to bet he'd played her mom with the same bag of tricks. And yet she couldn't be certain, could she? Because she couldn't really know what they'd whispered when they were alone together, her ex-husband and her mom. She'd tried, picturing them a thousand times, but no matter how detailed, no matter how thorough her invention, an aura of mystery prevailed because she could not hear them. She could not make them speak. She might see them exactly, their lips and tongues moving, but their words were their little secret.

She turned on her side, then sat up and flopped, going one way and the other. The shock of her initial response was back. Only now it possessed a complicated, mythical scope. With her mother dead, memory showed Bobby escorting her corpse in a plum-colored tunic, the fantastic dimness making her disintegrating body slim and youthful. At a table for two, their mouths moved in a silent duet, while a steady stream of maniacal candlelit smiles fled across her mother's face in a sequence that went from sad to haughty to teasing. She overflowed with delight, radiated gratitude. She was surprised and then pleased. She was flirtatiously wounded but coy. Flirtatiously alarmed. Demure. Momentarily regal and, for an instant, lewd.

Janet needed another drink. Maybe she should get out of the house. Go to the mall or somewhere for lunch. See a movie. She must have dozed, because once on her feet, she felt somewhat refreshed, and the bizarre scraps that lingered from her fading thoughts seemed to prove by their peculiarity that she must have been dreaming.

The drink was lovely but left the fifth empty. From her dresser, she removed underwear, socks, jeans, a pullover, and a ratty old hooded Chicago Cubs sweatshirt. But then, seized by an impulse of groundless dissatisfaction, she flung it all away.

Soon she was rooting through her closet in an aggressive, ambivalent hunt. The outcome was a very different style of top, this one an elegant slate-blue fleece sweatshirt from Victoria's Secret, sharing a hanger with matching checkered leggings. She switched her bra and underwear for items with a little more kick, silk lace, some frills. Bobby had loved buying her this kind of outfit, and there was always a detectable shift in Wayne's interest when he realized what she had on. As she perched on the edge of the bed to tug on the leggings, her gaze fell across a jump rope with heavy red handles coiled in the corner. Reminded of the hardware store and the garden hose, she smiled at the memory of her run-in with Big Baby Dog and his sleek sidekick and then little Robbie Oberhoffer. She stood, the sweatshirt tumbling down her upstretched arms, brushing her bare ribs in a pleasant flutter. At her bathroom mirror, she added light lipstick, some blush, mascara, a little undereye concealer, and for some reason began to doubt that Robbie Oberhoffer had been her student that very first year. She was sure, then unsure. To settle the matter, she checked the manila envelope of class photographs she kept in her bottom dresser drawer. And there he was, right where he belonged, brightening her beginning, a button of a boy, second from the left, front row, thumbs in his front pockets, nine and freckled. She had to smile, remembering Mr. Lanky from the hardware store. In her classroom, he had been one of a select few who radiated their wish to become something they couldn't name and probably would never manage. But who did? And what was it, really? In the photo, his fledgling body stood poised on the brink of turning into a teenager for whom it would be a short step to full-grown asshole like Bobby or Wayne. But there'd been something in Robbie. His father had done roadwork for the city. Maybe a foreman on one of those gangs by the time he was done. Robbie knew the value of hard work. A dutiful, earnest quality had reached out to her in those days, just as it had this afternoon. He'd written a story about a boy and a bear, and when she'd complimented it, he'd felt obligated to reveal that it was really about him and his dog, Nails. In the story, the dog had appeared as a bear, he told her, sharing his secret. The bear and the boy were best friends, and they had adventures. She remembered enjoying the whimsy and sly humor and wondered if she still had the story in a box somewhere. When she'd asked him to read it aloud to the class, he'd anchored his feet, looking ready to fight. There'd been a part about alligators in the neighbor's swimming pool and hidden messages on the radio that only the bear could understand because they were in a special animal code that was "sublinamal." That was the way he'd misspelled and mispronounced the word. She remembered even that. And then he'd shown up by her car today after she'd given him that hard stare before she knew who he was. She'd better learn to be more careful about who she gaped at. As she'd discovered the hard way, her students grew up, and you never could tell.

To spruce up her hair, she bowed, sending the length tumbling forward. Working with her favorite round brush while applying spray to the underside, she remembered how she'd collapsed and sat on the curb. Fucking Bobby. And Wayne, too. With their dicks and their egos. One in each hand, they're stroking away or getting you to do it for them. Stroke me, stroke me, she thought, trying to find her hip-length brown quilted jacket. And she needed different shoes. Quickly, she settled on black suede flats before hesitating at the door, making certain her purse contained the essentials—billfold, car keys, and keys to both her apartment and Bernice's house.

She decided to go to the liquor store on Anderson Court. It was a little out of the way, but after imagining Bobby on the prowl in her neighborhood, she felt sensitive about anybody, even clerks, tracking her drinking habits. She browsed a while and eventually pulled down a liter of Jack Daniel's. Acting casual and curious, she waited for the nerd behind the counter to turn from the overhead TV.

"Is this any good?" she asked, tapping the bottle. "This— What is it? Whiskey?"

His attention kept jerking to the TV, where cars squealed into an alley. "Jack Daniel's. Sure. It's whiskey. A lot of people like it."

As he started to ring her up, she waved at the shelf behind him. "Let me have one of the little ones, too." Pints and half-pints stood side by side, and she hoped it appeared she was accommodating an afterthought. "The cuter one."

He shot her a discontented smile. "They're both cute."

"The smaller." She took her time removing her billfold from her purse.

"That do it?"

Tired of her fake naïveté, she pocketed the half-pint and showed him a devilish grin. "For now."

In the lot outside, she wrapped the plastic bag tightly around the liter, then placed it on the floor of the backseat with the blankets and towels over it. She drove straight to the mall, where, after breaking the seal and taking a gulp, she arranged the half-pint in her purse so it could go with her into the cineplex.

Posters were displayed like paintings in a gallery, and she perused them before deciding on *Mercury Rising*. She bought a vat of popcorn and, blinded by the blast of light from the screen, waited until seats manifested in the dimness. Because she'd arrived late, the story had complexities she couldn't immediately untangle. But the couple in front of her seemed even more confused, arguing plot points and wondering whether or not to walk out. They stayed put, though, and grew attentive while Janet sipped her bourbon, munched popcorn, and conducted her own debate about the wisdom of leaving and returning when the next show started so she could see it from the beginning. But then she gleaned enough to understand that the little boy was autistic and had deciphered a government secret, provoking the wrath of a ruthless, arrogant bureaucrat. Bruce Willis was playing a down-on-his-luck but good-hearted FBI agent whose damaged spirit had not been fully broken. She knew enough to enjoy the far-fetched action sequences, especially the shredding of a villain trying to kill Bruce and the boy. The bureaucrat's obsession with the bewildering dynamics of trust and deception struck an interesting chord. Brilliant, alone, and prey to a cold-blooded assassin, the little boy had only Bruce Willis to count on. His mother and father had been murdered, a fact that made the overwrought music with its insistence on fear, grief, and mourning hard to resist. Calling the whole thing stupid could not keep tears from trying to break out. She imagined the entire theater filling with unhappiness. The effect was weirdly sweet as the credits scrolled and a dozen or so people straggled out. When the ceiling lights came up, she was alone amid popcorn debris, candy wrappers, and drink containers. She had the jittery, uncomfortable sensation that her interior was no longer correctly situated in her body. A young man carrying a big green garbage bag tramped down the aisle, and his glance ordered her out.

In the lobby, she thought she might go to another movie, yet she ended up in front of a cutout figure of Bruce Willis. He was thinner than in real life, she bet, and maybe shorter, because they were face-to-face. His overall expression attempted intensity along with wounded knowledge, which was probably his idea of the character's tragic condition in the story. But then she saw something else. She placed her hand on the cardboard shoulder. With a few more pounds and some hair removed, he could pass for Bobby Crimmins. They shared the smirk of an essentially snide mind. Peering into the unblinking mockery of his gaze for an interval governed by something other than time, she turned on her heel. A set of cadenced, militaristic sensations rallied her and carried her to the escalator. The glass doors parted, and she hurried into the afternoon light, having decided to go to Bobby's office. She'd pay him a litle surprise visit. Give him a taste of his own medicine.

The lot was crowded for a weekday afternoon. When she sprinted in front of a slowly moving black sedan, braking wasn't enough for the woman driver, who had to honk. Janet smiled, happy to be of service, and in those same seconds detected a familiar shape that turned out to be a silver Mercury Grand Marquis floating along the adjacent lane. Then the old man at the wheel glanced at her, and the moment drifted outside the norm, rising briefly into a cloud of magical premonition. Logic hastily sought to counter the likelihood that he'd actually seen her with the proposal that he had simply looked in her direction. Besides, he was inside a moving vehicle obscured by parked cars, so how could she be sure what she saw. Still, her pulse quickened with a surge of excited agreement as she gave in to the impulse to hurry to her car.

The Mercury had progressed to the exit, where traffic held it up long enough for her to arrive behind it. The old man cruised onto the street and went right. Bobby's office lay to the left, but she followed the old man. Something about their paths crossing this second time intrigued her, as if his repetition in her day offered a key that, if decoded, would show a meaningful pattern.

The steady traffic plowed on into the shimmering afternoon. Realizing they were headed into the countryside, she felt prompted to examine the old man's license plates. He had Illinois tags, but they were going away from Illinois and off into western Iowa, leaving behind the strip malls and restaurants marking the outskirts of Belger. She felt like the boy in *Mercury Rising*, discovering secrets. Random clues could be followed to conclusions rich with insight into the way her life was unfolding. A sudden alert cut through her, a spine-tingling blast, as she associated the movie with Bobby's car and the old man's car. Whoa, she thought. Mercury, Mercury, Mercury.

Whenever massed trucks or some haphazard conglomeration of cars obscured the old man, she maintained her speed and lane, eyeing the interference. As she lost contact for perhaps the third or fourth time, the momentary void filled with a spooky proposition that the Mercury had vanished or that it had never been there at all.

On either side of her, endless farmland spread its repetitive corn stalks picked clean and turning brown, while the interstate stretched on like a ruler laid flat to a vanishing point. She checked her speedometer and, as if to crush the life out of some annoying creature, stomped the accelerator. The car gave a burst. The needle wobbled at seventy and swayed on to eighty. Ahead, the horizon remained unchanged, and the feeling that she was getting nowhere fast began to weigh on her. She was rocketing down the stretch of road at nearly ninety miles an hour.

An exit offered escape onto a parallel two-lane, where she pulled to the shoulder after a few hundred yards. The neck of the half-pint extended from her purse. She felt like she'd been dreaming and laughed at the rather bizarre and certainly risky possibility that she'd been asleep at the wheel. But the hint of something nocturnal resonated, insistent and calling. It promised that she could penetrate the strangeness of the last half hour if she thought about it hard enough.

Satisfied that no traffic was coming, Janet took a drink. It annoyed her to be nagged by this thing she couldn't put her finger on. She ducked for another quick sip. It had to come to her, whatever it was, demanding to be known yet refusing to emerge, pressuring her with the eerie boldness of an apparition.

Easing back onto the road, she searched for a way across the four-lane so she could head back to town. Eventually, she found a viaduct, and halfway over, she allowed her gaze to flow to the horizon, where the old man was long gone into the vista of corn and sky. Bobby, she thought. It was him. She had set out to see him and ended up here feeling bereft of something that had been hers long before Bobby, long before Wayne, long before anybody.

16

That was nice of Irma to call," said Hazel in a sympathetic tone.

Lord, save me, thought Bernice. She sat with her head against the window of the Toyota, watching Newton Avenue go by. After the lunacy back at the house, all she wanted was a little peace and quiet. She'd run around, showering and getting all gussied up with Hazel counting the seconds—new Depends, some well-aimed deodorant, loads of Cashmere Bouquet, a clean bra strapping her in, and those big earrings back on and pinching already. She'd skipped the brooch, but while tucking it away for safekeeping in her jewelry box, she'd bumped into the fake pearl necklace Toby had presented her, all smiles and even giving a little bow, on their twenty-fifth wedding anniversary. She'd sort of felt Toby was with her, his big hands bungling the clasp as she put it on. Then it was back to the race—different pair of orthopedic lace-ups, new knee-highs, and finally, her gray jacket, which, surprisingly, had come through yesterday none the worse for wear. But somehow, in spite of all her hard work, she'd done something so harebrained she couldn't believe it. She'd put on her baby-blue pantsuit. If only she'd taken a second to think. It just wasn't right. It didn't feel serious, the way it was so comfortable and almost fun. She was really down in the dumps with this sense of being somebody who couldn't get out of her own way. A bull in a china shop, crashing around. But there wasn't a thing she could do about it now, because Hazel sure wasn't going to take her back. Not that Bernice had a better idea, anyway. She'd put all her eggs in yesterday's basket with that beautiful blouse and skirt, the brooch just so. Not that she could be blamed for the way things had gone last night. She'd done her part—done her best. Not that she was perfect, because she sure wasn't, and she wasn't ever going to be perfect, and she was tired of trying. She would just have to hope her baby-blue pantsuit was good enough. It was sort of sky-colored and innocent, after all.

"Bernice?"

"What?"

"Did you hear me about Irma?"

She nodded and tried to concentrate on the neighborhood outside her window. Aside from helping distract her from Hazel, the view seemed worth her while, since this might be the last time she ever saw it.

"That it was nice she called. Don't you think?"

"I guess."

"But I don't know why you jumped down her throat. Did she say something to get you going?"

Hazel had to know she was trying to put that bollixed-up phone call out of her mind, didn't she? Of course she did. But because she liked to air her dirty laundry in public, she figured Bernice did, too. The next corner was Prescott, a narrow bumpy cross street, and old Mr. Baumhover was out raking leaves in front of his boxy brown house. Hazel might be putting on a buddy-buddy front, like her biggest concern was Bernice's welfare, but Bernice knew better. She was mortified that she'd let Hazel witness her and her daughter with their claws out, the fur flying. It must have given her quite a thrill.

"What in the heck is Bernice up to? That's what I kept thinking. And I'm still thinking it." Hazel cleared her throat, like she needed to be pitch-perfect to deliver her next shot. "At least talk to the poor girl, I thought. Lord, you're her mother."

Now, bickering with Hazel was about the last thing Bernice wanted, but in spite of watching intersections and houses, she was fuming, her brain taken over by riled-up remarks, until it would have taken a much bigger person than Bernice Doorley not to say, "I talked to her."

"Thank goodness. Lord, I was starting to think you'd passed out over there."

"I don't know what you're blathering about."

"I guess you could say you talked to her, but it'd be stretching the point."

"So stretch it. Let's leave it at that."

"You know what I'm getting at, Bernice."

"I shouldn't have been forced to talk to her, and I wouldn't have if somebody hadn't been such a busybody they picked up my phone."

"Oh, sure. Blame me." With a shrug Hazel claimed to be innocent, abused, and used to it.

The tunnel of trees overhead mingled their tips in a splintered dome that did little to block out the sun, which flashed, all at once blinding. Bernice squinted and looked away into a space speckled with floaters, a bunch of insects that weren't really there. And then a snatch of bark shot by, as clear as a photograph, and she recalled the sad way all these trees were dying. There was a plague of some kind. Bugs or beetles. As far back as she could remember, these big tall trees had stood in their grand rows on both sides of Newton Avenue, but now there wasn't a single one without sickly, scabby bark. The blight wasn't going to be satisfied till it took them all. "You can see the rot in almost every one of those poor trees," she murmured.

"It's a pity."

"You'd think somebody could do something about it."

"I guess they can't. Or they would. It's sad, all right, but we won't have to let such things trouble us much longer. It'll all be behind us soon."

Bernice nodded in agreement with what struck her as wisdom, but after a second she wasn't even sure she'd understood what Hazel had said or meant to say. She rearranged her grip on her purse, taking a long hard look at Hazel. She had this sense of an unpleasant, unacceptable something that Hazel was trying to slip by her, like a snake in the grass.

Occupied by a series of potholes, Hazel was too busy to notice until the silence grew lengthy. She glanced over, but a jarring bounce drew her back. "Ouch," she said, speaking for her car. Bernice didn't give an inch. She was determined to let her stare do her talking, and if that meant things in the car got frigid and uncomfortable, so be it. When Hazel peeked a second time, she knew something was up. "What? What? Why are you looking at me like that?"

"What was that you said?"

"About what?"

"About those poor trees."

"You know what I mean. You know what I said."

"I'm saying maybe I don't. Maybe I do, but maybe I don't."

"C'mon. The end of the world, Bernice. The angels sweeping in with their sickles and whatnot. On them horses. Once that gets going, well, those trees and their problems won't concern us much, I don't think." Now that she was giving her little spiel, Hazel smiled contentedly straight ahead, like Bernice wasn't even there. "What's that way he has of saying it? I don't know if it's from the Bible or not, but it sounds like the Bible."

"Who?"

"Reverend Tauke."

"I don't know. Saying what?"

"I'm trying to remember. Though you get my point. Once the Rapture finally comes, we can just forget about the trees and a whole lot else. Put all those worries down."

Bernice started stroking her purse the way she might pet Ira or Elmira, somebody dear, on her lap. The fact that onrushing disaster made Hazel cheerful shoved Bernice up against a large troubling question that she couldn't put into words. But with one sad tree after another rocketing past, she had to wonder what it would be like to have no interest in what lived or died. She supposed there must be benefits, because plenty of people were eager to get a taste of that way of thinking. But when Bernice tried to put herself in their place, she couldn't come up with much except shortage and scarcity, an empty pantry with dust on the shelves. Just nobody home, she guessed.

"What'd Irma want?" Hazel asked. "Did she have something particular in mind?"

"Oh, you can bet she did. And not to pass the time of day. No, that wasn't what she was doing."

"What was she doing?" Hazel asked.

They were stuck at that goofy red light where five streets converged in a boneheaded affair that had been causing accidents since the beginning of time. Once a Western Auto had occupied the right-hand corner. That Burgmeyer had owned it, the older of the five brothers with the son who went crazy and tried to murder some total stranger. At least that was the way it had looked from the outside, though there might have been more to it. The first Dairy Queen had been on the opposite corner. She remembered the white-painted walls, so shiny on opening day, and the line of people that went clear around the block with everybody talking about the attempted murder in the alley behind the Western Auto just across the street. Both were gone now. Turned into gas stations with mini-malls. What did anybody need with two of the darn things? A Dairy Queen would still be nice. People always liked ice cream. The idea was probably to have a station convenient in both directions, though she hoped people hadn't grown so shiftless that they couldn't cross over to fill their tank. She could imagine crowds gathering at Dairy Queens from one end of Belger to the other. Or maybe she was remembering when that first one came to town and all of a sudden regular ice cream was old hat. People gawked at the white creamy stuff oozing from that silver nozzle in a spiral to fill the cone and pile on up. And always that little curlicue like a pig's tail at the very top. Then some sprinkles or maybe not.

"Lord," said Hazel, "talking to you is like pulling teeth."

Bernice went so far as to give Hazel a lackadaisical shrug, then hugged her purse tight, as if such a pose were an accepted signal for Hazel to leave her alone.

"I was there, you know," Hazel said. "When you two went at it. The least you could do is let me in on what Irma had on her mind, calling like that at just such a moment."

"It's nothing for you to concern yourself about."

"I think maybe it is, because I think she caught wind of all this we're up to, and that's why she called."

Hoping to close the subject, Bernice said, "That's what it was, all right."

"Just what I thought." Hazel turned onto Koster Road. They were taking the back way to Reverend Tauke's and soon would pass Trentwood Cemetery and, after a while, move along the rear of the Catholic girls' college, Saint Agnes. "But I'll tell you what I didn't understand," Hazel said, "and the truth is, I still don't—is why you jumped down her throat instead of talking to her about what's going on."

"What do you mean? Talk about this—what we're doing?"

"Well, she called you up, Bernice. I couldn't help but wonder what made her do it. Maybe it was meant to be. Maybe it was to give you your last opportunity."

"For what?"

"Well, to let her in on what's going on."

"Such as."

"Bernice, you are not as thick as you're letting on. The Rapture. Maybe she was supposed to call you. Give you a chance to put your house in order."

"Am I in the ballpark that you're thinking I should have told Irma I'm about to go off with Jesus?"

"He could have sent her to you, you know. Made her make that call."

"Jesus."

"Or one of his angels. Whispering in her ear to ring you up. I'm talking about the funny way things happen."

"You can say that again."

"I don't see what's wrong with thinking that could be, because it could be."

"You know as well as I do that Irma would call the little men in white coats. Next thing I know, they'd be drivin' up to my door and hauling me off to the loony bin." Bernice sighed and became aware of how she'd started fiddling with her necklace, kind of consoling the beads.

"You told Janet Cawley."

"What's Janet Cawley got to do with it?"

"You told her, and she's not even your daughter, now, is she?"

Bernice tugged some slack in the seat belt. "Let me see if I can show you what's wrong with where you're going with this thing, because you should stop before you get there." Nudging her backside to the door, she folded her hands over her purse. "I know Janet Cawley's not my daughter, and I know I told her. Because that's why I told her. Because she is not my daughter."

"Well, if we're gone tomorrow and you don't ever get to speak to Irma again, this would have the look of a missed opportunity."

"Hazel, the way things work between Irma and me, that kind of conversation is not in the cards."

"Why?"

"It just isn't."

"That's the past you're talking about."

"Yes, it is."

"So maybe this could have been different. What I'm thinking is maybe there didn't have to be this big fight. What if that's what happened? No big fight."

"I don't know. You tell me."

"How can I? That's what I'm getting at. You made sure to pick a fight, and now we'll never know."

"She was getting ready to lecture me. I just didn't have it in me to sit there with her up on her high horse, ready to let me know in no uncertain terms what a senile old fool I am. No, thank you."

"So she probably didn't get a word in edgeways."

"I told you. I didn't want to hear it."

"I may be sticking my neck out, Bernice, but you can't know whether you wanted to hear it, because you are not privy to what she was going to say until after she says it. And from where I stood, it looked like you jumped in before she got ten words out."

Bernice was grateful that Hazel was at least partially busy with driving. Not that she wasn't still a handful. "With some people, one word is more than enough, Hazel. You know that."

Hazel harrumphed as if an obvious insult had come her way. "Now, everybody in the world knows you two had a terrible falling-out, but nobody knows why, and not because they haven't racked their brains. It's because you never told a living soul."

"Because I don't know."

"That's what you say."

"And why do you think that is? Why do you think I say that?"

"But what if this was your chance to find out?"

"I don't think Irma knows, either. We both just went off the track. Wheels in the dirt. And then we got farther and farther off. And it's been a rough road ever since."

"I guess that could be."

"Trust me. It is."

"Well, you should know. But I'm thinking there are times when we know a lot more than we let on. So I'll just say that and let it go. Make of it what you want. But time goes by and feuds—even the worst kind—ought to end."

Bernice opened her purse and gazed in as if hoping to shrink and take cover inside. "That's a nice sentiment, but it don't apply. We get along fine just as long as we keep our distance."

"That don't seem right. Not between mother and daughter."

The way Bernice snapped her purse shut, it might have been her teeth taking a vicious bite. "You know why you think that way, Hazel? If I had to guess, I'd guess it's because you don't have a daughter. So you are the owner of some half-baked ideas on the subject. Kids and all. Up to a point, you don't really know what you're talking about. I mean, without having any." From the look that flashed in Hazel's eyes and the noise she made, Bernice might as well have just slapped her across the mouth.

"If you'd rather I shut up, Bernice, say so."

"You're free to say whatever you want."

Hazel took the next corner, like following the road made her furious. Momentum flung Bernice against the grab of the seat belt. All of a sudden they were on Spencer Drive, which sent them along the front of Saint Agnes College. "You just made a wrong turn, you know."

"I like to go this way."

Young girls in bright fall jackets hurried over the lawn and along pathways curling amid stone buildings.

"This way's going to run you smack into mall traffic."

"That don't worry me."

The hilly campus displayed scattered trees that clung to spare leaves. Vacant flower beds stood amid stubborn shrubbery edging the gray foundations of the buildings. Bernice knew trouble was on its way as she pretended to admire the view. She'd stirred up a hornet's nest, but no matter what the consequence, nothing could be as bad as if she'd let Hazel give her advice about Irma.

"I just think that's a dirty low blow, if you ask me," Hazel said. "I really do."

"What is?"

"Getting on me about my misfortunes in that arena."

"I'm not getting on you."

"There's no need for that kind of cheap shot." Hazel was flushed, her jaw grinding. "Let's not mince words. That was a cheap shot."

Bernice slipped the earring from her right ear and stared at it as if there might be some good advice inscribed on it somewhere. "I'm just trying to tell you something, and you may not want to hear it, but this whole business with kids, and they're little and cute and then they take over with their demands, and then they grow up. It's not all it's cracked up to be."

"That may well be. But what I'm waiting to hear, Bernice, is word one of why you think it's all right to stab me in the back."

"Oh, Hazel!" Maybe there was more she ought to say, but the closest thing she had to an idea was a mess she didn't want to go near.

" 'Oh, Hazel,' what?"

"Just stop it. There's no need for this. Let's just drive." She sat there rubbing her ear.

"Okay." Hazel stomped her foot, and the Toyota leaped. "But what there's no need for, Bernice, if you want to know what there's no need for, is you reminding me I never had any kids. Like it's something that just slips my mind. That and your bragging and getting your digs in at me."

"I'm not trying to get any digs in at you. I don't know what you're talking about."

"My barren womb."

"Oh, don't get so dramatic."

As if the only way to believe such a preposterous remark had been made was to hear it again, she said, " 'Don't get dramatic!' Why not, Bernice? You are."

Bernice wiggled into the corner and turned to the window. A slight girl was running for dear life down a steep slope on the campus, her black hair streaming over her knapsack, and she wasn't wearing a jacket or even a sweater.

"Call me dramatic. Look who's talking," said Hazel, sounding like the most disgusted person in the world.

"You're beating a dead horse. Now get off it."

"Easy for you to say."

"And you're driving too fast."

"Who says? You?"

"No. The speedometer."

"Fine. I'll slow down. But why am I so dramatic? Is it because I actually had the nerve to say a couple words about myself? About my own life? I did have one, you know. Like it or not."

"Fine."

"That's what I think bothers you."

"If you say so." All of a sudden, Bernice was hungry. She felt like she could eat a horse and, as luck would have it, a minimall was on the right. "Could we pull in up there? I'm starving."

"There's going to be food at Reverend Tauke's. People are bringing dishes."

"It'd only take a second."

"You're fine," Hazel said, racing past, making the intersection and light. "We'll be there in a jiffy, plus I have some snacks here that I keep." She indicated her purse balanced on the console between them.

"Those are for your diabetes."

"You can still have one."

"No, thanks." Bernice pivoted, eyeing the retreating advertisements for hot dogs, chips, and coffee. Another thing she'd never get to do. "Irma," she said, without knowing why for a second or two.

"What about her?"

"What?"

"What about her?"

"I don't know." Did she have to explain everything? Even when she didn't understand?

"Why'd you say it then?"

"Her phone call. We were talking about her and that phone call."

"Oh, right."

"And the whole deal of kids, but you don't have any. Can we say that? It's not a crime, but it is a fact. You don't have kids."

"I don't think I was saying it was a crime. I think what I was trying to get at is that it was a tragedy."

"Okay. Sure. That's how you see it. It's a tragedy. I can see that."

Hazel appeared to shrivel in size, her head sinking, as if someone were pushing down on the top of her skull. "So I should never bother to have a thought about kids? That just doesn't seem right. Because of my limitations? I don't think I can go along with that."

Bernice spied a stone bluff that seemed to be floating straight at them and realized they were drifting toward the shoulder. "Hazel! Watch where you're going!"

"I got my eye on it."

Bernice planted her hands against the dash, like she could slow the car. "You still got to steer."

Already grappling with the wheel, Hazel fought the dips and warps in the pavement. The boulders sailed close but went off to the rear, and the way ahead looked okay, except that Hazel had situated them funny.

"Now you're going down the middle."

"You keep this up, I'm going to put you in the backseat."

Clutching her purse tighter, Bernice crossed her ankles. "I think I told you I almost had a terrible accident earlier today. So I'm a little hyper on the subject."

"I gotta pee," Hazel said and she started swiveling her head back and forth.

The way the poor thing was carrying on, Bernice couldn't imagine what Hazel was seeing except some crazy blur. Nodding in sympathy, she said, "Again?"

"And bad. I got to stop. I won't make it to Reverend Tauke's."

The nearing intersection offered a mess of options, lanes and lights and white painted arrows hooking to the right, which Hazel took as giving her license to turn and speed under the blinking amber.

"Easy now," said Bernice.

"I ain't peeing myself."

They bounced up a driveway into the Jefferson Mall, where the Harvest National Bank and Trust was the first establishment coming up on their left. "They got a bathroom in the bank," Bernice told her. But Hazel roared on by, her eyes dead ahead while she jiggled and jerked. "Your Depends will keep your dress safe, and if we need fresh ones, we can—"

"I'm not wearing any."

"What? Are you crazy?"

"I'm not wearing any! Don't make me talk!"

Now Bernice understood the full-blown nature of the crisis they were in, and she planted her feet square on the floor. "Where you aiming?"

"Loefler's," Hazel said.

Loefler's was a family-owned restaurant, a cafeteria-style joint with pretty good eating located near the main mall entrance. Bernice could see the low roof up ahead, the red and green letters of the name in gigantic handwriting. Hazel was zigzagging through lanes of parked cars. "Now, don't kill anybody." Hazel honked timidly while Bernice kept her eyes peeled for unsuspecting pedestrians or cars.

"I ain't gonna make it."

"Sure, you are. We're almost there." Bernice felt like a copilot, though she had no idea what a copilot did.

Reaching the street that fronted the mall, Hazel threw the car into park. "Oh, boy. Oh, boy," she whimpered, battling the seat belt.

"Don't forget your purse."

"Right, right." She flung open the door and scooted to the walkway, where her attempt at normalcy left her crooked and humped over.

The Toyota was pretty much crossways, and Bernice hadn't even begun to consider what came next when the blast of a car horn behind her made her just about jump out of her skin. Inches from her rear bumper, a gaudy Buick was revving its engine and flashing its high beams. Wouldn't you know it? Even though Hazel's door was open and sticking out, there was plenty of room to get by for anybody who really wanted to. But apparently, this jerk preferred to sit there and stew. Just her luck. As she hobbled around to the driver's side, he rolled down his window in case she didn't know he was there.

"I'm going, I'm going," she told him.

"At least act like you have a nickel's worth of sense, even if you don't."

"You could go around. There's plenty of room."

"I'd like to know where." His face was nothing but blubber, all these folds fighting each other, his puffy lips sucking in air so he could snarl, "Just move it."

Oh, how she wished Toby was with her so he could teach this bum a lesson. Toby would've just left the door jutting out and hoped the guy tried something. But she didn't have the nerve. The Buick let loose a barrage of nastiness she couldn't believe. Did he think she wasn't going about things as fast as she knew how? The engine was running, so she didn't have to worry about that, and the gearshift looked pretty much like what she was used to, and so, ready at last, she checked behind her and then in front and almost died of fright when the Buick roared by on her left. Just like the big lummox could have done all along. What got into some people? But she'd better get a move on if she didn't want another jerk, maybe even a worse one, if that was possible, to show up.

The road went straight along the front of the mall, and she drove slowly, her fingers locked around the wheel, her whole body tied up in knots. She hoped Hazel had made it on time. Didn't want to think about the poor thing peeing all over herself in some public setting. Wasn't nothing easy anymore. She filled her lungs and let out a big sigh.

The end of the lot sent her left, and she flowed into the turn. Smooth as butter. It was a beauty, Hazel's little car. And Francis, her nephew, had just given it to her. The mere thought of that fact produced a wave of goose bumps. He'd handed over a brand-new automobile to his aunt. He was well off, sure. District manager for a chain of stores selling computers and TVs and those other kinds of players, VCRs and CDs and that other one. But still. Just to give somebody a car. The man wasn't made of money. Hazel must have done something right.

She wasn't sure whether to park and go look for Hazel or keep circling. It was hard to decide what was best, and wishing she had somebody to help her, the picture came to mind of that young girl running at the college with her long black hair and no jacket and this pained look like she would die if she didn't get where she was going. Probably late for class and looking so desperate. Bernice wanted to go back and give the poor kid a bit of advice about the things that mattered and the things that didn't. The engine was so smooth and quiet, Toby would have said, "This engine is purring, Bernice." Even the smell of the brand-new upholstery was pleasant.

Coming all the way around to where they'd hurried in not long ago, she angled toward Loefler's. It was all so smooth. At the front of the mall, another left would be needed. Fine by me, she thought. She'd be happy to oblige, just doing what she was doing, nudging the wheel and gliding like skates on ice. That was the feeling. Free and smooth and light, like Droessler's pond in winter when she and Isabel and Hazel and the Madigan twins and, oh, all the young girls flew hand in hand, squealing over that brightness. Their breath puffed out in streams into the air of the forest surrounding them with a fantastic tangle of ice-coated branches as far as the eye could see.

17

E VEN THOUGH THE DAY WAS still bright, Janet traveled through moody twilight. After a lunch of minestrone soup and a salad at the Olive Garden, she was coming to the end of the five-minute drive to Sun View Center, the small office complex where Bobby Crimmins had his office. Her stomach had turned queasy in the middle of her third cup of coffee, and the continuing discomfort argued against what she was doing as she slid into the empty space that waited beside the specter of Bobby's Mercury Grand Marquis. Chills, like snow melting, went down her spine. Unlike what had happened before, this situation was real. Bending low to frustrate anyone trying to see what she was doing, she took a sip of Jack Daniel's, and staying down, she stored it carefully under the passenger seat. In a voice that was familiar and trustworthy, she reminded herself, "You need to do this. He's always messing with you." She could feel him seeking to dishearten her right this second by warning that she was headed for trouble if she kept on.

Still, she pushed through the entrance and jabbed the elevator button. Every breath, every second, carried her closer to where he waited, content and proud of his skill to inflict harm and call it fun, as long as there was somebody willing to laugh till they cried.

Delivered to a carpeted hall of doors decked with names and logos, she paced until she saw Crimmins Real Estate over a metallic icon of a rooftop. What a joke, she thought, leaning on the door, which yielded with an animal sigh.

The receptionist was new, a frizzy blonde younger than Janet in a dark suit behind a small desk tucked into a corner. She looked up from a Rolodex, some documents in disarray alongside her personal crap. Her fake smile grew tentative it seemed as a mental filing system threw up a check mark. Though Janet was sure they had never laid eyes on each other, the woman was struggling with an impression of familiarity. Janet smiled, thinking how interesting this was. Had Bobby shown her a photograph—some sort of wanted poster?

The receptionist's fingers nudged the frames of the Vogue glasses that were less expensive-looking than she probably hoped. "May I help you?"

"If you would. I'd like to see Bobby Crimmins."

"Do you have an appointment?"

"You know," Janet said, and paused as if sharing a secret, "I don't. But I know him. And I saw his car outside. I only need a minute."

"But you really should have an appointment. His day is fairly booked. He has a million phone calls to return and—"

"A million?" She let out a sarcastic sputter.

"Well, that's a way of saying he's very busy. He just came back from—"

"Shhhhhhh!" She put her finger to her lips in a show of authority, even threat. "Maybe two minutes. Tell him, will you? 'Janet's here. She'd like maybe two minutes.'"

With the phone to her ear, the woman stalled in her approach to the intercom button. "Janet who?"

The Funny One, Janet thought, and then she said, "Cawley. Okay? The former Mrs. Crimmins."

Rapid blinking signaled factual understanding, while the arrival of a graver bit of information raised and lowered the receptionist's chin. "Just a minute," she said, setting down the phone.

"Remember, I'll be quick."

"Yes. Of course." She peeked back nervously from Bobby's door, as if she expected Janet to spring after her when she darted in.

Janet drifted, waiting. She wanted to be calm. She wanted to be steady. She did not want to pace. She imagined Bobby receiving the news of her proximity, his face glistening with a hunger for their showdown.

She visited the high wide window, the bland, sturdy drapery. Because of certain specific actions on her part preceded by certain specific decisions on her part that she could not now retract or disown, an event was about to occur for which she felt suddenly, shockingly ill equipped. Her hand, which she raised before her eyes, trembled. What should she do? What would her mother do? Janet noted a radiant figure beyond the window, and then as if it were a suit of clothes, she slipped inside. She let her hands flow in a wave reminiscent of a conductor before an orchestra, a queen before a worshipping world.

The receptionist had returned. She was watching Janet, having taken up a sideways stance bracing open the door. "He'd be happy to see you," she said in a voice so reverential it was revolting. "But remember not to take too long. Bobby really has a jammed-up day. So be considerate, all right?"

"Certainly. Thank you so much."

"You know how generous Bobby can be with his time."

"Well, if I stay past what's right, you can knock and stick your head in and remind me, okay."

"Bobby wouldn't like that. It'll suffice if you just keep in mind what I said."

Janet took hold of the knob, and after establishing her back to Bobby, she eyed the blonde and mouthed slowly: *Fuck you.* Stepping in, she met Bobby, disguised as some ordinary, soft-bellied, slightly balding, amiable fellow, rising from behind his desk. She made the gesture, the graceful wave of her hands flowing outward in queenly acknowledgment of her subject, but she was sadly inadequate, a hollow facsimile of her mother.

"Hi," he said.

She tried to endow the removal of her jacket with the flourish and flavor of an unveiling but felt graceless, her thoughts mired in a gray slop that spread to her sluggish tongue.

"Sit down," he told her. When she stayed standing, he stepped toward her. "Should we— What? Shake hands? You don't want a hug, I'm sure." Within inches, he waited, enacting miniature impressions of the various options. "Or do you? A hug? What? You're the boss."

She glanced to the window, where a square of sky waited, and it seemed her heart went flying toward that glare.

"I like the outfit," he told her. "It's casual, but something almost Victoria's Secret. Am I right?" She could see he was nervous, but it meant nothing to her. "Anyway, you look good. Sleek. I hope you don't mind me saying that."

She put her hand on the chair in front of his desk.

"Sure, sit. Okay." He scurried around to his high-backed dark brown leather office chair, but he didn't sit. Instead, he examined her nervously, shrugging at the way she was standing and staring at him. "Hey," he said. "Janet, what's with the enigmatic routine? C'mon."

She narrowed her eyes as if he fascinated her unexpectedly and she was intent on bringing his appeal into perfect focus. She bent over the desk, her flattened palms and elbows supporting her. Her jacket fell to the floor.

"What? Is something wrong? Did something happen?"

"I want to suck your cock," she said.

His eyes widened, the skin around them collecting in folds that seemed to declare he knew a good joke when he heard one. "Sure you do," he said, and chuckled.

"I mean it."

He scoffed, working at disbelief, while a reflex hope that she was sincere peeked out before he could stop it. He hid then, turning away. She expected he would collect himself and present a reconstituted, highly urbane figure. Which was fine with her. She had her own need for a break, because she'd spoken without the slightest idea she was going to say such a thing. And now she was realizing that she meant it. That she wanted him in her mouth. Wanted to look up as he swooned, wanted to stroke on in regal mastery, reducing him to gasps if she paused. Turning his verbal arrogance into grunts. Leaving his vanity wallowing in animal slobber. He was scowling at her when she caught sight of him once again, suddenly, strangely, as if an implausible time period had passed or one of them had left the room and someone else had come back. His eyes were evolving toward a laserlike interest that wanted to get inside her, but then he got a taste of what he might find there, and he flinched.

"C'mon, Bobby."

"What?"

He scanned the room as if some third party might be found to confirm that she had in fact said what he'd heard. Then it struck her that if he believed she was mocking and teasing him, he might also believe she had collaborators hiding nearby to enjoy the fun. "It's your office."

"What's that supposed to mean?"

"I'm just here. It's your office. I'm just here."

"Still a wack job, huh?"

"You're not going to pretend we never had any fun."

"Look, this is just—"

"What?"

"I don't believe you. To put it mildly. To put it bluntly. Sorry if I'm harsh, but this situation calls for harsh."

"Harsh is okay. You know that." She was inching along the desk, gouging the meat of her hip, sliding over the polished sheen.

"Just stay where you are," he said.

"Why?"

"Some of us have grown-up lives. Care to guess who?"

"You're being mean. Don't be mean. You knew this would happen someday. Don't pretend you never thought of this. You had to think about it. Just as much as I have."

"You sound like a goddamn porno book."

"Good. Because I feel like one."

"What do you really want?"

"I've been thinking about this for days. You know. Remembering. Remembering you for weeks. You know, trying to get up the nerve."

"Jesus Christ."

"Tell me what you want me to do. I'll do it."

"I mean this now. Just stop. Talk to me for a second, okay? Don't be so—don't be so—" He couldn't finish, his head shaking, his brain clearly fogging, everything floundering.

"Don't be so what?"

"Whatever. I don't know. Just don't."

She was close enough to spy the slantwise bulge in his pants where his dick was eager, even if he had his doubts. She'd have him in a second. He'd never be able to resist if she knelt before him, stroked his thighs, tugging his zipper down, lifting him out and taking him in her mouth, and when he was whimpering, when he was clutching her head the way he did, she would close her teeth like cleavers slicing. Like cleavers cleaving until they met. Snapping the prick's prick in half. She'd have it in her mouth then, her regal mastery reducing him to agony. Turning his verbal arrogance to screams. Leaving his vanity in bloody slobber. Astonished, helpless animal gore filling her mouth, and if she swallowed—

Again she traveled back, ascending from a cavernous hidden world to Bobby's office, where he stood behind his desk studying her as if she had burst into flame. Alarm mixed in his expression with tender worry, a genuine concern whose presence she could not explain and whose discovery in him dismayed her. "I need to sit down," she said, speaking quietly, hoping she made the impression of someone who knew enough to give in when she had failed, when sweat was seeping from every pore.

"I don't know what you're doing, Janet."

"I need to sit down." She retreated along the path she had forged, only now his desktop felt like a cliff of ice.

"I'm going to call Patricia in here now. Right this second."

"Who?"

"Patricia."

"Who, Bobby?"

"My receptionist. I think—"

"No. Please."

"I think I should. Whatever it is that's going on here is something I'm not comfortable with, and for both our benefits, I—"

"No, Bobby. Please. I'm sorry." When the back of her thighs bumped the chair, she knew she had found a sanctuary where none existed. She sat as if sitting were a form of rescue. "Let me calm down here, okay? But don't bring her in. Don't call Patricia."

"I have to tell you the truth, Janet. You're scaring me. You scared me a second ago, like I don't know what, and you're still scaring the hell out of me."

"I'm sorry."

"What are you doing?"

"I don't know."

"You came up here. You came walking in here."

"I know."

"You had to have a reason."

"A person would think so. I understand how you would think so. I would think so, too, and there may have been one—I think there was—but I don't know what anymore. I was thinking about you all day, and I—"

"Don't start that crap again."

"I don't mean thinking that way. But thinking in a different way."

"What way?"

"Different. I was mad at you."

"Okay. Now I believe you. You were pissed."

"Yes."

"That figures. Now I'm starting to see what was going on here. You were really pissed, and you came up here to what? To do something."

"I don't know."

"Get the goods on me. That's what I think. I certainly do. Get me into some kind of position, this compromising position, and then accuse me of God knows what. I'm calling Patricia."

"No, no."

"I'm not going to get caught in some bullshit conniving mess. Okay?"

"Okay."

"You understand."

"I need to put my head down." With her forearms crossed to provide the semblance of a pillow, she let her head sink. Entreating him with her upward gaze, she settled like a schoolgirl about to nap on her desk. His puzzlement was not something that could stop her, and his lack of interference, along with his continuing silence, seemed sufficient consent. Her arms cradled her forehead, their weave aiding her closed eyes to create a velvety darkness that deepened so she experienced herself in a realm of rest and peace. After a while in this hush, she felt she could say, "Maybe if we talked a little. I think I need to talk a little."

"Okay. I guess. But what's wrong with you?"

"Nothing. I'm okay."

The simple patter of their voices promised, if attended carefully, to calm the whirlwind that had almost carried her off. Inhaling, she felt grateful that the frenzy of her heartbeat was slowing enough to let her languish there contentedly.

"Janet," he said, as if doubting the wisdom of informing her that his patience was wearing thin.

"Yes," she answered. "Yes, Bobby."

"This is my office. I need to work here."

"I know."

"But you're just laying there."

"I thought we were going to talk for a little."

"Me, too. I said we could, but— We agreed, but—"

He stopped and she waited. "What?"

"I mean you just laid down."

"I need a little rest. Thanks so much."

"So let's talk, okay? If we're going to."

"In a minute. Just one minute. You're being so sweet. You really are."

"Here's what I'm thinking, Janet. Maybe we should go somewhere. I'm wondering about later on. Maybe we could meet for dinner. Even tonight is possible. You need to talk. Fine by me. I probably have my own complaints and, you know, chestful of heartbreak to unload and, you know, just air them out. I'm all for it. That's what people do. They have lunch or dinner and try to talk things through. Even divorced people, and maybe they learn that if they'd known how to talk before they got divorced, they would not— I mean, maybe they would not have ended up in the mess they did. Not that I mean us. I don't mean us. Don't think I mean us."

"No."

"Because I don't."

"Dinner might be nice, but I think talking now would be better. That's my vote."

"You know what I'm saying, though."

"Dinner seems a long way off. That's just what I'm feeling."

"Okay. I guess we could start now. But like this? You're just going to lay there? With your head like that?"

"Yeah. You could sit. You should sit, I think."

"I'm not so sure this is a good idea."

"It's okay. Go ahead, Bobby."

His clothing murmured, his chair squeaked, and she imagined him in his stately leather chair as he said, "Talk about what, Janet?"

"Mom."

"Oh."

"Oh," she said, discovering that his utterance introduced a way of speaking that she had been missing for a long time. "Oh. Oh. That's what I say. Oh."

"You're just going to have to speak up, Janet, okay? Because you are talking into the desk and into your arms, and—"

"Okay."

"It's only fair that I get to hear you."

"Sure."

"I mean, you have to know that I felt badly about what happened. I think if you know anything about me, you know I still feel bad. You know how fond I was of her. I tried hard to make things right."

"How's your work going, Bobby? Is everything okay?"

"What?"

He sounded startled, which she understood, because obviously, this was a question she should have asked when she first walked in instead of only getting around to it now. "Your work—your business."

"Why?"

"Is it going the way you'd like it?"

"It's fine."

"Good. I'm glad you're a success. You deserve it. You really do."

"I'm doing well. Yes. Thanks."

She felt mellow and pliant and full of appreciation for someone, or maybe everyone, including Bobby. Boundless warmth, along with contrition and tenderness, engulfed her, leaving her bewildered that she or anyone could ever try to live in any other condition. "Bobby?"

"What?"

"Could I have a drink of water?"

"What do you mean?"

"Some water in a cup."

"Well, sure, I know that. But the cooler is out in the hall. Is that what you want me to do?"

"I'd really appreciate it."

"All right. It's just in the hall. You take it easy."

"I'll be good."

"What?"

"I'll be good."

The rustle of his departure faded, and when she didn't hear the door close, she figured he must have left it open. How many thousands of times had she imagined Bobby and her mother bound together by an affinity sparking back and forth between them in the candlelight of the restaurant table they shared? They'd cruised the streets in Bobby's car, their mouths shaping the words of their appalling rapport.

"Here," he said, the cool side of a paper cup nudging her hand and dribbling onto her fingers.

Janet kept her eyes closed as she emptied the tiny cone-shaped container. She wanted every last drop before laying her head back down. "It really upset me, Bobby, when you were with Mom. Why did you do that?"

"I don't know what you mean."

"Those restaurants and all. The way you took her out, like on dates."

"Why call them that? They weren't dates."

"What were they?"

"That isn't fair. And you're talking into your arms again."

"Sorry."

"Because putting it that way isn't fair. And I don't think we're going to benefit from going all the way back there to all that and then calling them dates. Not either one of us. You know. Raking over those dead coals."

"You said we could talk."

"I know what I said. And you know why I did that. I liked her."

"Yes," she said. And Mom had liked Bobby. "I used to make up all these plans to ask her what was going on with you two, but it was her obligation to set the right mood, I thought. So I could feel I had the opportunity to ask. She should have done that, I think. It was her job. She was the one who could make that happen. The only one who could give some sign. That she needed to talk, too."

"I can tell you that she really wanted to talk to you about it all, Janet. She knew it was bothering you."

"Why do you say that?"

"Because it was, wasn't it—bothering you? She believed that, anyway. That was how she felt."

"But how do you know what she felt?"

"Well, she told me."

Why couldn't he see how selfishly he'd behaved? Why couldn't she find the words to declare what she had believed back then, and still believed—that her mother should have supported her over this man. All her life, she'd been waiting for a moment that would force her mother close, and when she'd divorced, she'd believed that time had come. Shared experience would reveal their similarities, their kinship—divorce would be their bond. But he had made it impossible. "I never dreamed you would do that, Bobby. It wasn't something I anticipated. I could never have anticipated it. Nobody could have, I don't think."

"It seemed natural enough at the time."

"Not to me."

"I liked her."

"She was my mom."

"Well, sure."

"So why, then? Did she say why?"

"Why what? I wish you'd sit up."

"I'm fine."

"Well, I'm not. This is too weird. It's creepy, okay? It's creepy."

"I'm sorry. I'm fine. Don't worry about it."

"It's not that easy."

"Help me—I'm asking for a little help, okay—all of a sudden you were spending all that time together. I always wanted to ask you about it."

"Well, you should have. And now you have."

"I mean, talk about creepy. That was creepy."

"This is going nowhere!"

His chair made a metallic fuss signaling that he'd started to stand, but then it whooshed and she knew he'd sunk back.

"But what's the answer, Bobby?"

"To what?"

"The secret between you."

"There was no secret."

"It seemed like there was."

"It was all in your head."

"It was not. Don't tell me it was all in my head. You took her to dinner. You went on drives. That wasn't in my head."

"No."

"That really happened. Don't say it didn't."

"Okay. But there was no big mystery. No big anything. I just wanted to make sure she knew me. You were going to trash me, I figured, paint me in an unattractive light, so I wanted to defend myself. Present my own case. I wanted to make a situation in which I could be a hundred and ten percent certain my true nature was clear to her, and if I managed that, well then let the chips fall where they may. Because we had this connection. We both felt we were kindred spirits. It was just something meant to be. It was this totally independent thing completely separate from you and me—from our catastrophe. Because we had something, Janet, your mom and me. We really did, and it was really something."

Peeking, Janet was treated to Bobby in a blissful trance. The glaze of his reverie was spellbinding, his happiness a window into the puzzle that had confounded her for so long. All those wordless vignettes in cars and restaurants and bars were simplified. No longer would Isabel and Bobby haunt her with their mysterious smiles, their mute and fervent hand-holding, like silent movie stars. She knew now that Bobby had enchanted her mother with mawkish soft-focus catchphrases such as "kindred spirits" and "soul mates" and "meant to be." She could hear him spinning his web. It was ridiculous. They were ridiculous. She wanted to believe that her mother must have seen through his charade, but she knew better. She had hoped and waited, but poor Isabel had been lost in Bobby's spells just as she had been lost long ago to her husband, Janet's father, who had dazzled her when she was young and hopeful. "Do you know what she said the only time I ever got her to say anything about it, Bobby? Do you?"

"I might. But I don't think so."

"She called herself an old hag. She was an old hag, she said, and so the attention of any young man was a treat and not something she could scoff at, even if the man was her 'daughter's discard.'"

"That's it, Janet. Right there." His voice quivered with the strain of withheld accusation. "That's what I found so appalling in your behavior. You just had to ruin it for her. I still don't understand. What did it matter to you? You didn't want me. Why couldn't you just let her have a little fun? That was the thing. We had fun. But the way you felt and the way you made her feel weighed on us. You were so obviously unhappy that everything we tried to do always had all this guilt attached. And it was pointless. Just dog in the manger. We talked about it—tried to put it into perspective. But it just made it so damn difficult for her to take any pleasure in something that could have meant so much to her. It was really unforgivable."

The floor beneath her could have been ice over dark water. He was right. She had been finished with him. The problem was, she had not been finished with her mom. Hadn't ever really started. Never had and never would. "I never thought of it that way."

"Of course you didn't. That was obvious."

"What was?"

"The way you couldn't think of anybody but yourself!"

She squirmed and tilted, wanting to see him clearly. At her mother's wake, he'd been among the first to arrive, and he had strode in looking prepared to shove aside any opposition. But most people liked him, so he'd stayed late, chatting in one corner or another with almost everyone. Janet had registered from the first second the dogged gleam he exuded, but for hours she hadn't dared look at him directly. When she'd finally managed, he had seemed ghostly, seated in the corner under a large old-fashioned lamp whose pleated shade was decorated with faint impressionistic trees and a hem of fringe. He would set the fringe into motion every now and then with the brush of a finger, causing shadows to flicker over his smile. He'd held court at the center of a gaggle of elderly women, Viola Morton, Mildred Matz, Hazel Vanasek, even Bernice Doorley, along with a few others, all of them attentive, all beguiled. Apparently, only Janet was immune to Bobby's allure, and she could remember envying their susceptibility. "I think I'll go," she said.

"Are you all right now?"

"Oh, sure."

"Did you get light-headed before? Dizzy?"

"In a way."

"Because you were out of control."

"Maybe."

"Are you seeing anyone, Janet? Do you mind me asking?"

"What?"

"It's none of my business, but on the other hand, you're here."

"You mean like a boyfriend?"

"No. Oh no, I'm not talking about that. That doesn't interest me. I'm talking about counseling. Because this is maybe even a cry for help, coming here like this and acting outrageous. You should be seeing a counselor. Maybe grief counseling. They have that, you know. It's a specialty for some, and they study for it. Have you thought about that? Because I think it might be a good idea."

"Are you seeing someone?"

"You mean like that?"

"No. The other way."

"Yes, I am. As a matter of fact." Solemnly, he used several seconds to alert her that she should anticipate profundity in his next remark. "And I'm doing the other thing, too. Counseling, as a matter of fact."

"You are? Really?"

"And it's very helpful. I started not long after we divorced, and I just stayed with it, and it's very helpful. I could ask my guy to recommend somebody for you, if you wanted."

"Maybe."

"There's medication involved, too. Or there can be. That can work wonders. It's not only boring talk."

"Are you taking some kind of medication, Bobby?"

"Yes, I am."

"You mean like Prozac?"

"Like Prozac but not Prozac. Same pharmaceutical family."

"And it helps?"

"Yes, it does. It really does. I'll call you with a recommendation after I talk to my guy. I see him on Thursdays."

"Thanks."

"Okay, then. I'll do it."

"I'd appreciate that. Thanks so much," she told him.

18

BERNICE COMPLETED HER THIRD LOOP, seeing neither hide nor hair of Hazel, and she'd stayed on the ball the whole time. In the vicinity of the main entrance, she let the Toyota idle while a dozen or so people trudged in and out. If she spotted a familiar face, she could ask whether they'd seen Hazel Vanasek. But it was only strangers, coming and going. Lord, there were a lot of them, even in a little place like Belger. And she had lived here all her life.

When a parking place came free nearby, she figured it was time for a change of plans. Her knees all but creaked as she stood in the crisp air. Carefully, she pushed on the key ring gadget the way she'd seen Hazel lock up. Flashing its lights front and back, the car gave her a start. Just for the heck of it, or maybe to prove she knew what she was doing, she hit unlock and then lock again, enjoying the sight of the buttons jumping up and tucking themselves away, something smarter than her reaching out through the air to see to it things were taken care of.

She kept her eyes open for vehicles zipping about, and hurried to the entrance. When she was safely inside, the noise of the lot was replaced by Muzak falling from on high to touch her with a nostalgic tint that, pleasantly enough, made her feel she'd lost something dear. It was this big-orchestra rendition of a song she could remember liking long ago. Toby had loved it when it was first sung by that crooner guy. Not Frank. Maybe Andy or Wayne. No, no, it was probably that rascal Dino. With a part of her brain revisiting fragmented song lyrics, she scouted the benches stationed along the wall and between the commercial booths lining the center of the corridor. But no Hazel. Not a clue.

The only friendly face belonged to Mary Walding, who looked busy with a customer in the first booth, which was a mini-version of Heartfelt Sweets & Nuts, the big candy store located deeper inside. Poor Mary had cancer in her lungs. With one cut out and chemo ongoing, she looked rickety. Her pasty, pale skin was made even more sickly and hard to miss by the colorful scarves dangling off racks in the shop behind her. When Mary looked up from the chocolate-covered raisins she was scooping into a white paper sack, Bernice said, "Hi, Mary. Working hard, I see. You haven't seen Hazel, have you?"

"Hazel Vanasek? Sure. A while ago. She was headed for the bathroom."

"You see her come out?"

"Why?"

"I can't find her."

"Come to think of it, I didn't."

"Okay, then. Thanks."

Next in line was an old man who must have thought he was the king of England, the way he summoned Mary by tapping on a glass bin with his cane.

"Stop by later. Let me know if you found her," said Mary.

"Okay." Bernice smiled and waved and headed for a narrow passage across from Mary's workplace which led to the women's bathroom. It was all brightly lit white tile on the walls and floor when she opened the door, and the second she walked in, the anxiety she'd been keeping a lid on broke loose, and she couldn't stop feeling that each step was bringing her closer to something she didn't want to find. Such as Hazel fainted, or dead. That would be the worst. Poor dear Hazel dead of diabetic shock. Or dead of a heart attack. Just slumped over behind one of those doors all in a row.

For a split second she thought some humped-over white-haired old bag in a baby-blue pantsuit had followed her in and now stood watching her from in front of a line of minty green doors with somebody dead behind one of them. Or maybe behind all of them. But of course it was just her reflection in the mirror above the sinks, along with some crazy, mixed-up thinking. The space around her seemed bigger than when she'd come in. It seemed enormous somehow and empty as a tomb and so quiet she could have heard a pin drop. She moved, wanting to cause a stir, and she was glad to hear the click of her shoes. The cleanliness and silence felt unfriendly, even ominous. What she wanted more than anything was to get out of there. "Hazel?" she whispered. When nothing came back, she bent over to see under the doors, straining for a glimpse of Hazel's navy pumps.

The first three or four stalls were empty. It hurt to walk half doubled over, but she didn't dare crouch any farther or she'd fall on her face. She sure wasn't going to get down on her hands and knees. Something about her circumstances was jam-packed with aggravating demands that something or somebody had no right to ask of her. Suddenly, she'd had all she could take, and turning to go, she heard a scrape. "Hazel?" she said. The possibility that Hazel was hiding for some crazy reason annoyed the heck out of her, at the same time that the off chance of some complete stranger listening brought on a hot flash of embarrassment. "Hazel Vanasek. Are you in here? Because I would appreciate an answer, if you are. And if you aren't, I'm going." She waited and, hearing what might have been a sigh, didn't know what to do. "Okay, then."

"Hello."

"Hazel?"

"Hello, Bernice."

"Hazel, for goodness sake, what are you doing? You could've scared the life out of me."

"That you, Bernice?"

"Well, it sure is. Care to tell me what's going on?" Her question, aimed at prompting an answer, seemed to end the conversation, the silence lengthening until she felt foolish. "Didn't you hear me calling?" Again she waited with nothing to go on. "Hazel?"

"I'll be out in a minute."

"You been in there a long time."

"I'll be out in a minute."

"Are you okay?"

"Oh, sure."

"I thought maybe you fell in."

"No."

"What's wrong?"

"Nothing."

"I mean, what's taking so long?"

"Why don't you go on out and wait? I'll be right there."

"Mary Walding said she saw you come in here quite a while back."

"Yeah. I saw her. We said hello."

"She don't look good at all."

"You're right about that."

"Okay. You want me to go out and wait? Is that what you said?"

"That'd be good, I think."

"Okay. I'll be just out on one of the benches. I might buy a little something from Mary. You want a snack? They have those sugar-free ones."

"No, thanks."

"You're sure you're okay, though? Did you check your blood sugar?"

"Stuck myself good. It's fine."

"Maybe I ought to pick you up some nuts. They got cashews or mixed nuts."

"No."

"There's regular peanuts."

"I don't want anything."

"Okay."

"You could get me a cup of coffee."

"Okay." Bernice was standing near the door. "You know, that sounds like it might hit the spot. Coffee. I'll have some, too."

"Get it from Loefler's. They make a pretty good cup. Better than most."

"Sure, and they're right there."

"They're worth goin' out of your way for if you have to. You know how I like it—cream and Equal. Or that other sweetener's okay. You know the one I mean."

"Sure, sure. The other one. Now, you hurry up, Hazel."

"Don't worry. You sound worried."

"I was startin' to. I admit it." She really ought to have her head examined, chewing the fat like this with nobody she could see in a big empty room. "Okay. I'll just be out there, then."

"See you in a minute."

Bernice crossed straight to Mary, who was tending a young couple so wrapped up in each other that a person would have thought there wasn't anybody else on earth. Mary was working to hide her fatigue, but her hand trembled as she raised a silver scooper of gumdrops and poured them onto the scale. The fact that Mary did all this without even a glance in Bernice's direction started her fretting that she'd done something earlier to offend Mary. The couple whispered to each other and strolled away, and Mary offered Bernice a tattered smile before dropping onto a chair in the corner. "Find Hazel?" she asked.

"I did indeed."

"In the bathroom all that time?"

"And don't seem to have a suitable explanation that I heard yet, either."

"Maybe she was sick."

"She says not. Wants coffee now. Can you believe it? Got me running. And it's got to be from Loefler's and nowhere else. Lucky for me they're close by." Watching Mary cope with those snooty lovebirds had ended any interest she had in making a purchase. The forlorn way Mary sat made it seem sinful to ask her to do anything at all, let alone to bother her with something so frivolous as sorting candy. "Anyway," she said in a manner she hoped would communicate she was thinking about going.

"Did you want to buy something?"

"No. Oh, no. I better get a move on. I think she wants that coffee waiting." She'd barely taken a step when Mary called to her.

"Take a good look," Mary said.

"What?"

"At me."

"What's that, Mary? Okay," she said, and hurried back.

"I guess you heard about me."

She searched the air around and above Mary's head as if guidance were known to hover there, a sign making clear the kind of response Mary wanted. But all Bernice discovered was the shockingly fake wig Mary wore. "Well, some," she said.

"I'm not long for this world."

"Oh, c'mon. Don't say that, now."

"Somebody's got to."

"Look at you here working. Now, what about that?"

"They got me on this chemo—it's something they shouldn't give a dog."

"But it must be helping. You're up and around."

Mary's fingers danced along the hem of the wig, and then she tugged, deliberately making the whole thing uneven. Her harsh laughter declared the mishmash on her head a joke she was playing on somebody she disliked intensely. "What bullshit, wouldn't you say? I'm like one of the Three Stooges. The bossy one."

A young girl in the ugliest outfit Bernice had ever seen—pink jeans topped off by a pink turtleneck—had just completed a long-drawn-out study of the cashews and mixed nuts. Her ample bosom and spoiled expression left no doubt she expected the waves to part for her.

"You go on, Bernice," Mary said. "Get your coffee. I got business. You keep Hazel waiting, she's liable to bite your head off."

"She can be a trial, all right."

"The thing with me, Bernice, is for me to say goodbye to people when I get a chance. Have a chance to see them, you know. So goodbye, Bernice. Say a little prayer for me."

"You say one for me, too, Mary."

"I will. Goodbye."

"Goodbye."

The young girl had high cheekbones, and her deep-set green eyes darted between Mary and Bernice, almost trying to pry them apart with her huffy glare, as much as to say she didn't understand how they could keep on talking while she stood in front of them waiting. But then Mary turned to her and said, "What can I do you for, sweetie?"

Bernice scurried to Loefler's, where, feeling urgent and tardy, she purchased two coffees to go in sturdy Styrofoam cups personalized with the Loefler's logo. The cashier wanted to chitchat about her mother, whom Bernice knew from Toby's bowling league at Tigge's Lanes. She was feeling pressed for time, but the girl couldn't take a hint. Finally, Bernice told her how all that seemed like another lifetime, then made a beeline for the door.

Mary was gone. A young redhead with chubby cheeks and dangling silver earrings was in her place, bowed intently over the cash register. Cocked atop the girl's red hair was a green and white sailor's hat with the store logo on it—a shiny brown heart-shaped nut. Mary must have had the good sense not to wear such foolishness, but this poor kid didn't know any better. In fact, Bernice saw, she had on a whole color-coordinated costume, vest and skirt. What was the world coming to? Wasn't it enough that people showed up and did their jobs? Did they have to look like they belonged to the boss, body and soul? She was about to go up to the girl and ask where Mary might have gone to, maybe even say something about the outfit, but Hazel appeared, beckoning for Bernice to join her on one of the benches against the wall.

"Mary's gone," Bernice said.

Hazel gave the redhead the once-over as if she needed to verify for herself the accuracy of Bernice's remark. Then she reached for the coffee and fiddled with the lid. "Where'd she go?"

"I don't know." Bernice settled beside Hazel. "We talked a minute, and then I went for the coffee. When I came out, she was gone."

"Maybe she was finished for the day."

"Maybe."

They both examined the booth, as if they believed Mary might have left evidence behind to inform them of facts deeper or more truthful than the things they seemed to know. "What did she have to say for herself?" Hazel wondered.

"She feels terrible. And she was talking kind of funny, I'd have to say."

"What kind of funny?"

Bernice thought a little but doubted her mind was headed anywhere worthwhile. "Just funny," she said. "Mary don't have good cards."

"No." Hazel sighed. "She's at death's door."

"That's what she said."

"She said that about herself?"

"Pretty much."

Hazel gave the impression of considering a point whose value and seriousness she suspected mattered only to her, and even she knew it didn't amount to much.

The bench was square to the wall, so there was no avoiding the parade of fools traveling in and out to spend, or having spent, their hard-earned cash in the rabbit warren of wonders down the hall.

"I just want to drink my coffee," said Hazel, "and then we'll get back on the road. You see what I mean about Loefler's, though." She raised the cup like a trophy, and the taste she took earned a smile. "Better than most, don't you think?"

"I'd have to agree."

"Those franchise places—hot water, sure, they'll give you that. And maybe there's coffee beans on the premises, but they're not going to let the two of them meet up and mingle."

"Not if they get to do things their way," said Bernice. Lord, she was mad all of a sudden—mad as all get-out. Ready to throw a rock through somebody's window. "Let's call a spade a spade. All they're thinking about is how to put up another one of their gyp joints, dress some poor souls in funny outfits, and run anybody worth their salt out of business."

Just then a figure shot past. A beefy man stuffed into hunting clothes, patting his pockets. One of the Linebargers, Bernice thought, and he was having one heck of a nicotine fit. "Smokers," she said.

"Can't wait to put another nail in the coffin."

"Not that quitting's easy. Cold turkey. I was climbing the walls, and you, Hazel, were not fit to be around."

The slow way Hazel lowered her container to her lap, almost tenderly and in both hands, was like a tap on the shoulder, alerting Bernice that something she'd known would have to come up sooner or later was about to arrive. "I don't know what come over me on that toilet before," said Hazel. "Once I got in there, I just plopped." The tilt of her head sent their thoughts back to the bathroom. "And I still feel wrung out, you know. Just good for nothing. Not my regular self at all."

"Did you have diarrhea or anything like that?"

"No. Just felt punked out."

"And you peed like you went in to do? And everything was okay in that area? Didn't burn or hurt?" Even though Hazel was shaking her head to advise Bernice that anything she might come up with would turn out wrong, Bernice kept trying. "And you really checked your blood sugar?"

"Not everything is diabetes, Bernice!" She seemed to discover an extremely disappointing flaw in Bernice. "I can have another kind of trouble, you know."

"Well, sure."

"I got no get-up-and-go! Just good for nothing. That's what I'm trying to tell you. I run in there like this fool. My Depends been giving me a nasty rash, so I take 'em off every chance I get and leave 'em off till the last minute. I meant to put them on before I left this morning, but with everything else, I forgot."

"You should've asked me at my place. I would've been happy to loan you a pair."

"Coulda-woulda-shoulda." Hazel lifted the coffee but was completely disgusted when she saw how little remained. She sat staring at the cup. "I run in there, and I got in that stall just in time, and good heavens, the way I was feeling, you'da thought I'd pulled off something really big. Got into the toilet across from Loefler's without peeing my pants. Holy cow. Stop the presses. And I had a heada steam up before, didn't I?"

"You sure did."

"Full of piss and vinegar. And then all of a sudden I'd just as soon sit there. I had to fight not to just lay down on that floor right then and there."

A young man in shiny black shoes clattered past. He could not wait to get out the door, where his lighter refused to work no matter how he shook it. Linebarger, who was still killing time, offered the burning end of his smoke.

"I'm like that sometimes," Bernice said. "Just wantin' to flop."

"Well, I can't say I care for it much."

"What about the Muzak?" Bernice wondered. "You ever ask yourself that?"

"What about it?"

"It always makes me a little blue. You know, the way they pipe it in and you don't even know you're listening except you feel sad."

"I can't say I ever had that experience, Bernice. And sometimes they play bouncy music, don't they? Sure they do."

"Sometimes, sure—" she wavered, questioning her point but unwilling to give it up.

Hazel lifted her wristwatch to the level of her chin and stared at it. "We should probably get going. I just need a minute or so more."

"Okay." As if to leave no doubt who was boss, the Muzak turned jaunty and upbeat, and Bernice felt put in her place. She didn't think her mind had been changed, but she could no longer see any way to get her idea across, and her disappointment, a lot darker and heavier than she could have expected, made her sad, and a big part of her sadness was for Hazel. "It was probably all that back there, then. Don't you think?"

"Maybe." Hazel took a tiny sip. "Back where? What?"

"In the car."

"All what?"

"What we ended up talking about. You know—your tragedy."

"Oh. That business. That's all old hat."

"I'm just saying it probably shouldn't have come up, and it probably wouldn't have if I'da kept my big trap shut."

"Well, it did." Hazel drained the cup. She began rolling the empty container in her palms. "I'm thin-skinned, I guess. You'd think after all this time. But it don't take much. It's right there. Ready to jump out. Right under the surface. This big angry thing. Like some monster. I'm talking about the feeling. And water. The feeling that it's waiting to jump out and get me. I'm thinking of water, and movies, too, I guess. That's what I mean. You know, the way they do in scary movies."

"Something jumping out at you. Sure."

"You remember that one?"

"Which one?"

"It was this one way up in a jungle. Creature in the black water, and they're going up a river in a little steamboat."

"I think I do. They were scientists. And he lived there, the creature."

"That's the one. Scary."

"That Richard somebody was in it, and that other one. He was Tarzan for a while." Bernice wondered if they were all dead now, even the one who played the monster. "Did they go in there looking for him?"

"I don't think so. I don't think they even knew he was there when they started up the river."

"And the creature fell in love with that pretty girl."

"They always do."

"Three-D, that one, right?"

"Yes, it was. You wore those glasses. What a hoot." Hazel yipped. "We thought they'd taken fun to the limit when they came up with three-D movies."

"It's somethin', when you think about it. And they're still at it. The things they come up with. Now it's computers. I see one, Hazel, I tell you, I run the other way."

Hazel had stopped rolling the cup and begun to pick at the rim. "It was something, wasn't it, when that creature took the pretty girl off. She was dark-haired and big-busted. Remember? They were all looking the wrong direction, and he came up and grabbed her right off the boat. I can still see it. He's got her, and they're overboard. So crazy to have her, he don't care if he drowns her. She was so white, I remember, and in a white suit, and he had these fish things. Gills and fishy eyes. And dark—he was dark, and down they went. It was like they were flying. Except it was down."

"No wings, though."

"No. But still."

"He did have those things on his hands and feet, and he flapped them. Webs. Like little wings."

"Down they went," said Hazel.

"That was the three-D part. They always had things coming and going at you, or flying off."

"I don't know why they stopped makin' them things."

"Musta been money."

"What else? Though it sure seemed like they should have made money."

"If they'da bothered to ask me, I'da give them thumbs-up." With a raised fist, Bernice cast her vote, smiling and waiting for the next fun thing to pop out of Hazel's mouth. But nothing came, and she seemed to go off somewhere all alone, leaving Bernice behind, even though they both were still on that bench in the mall, people walking by. Suddenly, something was so wrong. The silence was killing. Bernice couldn't take it. She cringed at the sight of her coffee cup half full, while Hazel's was bone-dry. To hint that she needed to say something, she cleared her throat, and Hazel shot her a look that begged her to hold off, because there was something Hazel needed badly to get off her chest first, if Bernice would only let her. Bernice widened her eyes and tilt in close to show she was willing.

"I think there was this one part," said Hazel, "where the Creature from the Black Lagoon had that girl under the water, and they were so far away she was just this speck—this little white speck. You couldn't really see him at all, but you could see her, and she was in this big dark place, and he was going deeper, and she was waving her arms. Do you remember that?"

It was odd the way Bernice saw it—not right in front of her, but still with the bright thrilling detail of a movie screen, even when there was none around, just her memory lit up by something anybody would have thought she'd forgotten long ago. And it was exactly the way Hazel said, too, every little detail except one. "You know, Hazel," she said, "I don't think the part about waving her arms is right. I don't think that happened."

"I could be wrong."

"She passed out is what I remember. Otherwise she would have been waving her arms—waving them like crazy—except she passed out."

"Of course she did. That's right. In the clutches of that creature, she just faints dead away. Well, who wouldn't?"

"Three-D," said Bernice, remembering.

"One of the best things they ever came up with, if you ask me."

The first one Bernice and Toby ever saw had come along during that stretch when he was so unhappy and bothered by something he couldn't say a word about. "First time, me and Toby were ducking and screaming at whatever came at us, these arrows and whatnot. I guess that one was cowboys and Indians, so they flung things out at the audience every chance they got." She'd been completely without a clue what was eating at him, but he'd spent hours locked up in his own head day after day, until it got so bad she was scared half the night he'd run away like Edgar, and then at the 3-D movies, he just woke up and the light came back into his smile and it was real again and not that fake front he'd been putting up for weeks on end. They had a box of popcorn, and when she reached for some, he took hold of her hand. Funny. Guns booming like thunder, smoke and arrows thick as hail over that river. "Toby loved them," she said. "You'da swore he invented them. Or they were going to make him rich. And you know what we did? We had so much fun, we celebrated by staying on for the next show. Watched the whole crazy thing again."

"Here's one for you," Hazel said, the tatters of her cup dangling from her fingers, particles spread below. "You know I can't manage to think of that poor girl in that creature's arms without seeing her waving for help. I just see it that way even though I know better now."

"I think I'm right about the way it went."

"I do, too. Now that you said it, I don't have a doubt."

"Well, you're just adding in your little bit. Nothing wrong with that."

Hazel shifted like she might stand up, but then she quieted, all her bustle no more than restlessness. "You know what I remember most from back then is this useless feeling. Just feeling useless."

With only that to go by, and no sign Hazel considered her remark incomplete, Bernice was hesitant to make a sound. She'd be skating on thin ice no matter what she said. Stalling and about to have a little coffee, she thought better of it. "You want what's left of my coffee here? It's cooled, but not too bad."

"Don't you want it?"

Bernice passed the cup with a smile. "I've had my fill."

"Better than nothing." The big swallow Hazel took seemed just the trick to move her on. "Miscarriage after miscarriage. Like I was some old heifer couldn't breed. Just a useless tub of guts. That was the feeling."

"Oh," said Bernice. "That's no good."

"Well, no. It's not. And sure, it's a long time now, but it can still come over me. When it does, well, they ought to drop me off at the slaughterhouse. Raise that sledgehammer and bang me square on top of my head. Or else somebody point me to the gun rack. And I'd prefer the one with the twelve-gauge."

"Goodness, Hazel, I don't think I had any idea it was still such a sore spot."

"I try not to let on. Can't imagine there'd be many wanting to put up with me if I was beggin' for sympathy all the time."

"I don't think that's what you're doin'."

"Well, it is and it isn't, if you want to know the truth."

"It's natural what you're saying, I think. I see that now. Especially with all doctors can do these days."

"I don't blame the doctors I had. They did their best."

"I'm not blaming them. I'm just saying with eggs and clinics and all they can do. Just knowing they're figuring out all these different ways that you have no chance to use—that's got to be rough."

"I guess. But that's not what I'm saying."

"Oh." Bernice reminded herself to step gingerly.

"There was some good doctors back then. You know that."

"Sure."

"McGhee. Doc McGhee. I wouldn't trade him for ten of them put to-gether today. The man cared. He really did. You'da thought the baby I was tryin' to have was going to be his. He kept tellin' me it was going to work. Each and every time. He was the most optimistic man. Jackie liked him, too. Jackie was shy and kept wantin' to take the blame, but it wasn't him. He'd get me pregnant half the time if we just slept in the same room. But I couldn't keep them. It was in me—some faulty machinery somewhere. They never did figure out just what."

"That's my point. I think they probably could today. Maybe even do something about it."

"I guess."

"So there's no blame in you sayin' it rubs you wrong, knowin' you could have been saved all that grief."

"I ain't sayin' that, though. I don't mean to, anyway."

"But Hazel, there's probably something they're giving people right now that would have been just the ticket for you."

"Maybe."

"Odds are, don't you think?"

"I couldn't hold them. That was the long and the short of it. Simple enough for most people. Doc McGhee would take me by my two arms. Up high, you know, near my shoulders, like he was going to pull me in and hug me, but he'd look me in the eye and make me say, 'Next time.' He wouldn't let go until I did. He'd say it. 'Next time's the right time. Next time's the charm.' And so I would, too. I'd say it. That's Doc McGhee for you, what a doctor he was. The genuine article. His eyes had something in them could light a person up. Make you feel this spark. Then, of course, his boy got killed in Vietnam. That was a low blow. You remember the fu-neral?"

"Oh, sure," Bernice said, though the question didn't stir much up.

"God, it was sad," Hazel said. "He was one of the early ones. His boy. Jimmy. It was sort of still a little war, and a surprise anybody died in it at all, let alone somebody from Belger. We should have known, I guess, but it was all so far away and not even on TV that much. It was 1963 or '4 or '5. Something in there."

"I think you're right."

"Oh, I'm right on this one. It was real early, I remember that. And naturally enough, Doc McGhee had all these women patients, and just about every one of them in attendance. People crying. Lord. They didn't want to intrude. But still. They couldn't help themselves. The flag and all that. They fold the flag in that special way, and you know how you feel it's a beautiful thing, a beautiful gesture. They give it to the parents. To the mother. Well, Doc McGhee just stared. I can still see his eyes to this day. And the way he looked at that flag in his wife's arms, well—I never seen such a look before or since, and I hope I never do. She hugged it. Cradled it, you'd have to say."

Bernice nodded like she was witnessing exactly what Hazel said, but the truth was all she had was some dark suits and dresses, flowers and gravestones, that could have belonged to anybody's funeral.

"They shot those rifles," said Hazel. "And he gave a little jump with each one. I couldn't help it—I started thinking, He's done for. Oh, no. Oh, no. A baby was cryin'. Little kids, too. Some of them upset because their mommas were cryin'. People pulled kids out of school so they could be there. So they could pay their respects. And every last one of them was one Doc McGhee had seen to their getting born. Every last one."

Bernice nodded, hoping for something heartfelt, trying to contribute. "He hung on, though, you'd have to say. Fought the fight."

Hazel turned a look on her that made her feel like a dirty corner that needed to be cleaned out. "He wasn't a quitter, if that's what you're sayin'. I'm not saying that. Not a bit of quit in that man, let me tell you. They got him when he wasn't looking. Cut him off at the knees. Never the same— everybody said it. He didn't know what hit him. I remember I wanted to do something for him. I actually thought I could. Stupidest thing. Then it was over, the whole deal, the whole ceremony. Just like that. The end came, and you felt like you must have missed something. We were on top of this little hill—you remember how it rolled, the grass. So people were going down on their way back to their cars to head for home or off to work. A lot of people went up to him, you know how they do, to say a word, and I started up. I had this idea. I'd take hold of his arms the way he'd always took hold of me, and I'd do for him what he'd always done for me. But what was I going to say? 'Next time's the right time.' I don't think that would have done the job. Maybe it was good sense, or maybe just dumb luck saved me. But I stood there tongue-tied from stupidity or by the grace of God, and I know I must have looked plain strange. Somebody—I don't know who—they were behind me in the line, and they pushed me out of the way. Just gimme a shove. Not exactly gentle about it, either. I had half a mind to tell them off, but then it came to me I ought to wait around and thank them, because it was right, what they did. But I didn't do that, either. Couldn't do anything, I guess. I just joined in with the others goin' on down the hill. It was a beautiful day. People were hanging around where the cars were parked, and the road went off, and then they all started driving away. It was somewhat like this one. The day, I mean. This bright, clear fall."

19

WELL, THOUGHT JANET, AND THEN she waited. The moment wasn't calm, but it wasn't riotous, either. In fact, her situation offered few clues to its nature until a sound approached and became the words *Now what?* She didn't know but hoped she might, because her mood was full of regret for misplaced things that she felt she could locate if only the dream lasted long enough. It was benevolent of the dream to name itself. Knowing that she slept explained the unpredictability of her impressions. It gave her the feeling that she had time to search on and on, though it also pushed her toward a consciousness of shapes and light and, finally, the fact that she was sprawled sideways on a couch with a television flashing in front of her, and a crazy duo of living voices screeching and growling elsewhere.

"Stop that damn foolishness, you don't want me to kick you into the other world, dipshit."

"You don't want to be in my reality. Don't get lost there, bro, because I am the rule-maker."

On the TV, a man in a dark suit stood with a crowd of somber faces stacked behind him. He glided up to an automobile fender, a wedge of red bricks. His accent was British, his tone solemn. "It's beyond recognition, mangled beyond any possible recognition. As for the rumors that the paparazzi chased the Mercedes into the tunnel—if borne out as fact, these are circumstances that could bring criminal charges."

"Do you believe the mood is such that actual charges could be made?" inquired an offscreen voice, also male and British.

"I do indeed," the first man answered, and several bystanders nodded.

"Yoooo, whassssup, dickhead?"

"You ain't nothin', motherfucker."

The voices, coming from a nearby room, crumpled into gurgling pools of laughter.

Janet licked her dry lips. She blinked, praying to arrest the steady throb of her headache. "Of course, the investigation is only in its beginning stages," the man informed her, seeming to yearn for her as he gazed out of the screen. "But witnesses abound to the desperate effort the driver made to escape pursuit. This appears to have been a manifestation of the recent mutation of the traditional paparazzi—as if they weren't sordid enough—into this new breed of 'stalkerazzi,' with cameras on motorbikes and other vehicles racing after targets like a band of savages."

"You ain't nothin', motherfucker," the shrill voice shouted from the other room, which Janet knew to be the kitchen. A portion of a sink was visible through the doorway.

"You don't wanna find out about my nothin', fool, because my nothin' is some badassed shit, fool."

"Like a pack of wolves running prey to ground," intoned the disembodied voice while the onscreen man filled with woe.

"I got a name you know," shouted the growler in the kitchen.

"That's right."

"So use it."

"I thought I was, fool."

A toilet flushed, and Janet sat up. Disorientation made her shake her head, a mistake that drove the screwdriver in her temple deeper. She raised her palms before her eyes. Hadn't this already happened? It was months ago that Princess Diana had died in a car crash in that tunnel. Replayed over and over, the news had catapulted Janet into unexpected shock, then into a period of genuine grieving. Why were they announcing it as if it had just happened? She'd thought Diana a silly woman. Beautiful. A thoroughbred of sorts. But silly, until she died.

A door slammed. The blinds were drawn, the curtains pulled, explaining the twilight atmosphere in which she sat feeling dwarfed by the gigantic TV. It was a massive rectangle of crystal-clear shimmering on fire with details. A hammer, a saw, nails in a box, gray duct tape, and lumber lay near the wall. Looked like Big Baby Dog and his hardware store project hadn't gotten all that far.

A skinny black woman was coming down the hall. Her actual shape was hard to find within the oversize ruby-red robe she wore, the folds undulating, the hem dragging. "Woke up, huh?" she said to Janet. "I loved that Diana, didn't you? She was a princess. But just full of trouble. Everywhere she turned, somethin' worse was waitin'. Just as messed up and lost as the person next door. Well, maybe not as bad off as all that, but bad off. I loved her."

Someone was shouting in the kitchen. "You remember what I tole you, because you are gonna end up coughin' and shittin' and freezin' to death by some burnin' barrel this winter, because—do you hear what I'm saying? You are way past dumb."

"Says you."

"Check it out. It's my warning, you hear me. You better worry or take the time to turn around and get you a brain."

Along with the voices, Janet registered a hollow booming and then a mechanical replication of human screams.

"Worry? I got nothin' to bring on worry. Not from somethin' like you."

Artificial machine-gun fire built a barrage that had one of the two men yowling with glee while the other grunted and the programmed human anguish escalated.

"What the fuck is this?" screamed a shrill male voice.

The answer was a triumphant, murderous howl. "You see what I'm sayin'? Check it out!"

The woman flopped onto the couch beside Janet, battling her robe to keep the collar from rising over her head. Her inky hair was pulled back into a tight nub secured with token elegance by a crooked, sequined scrunchie. She smiled at Janet and, aiming the remote, ignited a flurry of speeded-up motion. Automobile tires squealed in the kitchen, and more gunfire erupted. The woman shut down the play capacity on the VCR and concentrated on fast-forward. She smiled at Janet as if promising she would bring them something good.

"What the fuck is this?" the screecher in the kitchen wanted to know.

"Man, you are dismal. Stop cryin'."

"I ain't cryin'."

"You gettin' ready. You know what I mean. And it ain't gonna do no good."

"I ain't cryin'."

"I whipped your ass, you know what I mean, you see what I'm sayin'. Gonna be on Dan Rather. Mike Wallace."

"Just shut your mouth."

"And that other one, too. Katie Couric. Bryant Gumbel." Big Baby Dog was the growler of the two, but the other one wasn't Mr. Bats, she didn't think.

"You disrespectin' me, man."

"You my homie. You my nigger. You know what I mean. You yell all you want. Shoot your mouth. Trash-talk and throw bullshit. You know what I mean. Check it out. Don't matter what you think or what you fantasize."

Beside her on the couch, the woman elbowed Janet and said, "There, see."

Janet had been distracted from the TV to concentrate on the kitchen, though she could see neither the men nor the video game making them so crazy.

"Lord, man, you are one bothersome nigger, talking nonsense to me about what I can fantasize. You stay out of my business."

Diana had been fast-forwarded to Africa. In midmotion, she settled onto a bench under a tree rising from bare brown dirt near a tin wall. Surrounded by black children, she glanced at the camera, then back to the children, her arms opening as if to embrace them all. But she lifted only the nearest, a young long-limbed girl in a white dress printed with red dots, who landed in an ungainly slant across Diana's hips.

"Look where she is," said the woman beside Janet. Brenda. That was her name. She was nodding, her mouth puckered like that of a baby about to cry. She was so skinny, her head might as well have been supported by nothing but the piled-up red of her robe. "She was a real princess. Come from the people. Loved the people. I just thought it was such a hurtful thing. Wasn't it a hurtful thing when she was lost?"

Janet nodded, and Diana unleashed a smile bordering on the supernatural while the girl on her lap gazed up in awe.

The gunfire and mechanized screaming from the kitchen were more or less constant now, and the player who wasn't Big Baby Dog was saying, "I'd like to fuck that Katie Couric. And that Joan Lunden. That's the one. That blond bitch. So cool. Jus' hidin' her heat, man. Just fuck her good."

"You got her message, though, right? On the phone machine just this morning. Joan Lunden called you up."

"She did?"

"Yes, she did."

"Well, I didn't get it. You didn't tell me."

"I forgot."

"Well, fuck her, let her call again."

Now Janet remembered the overwhelming arrival of sleep on this couch before she'd even taken one of the 'ludes she'd come to buy. Just went out from all the Jack Daniel's. It soothed her now to feel she was figuring things out, connecting divergent puzzle parts. The couch had an odor, a close animal brew, along with something rank that led her to picture pizza decomposing on the floor. Her sense was that even when the details of her immediate past had been unavailable, as they had been moments ago, she'd known them somehow, but still their review interested her, and she went along step by step while the uproar in the kitchen and whatever Diana was doing onscreen provided vague accompaniment. All that talk about counseling in Bobby's office had been the start. Bobby had been so smug, talking about *his guy*. Like he owned the jerk. Like his recommendation should cancel all doubt. He was Bobby's guy. This concerned, earnest offer. Once she'd climbed into her car, a backwash of resentment carried her across town as she thought how he was one hundred percent right. She needed some counseling. She needed her prescription refilled. But she didn't need Bobby's help—she had her own guy. Big Baby Dog. She wished Bobby could see her now. What a prissy, tight-assed face he'd be stuck with. The wimp hadn't even been willing to smoke weed. Not even after she told him how it made her horny. How it exaggerated minutes into luxuriant intervals as long-lasting as hours of foggy, slow-motion indulgence.

"I still can't believe it happened," Brenda said, poking her face in front of Janet. "You know, in the real. In the world out there."

When she pulled back, the TV delivered Diana in a lovely pink ski outfit, wheeling away from a batch of other vacationers exiting a lift. She waved coyly and sailed off down a wintry slope. Janet winced at the ferocity of the sunlit snow, the pain in her head sickening. "Brenda, do you have any aspirin?"

Gnawing on a forefinger thrust into her mouth up to the second knuckle, Brenda shifted and jabbed her free hand repeatedly into and out of some part of the couch blocked from view by the robe, her eyes glued to the TV. But up came a bottle of Advil offered in her palm.

"Oh, thanks."

The kitchen had been invaded by sirens and squealing tires and Big Baby Dog shouting, "I own you, fuckhead. You are in the shit! Check it out. All I got to do is flush."

Brenda grunted, kind of woeful and beaten. Diana, on a horizon of snow, sank beneath a steep embankment. Janet stood, having spied two cans of Coke in the plastic loops of a six-pack against the baseboard. It really was sad about Diana. Maybe all little girls dream of being a princess, but she'd done it. Maybe her prince wasn't so charming, but he was a prince. Except the whole thing got screwed up. Or she screwed it up. With three Advils in her mouth, Janet drank warm Coke and suffered a wave of nausea.

Big Baby Dog screamed, "Give it up, give it up, give it up!" His voice rang as synthetic as the programmed gunshots and pain.

Janet was collapsing by the time she managed the couch. Blinking, her brow prickled with sweat, she was surprised to see Diana back in

Africa, strolling along a jungle trail. She wore a series of bizarre putty-colored slabs topped by a helmet that she should have had on the night of the crash. The announcer declared, "Following her separation from Prince Charles, the princess announced that she intended to scale back her charitable work. But to many observers, it seemed that as her own life became more difficult, she gave more and more to those who suffered."

The racket in the kitchen soared into a lengthy, rolling metallic clatter that concluded in breaking glass.

"Yooo, fool!"

"Like I know I'm fucked up. I know it."

"Look what you done! That's what?"

Diana was dismayed but not despairing atop a hillock overlooking miles of arid scrub while the narrator commented, "As in Angola, where, crusading for a ban on land mines, she not only courted political controversy but put herself at some risk."

"That sucks. It sucks, dog!"

"How long you been this dumb?"

Brenda expressed a lifetime of weary annoyance and worn-down pity with a slow turn toward the chaos in the kitchen. "The both of them fools in there need a role model," she informed Janet. She shook her head and returned to the TV, where a man and woman, both in dark clothing, sat oddly far from each other behind a long, rickety desk.

In the kitchen, another metal object landed and clanged.

"You know where the broom is, so you get on with your janitorial duties."

"Yeah, what's up? What you gonna do? You gonna shoot me or somethin'?"

"Maybe I'll just call the po-leese!"

"You go right ahead."

Janet concentrated for a second, wanting to make certain she recalled the woman's name correctly before she spoke. "Brenda?"

"Hmmmmmmmmm?"

"What's going on in there?"

"I tole you, Janet. They got no father figure. They all in the system, so you want one, you got to go to prison. But then you in prison. You and your role model."

"I thought you was telephoning the police!"

"Maybe I will," Big Baby Dog shouted.

"Whatsa matter, you don't got enough minutes?"

"I got my minutes."

"Can't get no service?"

"Ain't nothin' to me what you say."

While lighting a cigarette, Brenda said, "I taped fourteen hours of Diana. Had VCRs goin' on all these different TVs on different channels, because they did and said different things. But it don't last, the tapes and the pictures on it—it all gets rotted away by time. That's what I hear. And they can break, you know. I got to get some backups before I lose it all. He says he's gonna get me one of those machines got two decks and all the tapes I need, but he don't ever do it. I git on him, and he says it's on his list. We go on that way, but I don't think he will. If they started breakin' on me, I just can't bear it."

The man in the dark suit was tilting toward the distant woman while Brenda watched intently, fearfully, as if it all might vanish before she took another breath. "Well, for my part," he offered, "seeing that coffin slide into the hearse was a blow. Knowing everything I know, having seen all I've seen, I still felt it, you know, Sarah. A hard blow to the pit of the stomach."

Sarah prepared her response by thoughtfully consulting a series of inner notations that created a reverential pose. Somehow it was clear she intended to simplify the experience that had left her companion so befuddled. "Well, I think it was the truth, Henry. It made it real. The coffin sliding into the hearse made it real."

"Did we miss that?" said Brenda. "The coffin goin' into the hearse. We didn't see that. I don't think. Did we?" Aiming the remote, she hurled the mannered couple at their makeshift desk backward. "She said that part right, though, I think, don't you? The coffin makin' it real." The images stopped, doubled in a scarily confused overlap, and were replaced by an American talk show with a black-haired hostess stroking the hand of a large woman stuffed into ill-fitting clothes.

"I gotta go," said Janet, standing.

Brenda gestured energetically at the TV as if strengthening the remote's power to achieve her goal. "Hang on. Don't you wanna see the coffin?"

The talk show shuddered and vanished, and there was Diana in a parking lot, carrying a gym bag. She wore light brown shorts, a sleeveless sweatshirt. Her cheeks were flushed, and the bounce in her stride, along with her sly acceptance of the cameraman recording the carefree gesture she used to fling open her car door, belonged to someone who would never end up in a coffin but would live forever.

"Hey, Janet, girl, look at you—you still here! I thought you took off." Big Baby Dog was crammed in the kitchen doorway. "Or did you feel the need to come back?"

"No, I ain't left yet. Leaving now."

"Don't you run her off, Big Baby Dog," said Brenda.

"I ain't runnin' nobody anywhere." He had on the same black pants, but his sweatshirt was gold with the decal of a car crash shooting flames. Janet was about to turn for the door when worry transformed Big Baby Dog, his huge arms flopping against his sides and leaving him sad-looking as he searched the room for something. "Where you leave your purse, Janet? You don't want to go without your purse."

"What?" He was right; she didn't have it. "Oh, no. Thanks." She scanned quickly the floor, the corners, unable to remember.

"Where you put her purse, Brenda?"

"I ain't put it anywhere. She put it here." She patted the back of the couch. "She took a nap."

"Oh, right." Janet hurried around behind the couch, where her purse waited on the floor. She stood, slinging the strap over her shoulder. "Thanks."

Big Baby Dog nodded but seemed to grow even more concerned, gazing at Brenda and the TV. "You watchin' that Diana crap again, Brenda? You are one crack-addled fool."

"Me and Janet doin' jus' fine. You go on back and shoot some more of them little people can't shoot back and blow up things in that fucked-up world. You fit in just fine, so be fine with it, but we don't need you barkin' your craziness at us."

"Any barkin' 'round here, you the dog."

"Me and Janet fine with the world is all I'm sayin'."

No longer wearing his baseball cap, he came off balding and middle-aged. "But how can that be, you are watchin' what you are watchin'? Because you are simple with that woman. You are just pathetic. Ain't you got no real friends? That woman ain't ever your friend."

"Who you talkin' about?" said a lanky teenager in baggy maroon pants, red sneakers, and a faded gray pullover. Peeking out from behind Big Baby Dog, he had only one tiny gold earring and a single thin gold chain. Half of his hair was cornrows, while the rest stuck out in a springy, uneven wedge. The pale splotch on his cheek made him look like somebody had dabbed him with bleach.

"That woman was everybody's friend," said Brenda. "Everybody on the face of the earth."

"Who you talkin' about?" said the kid.

"Ain't my friend," Big Baby Dog grumbled.

"Who you talkin' about?"

"Diana, princess of Wales."

"Who?"

"See? He ain't even heard of her, have you, Jamal?"

"Who?"

"Diana, princess of Wales," Brenda told him.

"Who's she?"

"Right there!" said Brenda, pointing. "Right there!"

"I'd like to fuck her," said the kid, slipping around Big Baby Dog so he arrived facing the TV, his hand grabbing his crotch and then fluttering in a pass that left his zipper down, the head of his stubby cock peering out of his fist at the end of a tattooed forearm. "I could fuck her good. Skinny bitch."

"You are one low animal, Jamal," Brenda sighed.

In her car, Diana shot down a wooded lane as if to outrace Jamal and his vulgar aims.

"Where's she goin'? Her and that Joan Lunden. Fuck 'em both."

"Just some sort of snarly, sweaty low animal."

"That ain't how I see it."

"Don't matter how you see it if you are a low animal. Nobody is gonna pay you any attention."

"Except I ain't."

"Words is just words."

"Shut up."

"You still a fool."

Janet had fixed on the dark curl of Jamal's purplish uncircumcised cock nosing from his fingers with what looked like a wart on the side, and she was about to avert her eyes when her interest was discovered. The sleepy anger in Jamal's gaze turned menacing as he fixed her and tried to freeze her so her glance could not slip away.

"That's right," he said. "Fuck you, too, even if you ain't blond. I ain't prejudice."

"You let Janet alone, now."

"She got no problem. You the problem," said Big Baby Dog. "You know what I mean. You fine with all this, ain't you, Janet? I know you are. That one over there don't know nothin' 'bout nothin' except tornado. You know what I mean, ain't that right, Bernadette?"

"What?" said Brenda. Confusion jammed her half-buried pupils into a squint, though outrage fed their gleam. "Who the hell you calling Bernadette?"

"What?" said Big Baby Dog.

"I ain't no Bernadette, fool!"

"Who you callin' fool?"

"Who you callin' Bernadette?"

"I gotta go," Janet said.

"Bye," said Brenda.

"Did you take your rock?" asked Big Baby Dog.

"I didn't buy any rock."

"I'm talkin' about my gift."

"I don't want any rock. I told you."

"She tole you," said Brenda.

"Jamal, get Janet her rock."

"She don't want it." Jamal shrugged.

"Get it."

"She don't want it." He stepped toward the couch.

"Go on, now."

"She just said she don't want it."

"I heard what she said, and I heard what I said, and what I said is all you got to worry about!"

"Why should I get it, she don't want it?"

"Damn you, you fucking motherfucker, Jamal, you want me to bust open your head so I can shout straight into your sad-assed brain? I said get it!"

"Okay. Take a breath."

"Don't you tell me to take a breath, you funky-assed useless nigger. Get the rock!"

"Okay, okay."

"And fix your goddamn hair!"

"Ain't nothin' wrong with my hair!"

"Look in the mirror. You look crazy! And then get sweepin' up that mess you made in my kitchen."

"I have to go," said Janet, intrigued by the way she kept repeating her intention without following through, as if she needed permission.

"Crack cocaine is what you're lookin' for, you dumb bitch," Big Baby Dog snapped at her.

"I got what I came for."

"No, no, no. I'm talking 'bout your deep down. There's a down, you know. You go there, you're down. You got one. I got the feeling. You know what I'm saying. You know what I mean. You got a down in you, and it's down. Me, too, Janet, me, too." He had manufactured a glaze over his eyes while bringing a syrupy deceleration to bear on his speech until his words slogged on, almost slurring. "Do you understand my idea in what I'm sayin'? Because there's an idea involved."

"I think I do."

"Okay, then."

"Not today," she said.

Jamal returned with his zipper reset, his cock contained, a vial rising toward her as he opened his fingers like a magician at the end of a trick.

"Not today, Big Baby Dog, okay?" Janet said.

"Okay. But maybe some other day."

"Maybe." Wary that her hand might move on its own, simply ride out in dim obedience to the desire lurking in the vial, she hooked her thumb in her pocket.

A peal of trumpets introduced an orchestral flowering. Intense glitter from the TV fluctuated rapidly over Brenda, the red swell of her robe awash in the reflection of an image hidden from Janet who, having made her way into the hallway, stood behind the glowing console.

"I'll keep it," Big Baby Dog said. "It be here. That's what I'm sayin'. You know what I mean. Check it out. And a gift, too. Lemme say it again. No limited warranty. Just here for you. Free. You know what I mean. You see what I'm sayin'. Janet's piece of tornado. Waiting. Like it knows and loves you. Like it's your pet little dog. Okay?"

"Okay."

"Like your very own pet rock. People really have them. Real people. You know what I mean? That's what I'm talkin' about. Real pet rocks."

"I've heard of that."

"Me, too."

"Okay. Okay."

"I like how you say that. I like how you say that word. 'Okay.' That's right," said Big Baby Dog, striding to Jamal. He seized and held the vial before his eye like a jeweler evaluating a gem. "That's what I'm talkin' about. Be a ringer. That's what I'm talking about. You know what I mean."

"Sure." Behind him, Brenda poked and punched the folds piled around her with a fidgety frustrated need.

" 'Course you do." Big Baby Dog smiled.

Brenda was frenzied, shifting and groping into the gaps around the cushions. Janet could not help but feel a sympathetic desire to help

Brenda and was about to ask what she could do when Big Baby Dog coughed loudly, startling her. She felt scolded when his glowering gaze took hold of her. He curled his gnarled fingers one after the other until the vial vanished inside the knot of his fist. "For fuck's sake, Janet, I'm talkin' to you."

"You be nice, now, Big Baby Dog," Brenda said to him.

"You be nice, you sad-assed stupid bitch. You the one."

Having found the remote, Brenda leveled it at the TV, and the orchestra went silent while the flurry of faint colors continued to dance out from the screen.

Jamal flopped down beside her. "What you watching?"

"What?"

"What you watching?" He sounded fed up with having to find his way amid so many stupid people.

"Why?"

"Because I don't know what it is."

Brenda shook her head disgustedly, and Janet realized Big Baby Dog had come to stand beside her, the two of them gaping at Brenda and Jamal on the couch. Jamal squirmed around like he was mocking what Brenda had just done, but then he wrestled from somewhere the last Coke can dangling in its plastic loop. His face underwent a series of dark distortions, ending in a scowl, as he punched Brenda in the arm. "What you doing drinkin' my Coke?"

"Don't you be hittin' me, dumbass. What you hittin' me for?"

"Don't you be drinkin' my Coke, you don't want me givin' you a smack."

"I ain't."

"It's gone."

"That don't mean I did it."

"Was two. Now one. Whata you say to that?" The can he thrust before her eyes was all the proof he would ever need.

"She did it. Janet. She needed to drink her Advil."

"Who?"

"Janet. I jus' tole you."

His expression became sad, shades of hurt and puzzlement making him appear almost innocent. Janet didn't wait for him to speak before speeding out the front door.

The brazen light assaulted her. The late afternoon was odd, the wind cool, the sun fiery. The house stood on a hillside. Surely the original owner had not foreseen the unhappy situation that would arrive after the building was turned into apartments, with Big Baby Dog trashing the ground floor and somebody worse upstairs. She imagined the first pristine moments with the paint freshly applied, the grass mowed, the concrete stairs bordered in flowers and swept clean rather than littered with discarded beer and soda cans. She had to dodge brown shards from a shattered malt liquor bottle, and anxious suddenly that her car might have been stolen or vandalized, she jogged by bedraggled white plastic garbage bags bursting with clutter and stench.

When the door slammed behind her, she saw Jamal in a blur of motion. Not yet accustomed to the daylight, she had no idea what his flurry of actions meant until an explosive splat beside her became a spinning Coke can spraying its contents. "Take that one, too, why don't you, you bitch. You hear me. You hear me!"

He could have killed her. Could have brained her, for crissake, throwing that unopened Coke can at her. Because she drank one? He bopped sideways with the loose-limbed swagger of a rapper, his hands flying about in codified contempt. When he ended up against the house, the glare dimmed enough for her to see him glowering. Then he nodded with the satisfaction of someone who believed his momentous deed long overdue. "That's right," he said, and strode off. "You see what I'm sayin' to you now, you messed-up bitch, think you can do anything you please. That's right!"

What was right? She wheeled toward her car, parked at the curb in the shadows of a large oak. She saw no broken windows or scrapes in the paint, but that damn Coke had spattered her shoes and stained her leggings. She circled the car to the driver's side only to have outrage whirl her with such mastery that she was stomping up the stairs before she had time to take note of what she was doing, let alone consider the wisdom of flinging open the front door and barging in.

"You idiot!" she shouted. "What the hell do you think you're doing?"

"Hey," said Big Baby Dog, who was on the couch with Brenda.

Janet examined the room but saw no one else. "That idiot partner of yours almost killed me."

"Who?"

"That one! The other one. He's crazy!"

"I ain't got no partner," he told her.

"You know who I mean. The idiot with his dick in his hand. He nearly killed me."

"She talkin' about Jamal," said Brenda.

"I know who she talkin' about."

"Jamal's in the bathroom," said Brenda

"You don't want to pay Jamal no mind, Janet," said Big Baby Dog.

"I'm telling you for your own good—whatever he is to you, he's useless. What if he had hit me? You know what I mean? For no reason. You know what I'm saying! Where the hell is he? I want to know his reason. In the bathroom? This bathroom?" Janet bolted toward the door like she might pound on it. "He's dangerous. To you, I'm talking about. You see what I'm saying? If he'd hit me or killed me, you don't want that kind of attention in your front yard, I don't think."

"That's an important point you are makin', Janet." Big Baby Dog struck a brief, thoughtful pose. "Jamal! Get out here!"

His voice came muffled through the wall. "What for?"

"Just do it."

The toilet flushed, the unseen pipes squealing. Jamal emerged, his frown a knot of attempted menace that left him looking worried. He seemed besieged by complexities. Tucking in his shirt and zipping up, he peeked at her, his mucus-filmed eyes burning with how much he hated her for standing there like she was.

"What you doin' throwin' shit at Janet, Jamal?" Big Baby Dog said.

"What'd I do?"

"I just tole you."

"What if that thing had hit me?" Janet demanded.

"What thing?"

"That Coke can!"

"What Coke can?"

"The one you threw at me."

"You all right," he said, and shoved her aside as if he needed a wide path to the couch. "I thought maybe you wanted it. Maybe you still thirsty. You took the other one, you know."

"You're such bullshit," Janet told him. "You really are. Just bullshit."

The luster of the TV still flared over Brenda, and then it painted Jamal as he squeezed in between her and Big Baby Dog. Either the VCR was on pause or the volume was muted. Brenda was smiling at Janet. "I don't want you hurtin' Janet, Jamal," she said.

"I didn't."

"Janet comes here to do a little business, she got to feel safe," Big Baby Dog told him.

"I didn't hurt her."

"Janet talks to me in the hardware store, you know what I mean. That's what I'm sayin'. Happened today, even, and I got to say, it made me feel good right in my heart." He placed his hand as if in preparation for a vow or to swear allegiance. "We just had a nice little talk."

"About duct tape," Janet said.

"That's right. About duct tape. Colors and stuff."

Jamal jutted his chin three or four times in the direction of the TV before he said, "Turn it back on, Brenda."

"Okay." She nodded, raising the remote.

"You just put that thing down, you don't want me throwin' it out the window, Brenda!" Big Baby Dog growled. "Hear me?"

"Okay," she said, lowering the remote.

"Jamal, dumbass. You listen. You ought to be payin' attention to what I'm sayin' and not just wantin' to watch the damn TV. Somehow what I'm sayin' ought to be of interest to you, since it's about you."

"Well, it ain't. It ain't of no interest."

"You ain't even heard it yet." Big Baby Dog looked expectantly to Janet. Clearly, he believed she shared his conviction that they were two of a kind, Janet and Big Baby Dog, both cursed with the burden of reason in a nonsensical world. "What you got to know about Jamal, now, Janet—what you got to understand—is that he ain't gonna see all that many more Sundays in this world. Everybody knows it. He ain't gonna get much older. Can't happen. You see what I mean. You know what I'm sayin'. Ain't that right, Jamal."

Jamal puckered his lips and put his head into wavy motion as a way of signaling his complete disregard for Big Baby Dog's opinions, especially any attempting to comment on somebody as hip as Jamal knew himself to be.

"See? Check him out. He got to get a brain, but he can't. Trouble jus' jumps on him. He's one young nigger ain't ever gonna get to be an old nigger. How many times you been shot, Jamal?"

"Why?"

"He been shot a lot a times, Janet. God don't want him dead is the only reason he ain't dead. And he ain't done with gettin' shot. It's jus' a sad fact. I won't ever be the one shoots him. That's my vow, and I give it." He gestured at something that turned out to be the lumber and tools from the hardware store. "Like all that stuff we bought at that fucked-up store—it was for him. You know what I mean? Jamal says he knows how to build stuff. He knows how to carpenter. He'll build shelves and a nice unit, but he don't know shit. He's full of shit. You see what I mean? That's what I'm sayin'. Now, I ain't gonna shoot him over it. No, I won't. But it's gotta come that one day God's gonna wake up done with him. Jus' as sick of his foolishness as everybody else."

"Turn it on, Brenda. I want to see it now," Jamal said, and this time his fluttering fingers closed in a fist before the gesture ended.

"So I'd just say don't let nothin' 'bout Jamal worry you, 'cause he won't be troublin' anybody much longer, ain't that right, Jamal?"

Jamal glanced at him and then sat glowering and pensive, staring at the wall, as he absorbed Big Baby Dog's forecast of his doom. "They run him out of Omaha and some other spot before that. Big spot. And I'm not talkin' about the police, either, or the citizens. No, I'm talkin' about the gang run him out. The Bloods. And he ain't but sixteen now, so he musta started runnin' he was twelve, thirteen. But they run him out because the fool couldn't do nothing but fuck things up. Ain't that right, Jamal? And before they run him out of Omaha, they run him out of California. Where else they run you out of?"

"I don't know."

"Sure you do."

"Why you wanna know?"

"I'm tellin' Janet here."

The flicker of contact Jamal endured with her left no doubt about her power to fill him with things bleak and exasperating. "Ain't her business."

"I'm talking about that first place where they nearly killed you. The one before California."

"Ain't none of her business, Big Baby Dog."

"He ain't been here but a week. How long you been here?"

"Why?"

"How long you been here, dickhead?"

"I don't know. They send me, I come."

She couldn't see the TV, but she heard drums, faint, almost delicate, and figured Brenda was sneaking the sound back on. She imagined pageantry. Big Baby Dog looked disgusted because of all the things he could not control. Along with the drums, Janet heard voices whose timbre conjured crowds of stricken people straining at barricades along a thoroughfare, the hearse with poor dead Diana gliding at a deliberate pace trailed by dark-suited mourners. She imagined rows of tear-stained faces, some old, others young, some gruff and weathered, others upper-class and refined. Flowers flew through the air.

The hard white nub of crack cocaine lay in its vial on a small table beside the kitchen doorway, and she walked to it and put her hand on it, pinching it between two fingers. It seemed an artifact, a preserved chip of bone. Wondering if the thing she was about to accomplish was what she had come back to do, she turned toward the couch and said, "This is mine, right, Big Baby Dog?"

He was smiling. It seemed she had made him very happy. "That's the one. I tole you. You got a pipe? You know how to do it, right?"

"I think so."

"You just cook it in a pipe," Brenda told her.

"Give her a pipe, Brenda." Big Baby Dog nodded. He was shifting in a way that made it seem he intended to lie down on the crowded couch.

"I got some in the kitchen someplace," Brenda said.

"Well, go get one and give her one."

"Okay." Brenda bent forward, ready to rise, but she froze and sat there, tilted, looking troubled, thinking hard.

Big Baby Dog stared at her, and Janet did, too. It struck Janet that the thing stymieing Brenda was simply the concept of getting to her feet. Whatever she was considering, she appeared face-to-face with insurmountable difficulties. Any chance of standing disappeared as she sank back. "Jamal, go get Janet a pipe. You know, they in that drawer. The one in the kitchen."

"She just say she don't need it."

"Just go on, fool." Big Baby Dog flung out a fist that smacked Jamal on the side of the head. "I'm sick of telling you anything I tell you more times than a deaf man. You wearin' me down, boy."

Jamal stood slowly, rubbing around his ear and pushing up through the weight of his resentment and bitterness and the way they were about all he had to express who he was. It was his elbow this time that fluttered toward the TV. "You put it on pause, okay, Brenda, or I ain't goin'. I don't want to miss that parade."

She aimed and twitched the remote, and the TV went silent. "It's the drawer under all those shelves with the dishes—the same place we got you a rig yesterday."

"Oh."

"That's where it is."

"I mean it, Brenda. Don't you turn it back on till I'm back to see what happens."

"Jamal," Big Baby Dog growled. "For fuck's sake!" He looked bitter and worn out and sad.

Jamal went and Janet waited, glancing into the little she could see of the kitchen, where Jamal bobbed about. Her hand, clutching the vial, slipped into her purse.

"You know how to cook it," Brenda said, picking something off the nearby end table. She rolled her eyes as if identifying an outrageous prank. "We call it a pipe, okay."

"Check it out." Big Baby Dog grinned. "She gonna give you a tutorial, and she is an all-star Rockette. She been everywhere a puffer can get to. A rock star, space base. She been a puller, been strawberry. So you just keep on her tight." Half standing and angling toward the kitchen, he bellowed, "Don't want no Brillo, Jamal! You hear me! You bring Janet a copper screen and a padded-up rig."

Brenda was inserting a brownish pebble into one end of a small glass tube. "Little rock goes in it under the Brillo. You got to filter. Nice little padding to protect you from gettin' burned." Her fingers were daintily fitted to a snatch of orange cloth, or maybe rubber, held in place by yellow elastic bands. "You got Vaseline, some people say put it on your lips. Matches okay, but best you have a lighter." She only pretended to pick one up. "You got to tilt so the rock don't fall out." It was all pantomime as Brenda reclined and rotated the tube over the imaginary flame. "Don't want to scorch, see. Suck it deep and hang on."

"And get somewhere safe," said Big Baby Dog. "Home in bed. Or with a friend."

"You got to learn to be moderated. See how I was just playin' it, because I am moderated. Wasn't for a long time. But you got to be. Tornado, now, you got to know, he don't care much for moderated. But you go the other way, and you end up sittin' on a curb somewhere, your best friend a hydrant."

"Brenda, what the fuck you talkin' about?" Big Baby Dog had let his face get twisted into a fed-up pout, his shoulders up by his ears. "Janet, don't pay her no attention."

"I am just tryin' to be her friend and be the voice of my experience."

"She don't need to hear it."

"I like Janet."

"We all like Janet. But you an addict, Brenda, for fuck's sake, talking about moderated. Janet don't need to hear that. Janet's just gonna have a little joy ride, ain't that right, Janet?"

"Sure," she said.

"Just get on and get off."

Nodding, she wondered aloud, "How much does this go for under regular circumstances?"

"We don't have none of them, you know. Regular circumstances. You know what I'm sayin'. There's this for one somebody, and then there's some other one. Can't say who. You know what I mean. But there's every which kind, you might say, and you would be right to say it. But you and me got no need to figure that foolishness right now."

Jamal returned, pausing on his way to the couch long enough to contact Janet's eyes with his own as he held out the gear for her to take. It required delicacy for her to pincer the items from his open palm without touching his skin. She saw softness in him, something malleable and lost, but none of it was sufficient to dilute his hatred of her.

Inching the crack and the pipe into her purse, she turned to go. She was near the door when the TV came back on. Drums again, and sober voices, the hearse and the dead princess passing along a street.

20

SOMEHOW HAZEL'S SPIRITS HAD LIFTED. It was hard to piece together how she'd put the bathroom episode behind her, but she had. She was smiling at the road like somebody being paid a ton of money to cart Bernice around. Maybe talking about Doc McGhee had done her good, though Bernice couldn't see how. She'd been almost cheerful when they went for more coffee, and then after the drugstore, where they'd picked up a pack of Depends, she had a real bounce in her step. Those were big generous cups they gave you at Loefler's, and Hazel had downed her own, some of Bernice's, and had just finished another. Still, a caffeine buzz couldn't be the whole story. Bernice was trying without much success to recall if she'd ever seen anything quite like this before, where coming unglued gave a person a whole new lease on life. It was a turn of events she ought to welcome, but the trouble was, she could feel her own mood teetering and getting ready to knock her off her pins.

The sun had changed into a violent-looking smear half buried way off in the west. Brown drifts in a field were maybe a million of piled-up leaves, the ruined trees these black shapes like the drawings Irma used to make, and some not half bad, either. Even the art teacher said so. Suddenly, the piles were flying like something solid going to pieces. Every single leaf was helpless in a crooked, tumbling struggle, and watching them sharpened her own nosedive, with nothing she could do to fix it. Not that she really wanted to change things or thought she could. Maybe it was just time. Maybe she was getting ready. Starting to become something she'd never thought she could tolerate. But maybe soon she'd be one of those people who didn't care whether things were alive or dead. Maybe this was how it started. Just sitting in a car feeling yourself sinking. Because there was a lot in this life, when you got right down to it, that a person could do without. Like poor Mary Walding lugging those silver prongs around and sticking them into bins of candy, then having to fit all those pieces into a white paper bag without spilling them, and all the while her hands were shaking. And then she had to drag herself up and smile at that snotty little thing in her outlandish outfit and call her "sweetie," saying, "What can I do you for, sweetie?" And saying goodbye to her friends, even those she wasn't really all that close to, such as Bernice. Because she didn't know Mary all that well. But still. Did that matter? Or was the point that they could at least see each other and say, *There's Mary. There's Bernice.* Which wouldn't be the case with billions of other people in the world who would just gape at you with no idea who you were and no interest in learning. So it was that kind of goodbye. Like you'd say to anybody you knew at all, if it was the last time you'd ever see them. And that stupid hat with the shameful logo she was supposed to wear but didn't, because she was brave enough to buck the system. And poor Doc McGhee. What a low blow that was. A great man cut off at the knees. And he was a rare bird, like Hazel said. He'd been Bernice's doctor for Irma and then another pregnancy that didn't work out. So she knew a little about that, too. She'd been there at the funeral but hadn't really remembered the way Hazel had. It made her sick to think how she'd forgotten all about it. How could she be so useless and shallow? Here she was, able to remember that Creature from the Black Lagoon and the ups and downs of his dumb life, but the saddest day Doc McGhee would ever live through wasn't important enough for her to set it up in a place where it could be found forever. And he was real, not some movie monster. She felt rotten. Just plain disgusted with herself. As a matter of fact, she didn't know which made her feel worse, the way poor Doc McGhee had suffered or the fact that she'd turned out to be the kind of coldhearted person who could let such precious human trouble slip away like it might as well not have happened, for all she cared.

The sky appeared a vast stretch of concrete marred by bubbles, cracks, and claw marks. Mother Nature was spreading her barren touch. What did it matter what happened to people if nobody cared? If everybody forgot the terrible things. And the good things, too. Or the terrible and good together in one mix, like poor Mary saying goodbye. And Jimmy! What about that? Good Lord. Jimmy McGhee, whom she knew nothing about, except for that time he hit the home run in Little League and wore this beaming smile running all the way around the bases. But then when the game was over and they lost, he sat in the dirt sobbing, just heartbroken because he'd made some mistake and the ball had gone right between his legs, an error, Toby called it. "Cost them the game." What about him ending up in a jungle with bugs and snakes a million miles from where he belonged? And for that matter, what about the heartbreak in the dirt? Poor little guy, crying his eyes out over his error, like it was the end of the world, even after hitting a home run. Misery, Bernice thought. There was plenty to go around. More than enough to make a person think twice about the whole damn deal of living in this world. And Hazel today. That wasn't something to skip. Because maybe she'd managed to find a way out of her tailspin, but locked up inside that bathroom stall, she'd been pretty much down for the count. She might be acting like she didn't have a care in the world now, but not so long ago she'd been a wreck. Couldn't even poke her head out.

"Hazel," she said.

"Yeah."

"How you doing?"

"I'm okay."

They were coming to the end of a block where a stop sign and heavy traffic kept them waiting.

"Bernice," said Hazel.

"Yeah."

"I want to ask you something, okay?" She smiled, and Bernice smiled back. Given the chance, Hazel turned right.

"Okay."

"When you were talking about what the doctors today could maybe have done for me, what did you have in mind?"

"Oh, I wasn't thinking of anything in particular."

"You sounded like you were."

"You see things on those shows sometimes."

"On TV, you mean."

"On a news show, maybe. Or there's a piece in the paper. You must have run into some."

"That's what I thought. That kind of stuff. With the test tubes and all like that."

"That's some of it."

"I don't think I'd care for that."

"Well, it's not something a person would set their sights on. It's pretty much a last-resort type of thing."

"Sure."

"But there's people doing it more and more all the time, and the kids turn out fine."

"That's what they say. I know all that. But it don't seem natural."

"Well, no. It's not natural."

"So they get an egg out of me and some of Jackie's stuff and put 'em together, right?"

"I'm not saying I understand it, Hazel. I'm no doctor."

"So Jackie's gotta go in some room, and you know—they give him *Playboy*-type magazines and he has to go in there and you know. See, now, that's just not something I'd be crazy about."

"I think he probably would've had some idea how to get it done."

"I can't argue that. But he'd be mortified doin' it with everybody knowing what he was up to. Lord."

"Well, it's not something you have to worry about now."

"I know. I'm just trying to think it through. Maybe he could have done it at home. That woulda helped him out."

"I don't think so. I think it's got to be at the place. The clinic or what-ever. So they're alive."

"There's some I hear where what they end up doing is taking the egg, and they get it fertilized, and once that's set up, they stick the whole deal into some other woman. Some third party. Not the wife."

"That's one of the ways."

"Somebody who's healthy and who can carry it. Right? So she's the one pregnant. She's got to go through the nine months. What's in it for her? I'd like to know. I guess money changes hands."

"More often than not. Though there's friends do it for their friends, too."

"Like you for me."

"Well, sure. Or your sister."

"Glenda. Sure. She would have. What about you?"

"Sure."

"You're lyin', Bernice." Playful yet sharp as a tack, Hazel lit up with her little indictment. "I mean, you couldn't answer that fast and not be at least partway lying. See what I mean?"

"What does it matter?"

"Well, only in as much as I'm trying to think it through, like I said. In a real way, you know. Because that'd be the likely thing, in my case, since the trouble was never us getting pregnant, but I couldn't get all the way to the end. So this other woman would give birth, and we'd take the baby home."

"I think that's about it."

"What about nursing? She'd have to be the one to nurse."

"Or nobody. Formula. There's formula."

"I think it'd have to be her."

"If anybody, sure. It's a good question, though. It'd depend, I bet."

"You can say that again. Probably charge you an arm and a leg, too."

"There'd be all kinds of things to take into account."

"The truth is, Bernice, I can't say the whole deal holds out much appeal. Just not our kind of thing. What we kept hoping was that the regular way would work out. And I'd bet my bottom dollar that even if that kind of business had come our way, me and Jackie would not have gone for it. You know, doin' it some funny way."

"Like the regular way was somethin' to write home about," Bernice said.

Hazel's lips parted with her reaction, but she held back, and Bernice was relieved Hazel had decided to keep her first thought to herself. She looked away, then peeked to give Bernice a sly but thorough going-over.

"It was pretty funny, too, if you ask me," Bernice told her.

Hazel's grin was more manufactured than racy, though racy was obviously what she was shooting for. "Oh, now, Bernice, you had yourself a good man, and you know it."

"Nobody's saying that wasn't the case."

"So why pick at him? Poor man's not around to defend himself. You had your fun, I bet."

"Oh, sure."

"Me and Jackie did, and that's the truth. He was more than a little fond of it."

"Oh, yeah. Toby was, too."

"So what are you complaining about?"

She didn't really know. Not that the word struck her as fitting. In fact, it felt completely off base. But if she wasn't complaining, what was she doing?

"I'd bet dollars to doughnuts Toby was a sweetheart once you got him going," Hazel said. "Plenty of girls thought he was handsome as all get-out, let me tell you."

What girls? Bernice wondered, remembering Toby as a sweetheart she'd gotten going every now and then when she might be going, too. He'd get to grabbing at her, and she'd start grabbing back. All this grabbing, and then this feeling of mouthwatering shimmer in his skin. There'd been some times of hopped-up sensations, all right. A person could get carried away. It was like drugs when the surgeon was going to cut you open, so he put you under and you were glad to go. Or this dizzy kind of spell, turning Toby's thickness and hairy parts into riches with little tickles jumping out of him and into her, skin to skin, like it was time to face the fact that there was more to them than what they'd thought, and one or maybe both of them was electric and maybe magnetic, too. Male and female sockets, all right, with this low-voltage current humming through her. Screwdriver and screw. All these handy tools. And animal noises. Couple of growling dogs. Or she'd be sounding like a train blowing its whistle. Or maybe she would be talking away but making no sense. Babbling, you'd have to call it. What was that all about? Who knew? Because when it was over, she felt like some crazed stranger had filled in for her. Just showed up and took her place. This crazed stranger in off the street, or up from the basement, or down from the attic, just stepping in from some put-away place to nudge her aside and take charge. Not the least bit shy, and pretty handy. Crazy as a loon, and cutting in to run the show until things wound down, when she would pack up and head on back to wherever she came from. Just take off, because she wasn't one for walking around in a housedress and apron, washing dishes or cooking a decent meal. That wasn't for her. Not by a long shot. She wasn't one to put dirty laundry in the machine or stand out in the wind with clothespins in her mouth, hanging up pants and shirts and sheets to dry on the line. Once you had your clothes back on, you were better off without her.

"Won't be long now," Hazel said, grinning. "Another few minutes and we're there."

It was true. Reverend Tauke's place was getting close, and the realization made Bernice all the more miserable, because she was nowhere near being in the right frame of mind to arrive. She wanted to get out of the car cheery and upbeat, like everybody did. Why'd she have to start thinking about Toby like they were a couple of soap-opera people in those afternoon stories where things went pretty far these days? They didn't leave much to the imagination, and her and Toby must have been like that, even if it was hard to get the feeling back. Like drinking schnapps, maybe, this sweetness all over. Or somebody racing their fingers up and down her spine when she was little and then squeezing her neck so goose bumps danced. Or the time she'd touched that loose wire. It had to be something like that, didn't it? She didn't know, but given her dreary mood, which she couldn't escape and which in fact seemed to be getting worse, she might as well have been standing on the sidewalk watching somebody rob her house.

The fields looked aged and empty, the trees brittle, the sky drained and wintry. Maybe, she thought, it was good that she was down in the dumps, considering what she had in store for her. Maybe it was good she'd had that hurtful conversation with Irma. Even good the way she'd taken her frustration out on poor Sappy, punching him square in the nose. Used her fist, too. The disbelief that had overtaken his goofy, sweet-natured eyes wasn't anything she cared to see right this second, but there it was. After that phone call with Irma, she'd been on pins and needles. Jumped into the shower and then worked up a sweat rushing to get dressed. She was bent over, the life just about squeezed out of her as she put on her shoes, when Sappy had scampered up to poke his nose in and start licking her hands. She'd pushed him aside, and back he'd come. Watching from the door, Hazel had let out this exasperated groan, just throwing daggers. Already going as fast as humanly possible, Bernice tried to speed up, knowing she was forgetting something that for the life of her she couldn't recall. "Bernice, please! Can we go?" Hazel had snapped, tapping her toe like some snooty four-star Napoleon at the end of her rope because Bernice was stupid or stalling, and Bernice had just surrendered, veering for the door with Sappy bouncing along, his adoring gaze angled up. "What are you so happy about?" she'd said, and as he'd jumped to coax her one more time, she'd balled her hand into a fist and cracked him across the snout. He'd yelped and cowered, and that was the last she saw of him.

"Bernice?" said Hazel, glancing up from the road.

"What?" Bernice snarled, all but foaming at the memory of Hazel, the gold-braided honcho with her nose up in the air, the Queen Bee who should have been the one to get smacked instead of poor Sappy. "I said, 'What?'"

"Don't bite my head off."

"Could we just be quiet for a while?"

"We were."

"I think we've said enough for one day."

"I was just going to tell you something."

"I don't want to hear it." And she didn't. Here she was on her way to heaven, the whole thing over and done with, angels swarming and the end coming on like the sunset, like the winter, like the evening, like the dark itself, and all she had to show for it was a daughter she couldn't talk to. Not a civil word. And the memory of hitting Sappy. She had that, too.

"We don't seem to be able to get through five sentences without getting on each other's nerves, Hazel. So just let it rest."

"Okay," said Hazel. "Fine. Except I don't know what you're talking about."

Of course she didn't. How could she? She never had. And that was just fine. Nobody ever understood a word out of her mouth, and they probably never would. Not Hazel, not Irma. Probably not even Toby. And that was just fine. So she had nobody to say goodbye to except some perfect stranger like Mary Walding, who didn't really care but was just scared and thinking about herself. And that was fine, too. So what if there was nobody to miss Bernice, or wonder where she'd gone, except a bunch of animals, who wouldn't care, either, once somebody bothered to show up and throw a little food their way. They were selfish as a bunch of children. A bunch of babies. Just like Irma. Only Irma didn't appear selfish or petty or neglectful just then, showing up as a shiny, adorable bundle in her brand-new little-girl flesh wrapped up in the gaiety of her dress. Seated on the floor with her tongue between her lips, she maneuvered a pencil, while the hard work of drawing pushed her face into a frown. The lines of a limb marked the page. Of a trunk. Little knots, even. Bernice swallowed the tears that were building, but they tangled in her chest and refused to stay. She pinched her eyes shut against them and saw herself in the arms of that Creature in his Black Lagoon. She was young and wearing a white one-piece bathing suit, and his embrace was powerful as he bore her off into the darkness.

"It's okay, Bernice," said Hazel.

More from Hazel's sympathetic tone than from her own sensations, Bernice understood that she'd lost the battle to keep her feelings in check. "I don't know."

"It is."

"I don't know. I really don't."

"I'm telling you. Just look out the window. Look at that sky. That's Him. He's shining behind it."

Bernice removed her glasses to wipe her eyes, and the gray vista blurred and streaked in a jumble of fading colors. "I don't see it."

"The Lord is in the daylight. It's Jesus, so bright. Not even the clouds can hide Him."

"I don't see it."

"Just look. Right up there in that sunlight." Letting both hands lift from the wheel, Hazel pressed her palms toward the windshield as if raising a platter. "Hallelujah."

"Just drive and don't be some damn fool," Bernice said, and Hazel responded with a far-fetched smile that forced Bernice to plow on. "I'm being serious here, Hazel, okay? I told Janet Cawley something like that— like what you're saying—when I went up to her house the other evening, and I sat in her kitchen eating Oreos, and I looked out at the sunset and said what you're saying. But I was lying. I lied about what I saw. I don't know why. I felt like bragging, I think, or something."

"He's there, Bernice."

Sunlight strained behind the gray stubborn blankness that cracked into splinters and shards of color, like someone had kicked in a stained-glass window.

" 'When time shall be no more,' " said Hazel.

"What?"

" 'When time shall be no more.' That's what I wanted to tell you before."

"When?"

"When you about bit my head off. But that's what we were trying to remember. Remember when we were trying to remember the saying Reverend Tauke says and the way he says it and we couldn't."

"That's it?"

"Yeah."

"And you never remembered it till now?"

"Just a bit ago, when you snapped at me. But that's it. And it's not from the Bible. It sounds like the Bible, but I don't think it's from the Bible. Where is it from? Do you remember?"

"No." She associated the phrase with one sermon or another, but she wasn't the least inclined to help Hazel look for her answer. Instead, she fixed on the school bus going by, and then on two little girls huddled at a gray roadside mailbox up ahead. They wore shiny jackets, one yellow, the other red, their book bags dropped in the grass. They tugged open the mailbox flap and peered in. Bernice didn't dare ask Hazel to stop, though she wanted to learn what the girls hoped to find. Had some long-awaited item come at last? A toy? A letter? A mysterious map or fairy-tale diamond?

But the car flashed on, and the girls flew off behind her. Hazel chuckled, her gaze upraised, as if she was enjoying a spectacle both awesome and heartwarming. Ahead, the road advanced beneath an expanse of dazzle and white drifting clouds that seemed to map an unfamiliar world of invisible pathways, secret countries, armies of angels. Cumulus. That was one of them. Others were Timbuktu, Istanbul. Thunderheads. Precipitation. She was getting it all mixed up.

"It's from a song," said Hazel.

"What is?"

" 'When time shall be no more.' "

"Oh, sure." The melody came to her instantly, though not with every note in place. It had a certain appeal, all right, but she wasn't sure it was all to the good. *When time shall be no more.* Well, maybe, she thought. Like jumping off a cliff, because Jesus would catch her. Like she used to run and fly off the high dive at the public pool in summer, thinking, Lord help me. Couldn't do it except by belittling and chasing herself with scolding thoughts. Or swinging on that rope that creaked as she swooped out over Droessler's pond. Just closing her eyes and holding her nose as she fell with this exploding slap into the water. The splash rose in bubbles while she sank through the airless dark until she came to where that black creature waited with widespread arms. Now, what in the name of heaven was the point? she demanded. Of thinking such a thing? And not just once but to keep thinking it! Good Lord. She really wished she knew. Because there he was with his fishy eyes and his heart bursting with love for her, and once again she was young as they sailed into deeper and blacker water.

"Tell me the truth, Hazel. Be honest now. You don't see Him up there. No more than I did. You see clouds, and some are gray. And there's whiter ones, and they got these shapes. Different shapes, and they're clouds in the sky, and that's what you see. That's what I see, and you see it, too. You don't see a face or something."

"He's there."

"I'm asking you, do you see Him? His face and eyes and nose and like that."

"No."

"Okay, then."

"It's sort of an inside-outside thing. My insides see him up there in the clouds that my outsides are looking at."

"Oh, Lord," said Bernice. "I want an answer."

"That is an answer."

"Because I'm scared, Hazel. That's what I'm saying. I mean, let's just think what we're talking about. What's going to happen."

"You're having doubts. But Jesus will take care of us."

"But what if He don't?"

"Those are your doubts, Bernice."

"I know that."

"You'll feel better when you get there and we're all together."

"Even if He takes care of us. Even if it all happens in the best possible way, Hazel, it's still scary, don't you think?"

A field of hacked-down corn spread golden rows all the way to the big oak standing just below the horizon. The muted sky showed through a mist of leaves, which suddenly exploded, turning into birds, black-winged dots flying off.

The road ahead curved into a long downward arc on its way to Reverend Tauke's church, visible off to the right. The sun burned above the peaks of the buildings that had once been a farmhouse and barn. It was a pleasant sight from the road. Always had been, even back when it belonged to the Tiedeman family all those years—who knew how many generations. Bernice remembered her first service and how amazed she'd been to find everything so clean and cared for. The house had been turned into the parsonage, with Reverend Tauke's living quarters upstairs and the whole of the downstairs a communal gathering place. But it was the transformation of the barn into the chapel that had struck her as next to miraculous, planked flooring and rows of waxed, buffed pews with a raised altar area and red carpeting down the center aisle so that it was a perfect setting for sermons, testimony, and singing.

A three-foot white cross floated atop the peaked roof, catching the last of the afternoon light. Cars crowded the dirt parking lot in neat rows. The figure of a man stood gazing off past the fence around an adjacent pasture, where a small herd of milking cows lounged. A few people had formed a group a short walk down from the house. The man watching the cows was smoking, and another man, also smoking, ambled toward him.

As the Toyota slowed near the entrance, it struck Bernice that the old barn and farmhouse were still around somehow, like ghosts haunting the chapel and parsonage. "Which of the Tiedemans was the last to give up on that old place?" she wondered.

"It was Clyde made things go." The quickness of Hazel's answer meant she'd probably been having similar thoughts. "His parents built it, and he grew up there. And he made a mint all through the forties and fifties."

"That's right—Clyde. Big fat man, a little stuck up, as I recall. So his mom and dad were the first, but I'm wondering which was the last to go?"

"That'd be Marlin. His wife was Katie. You remember them."

"Oh, sure. Marlin and Katie. You're sure they were the last ones tried to make a go of it?"

"I remember the yard sale. That was a circus that left no doubt they were done tryin' to hang on."

"That's right. I remember now. What a big yard sale that was."

"One of the biggest I ever saw, and loaded with good stuff. Bargains everywhere you looked."

"Did we go together?"

"I think we did."

"Or maybe we just bumped into each other."

"I think we went together. If I remember right."

"It's coming back to me. And I think I see it your way. Who drove? You, I think. In that old Pontiac."

"I bought a rocking chair."

"I remember that."

"Sturdy, too. More than our money's worth. Jackie had plenty a nice evening rockin' in that chair. Put himself to sleep many's the night."

"I remember that chair. Had a pretty light stain."

"That's the one."

"Did I buy anything?" Bernice wondered.

"Probably."

"What?"

"I'm not sure. Lemme think a minute, and I bet it'll come to me."

"She was cryin'. I remember that. Katie was a sweet little thing. Always friendly, but just cryin' her eyes out all day long. Couldn't hardly take a person's money or make proper change when she made a sale."

"It was sad. The whole affair. Marlin looked awful."

"Katie had to cry for both of them was how it looked to me."

"You know that's exactly the way it went. That Marlin wouldn't cry."

"No, no. Not him."

"Not Marlin Tiedeman. Take more than losing everything to make him bawl."

21

LEAVING BIG BABY DOG STACKED on that couch with Jamal and Brenda, Janet hurried to her car, absently turning on her radio only to switch it off before whatever grating new band she'd bumped into had time to get on her nerves. She might have tried other stations but opted for silence, and then, delayed behind a beat-up truck full of crates tied down by a tarp, she felt she was being observed. The cops had to be keeping an eye on Big Baby Dog's place, didn't they? Tracking who came and went.

Over the next few blocks, she checked the rearview mirror and searched down every cross street and alleyway. What the hell had she been thinking to go there in broad daylight? Awaiting an answer, she was startled by getting the giggles. No reason to feel ill fated or cursed. She was simply prone to calamity. The furious, unexpected hilarity escalated, and the funniest part was her—the way she was a joke. What she'd done was idiotic, and the fact that it entertained her added to her absurdity.

Having spied a ragged old cardboard coffee cup and a couple of napkins on the floor, she waited for a red light before bending to pick them up. She wasn't stupid, just ridiculous, she thought while removing the crack and crack gear from her purse. She wrapped the vial in one napkin, the pipe and screen in the other. Impatient honking urged her to go, and while matching the pace of the blue Nissan in front of her, she slipped both padded items into the cup. She crumpled the sides carefully, folding them in, and stuck the whole contraption deep into the canvas trash bag hanging from the back of the passenger seat. She'd really better watch her step. Now she was driving around town with an open bottle of Jack Daniel's in her backseat and drugs and drug paraphernalia in her garbage. Not to mention the 'ludes in her pocket. It was a battle to keep the riotous laughter from busting out and to maintain a steady speed.

A woman in a dark blue blazer waited with a chunky yellow Labrador on a leash at the intersection. Seated and gazing in a semi-stupor until Janet passed by, the Labrador jumped to all fours and full alert, eyeing her. In her rearview mirror, she saw the pair enter the crosswalk, the woman's face hidden in sunglasses, while the dog trotted along, no longer interested in Janet, who thought, Oh, shit. Bernice. If she didn't hightail it on over there, she was going to have a houseful of crazed, starving animals, and worse yet, piles of dog shit to clean up. She could all but hear Bernice's scolding voice, as if she'd failed completely and Bernice knew.

The mini-mart on her right seemed a good place to turn around, but then the mix of self-service pumps, parked cars, and people traipsing in and out invited her to stay, as if she had washed ashore on an island of friendly strangers. She could have a cup of coffee and maybe, after the coffee, a clear mind.

She went straight to the three vacuum-packed thermoses, Our Breakfast Blend, Dark Dark Chocolate, and Holly's Hazelnut Delight, arranged on a shelf near racks of newspapers and magazines. Wayne Miller's voice came to her, pitched higher than normal but very relaxed. She found him a couple of aisles away, leaning over a glassed-in freezer, while two small children pestered him about flavors. Their disagreement was mild, the issue whether to get Cherry Vanilla or Chunky Monkey. When Wayne lifted the little boy, who wore a Worthington High athletic jacket like his dad, and then the girl, with the same dark hair as Wayne, onto the thick glass cover of the freezer, Janet felt for a moment that she, too, was peering down with them into the colorful array of ice cream containers.

But she snapped out of it and knew to get going. The fact that he hadn't seen her didn't mean he couldn't or wouldn't, and— She jumped at the loudness of the hiss as she pumped Dark Dark Chocolate into a jumbo cup. Not wanting to catch Wayne's attention, she slowed, hoping for less noise. The little girl was seated, watching her brother crawl the length of the glass, his eyes locked on what lay below. Mom had to be around somewhere. The wife would step up next.

Janet reached for a handful of sugar packets and felt, as much as saw, a blur of Levi's. She knew to head for the register.

"Hey, Janet," he said.

What choice did she have? She'd look like an idiot if she kept going. "Hey, Wayne, hi."

"I thought that was you." He sounded as if recognizing her was a complicated task he was proud to have accomplished.

"And it was. Where were you? Over there?" Together they faced the freezer, where the kids sat studying Daddy and the woman they didn't know.

Wayne nodded and then seemed to think it significant to confirm her guess about his previous location. "We were checking out the ice cream."

"Those your kids?"

"Yeah. But you know that. You've seen them before."

"Here and there."

"Say hello to Janet, kids. She's a teacher, like Daddy."

"Used to be." Janet shook her finger at him.

He exaggerated the importance of getting the details correct. "Used to be. Right. But at a different school."

"I know the ice cream we want," said the boy.

"Chunky Monkey," the girl squeaked, glancing at her brother, who nodded enthusiastically.

"Just a second." Wayne sent them a smile and then turned to Janet. "Getting some coffee, huh?"

"Hey. Needed a pick-me-up."

"You got enough there." With widening eyes, he dramatized his awe at her coffee-drinking prowess.

She examined the cup as if surprised to find it in her hand, then sent a mini-toast in his direction. "Well, it beats crack cocaine."

"I doubt that," he said, and found himself in need of a larger-than-life grin. "From what I've heard."

As his dimples came and went, she waited to say, "I guess I'm speaking from the angle of health. That vantage. You know. And staying sane."

"Well, sure." The kids were laboring to slide open the freezer lid. The sound Wayne made clearing his throat told her he was nervous, but the craving he allowed his eyes to expose canceled her earlier guess about Mom being close by. "Hey," he said, nodding.

"I think you said that, Wayne."

"Did I?" He ruminated for a short time, and the facts he uncovered made him sad, even though he smiled. "I guess I did. I miss you, okay?"

"Already? Wayne, Wayne, Wayne," she said. "It hasn't been that long."

"I guess I'm just trying to get a head start."

"Wayne, Wayne, Wayne."

"What?"

"You know."

"I don't."

"Cute kids."

He reacted as if she had told him to conduct a fresh evaluation of his children. He was still gazing at them when he said, "You have time tonight?"

"You mean after last night you want more?"

The little boy stepped to the edge of the freezer, where his daredevil pose declared him ready to jump. "Kids. C'mon, now. Stop that. Roger, don't you even think of flyin' off that thing, okay? I'll get you the ice cream. Two kinds, if you want."

She placed her palm against his bicep, creating the impression she intended to pull him back around. The tautness beneath his shirt gave a welcoming response, and yet he said, "Don't do that here."

The little boy took the leap, squealing through the air. His awkward lunge, intended to recover his balance, launched him into a rack of potato chips, pretzels, Cheetos. Rebounding, he toppled backward, landing hard while Wayne rushed in to steady the wobbling display.

"Sorry, Dad," the little girl said.

"You didn't do anything, Sarah."

"Oh, oh." Struggling off the floor, the boy began hopping on one foot. "I broke my foot, I think. I broke my ankle."

"You didn't break it."

"No, no. I did. It hurts really, really bad."

The impulse to put a calming hand to the boy's cheek moved Janet in the opposite direction. Wayne was helping his son lie down in order to remove his shoe. She couldn't make out what they were saying, and she sensed more than saw Wayne twitch and half stand, remembering her. He gestured to slow her down. "Hey," he said, and then he pawed through his hair the way he did when he wanted to signal that he was undergoing a lot of emotion, and she thought maybe he really was.

She waved and pivoted to the register while Wayne, behind her, tried to prompt an answer to his question about her availability. "Hey," he said again.

"I don't know if I'm the one to ask," she cast over her shoulder.

The heavyset clerk wore a tie with Donald Duck on it, and he interrupted a jolly telephone conversation to take her money and make quick change. She left without looking back.

Crossing the parking lot, she found the weather indecisive. She sensed something beyond the commonplace, not unnatural, simply grander than a windblown day, and it held her there, standing at her car door, staring into the steely texture of the air.

She drove most of the way to Bernice's house, sipping coffee, while Wayne receded in her mind. At first it was simple and straightforward, merely a replica of the way she'd left him. But then she spied a variation. Desperate to speak, his mouth opened, but only a moan came out. Preoccupied by the requirements of driving, she wasn't fully conscious of every visitation, and yet she underwent accompanying emotions. He might be alone or holding the hands of his kids. In a rowboat on blue-green miles of ocean, he bobbed about far from any shore, encircled by an excruciating glare. She was startled, glimpsing the tattered ends of a rendition in which he ran after her along a country road, and when he stopped, he gazed upward, leading her to think she was flying.

Halfway through an intersection, she awoke to danger. She'd run a stop sign, and only the improbable lack of any cross traffic saved her. Somehow, this alerted her to the fact that the figure she'd been abandoning the last few times was no longer Wayne. He'd worn a dark suit with a dark tie, a lavender shirt? Did he have sunglasses on? His interest in her emanated from a core deep inside his bony skull, and it languidly flowed to her and languidly wanted to enfold her.

But then she saw that she had parked. The faded yellow of Bernice's house looked dingy in the late-afternoon light, and Janet was on the verge of falling asleep. The coffee was gone, the container empty, but she could barely keep her eyes open. Her stomach felt queasy, her limbs numb and lifeless, hanging off her like sacks of concrete. She negotiated the lawn only to be swarmed by dogs the second she walked in. "Okay," she said, and swayed to the nearest chair.

When she shuddered and sat up with a shout, she realized she'd drifted off. Fearful of time—fearful it was running out—she checked her watch, her yawn turning into a groan. As best she could judge, it was only minutes since she'd come in the door. Two dogs sat before her. They were similar and related, if she remembered right, and their names were Goofy and something. She was almost positive. She patted her pockets for the notes Bernice had made her take down, but she'd forgotten all about them when she changed clothes. The dogs, their eyes big and expectant, watched her closely, earnestly. A rhythmic, invasive pressure against her leg turned out to be one of the cats.

She stood and saw the old dog sprawled on the big pillow that served as his bed. He was gazing at her. She wanted to recall his name and was glad when it came to her. "Hello, Admiral."

No matter how miserable she felt, her first job was to get the bunch of them outside, because nothing but luck had saved her from piles of shit. She would take the look-alikes first, Goofy and Doofy. Or Goofy and Doofus. Not that it mattered, but Doofus felt right. Her hand had barely touched the leashes when they squealed and bounded at her. Their zeal confused everything she was trying to do, and they knocked each other over. Admiral eyed her skeptically. Dizziness rolled through her, and she bent at the waist, hands on her knees, for a momentary respite before stomping her foot and shouting, "Sit!," which made them cower long enough for her to snap the hooks onto their collars. Instantly, they hurled themselves toward the door, almost jolting her arms loose from her shoulders. "Hey!"

No sooner did their paws hit the grass than they pissed. But to get them to take a dump required Janet to stagger behind them as numerous sites were examined and disqualified, until at last they found what they wanted and deposited similar turds in neat little piles.

The fact that Admiral hadn't budged encouraged her to hope that he didn't have to go. Feeding was next, but the procedure had been swept from her head. Obviously, the cats would get cat food. The grinding of the opener brought them snaking around her feet, but the opener was old, and getting the lids off seemed to go on forever. She had to take a momentary break. The little crank turned grudgingly, and the crooked blade left clinging, serrated edges. The tawny cat sprang onto the counter, and then the black-and-white one followed, their butts raised as they dove into their dinners. She would feed the dogs each a bowl of kibble mixed with canned slop. This time the opener with its arduous crank bore down on her oppressively. She had to rest and start up. It seemed hours before she could pry the lid off, being careful not to cut herself. And then with the can upside down, nothing happened, nothing emerged. She tried to jar the food loose, jerking it up and down in the air, using more and more force, until the futility made her think she might cry. I can't, I can't, she thought, just as the slop came free in a gush.

She distributed the fishy-smelling mess into three bowls. Goofy and Doofus couldn't wait to start gobbling, but Admiral recoiled after one sniff. He considered her disgustedly. He groaned and drove his head into her thigh. "Okay, okay," she said, watching him stagger to the revolting bowl, where he flopped, pointing his nose away in case she didn't understand.

Vaguely, she recalled a warning about this problem. Hot dogs and something were the vague solution. Was it cheese? He had to have pills, too. By the time she had water boiling, either Goofy or Doofus had crept up to Admiral's bowl and was chomping away. Unclear if the pills were to be administered at both breakfast and dinner, she figured it was better to give too much medicine rather than too little. Molding a hunk of cheese around two pills, she could not believe her misfortune when one squirted loose and skittered under a cabinet. Though she was on her knees and then her belly, the length and breadth of the haze into which she'd seen the pink blur tumble refused to give up its location. She could not cope with any more problems. She sagged onto her side with her eyes closed for a minute or more, and when she let them open, the tablet lay inches from her nose. She felt oddly bewildered but went ahead with what she had to do, picking it up and stuffing it into the cheese. On all fours, she offered the marble-sized morsel to Admiral, who sprang clumsily, driving a fang into her finger.

"Owww! What the fuck are you doing?" He gazed blankly. "Don't bite the hand that feeds you. Ever hear of that one, you fucking idiot?" Something opaque in his expression told her that he was probably half blind. The pain produced a bubble of blood. "I'm going to bed," she told him, and kicked the bowl containing the three cooked hot dogs close to his stupid old nose.

The white ceiling in Bernice's bedroom introduced a parade of weird sensations. Shutting her eyes helped for a moment but then, unhappily, seemed to boost her sense of smell, and the strongest odor was the stink of urine. She needed a 'lude and dug them from her jacket pocket. She broke a tablet in half—it was counterfeit, but looked like a 300—then worked up enough saliva to get it down. But she missed the table as she reached to place the vial, which sank soundlessly into the rug. The piss smell remained, drifting in from somewhere that no amount of scrubbing could ever clean. Sweet body powder mixed with mothballs. Too much detergent and too much hair spray. She began to imagine old skin in the rug, shed skin flaking the sheets under her. She began to see Bernice's old bare feet walking and stopping and turning. Little Red Riding Hood, she thought. Lying in Grandma's bed. Age and otherness had been steeped into the clothes folded in drawers, drooping off closet hangers. Janet was stretched out, and the thing her elbow bumped was Bernice's Bible. She lifted it but barely had the strength to move it aside.

Again she closed her eyes, tired enough to lose track, she hoped. The ceiling went away, and the dark of her mind offered little of interest, though gradually it raised a set of agitations identical to those the ceiling had proposed. Is this it? she wondered. Feeling this way, feeling lost and small with the wolf at the door. Having been left to wander through the forest to the old woman's cottage. Dogs and cats everywhere. Wolves pretending to be people, dressing up in Grandma's old clothes. Janet tried to explain that her thoughts were not making sense because she was sleeping. She wanted to illuminate this important principle. Ohh, where was the teacher to help? Where was that wise and generous and comforting teacher she had tried to put into the world, so she could learn how to be someone, after teaching all the little children and seeing how, when they did what she taught them, they grew up and became big, strong people? Then she could do it, too, couldn't she? But what had become of that teacher? And who was howling? Was it the teacher? The children? Or was it the wolf at the door, wanting to break in and bite her again?

Blinking, she realized the animal misery dwarfing her questions had a source somewhere outside the walls of the bedroom. She staggered into the living room, where Admiral careened wildly, fleeing demons. With his backward gaze widened by dread, he crashed into a chair.

Bernice's little house stood before her, full of furniture and dogs and cats and late-afternoon light. The cats reclined serenely, one on a windowsill, the other on the couch, their perfect indifference to Admiral's crazed behavior expressed in slowly twitching tails. Goofy and Doofus were alert, their attention divided between Janet and the old dog. Having fallen beside the couch, Admiral lay panting. Janet approached with Goofy and Doofus following, warily. There were no wolves or demons, of course. It was just bad dreams waking poor old Admiral, and her, too, some nightmarish figure chasing them both from sleep. She stared at him as he lay where he'd fallen, and wished she could explain.

When she reached his abandoned bed, she could not recall having decided to go there, to lift and shake the cumbersome pillow, and yet there she was, and out tumbled three turds to lay at her feet. Was it his shit he had run from, his shit that had terrorized him into such a wild, desperate need to escape all blame? He lay watching her sadly, Goofy and Doofus stationed at his side. The turds were perfectly shaped. They were like little ideals of turds. Using Kleenex, she picked them up, and their firm texture surprised her, as did the way they left no stain.

She returned from flushing them down the toilet to find Admiral traveling back toward his bed. He walked stiff-legged with his haunted gaze straight ahead. Each ungainly step threatened to tip him over, and it seemed to Janet he was thinking hard about how to manage his journey an inch at a time. The cats had not stirred. Both spaniels had climbed onto the couch, where they were arranging themselves for sleep.

She washed her hands and let the kitchen faucet run until the water, brimming over her glass, grew cold. She drank some and, carrying the remainder, paused on her way to the bedroom to look down at Admiral. Her hand settled on his old head, and he stirred in surprise. He seemed to think there must be something wrong, some threatening reason for her intrusion, and when there wasn't, he sank down. Her hand went with him, scratching gently. The light in his eyes flickered toward her, but he was preoccupied. She sensed that his awareness was friendly, though full of growing disinterest. Like her, he needed more sleep.

Seated on the edge of the bed, she drank the last of the water. There was dog hair all over the sheets and even a patch of dried dirt. Bernice probably curled up here with her animals every night. She wondered what the old woman would think if she came home and found Janet sound asleep in her bed. Probably throw a fit. Screaming, *I ain't dead yet, you little snot!* Still, the odds were against that happening, because Bernice was out at the old Tiedeman farm with her cronies, waiting to get taken up to heaven.

She lay back, closing her eyes, hoping for calm but feeling encircled by turbulence. And yet as she drifted, she sensed that a peaceful interlude might actually be possible. Her mind resembled an uneasy beacon whose anxious search went here and there, and on and on, until finally, it settled, having turned into a floodlight, enshrining Admiral dozing in the other room. Or maybe he wasn't asleep. Just resting. But he was down and silent and so very still as he lay with her at the brink of slumber. He was all in, too, maybe even more worn out than she was, and he was finished with something, and she could be finished with it, too. He appeared to contemplate a puzzle that had troubled him all his life, but he had come to a point where the allure of penetrating its secrets was no longer tempting enough to keep him involved. That was how he felt. As for her, he didn't know. It was not their fate to share everything. He was certain that she understood this and that she had known it for a long time. The truth was that he understood very little, lying with his chin on his crossed paws. But he was quiet. She could see that about him; he was quiet and wanted further quiet. She saw that he might serve as a kind of example. He might lead the way. Yes, you can watch, he sighed. Just wait and see. He wasn't watching her, though. His interest belonged to something else right now, something she couldn't see. He studied it very closely, and when she registered the intensity of his concentration, she felt a chill. He was waiting. She wondered if she should rise up, if she should say something to him. If she should call to him now.

22

BEFORE HAZEL HAD MANEUVERED HER Toyota even halfway into the slot at the end of the last row of cars, she started waving excitedly out the window. And when she piled out in a rush, Bernice, who'd hoped for a second to get ready, was totally flummoxed. Not wanting to be left behind, she shoved her door open, swung her legs out, and realized Hazel had parked on an incline that left the passenger side slanted uphill, turning gravity into this big bully pushing her backward. Plus, there was a mound right there that kept the door from opening completely. The instant she grasped the fix she was in, she called, "Do you think you could move this car out some from this embankment, Hazel?"

But Hazel didn't even glance back, having run up to Alice Kuhn and Jean Hines, the three of them hugging and grinning and ignoring Bernice like a bunch of schoolgirls too keyed up to bother with somebody having a problem. "Take an acrobat to get out of this mess." She didn't want to cause a scene, but her annoyance demanded that she shout, "I'm not some Flying Wallenda, you know."

With her purse clamped under her arm and her hands braced against the seat, she scooted ahead. About as ready as she'd ever be, she took a big breath to give her some gumption, and with it inhaled the smell of meat on a grill, sizzling grease and charcoal. Had she eaten anything all day? Too damn busy. All that came to mind was sitting with her little buddies in the kitchen gobbling ice cream last night. Lord, she hoped Janet was doing what she was supposed to and the bunch of them were okay. She wanted to squeeze Sappy and tell him how sorry she was for bopping him. She looked off hungrily toward the parsonage but got no farther than the sight of Alice Kuhn, who was prancing around in front of Hazel. Her long billowing skirt had maybe a gazillion green buttons flowing out from under a silver jacket that went to her narrow hips, frills on the shoulders, and a bow on the back that left Bernice shaking her head. The print was purple flowers as big as a man's hand, and they looked like lilacs, of all things. Did she think it was Easter and they were off to a parade? Leave it to Alice Kuhn. Bernice was disgusted, watching Alice pat her white hair and straighten her white hat with hands covered in gloves that matched the hat and were trimmed in the same sparkly silver. Poor dumb Hazel was agog. She looked about ready to break into applause. Jean Hines didn't have a chance in her straight-legged pants and chocolate-colored poncho. She was a dim bulb next to a million-watt floodlight. Not even her nice gloves and beret could make a dent. Not that she was as frumpy and butt-ugly as Bernice, sitting there stuck in that car in her stupid baby-blue pantsuit.

But she still had to eat, didn't she? Shabby or not, she was hungry enough to faint. Squirming her rear end and working her feet until they were about as close to under her as she could hope to get them, she strained without much success against the invisible hands of clumsiness and instability pressing her down.

"Are you as bad off as you look, Bernice? Should I call nine-one-one?"

Esther Huegel was herding her bulk over the rutted lawn in a navy blue sack dress, shifting and bulging. Her head was so huge it seemed that early in life she'd decided to thicken her body in pursuit of balance, and her lopsided grin was something a person couldn't be blamed for thinking was left over from a stroke. The line of her mouth took a sour dive, making it hard for people to believe she was really glad to see them, even when the welcome in her eyes came from deep down.

"Hello, Esther. How are you?"

"Just dandy. How's by you?"

"I been better."

"I saw you and I says, 'Bernice needs a hand.' "

"I think it might take more than a hand. Might take a crane to get me out of the fix Hazel has left me in."

"Oh, I bet we can manage, with a little help from the Lord."

"Amen," said Bernice.

"Amen. Jesus' name." Esther snuggled her heft sideways between the car and the mound of loose excavated dirt. "Grab hold, now." The width of her upper torso absorbed the length of her extended arms so her wrists barely reached beyond her breasts.

"I was gonna push. Lemme try pushing."

"Bernice, now, don't be stubborn. Do what I'm tellin' you and grab hold."

Reluctant and mortified at being stuck in such a humiliating plight, Bernice fell silent and was surprised by the way the hush made her unhappy. She wanted to come up with an argument that could make a case for doing it her way.

"Oh, don't get all gloomy on me," Esther said, wiggling her fingers in an inviting flutter. "C'mon, now."

All of a sudden she liked Esther. Affection spread, coming on strong, canceling everything but fondness. "Okay," she said.

"Thatta girl."

Esther was big and ugly but a blessing with her offer of motherly interest. For all her seventy-one years, Bernice couldn't hide from the simple fact that it felt nice to have somebody care.

"I'm strong as an ox, and I got plenty of ballast. Gimme your purse."

"Okay," she said.

Esther smiled and blinked both eyes in playful awe at the handbag's size and weight. She bent as far as she could but had to let the cumbersome thing fall the rest of the way with a thump. "Amen," she said. "Now, you just haul away like I'm somebody's fence post."

Esther's fingers were buttery, and Bernice petted them before sliding on to the mush of her wrists. Or maybe it was Jesus, she thought. Jesus and kindness filling her heart, because of Esther being so generous. That'd be like Jesus, to try and show Himself through this sort of surprising thing. The two of them like this—one grumpy and stuck, the other big and fat.

"On three," said Esther. "Okay? One, two—"

"Three!" Bernice heaved, searching for a glimpse of Jesus inside Esther, who grimaced and tottered while Bernice hung on like the car was going down in quicksand. Upright and wobbling, she was face-to-face with Esther's big breasts. She skittered backward, then threw her arms around Esther, who responded with a squeal and a firm embrace. They sidled along the fender until they reached level ground, where, modestly, they stepped back in unison. "I don't know what I'da done if you hadn't come along, Esther."

"You coulda been there for a while, all right. Till the angels grabbed you up." Esther twittered, birdlike and happy, while her hands approached each other from either side of her round belly.

"All that fuss just getting out of a car."

Esther's fingers strained the final inch to interlace. "How's the Lord been treating you?"

"Okay."

"Where you been? Hazel told somebody you'd be out here hours ago."

"Well, things didn't go according to Hazel's plan. Or mine, either, for that matter." She shrugged and picked up her purse. "How about everything here?"

"Ohh, well." Esther's gaze reflected a memory not exactly welcome, even though she smiled. "We had some goings-on, you can bet."

"Like what?"

"I got here early. Six thirty. Couldn't sleep, you know. Felt real sad. And I just had to get over here."

"Did you, Esther?"

"Yes, I did. Drove over first thing. Thought I might set a new speed limit. Didn't call or anything. And I been feeling fine ever since I arrived." She tapped her knuckles against her head. "But you know—knock wood."

"I wanted to get over."

"Didn't work the same on everybody. Jean Hines had a real crying jag."

"Did she?"

Esther nodded, sympathy battling distaste in the shine of her half-buried eyes and pouting lips.

"What happened?"

"Somethin' got to her."

"What?"

"Nobody knows. She wouldn't say. Just wanted to hold Reverend Tauke's hand. Even kissed his knuckles, you know. Blathering away like a baby. And I mean that really. Not an ounce of shame."

"Is that a fact?"

"Yes, it is."

"That must have been a while ago. Because she looked okay when I saw her just a second ago."

"Oh, yeah. He got her through it. You know how he can. Just as tender and thoughtful as a big old Saint Bernard." Esther shrugged before leaning closer. "If you ask me, the whole thing was unnecessary. You know, a show. You know how she likes to put on a show." Her head twitched with the hint of a conflict that generated a very different kind of shrug, this one full of surrender. "But that's me and not him. Of course, he's a saint. Thank goodness. He's the Shepherd. Amen."

"Amen."

"Jesus' name." Her big bosom swelled above her fingers. "Anyhoo— you're here now and out of your car."

"Thanks to you."

These gentle words of praise stirred yet another variation from Esther's array of shrugs, this one simple and upbeat. "I guess we all just do what we can, right?"

"Is that food I smell?"

"Sure is. Quite a spread. People brought all sorts of good stuff. I brought ham and cheese sandwiches."

"I smell burgers, don't I?"

"There's burgers."

"Good." Bernice regretted having failed to contribute, not that she'd had a minute to spare. "I guess I should have brought something."

"Don't you worry about that. Some did, some didn't. There's some people thinking about food, no matter what." Her sheepish grin admitted she was one of those. "I brought plenty."

"Well, bless you, because I'm starving."

"Are you starving, Bernice? Then you better get a bite, because Reverend Tauke wants us all in the chapel at four thirty."

They both glanced at their watches, and Bernice said, "Yikes."

"Fifteen minutes. You better hurry."

"Come with me."

"No, no." Her refusal lost its power almost before the words were out. "Well, maybe." As Esther looked over the terrain separating them from the parsonage, Bernice checked the same route and saw the front door emit a man who wheeled and reentered.

"You should have seen Marty Dolphin," said Esther. "You missed something big with that one. I'll tell you about it later, but he had a fit."

"He did?" They hadn't budged, and Bernice couldn't tear her eyes from the parsonage, as if worried it might disappear, taking the food with it.

"He came all the way out here to pick a fight, and you'll never guess with who."

She wanted to get going, but Esther's dramatic tone and bearing warned that this fight had been with Reverend Tauke. "He didn't, did he?"

"Yes, he did. Brought his two big boys to back him up. Said Reverend Tauke should apologize to everybody. Called him a fake."

"He did not."

"Oh, yes, he did. I heard him with my own ears. You know how crazy he can get."

"What a terrible thing."

"Reverend Tauke just took it. He just took it. Said he had apologized and would again if that was what Marty needed. Well, that sort of stole Marty's thunder, don't you see. It was then and there the fake business came up. Marty says he's gone through enough grief over 'some fake minister.' Well, Reverend Tauke gave Marty the saddest look. You know, just turned the other cheek, and that sent Marty 'round the bend. He stormed off. And I hate to say it, but he was cursing under his breath."

"That's just terrible," said Bernice as her stomach grumbled and they both heard it. "I think I'm glad I wasn't here to see that." The door slammed, and she looked fearfully toward the parsonage, where the man they'd seen before was coming out again.

"Bernice," Esther said. "I'm just slowing you down. You go on." She patted her belly. "I'm not one needs more grub." Her cheeks were squirming to get out of the way of her grin. "I'd probably just make myself late for the service. I think I'll head up that way now."

The frightful possibility that she might end up in church without a bite had Bernice setting off even as she asked, "Can I bring you back something?"

"No, thanks."

"Okay." To imagine being hungry and the hours stretching on for who knew how long—maybe even into eternity—made her a little panicky. Hungry for hours. And then hungry forever. But wouldn't Jesus feed her? Fill her up good. Loaves and fishes. Of course He would. What was she thinking? Starting to sound as crazy as Marty Dolphin. But still, try as she might, she could not sidestep the notion of the whole bunch of them airborne and arriving somewhere the way people traveling anywhere did, famished and in need of a bathroom, because they were supposed to have their bodies, weren't they? Was she the only one having these kinds of goofy thoughts? Her and Marty Dolphin, by the sound of things.

About to cross paths with whomever had emerged seconds ago, she saw he was just some teenager—that so-and-so whose name she could never hang on to, chomping away on a burger in a bun. "We need to get to service," he told her.

"I'll be right there."

"Well, you're going the wrong way."

That all but stopped her in her tracks. She didn't really know him from Adam. "I need something to eat. Unless you want to give me that burger of yours?"

He found that so outlandish, he had to snicker. "They shut the grill off, anyway."

"I'll find something."

She picked up her pace and didn't mean to look after him but did anyway. His pants were a fancy material, maybe silk, and they looked fresh off the rack, just like his orange windbreaker. Probably thought he was a sight to behold because he'd spent a truckload of money. And sniggering at her like that—was he trying to rub her the wrong way? Somebody should tell the wiseacre this wasn't the time or place to be making fun of his elders. Why'd they even have his kind around? As for finding the Lord in the likes of that one, the way she'd seen Him in Esther, well, that would be a tough row to hoe. She glanced past the boy, hoping to revisit that sweetness by catching sight of Esther, who she discovered hadn't gotten all that far. Esther was stalled in her climb, bent over and gasping, and Bernice had to say that Jesus seemed gone from her, too, leaving nothing but a fat old thing. And judging by her own nasty thoughts, Bernice had lost Him for sure. Lord, she thought, hurrying up the stairs. Help me now. I know I need to do better.

The figure of Reverend Tauke against a kitchen window with a white mug of coffee inches from his lips made her go weak in the knees. Dressed in one of the two dark suits he always wore, he appeared almost prayerful. Momentarily caught in her bitter thoughts, she was surprised to fill with giddy excitement, like that time in Chicago when she and Toby came around a corner into a crowd buzzing about how Lana Turner had just gotten into a limousine and driven off. She couldn't help the thrill of privilege she felt, bumping into Reverend Tauke this way.

Irene Krebs and her daughter, Lucy, were near the refrigerator at the far end of the room, sealing platters of food in Saran Wrap. Bernice tried to imagine Marty Dolphin yelling at Reverend Tauke and got even more nervous. Was he possibly communing with the Lord right now in this ordinary setting as the mug tilted to his lips and he drank?

She turned to Irene, who was lost in her work, and to Lucy, who smiled. A twice-divorced, excitable woman in her mid-thirties, she was known to Bernice by rumor, mainly, the most recent being that she'd messed around with her married boss at the Iron Bar Bank, where she was a teller, and before the whole to-do got settled, she had to give up a baby for adoption.

Lucy, perhaps offended by Bernice's scrutiny, turned away, but she spun back with a questioning expression whose purpose was revealed as she raised a paper plate containing a burger, coleslaw, potato salad. It didn't seem right to make a fuss about how she was starving with Reverend Tauke right there praying or whatever he was doing, so Bernice showed her gratitude by hurrying toward Lucy.

"Bernice," said Reverend Tauke behind her. "At last."

"What?" The way he said "at last," like he'd been waiting, made her heart jump.

"You're here. That's wonderful."

"Sorry we're late, but . . ." But what? she wondered, and drew a blank in her hunt for an explanation worthy of being addressed to him.

"I guess you're a little hungry," he smiled.

"I don't have to eat."

"Of course you do." His hand barely moved but granted a kind of magical permission.

"Thank you. I'd sure like to."

"Take your time. I was just waiting for Irene and Lucy to finish up." His brief interest in Irene caused her to avert her eyes as if he emitted a glare. "How long will you be yet, do you suppose?"

"Not long," Irene said. "Ten minutes."

"Let's make it twenty. I think I'll go for a little stroll and then wend my way to the chapel in about that time." He placed the cup on the table. "See you then." He swept from the room, a departing celebrity once again leaving behind forceful sensations Bernice couldn't quite put her finger on.

Lucy carried his cup to the sink, and Bernice settled with her food at the table. Her coffee arrived in Irene's skinny hand. "Thanks, Irene. How you doing?"

"Just fine."

"How things been here?"

"Good. You know, we been eating, praying, and talking."

Lucy chuckled in the corner, where she was draping a dish towel on a rack. "And then we been eating, praying, and arguing."

"There's not that much arguing," Irene explained gently. She had a soothing way about her, a manner of speaking both crisp and careful, as if she wanted to make it known that she trusted in good sense and good manners to ease most difficulties. "One thing or another gets into people's heads, and they start talking it over."

"Which, if I'm any judge," Lucy put in slyly, "gets to sounding like arguing. You know what they say about ducks? If it waddles and quacks."

Bernice doubted she understood exactly what either one of them was getting at, which left her muddled about their disagreement. "Was everybody here already? I mean except for Hazel and me?"

"Most everybody," Irene told her.

"There's some that aren't here. And they won't be coming, either. And we won't be seeing any more of them, I don't think," Lucy announced.

Bernice dug into her potato salad. Clearly, Lucy had a lot more on her mind than what she'd let on so far. "Some folks would just rather wait at home, I guess. I was almost one of them."

"That would not have been such a good idea, Bernice." Lucy had a threatening way to her all of a sudden. "Reverend Tauke said some things that I think maybe show he's changing his position on that point."

"That's one of the matters everybody's arguing about," Irene offered.

Lucy took a couple steps nearer. "He was talking this afternoon, and it sounded to me like he's changing his idea about where we can be for the angels to find us."

"Now, you don't know for certain, Lucy." Irene sounded amiable as she made her point.

"I'm not saying that I know it."

"Well, you sound like you do. Doesn't she, Bernice?"

Bernice was shoveling in food, gobbling and chewing so fast she was close to panting. She straightened, leaning back to free up her stomach.

"That's a good idea, taking a break." Irene smiled. "Don't want to have to Heimlich you."

Bernice swallowed and lifted her coffee. "I'm not sure I follow your train of thought, Lucy."

Irene clasped her hands and held them centered at her waist. "Lucy thinks Reverend Tauke is changing things so that we all have to be in the chapel tonight to be taken off."

"Goodness, Lucy, is that right?"

Lucy nodded. "I can't give it to you scripture and verse—I wouldn't claim that, but he spoke about people being called here today for a great reason. That was his word—'great.' And I think that's what it means. That those of us who came here today were called, even if they just came. Just showed up. And then what happened was he went on to tell a story about how our chapel was once a barn, and Jesus was born in a barn. He came to a barn. You know, it was kind of a parable."

Bernice nodded, giving Lucy her due, and then she took a close look at Irene, who parted her interwoven fingers. "It was a nice little story. A nice story to make us feel closer to Jesus, reminding us of His barn and ours, and it did just that."

"I'm not the only one who thinks what I think. There are others."

"Yes, there are."

"And plenty of them."

"But that doesn't make the bunch of you right."

"Mom, I said, 'maybe.'"

"Yes, you did."

"So 'maybe' means 'maybe.' I just think Reverend Tauke wants us to listen to his every word. We're all so lazy, and he wants us to listen hard and think hard, the way Jesus did with His disciples."

"Well," Irene said, and the precision with which she set down her empty cup asked both Lucy and Bernice to understand that she was about to speak in a way she believed was a step above everything she'd said so far. She needed a second to find the right first word, and in that pause, Lucy retrieved her mother's cup and started to rinse it in the sink. "Thank you, Lucy," Irene said.

"You're welcome."

A look of deep satisfaction came over Irene as she watched her daughter while addressing Bernice. "The truth is, we don't know for sure why he had us all come here today. I'm just thankful he did." Her voice lowered, gaining strength and influence by becoming softer. "Some say it's to comfort each other, or to maybe make our prayers more powerful by all of us being together and praying in unison. And those are reasons good enough for me." Nodding respectfully to Lucy, who stood with a towel drying the cup, she went on, "There's others, though, who believe something is changing, and they could be right. But I'm of the mind that we'll go when we go, and until I hear different in some clear-cut way, I think the Lord will find us wherever we might be. Here in this kitchen or off in Paris, France, or the North Pole. He'll find us, or His angels will." She waved her hands as if signaling her whereabouts lightheartedly, palms to heaven, her lanky frame rocking, eyes glittery.

"Hallelujah," said Lucy.

Irene's gentle pantomime, accompanied by Lucy's sweet voice, pierced Bernice, a blunt and nameless ache coming from deep down, and it had to do with how much had gone astray between her and Irma, she was sure, until she realized abruptly that she didn't have her Bible. "Oh my Lord, I forgot my Bible." Hoping against hope, she plucked up her purse. But her Bible had been left behind. It was on her bedside table, or in her bed, and at that instant, as she faced her carelessness, she burped and put her hand to her mouth. Along with the escaping gas came the memory of Hazel hounding her as she rushed around getting ready to leave, and she'd known all the while she was forgetting something—she'd known it. It was that darn Hazel's fault. First for taking Irma's call, which had turned everything topsy-turvy, and then for acting so fed up, standing like that snooty, bossy Napoleon at the door. She was about to tell the Krebses, just dump the whole thing in Hazel's lap, because everybody knew how Hazel could get a person in such a lather they didn't know which end was up. But instead, she shook her head, because it just wasn't true. She'd forgotten things all her life. Just a slipshod little girl, one day coming late to school without her homework, or having lost her books. Had she ever been so small? For an instant she tried to bring detail to the face of a large female. What had been her first-grade teacher's name? "I left it at home. How dumb can you get?"

"There's extras," said Irene.

"Sure. There's extras," Lucy told her. "Some out by the door and some up by the chapel entrance. You just help yourself."

Bernice raised a forkful of coleslaw. "I'd forget my head if it wasn't screwed on."

Still at the sink, Lucy said rather firmly, "You need to hurry up now and get your fill, Bernice. Our twenty minutes is just about up."

"Lucy's right," Irene added, drawing near to Bernice and waiting in that no-nonsense way she had about her.

"Those clouds look almost rock-solid, Mom," said Lucy, who had a view of the sky through the delicately curtained window above the sink. "Gray as rocks. Just about firm enough to walk on."

"Stepping-stones for the Lord. Not that he needs them."

"It's fun to picture, though. Him coming down a stairway in the sky, like a king walking down from a castle."

Bernice swallowed and worked her tongue free. "That about does it." Cramming her mouth with the last of the potato salad, she shoved her chair back.

Irene flew to the sink to wash the plate and cutlery, as if she'd forgotten they were paper and plastic, and Bernice got up, curious about the view they described into the clouds, and up came the name of that teacher she'd wondered about. "Mrs. Belcher," she said.

"What's that?"

"My first-grade teacher. Mrs. Belcher."

"First grade?"

"She's not here today, is she?"

"Oh, no. She passed."

"Probably would have had to by now. I mean, teaching you in the first grade."

"Was she a good Christian woman?"

"What?" Bernice had no idea, and looking into a bundle of sensations that seemed to hold her six-year-old self, she remained in the dark. "I think so."

"What got into you to bring her up at this particular juncture?"

"I just thought of her, I guess. You know."

Irene and Lucy shared a glance near the kitchen door, where they were putting on similar hip-length jackets padded in squares, one brown, the other tan. They shrugged at their mittens and smiled, stuffing them into their pockets, before draping identical striped scarves around their necks.

"Did you like her? This Mrs. Belcher?" Irene asked.

"Yes, I did."

"And she just pops into your head. See, that's what I'm thinking."

"What?" said Lucy, smiling at her mother. "Want me to guess?"

"Okay by me."

Lucy turned radiant eyes on Bernice. "Jesus sent her to warm you up. She's a teacher, and you liked her, and she passed over a while back, so she's there among the good people waiting for you. The ones who know you and care about you, Bernice."

"Waiting with the angels—that Mrs. Belcher," said Irene.

"You think so?" Bernice asked.

"Could be," said Lucy.

The Krebses, mother and daughter, slipped out into the gray afternoon while Bernice lingered. She picked up one of the two Bibles on the table by the door. Both were the version Reverend Tauke liked. She noted passages highlighted in yellow marker and the name of the owner, Homer Robinson, printed on the flyleaf. Nobody she knew. But the address where he'd wanted it returned, should it be lost, was on a street she recognized. Her brother Hank's friend Tommy Prescott had lived on Troutbrook Lane.

She emerged into the Indian summer that, even in the ebbing day, made buttoning up unnecessary. Irene and Lucy were well along, chattering, even giggling. They could have been bound for some mother-daughter vacation, just dancing through the airport terminal to their waiting jetliner.

The walkway sloped up to the chapel's open doors, where people converged from various directions. Her memory of Reverend Tauke's last remarks in the kitchen guided her to where the land crested, and there he leaned against the pasture fence with one foot braced on the bottom rail. The dimming light removed the ground from under him, so he looked both farther away and higher than he actually was. Intrigued by his stately bearing and the sense she had of serenity all around him, she had to ask whether it was something she was imagining, or was it really out there in the air, brightness like a halo in a picture book of the Nativity with Joseph and Mary kneeling in the straw beside the glowing baby Jesus.

When he took his first long stride in the direction of the chapel, she knew it was time to hurry. She didn't have as far to go as he did, but he had those long legs. She would have to work hard to get there first, so she could be waiting respectfully when he arrived. Holding her own and watching him closely, she was jarred by two shadows scuttling from under nearby trees. "I don't care, Mom. I don't know how many times I have to say it!"

It was Bonnie Frunke and her older boy, the one with the gimpy leg. He was all worked up, while Bonnie looked befuddled, her voice trying for authority. " 'Now we beseech you, brethren, by the coming of our Lord Jesus Christ, and by our gathering together unto him, That ye be not soon shaken in mind, or be troubled, neither by spirit, nor by word, nor by letter as from us, as that the day of Christ is at hand. Let no man deceive—' "

"Shut up, Mom. Just—please." The boy spat his words in a hoarse grumble.

"Let me finish!" she commanded. Resentment tipped his eyes to the ground. " 'Let no man deceive you by any means: for that day shall not come, except there come a falling away first, and that man of sin be revealed, the son of perdition; Who opposeth and—' "

"Okay, okay, Mom. Just— Please, you listen now."

"No."

"For one second."

"We have to get to service. He'll start without us."

They joined Bernice on the path, walking a few steps ahead and more or less matching her pace like they were all three together.

"Matthew twenty-five, verse thirteen, Mom," the boy said. " 'Watch therefore, for ye know neither the day nor the hour wherein the Son of man cometh!' " To give his reedy voice some oomph, he stomped his foot as he repeated, " 'Wherein the Son of man cometh!' Matthew twenty-five, verse thirteen, Mom. Okay?"

Bonnie swung her big eyes to Bernice. "He won't listen! Tell him, will you?"

"Tell him what?"

"That what he's saying—even if he's right somehow—is wrong, because he's saying it to me and I'm the wrong person. He's smarter than me, so he's picking on me because he can win with me, and besides, it's his favorite thing to do."

"You can't be serious." His hands went toward the sky, and Bernice understood he believed he was throwing away every ounce of patience and hope he had ever thought might help him understand her.

"Why? Because I'm your mother? That does not make it impossible for me to be serious. No matter what you might think."

"No. It's because what you're saying is idiotic." The boy, who Bernice knew was either Roy or Ray, said, " 'Watch therefore, for ye know neither the day nor the hour wherein the Son of man cometh!' That leaves no doubt. It couldn't be—"

"I can't take this another second. Bernice, please. Help us out!"

"I'm not good at this debate kind of thing."

He shook his head at Bernice, her admission clearly puffing him up. "It's as plain as the nose on your face. I mean, 'ye know neither the day nor the hour!' What else could that mean except that we don't get to know ahead of time?"

"So maybe it sounds that way," Bonnie admitted. "Okay, okay. But that's why you have to talk to somebody like Reverend Tauke. Doesn't that make sense, Bernice?"

"She calls me the Antichrist," the boy said to Bernice before she could answer his mother.

"I never did," Bonnie said.

"You implied it."

"No. Absolutely not! I said something, and you read that into it."

"What'd you say then?" He planted his feet, refusing to go on.

"I don't know. I mean, you're the one who says I said it."

"Why would I do that without good reason?"

"I wish I knew. I keep asking myself that question."

"It was implicit in the scripture you used, Mom. I had no choice but to point it out."

"I don't even know what we're talking about anymore."

"You're calling me the Antichrist. My own mother."

"You have got to stop saying that."

"All because I want to point out some scriptural inconsistency in Reverend Tauke."

"No. That's fine. But just don't do it to me, because it's wasted on me." Bonnie looked left and then right, like she was about to enter a street full of traffic. "I don't know anything."

He squared his stance, digging in. "Maybe I don't want to go. Did you ever think of that?"

"Where?"

"Where do you think, Mom? What are we talking about?"

"You have no choice."

"Dad doesn't get to go. Because he has beer. He drinks beer. Maybe I'd like a beer."

Bonnie Frunke sought assistance somewhere up the hill and then down the hill, and the expression she turned on Bernice made her seem the sole survivor of a terrible accident.

Anxious about the start of service, Bernice was relieved to see Reverend Tauke chatting with a small gathering by the door. But then he stepped toward her, every inch of his lean height fueling his gesture that urged Bernice to hurry up and bring the Frunkes. Before she could wave in acknowledgment, he turned and strode inside.

"We gotta go." They were gaping at her, Bonnie desperate, her son defiant. If these two kept at it, they would make her late for sure, but it seemed against every one of Reverend Tauke's teachings to leave them in such a mess, especially after the look he'd just sent her. "I know we're supposed to study scripture," she said to the boy, "and it's pretty clear you're sharp as a tack, Roy, but you still—"

"Roy?" he said. "I'm not Roy. Who's Roy? I'm Ray."

"Sorry."

"In fact, I'm Raymond. So what advice can you give me?"

He was within his rights to be irked at her stupid mistake, but she was both fed up and empowered by the force of Reverend Tauke's glance. "Raymond," she said. "Do what your mother says and go to church."

"Oh, Lord. You're all the same."

She strode off and Bonnie followed, and it wasn't a complete surprise that the boy, after a second or two of delay, turned into a sad sack trudging behind them.

Everyone was gone, the chapel doors shut, by the time Bernice scurried up. She could hear Revered Tauke through the thick wood, as if he had traveled to a distant, solemn place. With her finger to her lips, she shushed the Frunkes and parted the door from its frame. Reverend Tauke's voice, ripe with passion, became distinct and powerful: "'... of heaven will be like this. There were ten young girls who took their lamps and went out to meet the bridegroom. Five of them were foolish and five were prudent; when the foolish ones took their lamps, they took no oil with them, but the others took flasks of oil with their lamps. As the bridegroom was late in coming, they all dozed off to sleep.'"

Eager to hide her tardy entrance, Bernice took the first available seat at the end of the last row. Instantly, her meandering day struck her as wasteful. Did she have her lamp? Did she have her oil? Was she one of the foolish, foolish maidens? On the dais, Reverend Tauke prowled past the pulpit, past the plain wood altar, his voice thrusting into her.

"'But at midnight a cry was heard: 'Here comes the bridegroom! Come out to meet him!' With that, all the young girls got up and trimmed their lamps. The foolish said to the prudent, 'Our lamps are going out; give us some of your oil.' 'No,' they said; 'there will never be enough for all of us. You had better go to the shop and buy some for yourselves.'"

Bernice wanted to warn the girls, all innocent virgins, that they were making a big mistake. She saw their white gowns skittering through the encircling gloom, when they would have been so much better off if they'd stayed and waited for the bridegroom. At least they could have been there to greet Him. They could have flung their arms open, their eyes full of love, even if they didn't have oil in their lamps to brighten the way and show their adoration. But they did as they were told, trustingly. She saw them hurrying into darkness, and she pitied them, for she felt, running coldly through her heart, the hard lesson they must soon learn.

"While they were away, the bridegroom arrived," Reverend Tauke proclaimed in ringing celebration of how much smarter he was than the girls. His attitude rubbed Bernice wrong, but knowing she must be in error, she tried to ignore every negative sensation, shoving them all into a corner she wanted nothing to do with. "The bridegroom arrived," Reverend Tauke repeated, and paused to build suspense in the rows before him. "And those who were ready went in with him to the wedding; and the door was shut. And then the other five came back. 'Sir, sir,' they cried.' " And Bernice could not help but cry with them, for they loved him. " 'Sir, sir, open the door for us.' But he answered, 'I declare I do not know you.' "

She closed her eyes, arguing that she didn't want to think these stupid thoughts, only to listen. " 'Keep awake, then,' " she heard him command, " 'for you never know the day or the hour.' " His voice swelled, as if his own words were unexpected. "And yet we do! Don't we! We here do! How is that?"

He was at the pulpit. Behind him, wooden stairs led to the baptismal fount. Bernice had walked the bloodred carpet of the center aisle, rising to the water not six months ago, where he had taken her by the shoulders and dunked her.

Now he lifted his hands, palms directed at them all. "We know, because the bridegroom speaks of death. And it is not death that comes for us, but a gift, an opportunity to stride from our life on earth into our life in heaven. But without having to die as we have feared. Without death as we have always known it. Without suffering and sickness—some terrible ending. Or perhaps not so terrible, but an ending, and always followed by the grave. Burial and the same three days under the dirt. Three days unknown—an eternity in some way. And then the resurrection. This is what came to me in the voice that could not be my own. But I'm getting ahead of myself." He stopped, his last words sounding an instruction he must obey. But then his thoughtful expression vanished, and when he spoke, it was with the surprised realization that he had been silent for no good reason. "But why not? Why not get ahead of myself? What does it matter? Because we have been chosen to rise and get past those lonely, empty hours of night, those terrible three days that will not be ours, because Jesus has done it for us, and we have taken Him into our hearts and know that by accepting Him, we need not worry about oil or wicks or candles. He will come for us, and we will be plucked living from the earth. As a group of children holding hands. As we all did playing ring-around-the-rosy. Only this daisy chain will fly with each of us lifting his brother and so on, his brother lifting his sister and so on. We will have this bunch of angels as our wings." He directed them toward the tall narrow windows and the sky beyond, scooping air and casting it toward the ceiling. "This is what I know, and through me, as I tell it to you, it's what you can know, too. Who among us would not like to be carried away by angels?"

When he pivoted from them, she thought he would leave the pulpit, but he didn't budge, hovering midstep, held by something invisible. "I'm going to tell you something that I have never spoken of before." He came around slowly. "I'm going to talk about certain things—about when the first messages came—things that I never said before. When they came, it was just before bed. I was alone in the house. I said aloud, 'What's this? Whose words are these? I hear them, but are they for me?' All this out loud, and I was alone. I could hear myself but didn't know myself. I was walking, and I stopped. I looked around because there had to be somebody else in the room."

She thought his eyes narrowed. She thought worry snapped and chewed at him. He might have been lost and hoping someone would give him directions. "Pray for me now. As I'm talking. Listen and pray for me and with me. I'm trying to tell of the very first time of all. The next thing I said was 'I am; that is what I am,' not meaning myself, not blaspheming, but realizing who it was speaking to me, out of me. 'This is my covenant,' I said, and what you must understand is that I was repeating things told to me. I was told to say them, so I did. I shouted, 'I'm not the one. I'm not the one. I can't be the one to do this.' But I had to take the risk, because it is a risk, and when it was over, I woke up, sort of—that kind of feeling—and with a sense of warmth and certainty. Yes, I'm saying 'certainty' about all the things that I have told you since that day, when maybe I should not have had it, but how was I to know then? It was a hard day, a tough day. Some would call it too much. In the sense of more than I ought to try to bear. But even as I fought and worried, because you must know I did— even as I misread and spoke wrongly at first, my faith was pure, and the feeling of it was strong. It was so strong. And then I admitted my error— the way I was off by a day with my first announcements—okay, I was off—it was all new to me, wasn't it, and if I was off by more than that, or in other ways, well, the Lord would straighten it out if I had faith, because faith was what I had to have. That was the task. I had to have faith, and I had to talk of faith—I had to make faith here and now as real as the air we breathe, the shoes on our feet, our skin, our fingernails, and when I felt that, I knew for sure that the feeling was true and that the truth would unfold. Nothing like this had ever happened to me, and there was a feeling with it, and the feeling knew. It said yes. Because I was not the one. Because it was our Lord, and I knew it, and I worry all the time—it is my biggest worry—how do I make you know it?" He reminded Bernice of somebody, maybe even herself, as she searched lots of shelves and drawers for an important object that she was scared she would never find. His failure made him sigh. "I knew the truth of it, but as you have each been confused by my words, and as you have doubted and labored to understand how what I've said to you can be meant for you—" He stopped, and it gave her goose bumps, the way he seemed to see them all for the very first time. "You have all been driven to ask of yourself—how can the things I promise be meant for you, Donald, or you, Bonnie or Raymond? Or Lucy? Or Hazel, or Bruce, or Otto? Who among you has not said, 'I'm not the one. I can't be the one this is for'?"

Oh, why hadn't he said Bernice? What did it mean?

"This is it, I think now. All of you! This is how we are to learn to know one another. The speaking of the Lord to me and me to you. Of course it's confusing. Of course it is. But we are needed. You are needed. All of you. Needed and loved."

It was like someone pushed him without knocking him down. He staggered back and had to jump forward. "Look at the windows, will you, please? Look and see the light starting to go in the west. The day is ending, the dark coming, and inside this dark, I think, a light waits that will light up inside us. Right inside us. Unlike anything we have ever known. In Jesus' name. The hour is nigh. A blessing. Not of death but of our holding hands with angels. Of our rising. Our Rapture. Here in our little town, our poor, simple, even stupid in the eyes of the outside world—our stupid little town on the edge of this big flat state. A bunch of clodhoppers. An old word, I know, but that's how they see us. Those who see us from outside. They will not recognize our death without death. But I say we are clodhoppers for Jesus. Clodhoppers for the Lord."

Bernice had gone to a peaceful place where his voice mingled with her thoughts, and the windows continued to darken under an influence that felt connected to his gestures and words, perhaps even begun in them, resulting from them. He surveyed his congregation, and she wondered how they looked to him. Did they sort of glow, their upturned faces like clean white dinner plates? Smiling, he returned to the scriptures, drifting to his left while reading, " 'And look, I have set before you an open door, which no one can shut.' "

She sat up, eyes sharp, as she thought how this last notion was another way of saying "the Way, the Truth, and the Light." She felt close to him, like she was getting his message.

" 'Your strength, I know, is small, yet you have observed my commands and have not disowned my name.' " Detecting tension in his voice, each phrase a tightening knot, she felt he wrestled against something hidden. " 'So this is what I will do; I will make those of Satan's synagogue, who claim to be Jews but are lying frauds, come and fall down at your feet!' " He was shouting suddenly, and the picture that came to her wasn't one she cared for at all, the doors of their chapel flung open and all these Jews streaming in, stumbling, staggering. " 'And they shall know that you are my beloved people. Because you have kept my command and stood fast, I will also keep you from the ordeal that is to fall upon the whole world and test its inhabitants.' "

Oh-oh, she thought. There it was. The end of the world right out of the Book, like he was always talking about. What had it been? Test the people?

" 'I am coming soon; hold fast what you have, and let no one . . .' "

Seconds ago she'd understood what he was getting at. She'd felt she was becoming a good student in the most important school anywhere. But now she couldn't find her place. She was turning pages hastily, randomly. If he'd announced the chapter and verse, she'd missed it. She feared she might have fallen asleep when she was so peaceful before, though it didn't seem possible, and even if she had, it couldn't have been for more than a second. And yet what was he reading? Why was she so confused? Maybe she could peek to where Wilbur Brew beside her, or Agnes Lodder in front of her, had their Bibles open. The fading day was dragging the sanctuary into night, and the pages they held appeared covered not in print but in dust specks she couldn't make out, and she dreaded going on like this, never finding the right page. When the overhead lights came on, it seemed out of the blue, and she was grateful for the big lanternlike fixtures dangling on brass chains from the old barn's beams refinished in a buttery tone. She knew that nothing more extraordinary than someone flipping a switch had occurred, but she felt blessed in a way that relaxed her enough to ask Wilbur Brew for the correct place.

"Revelations three—eight, nine," he whispered.

Reverend Tauke had calmed down, too. " 'And my own new name. Hear, you who have ears to hear, what the spirit says to the churches! To the Angel of the church at Laodicea write: "These are . . ." ' "

So it was Laodicea she wanted. Bernice was scrambling closer, flipping the wispy, wrinkled pages as Reverend Tauke paused and began thumbing about, too, rapidly sorting segments, and in a matter of seconds, he declared:

"The Lord said to Moses, 'I am now coming to you in a thick cloud, so that I may speak to you in the hearing of the people and their faith in you may never fail.' "

Moses? she thought. She had barely landed in Revelations. Her bewilderment sent her to Wilbur Brew, but he was battling confusion as big or bigger than hers. She shrugged with no idea and no real clue except one. "Moses?" she whispered.

"Exodus," Wilbur whispered back and snapped his fingers like he'd just caught on to a trick.

"Moses told the Lord what the people had said, and the Lord said to him, 'Go to the people and hallow them today and tomorrow and make them wash their clothes.'"

Wilbur was right. It had to be Exodus. But with that established, she was unsure whether to hunt for the text or just listen to Reverend Tauke. Hoping for an example in Agnes Lodder, she found a prim, contented woman who made it seem simple enough to gaze up, with her good book resting in her lap under her folded hands.

"Exodus nineteen," Reverend Tauke said, sounding surprised and raising his Bible overhead. "Verses nine through sixteen."

That got everybody going to beat the band, Bernice included, and Agnes, too, the whole chapel full of fluttering pages like leaves underfoot, or everybody murmuring, or maybe the hard work of someone sick unto death fighting to breathe.

"'Be ready by the third day, because on the third day, the Lord will descend upon Mount Sinai in the sight of the people. You must put barriers around the mountain and say, "Take care not to go up the mountain or even touch the edge of it." Any man who touches the mountain must be put to death. No hand shall touch him; he shall be stoned, or shot dead; neither man nor beast may live. But when the ram horn sounds, they may go up the mountain.'"

He was speaking peacefully now, so soothingly and dreamily that she had to see him, and she was astonished to discover that he was no longer reading but stood with his eyes closed. "Peals of thunder on the third day, flashes of lightning. A dense cloud on the mountain, a loud trumpet blast, and the people were terrified."

23

JANET WAS DESPERATE FOR COFFEE. Her blurry impression of the old dog on his bed could have been a glimpse into a corner of her sleep-addled mind. With the teakettle full and the burner on, she rummaged in Bernice's cabinets until she found a tin of instant coffee, and as she did, she saw the dog dead in the night. Still in a daze, her thoughts traveled back, and her eyes followed to where he lay. She said his name softly, and when he didn't respond, she reminded herself that he was deaf. But then his motionless pose whispered that he was gone even before her fingers jumped back at contact. "Hey," she said, refusing the idea, placing her palm against his thinning fur and brittle bones. The teakettle whistled, and she made a cup of coffee and sat drinking and looking down. Goofy and Doofus gazed at her, seeming to share her stubborn disbelief. As if to assist her, the dog she called Doofus and believed was the male sniffed Admiral from head to toe in a serious, investigative manner. So now she was being forced yet again to cope with what ought to be somebody else's problem. Her exasperation was so strong that she seized her purse and jacket, intending to walk out, because being fed up and pissed off gave her the right. But the impulse stalled at the door, her hand on the knob. It just wasn't in her to let him lie there like roadkill in his own living room. She couldn't run out on him, as much as she might want to, and her ebbing annoyance was replaced by the faint, purring desire for a drink. She was already at the door, so it cost her next to nothing to shoot out to her car, fill her half-pint, and return to mull over her situation.

Admiral hadn't changed, a detail that compelled her to suppose he was serious about this death thing. That was her first thought after her first drink. The truth was, she had few options. She could deliver the body to some vet's for disposal. Or dump him along the road where city work-men would pick him up. The Jack Daniel's had begun, elegantly, to smooth the shambles in her head. Each little intake had the sweetness of honey, the vigor of a deep breath, encouraging her mismatched opinions to sort themselves out. If she just went off and left him, it might not be the calamity she'd first thought, because Bernice would show up in the morning, and she could take over. On the other hand, the idea of him alone and stiffening overnight felt creepy, and she began to worry about the other animals. Would they be scared? Or worse yet, would they turn into cannibals?

Goofy and Doofus had plopped down to contemplate the sad specta-cle of Admiral. She reached out to pet Goofy, then stretched for Doofus. "So," she said, "what are your thoughts? Any advice?" Doofus lay on his belly, his forepaws massaging his snout. Goofy nestled her chin deeper into the rug and met Janet's question with an earnest, kindly expression. Well, at least you're here, she thought, giving over to a vague prejudice against the disinterested cats. The tawny one dozed on the couch. The other was out of sight.

She nodded then, entranced by burgeoning well-being and rich affir-mation for a course of action that would soon be clear. Each little swal-low improved her awakening spirits. There was only one thing to do. She would take the dog out to Bernice, and Bernice could decide what she wanted. Whatever foolishness was going on at that church didn't have to be respected. Hazel Vanasek and that bunch collected in some pasture could be interrupted. Besides, Bernice would want to know what had happened. That's why Janet was here in the first place—because Bernice cared about her animals.

The need to protect her Honda's backseat in case the old boy oozed directed her to a hallway closet with shelves of bedding, towels and wash-cloths, cans of soup, unopened soap and toothpaste, all just so. Trying to determine which of the blankets was the worst for wear, she remembered sleeping in her car under that old army blanket. So off she went, only to be waylaid on the stoop, because she liked having that blanket to conceal her Jack Daniel's.

She pulled down a ratty item, faded yellow with an unraveling hem, and spread it on the floor beside Admiral. She propped the front door open and began the awkward task of wrapping and lifting the sagging carcass, far more unwieldy than she'd anticipated. It was as if she were lugging a gigantic baby with a long black tail. She smiled at the idea of some confused observer watching her struggle to walk, while the tail swept back and forth across her thighs. But then her fingers slipped. She crouched to regain leverage. The light was dim as her knee hit the cold ground. She better not forget her jacket. Evening was a distant bar, like an ever narrowing door in the west.

The dog's head bounced free when she stood, his snout dangling inches from her nose. It seemed he must take a breath. He was so close his features blurred. His pelt smelled faintly of Bernice's bedroom.

With her knee under his belly, Janet jerked open the car door and leaned to lay him down inside, where she lost her balance and started to topple in on top of him. She had to let go, feeling crazily alarmed that dumping him in this careless way might hurt him. She arched and stretched to escape a cramp before sagging in beside him. As she tugged the blanket flat beneath him and freed a portion to fold over him, she felt vaguely that she inhabited a melancholy fairy tale, an impression that deepened and sweetened with the brief visitation of her bottle.

Back in the house, she made sure there was water in the various bowls. If they had a choice, she figured the dogs would prefer not to spend the night in the dark, so she switched on a lamp. She was checking her belongings—jacket, purse, bottle, keys—when it struck her as a good idea to take one of Bernice's tubes of toothpaste. She scanned the rooms, evaluating their conditions against an ideal that was unclear, before turning away and thoughtfully locking up.

She hadn't gotten very far when a surly cop manning an intersection in an orange reflector vest commanded her to stop. Her heart pounded, even though he showed no further interest in her while waving a river of vehicles across her path. She hated sitting there with drugs and booze and that poor dead dog behind her. She contorted, levering against the floor to look back, as if verification could serve a purpose. The booze and the drugs were hidden from sight, but Admiral was dusty, his eyes vague.

Three gentle taps of a horn called to her. A bearded man in a gray pickup behind her smiled and shrugged for her to go. Appreciative of his tact, she gestured thanks and took off, veering way too close to the cop. She waved and mouthed, "I'm sorry," then tried to find the bearded guy in the hope that, having nearly run down a cop, she had at least made her gratitude understood. But there was no way to know, because he was headed in the opposite direction. She saw only the two dirty laborers riding in the back on either side of an overturned wheelbarrow under a rack of ladders. The traffic cop had her in his sights, however. So considerate of the guy in the pickup she'd almost mowed down a cop, shiny vest and all. Just about demanding that he pull her over. And then what? Jail, that's what. Disheartening and keen, her propensity to screw up one thing after another came at her in a shameful rush like the cop's glare. So what made her think her current plan would work out any better for her? That driving out to that stupid church was so smart? The only thing she could count on was that she'd have to cope with Bernice—and maybe not just her but the entire mob holed up out there, every one of them as batty as Bernice. The most likely outcome was her and Bernice off somewhere with a shovel, trying to bury the dog. Or Janet alone, hacking away at the dirt to bury the dog all by herself after Bernice told her to get lost. And she didn't even have a shovel, did she? No, she did not. Just an open bottle of booze. Just some 'ludes and a dead dog. Just duct tape and a hose and some crack cocaine. But her pocket felt empty, the 'ludes gone. She remembered putting them there, but as she searched her other pockets, she vaguely recalled Bernice's bed, the vial falling to the floor.

It was time to slide to the curb and think things over. She needed help. She needed a shovel, at least. Or somebody with a shovel. Like that guy in the pickup who had honked in that friendly way. He probably had a shovel. He might even have some 'ludes. He had a wheelbarrow, that much she knew. And ladders, if she remembered right. A couple of dirt-caked helpers. Probably worked construction, like Robbie Oberhoffer. Now there was an idea. Robbie Oberhoffer. He surely had a shovel.

Absurdity brought bubbling laughter. That would take the cake, all right, calling him up. And yet the suggestion delivered an accompanying excitement that made her wonder what was so audacious about it, after all. It wouldn't be like she was calling up out of the blue. If it wasn't for this afternoon—if he hadn't come up to her, shrugging and smiling—she never would have thought of him in a million years. But he was clearly a real solution. With his help, she could get the dog buried, whatever else happened. It wouldn't matter what Bernice did. They could drive out and tell her, and Bernice could do whatever she wanted. Or maybe she and Robbie would go off and bury the poor old dog. They could talk it over. He might have a thought or two about the right way to handle things.

It was curious, though, she had to admit, the way that trip to the hardware store was spreading its influence through her entire day. The errand that had sent her through those doors had been a stroke of good fortune. She could thank her lucky stars. Or Bernice or whoever had asked her to do that favor. Though she still hadn't picked up the CDs. But whoever or whatever lay behind it all knew what they were doing. Because Big Baby Dog had been there, and then Robbie, bringing back something about those vanished years—her idealism, his sweetness, the optimism of the classroom when she had first started out. With his involvement, the sad job of burying the dog might become something else, something good and beneficial between them, like those earlier days had been. If she was with him. If she reached him. If he was willing to help. If he was home. If he didn't have something else to do. A date. Or some other job. If he, if he, if he. Again she laughed, but this time because she was remembering him standing nervously before her desk, and then it seemed they were lifted and swept to a field at night, the two of them near a hole that he had forged in the dirt.

The Honda was at rest, having glided peacefully to the curb with little involvement from her. Nevertheless, there she sat under a tree, the long stretch of shoulder empty ahead. The engine idled. Traffic passed. Lawrence, she thought. Lawrence Oberhoffer. Having Robbie's dad's name come to her before she'd even asked for it was heartening. There were a lot of Oberhoffers in Belger. Locating the right household would have been a next to impossible chore without the correct first name.

She scouted the line of vehicles moving past to make sure no one would see her steal an almost dainty swig of Jack. The charge it brought made her sigh. Helping herself to a little more, she thought, The hell with it, and just let out a purr. C'mon, c'mon, just roll the dice. Her view of the road ahead melted under lowering lids, and for a moment she was a leaf in a breeze. The phone call might never be made, but at least she'd thought of it. At least she wanted to do it. She perked up, responding to a vibrant signal from somewhere remote in her thoughts. She sat more erect, her focus on her interior intensifying the way it might on a document she needed to read in dim light. Maybe getting ahold of Robbie wasn't the point. Maybe it was only her impulse that mattered, because it felt different from everything else today, and the difference was that it was hers and she wanted to follow it. Maybe the thing to pay attention to was the basic fact that she'd forgotten how some actions were truly her own. They were natural to her, devised in a place she could trust, and if this was one, if calling Robbie was one, it certainly couldn't be the only one. There had to be others, and they were what she should make her life from. As if refitting the bottle cap were an intricate task, she went about it deliberately before sliding the bottle back under the passenger seat.

The first available pay phone was in a run-down Dunkin' Donuts on Garret Avenue. Behind the graffiti-scarred wall, a toilet flushed as she thumbed the directory. A skinny teenybopper with a ring in her nose came out. Lawrence Oberhoffer had a listing on Red Hook Lane. She threw in some change and dialed. Her racing heart struck her as comical, even as it urged her to hang up. She attended each identical buzz as if to learn whether or not the house was empty, or to discover Robbie's whereabouts. She saw the phone ringing on a wall. Then it sat on a small brown end table. Seven, eight, nine. She hung up. Coins clattered into the tiny bin. So that was that, she thought, turning to go. But what if he'd just jumped out of the shower or raced in the back door only to be met by a stupid dial tone? What if he was standing there wishing he knew who had called? She had to ask about luck and the way half the time whatever happened was really, secretly an accident. People talked about chance. They worried and called it serendipity. Providence. They read horoscopes. What was a coincidence? A fluke? A shot in the dark? She had redialed before reaching this point in her speculations, and the line came to life with a clatter. "Hello. This is Robbie."

"Robbie?"

"Yes, this is Robbie."

"Hi. I hope I'm not catching you at a busy time."

"No."

Only then did she grasp his scramble to identify her voice, and she felt rude, even mean-spirited. "It's Janet Cawley. You remember from this afternoon?"

"Miss Cawley?" He seemed to grow young as he said her name.

"I'm sorry, I didn't mean to be mysterious."

"No, no, I just didn't know who you were."

"How could you?"

"Right. Hi."

"Hi," she said, and she wanted to shout in celebration of the instinct that had moved her to call back.

"Hey. All those years and then twice in one day."

"How's that for something?"

"I know."

"But what?" she joked.

"Somebody's lucky day, I guess." Hidden in his chuckle was a realization that wiped away his awkwardness.

"Here's the thing. And no is definitely an okay response, okay? Perfectly legitimate. Feel free to say no."

"How could I say no?"

"Well, you could."

"Not before I know what we're talking about."

Whatever he had discovered had left him sounding steady, even casual. "I just want you to know it's okay."

"Okay."

"Because I have a harebrained favor to ask. Or you could think it's harebrained."

"What is it?"

"A friend of mine—well, her dog died, and I'm—"

"Oh, man," he said, quick to sympathy. "That's terrible. What kind of dog?"

"It's a— I don't know. A mix of some kind. A mutt, you know."

"They're the best. A lot of the time they really are. The best." He turned quiet then, and his mood came to her, traveling all those miles to tell her that his next remark would broach something crucial. "Was he old?" And then, so rapidly he almost overlapped his own question, he said, "Or she old?"

"He. He was a male. And he was old."

"Real old?"

"I think so."

"Well, that's something. I mean, he lived his life. I guess you can't ask for more. You get your shot."

"Right."

"You know."

There was no mistaking his allusion to their earlier conversation about her mom and his dad. Interconnectedness threw another stitch between them, making her smile and open the palm of her free hand against the wall as if he were right there. "He was tough," she said. "That's what I think. I didn't know him well, but he had a sense about him. Character." She expected a quick response, was given silence, but in spite of the simplicity, maybe even the banality, of their exchange, something solid waited in the gap he'd left. "Anyway," she said, "here's the thing. I have to bury him. Or deal with him somehow. However I do it—however I dispose of him—I want it to be respectful, and so I need help. You know, digging a hole, or whatever I do. And— I just thought of you."

"Whose dog is it?"

"Bernice Doorley's. Do you know her?"

"I don't think so."

"Probably not. Why would you? She was a friend of my mother's. Real close at one time."

"I see. Hey, count me in."

"You'll help?"

"Yeah, yeah. Is she around? The owner."

"Well, yes. In a way."

"Is she with you?"

"No, she's not."

"Where is she?"

"Well, that, Robbie, is a long story."

This time the pause he took felt lighthearted, and so she let it go on, feeling coaxed and appreciated.

"Well," Robbie said, "maybe you can tell me later."

She understood him perfectly, but she said, "What?"

"The owner. Her story."

"It would take a little time."

"Fine by me. Listen. Where are you?"

"I'm in a Dunkin' Donuts—the one on Garret Avenue. You know it?"

"Yeah, yeah. That's not far at all. I'm on Red Hook Lane. My folks' place in Homestead Development. You're driving, right?"

"Sure."

"I need a quick shower, and then I could meet you. Or you could come by here if you don't want to wait there."

She glanced around like she was actually considering staying there. One of her mother's friends lived in Homestead with her daughter and family. Isabel had gone for a card game, and Janet had driven her. She remembered twists and turns, myriad circles, and cars depositing dolled-up old women like fragile children. "I'll come by. No need to have you driving all over the place."

"Great," he said. "So go on Garret to the entrance."

"I've been there."

"Great." He spooled out the directions, naming several streets and circles, counting the blocks for her, a nuance of excitement under his effort to make certain she got to him. "It should take you maybe ten minutes."

"Got it," she said. "See you then."

"Can I ask you something?"

"What? Sure."

"Where's the dog?"

"Oh, right. He's in the car."

"No kidding."

"Yeah."

"He's with you?"

"Yeah. He's in the car."

"Okay," he said, as if he'd just won a bet.

Prudence advised that certain precautions be taken, such as moving the liter of liquor, along with its more or less permanent accessories, the plastic bag and blanket, to the trunk. After topping off her half-pint, she spiked her freshly purchased black coffee. The notion of checking on the dog led her to slip in beside him, surprised by the allure that reached out to draw her close. A wedge of yellow blanket hovered over his brow in folds like those of a ruffled bonnet. Along with the gray around his snout and under his jaw, she absorbed in detail the red collar encircling his throat with his identification tags on a silver loop. Just like the junk in her wallet. Name, address, and blah blah blah. She passed her fingers over his snout. Emptiness inhabited him, but he felt dear, and she squeezed his ears as if to bring back the pink that was draining away. It was because of him that she'd called Robbie. She took a long drink. Quickened by booze, the coffee hit with a lovely surge that sent heat out from her center. She felt indebted to the poor old dead dog, who seemed somehow responsible for her changing fortunes.

24

T HE CONGREGATION CAME FROM THE sanctuary into the open air, where evening was a deepening presence. Adrift within the jostle and murmur, Bernice fastened the lower two buttons of her jacket. They had an hour until the next service. Her gaze fell across the parked cars, the parsonage, where several downstairs lights burned. Everybody was acting so excited, and to her way of thinking, sort of childish or fake. While some were commenting on the unexpected beauty of the weather, the main topic was the new hymn they'd sung to end the service. Or, as she saw it, tried to sing. Not only was it something new to them, they'd never seen or heard it before, and it hadn't gone all that well, though Reverend Tauke had acted overjoyed. Introducing it, he'd explained how it was theirs alone. He had created it for them, and so he hoped they would see how special it was. Taking the tune from a song he felt they all must have heard, "A Whiter Shade of Pale," he'd written his own words to fit it, and after explaining, he'd passed out xeroxed copies. The first verse went something like *I trip and call to Jesus, end up hopeless on the floor. / But then He touches me and—* Or maybe it was: *I feel Him touch me. My soul calls out for more . . . !* She had the option of referring to the folded-up sheet in her jacket pocket but she didn't feel like it. The name was "All Rising to the Lord," and Reverend Tauke had arranged to have tape-recorded karaoke accompaniment piped over loudspeakers. There'd been a lot of reluctance at first, and in the bustle around her now, there was still confusion, though some were acting thrilled, and many were humming the tune. Otto Fritsch, not looking where he was going, walked right into her just then, his head stuck in the printout, his lips moving as he worked to learn the words. She figured she'd have to do that, too, but she wasn't looking forward to it.

Pressure on her shoulder from behind turned her to Hazel, who opened her arms, expecting a hug. Well, it's my old friend Hazel, Bernice thought, her embrace lacking the slightest warmth. "Hello, Hazel."

They squeezed and patted, Bernice doing what she had to, and when they withdrew, the surprise was that Hazel looked on fire. Her eyes were scarily big and bright, while the sway of her head was the best she could do to express a state of mind she would not even try to describe. Bernice hoped to show something similar, though she didn't have the goods and suspected Hazel really only wanted to be admired. "How's the Lord treating you, Hazel?"

"No, Bernice, no. How's He treating you?" Her tone brushed aside any thought that Bernice's well-being was not her number-one priority.

"I'm good."

"Don't you just love the hymn he made for us?"

"Oh, sure."

"I broke down and cried a couple times, just hearing the blessing inside it, and everybody trying so hard to get it out. Like little children."

Bernice was a bit frightened not to go along with Hazel's picture of things. It felt risky to show even a hint of anything that wasn't upbeat and enthusiastic. "It's a good tune. And once everybody gets it down, well, it'll be something, all right."

"Are you really feeling good? I'm not so sure."

"Oh, yes. I am. I sure am."

"Thank God. I'm so relieved. Because I'm wonderful. Wonderful, I tell you. Just wonderful."

"You look it."

"I feel it. It came over me, you know. It just all came over me. Every square inch."

"Good."

"It's that Alice Kuhn. It was being with her, I think."

"Is that right?"

"The Lord came right out of her. She's an inspiration. And when we sang, her voice carried me up. As you well know, my singing voice is nothing to write home about. All my life I been told I couldn't carry a tune in a bucket, and if the truth be told, I can't. You know that."

"Sure."

"You can say it—I won't be hurt, because all of a sudden it doesn't matter. With Alice leading the way, with Alice beside me, I let go, just let myself join in, and I was halfway decent. Not that anybody cares. Good or bad didn't matter one iota. The more I sang, the more I felt at home. Did you see the way Alice came up to me when I first got here? I barely got out of the car, and up she runs. Well, she was looking for me. Can you believe it? Had this feeling! There she was. Do you see what I'm gettin' at?"

Pretty run-of-the-mill stuff, as far as Bernice could tell, in spite of the fuss Hazel was making. "Maybe you should tell me."

"Well, it was what the Lord wanted," Hazel explained, beaming, not the least bit shy to bear witness to miracles worked just for her. "He wanted her to be looking for me and to find me and the two of us to go in together, so I could find the things I'm talking about. She's an inspiration, and Jesus wanted me to feel that inspiration, and so He had her waiting for me."

"What happened to Jean Hines?"

"What? Why?" Her brow wrinkled, like Bernice's question was unfathomable.

"Jean Hines. She was waiting for you, too, wasn't she?"

"I don't think so."

"Sure. She was right there with Alice when you say Alice was waiting for you. That's what I saw. You hardly got out of the car, and the pair of them came running up to you together."

"I don't know where she went." Hazel glanced around, more puzzled than concerned about lost Jean Hines. "I didn't see her in church, did you?"

"No. But she was right there for all that do-si-do-ing Alice put on."

"Anyway, Alice wants us all heading down to the house. There's a gathering of people to testify, she says, and then she's going to organize groups to work on the new song—you know, help everybody get the words down. Sounds just right, don't you think? Alice says there's food and a big pot of coffee. C'mon with us."

Hazel was in a tizzy, her attention everywhere but on Bernice, and for a second her distraction was a mystery, but then her hands flew up in response to her wonderful discovery. "There she is," she said, pointing to Alice, who stood between Bonnie Frunke and her son. The three of them were down the slope in the direction of the parsonage, but not so far Bernice couldn't recognize merry satisfaction in the faces of the Frunkes as Alice swirled, showing off her dress. Good Lord, thought Bernice.

"Alice said she was going to think about the first time she ever heard the other song, the one ours is based on, because she always felt it was kind of spiritual. She says she remembers that it stopped her cold that first time. I remember it from back a while, but not the first time. Do you?"

"What? The first time I heard it? No."

"I don't, either. I think it's pretty neat, though, don't you?"

"It's okay. But I like the old ones better—the regular ones."

"You're such a stick in the mud. That's why we gotta practice it. So it gets to be regular. C'mon," she said, raring to go. "Time's a-wasting."

"I'll be along in a minute, Hazel." Bernice was not about to follow along with anything Alice Kuhn was leading, and she backstepped without looking or caring where she was off to.

"No, no. What are you going to do? There's nothing better to do."

"I just need to stretch my legs a little."

"That's silly. Just do what I'm telling you, Bernice, and come with me. You'll miss everything. You don't want to miss out, do you?"

While Hazel's words declared her eagerness to bring Bernice along, she had already started walking away because of desires in which Bernice didn't count at all.

"I'll be along," Bernice said, doubting Hazel even heard her.

The Frunkes—both of them—watched blissfully as Hazel and Alice fell into each other's arms. It was as if they'd been apart and pining for years, not mere mínutes. And something had happened to the boy, all right—he looked downright goofy. Anticipating the three of them wheeling toward her, should Hazel actually remember to mention her existence, Bernice pivoted away. She was trying to recall what she knew of any friendship between Hazel and Alice Kuhn, but as best as she could discover, there had never been one. Alice was a good fifteen years younger. Attractive but sort of corpselike, namely pale and thin as a rail; her husband had been a chiropractor, and she'd been his receptionist until he came down with a terrible cancer and went in a flash. After that she worked some at the gift shop up at Koopman Hospital, where Bernice had some dealings with her but as few as possible, because Alice struck her as somebody who couldn't wait to toot her own horn. And now Hazel was totally gaga over her, acting like some head-over-heels teenager forgetting anybody who might have once been her friend. Hazel would probably claim it was Jesus she was gaga over, and she could believe that if she wanted. But if Bernice was to come to her own conclusion, she'd have to say Hazel's current heartthrob was Alice. Well, she'd known that, hadn't she? Hazel ran hot and cold. Fickle. Not a snake in the grass, but the kind of person who changes with the wind. And that song, "The Whiter Whatever Whatever." Spiritual. Right. She snorted, her sense of scorn too heavy to become the least bit enjoyable. At the time it was popular, it was the kind kids listened to when they were up to no good, making out or smoking dope in the backseats of cars. Maybe that was Alice Kuhn's idea of spiritual, but it sure wasn't Bernice's.

Her restless gaze had come to a stop on the pasture where she remembered Reverend Tauke standing with the cows and looking so impressive. Viewed at a slightly upward angle, the fence appeared faint across the horizon. It seemed that Reverend Tauke's previous occupation had hallowed the ground, and she felt that walking up there might offer a solution to her cranky mood.

Mostly, the cows were collected near a water trough located to one side, but a pair had ended up in the far corner, with the neck of one crossed over the other. Somebody would have to herd them to shelter before sundown, but she couldn't think who owned that neighboring farm.

Visible beyond the farthest section of the pen, a mud road ran toward a distant barn that appeared, with the sun down and night near, to float and melt. Walking the way she was on rough ground made her sturdy shoes seem smart, her pantsuit down-to-earth and sensible.

When one of the cows left the main group, she didn't think much of it. But then she noticed that the creature was eyeing her while trudging on a course that would bring them together. Bernice veered and came up to the fence at a slightly altered point, and the cow adjusted and sidled on over. The big eyes made her uneasy. Not exactly thoughtful, they showed evidence of an idea of some kind. Huge and knobby, with twitching ears and moist, gaping nostrils, the cow's head jutted from her broad dark chest. White splotches spread backward from both shoulders. The cow's mouth moved then, the enormous lips mashing each other, and Bernice felt sad. She hadn't come up here to look at a cow. Not one acting like this one, anyway. Like it was trying to figure out how to say something. The poor dumb creature probably thought Bernice had brought food, and that was why it was so attentive.

Bernice shook her head, the scope and tenderness of her interest in the cow striking her as stupid, even sinful, and she glanced skyward to the clouds and dwindling light. Her Bible flexed under her fingers. She looked down at the dark rectangle of the cover the way she might at a curtain that could open on a whole different kind of world. She felt so ignorant about everything. First of all, the book she held. Even her own heart, the way it ached. Couldn't even say what it was she was feeling or what she was supposed to make of it all.

Hearing the cow breathe, she contemplated the black spooky face and felt pretty much like a dumb beast herself. Just dumb as a post. She wondered if she might raise the book to the rail. Let the cow take a look. Or maybe if that wasn't crazy enough, she could fling it up in the air. Let the pages do their own sorting until they hit the ground and stopped all by themselves.

What had come over her? Letting a cow read? Throwing her Bible? Nutty as a fruitcake. Crazy, blasphemous thoughts. And yet they re- minded her of the things Reverend Tauke had been talking about at service. The verses she came upon that way wouldn't be ones she'd decided on, so they would be like something delivered to her the way things came to him. They would be verses that maybe Jesus chose. Or one of His angels. Not that she thought the angels and Jesus had nothing better to do with their time than waste it on her. And not that she would be like Reverend Tauke. But without her even deciding, the book was before her, the rough rail giving support while the pages fluttered. The force of her confusion had her fingers riffling pages until they stopped abruptly. One last faintly transparent sheet settled over them. She could turn it or simply stand pat. But then her hand pulled out, forcing her to decide whether she needed to change what had just happened or leave it alone, even though she had not really made a decision in the first place.

The cow snorted, a moist, lengthy shudder blending a snore with a sneeze. "Shoo!" she said, and stomped her foot. The cow heaved a step backward. "Shoo!" she repeated, and the bulky body shivered while the animal's gaze tried to convince her she didn't want to act this way. She blinked, then closed her eyes, deciding to read what she'd found upon first looking: *You must face the fact: the final age of this world is to be a time of troubles. Men will love nothing but money and self; they will be arrogant, boastful, and abusive; with no respect for parents, no gratitude, no piety, no natural affection; they will be implacable in their hatreds, scandal-mongers, intemperate and fierce, strangers to all goodness. . . .*

Goose bumps coated her forearms. Wasn't this enough? Reverend Tauke had talked about trying to hear Jesus. And she wasn't even in Revelations. Wandering into Timothy, she'd arrived at a description of the end of the world. Her finger led her back to where she'd started: *the final age of this world . . .*

She was changing, she hoped. Or at least wanting to. Beginning to. She felt sad and a little lonely. What was she doing up here, anyway? Why had she turned away from Hazel and Alice and everyone? Did she think she was different from them? Did she think she was better? Her reaction to Hazel being happy had been so small-minded. She'd treated Hazel's joy as if it was foolish, or worse yet, a bitter pill Bernice refused to swallow. But who was she to look down her nose at Hazel? Or even at Alice Kuhn?

What gave her the right to think she could decide whether or not some-body was sincere or phony when they spoke of love and Jesus? Maybe she felt mean and petty about Hazel because she'd never known anything like that kind of joyfulness. Had no idea what it was. Her membership in Rev-erend Tauke's church had little rhyme or reason, if she got right down to it. Hadn't it all just kind of happened after that weirdness in her surgery when she woke up unable to move and full of crazy thoughts? Sure, she'd let him baptize her. She'd stood looking down into the blue inflated kid-die pool with its wooden frame so expertly built and stained with the same devotion as the stairs she'd climbed to get there. Reverend Tauke was waiting, his bare feet blurry under the waves. She wore old clothes, and the rippling depths rose up her legs. They were both sweating. She re-called droplets on her cheek. He wiped his big palm over his brow. She didn't like to connect her baptism to Isabel, but it was under a year after the funeral when she said the word "yes" after he asked if she'd received Christ as her Savior, listening close to what he wanted to tell her about the Father, Son, and Holy Ghost. He took hold of her shoulders, and she wanted to give over, body and soul, but then she started worrying about not having enough air in her lungs and when he put a cloth over her face, it scared her, even though she knew it was meant to help. She wanted to pull away and felt foolish as she sank back gasping with her eyes shut. She came up sputtering and hoping she'd done it right, repeating in her mind all the words they'd said, both his and her own, wanting to mean them but scared by the memory of something niggardly and miserly clutching at her all the while to keep her back. Maybe that was the problem, her lack of sincerity, of honesty, her lack of almost all the things needed for salvation.

With her next breath, Bernice realized her doubts were a kind of hex. Her poisonous response to Hazel came not only from her unfamiliarity with such joy but from her refusal to believe that anyone could feel such pure, uplifting bliss. Without ever really meaning to, she had come to be-lieve that deep down everybody had to be just as deprived and half starved as she was. They just covered it up better—they pretended better and so were even bigger phonies.

But what if she was wrong? What if there were only her and a few other good-for-nothings missing out? Like Marty Dolphin. She couldn't quite picture him yelling at Reverend Tauke the way Esther had described. How had he ever had the nerve? To say those things—to admit he was sick of it all and that he felt tricked! She knew the look of Marty Dolphin when he flew in a rage. She'd seen him blow a gasket at the bowling alley too many times to count when he and Toby were on different teams, and all of a sudden Marty was red-faced and ready to throw a punch and nobody knew exactly why. Which was exactly what Bernice did. Way too often. The thought kicked apart something inside her that she counted on to keep her standing. The legs went out, and down it came, because she had to admit she was just like Marty Dolphin—they were two of a kind— hair-triggered and confusing to everybody around her, even herself, when she got hopping mad for reasons that didn't make sense and didn't have to. And then he'd bolted, hadn't he? And where was she? After spending the day wishing Hazel would leave her alone, she'd had a conniption at the sight of Hazel and Alice Kuhn together. But admit she felt left out? No, not her. How could she envy something she claimed made her want to upchuck? So she'd run off, like Marty. Just had to single herself out. The queen of Sheba! And who was that? Some pagan whore! Up here with this stupid cow when everybody was together praying. But not Bernice Doorley. Hadn't just about everything that she'd ever done or that had ever happened to her sooner or later rubbed her nose in shit? And yet here she was, trying to make out like she was special. Just a big phony. Arrogant and boastful, exactly the way it said in Timothy. She searched the still-open Bible propped on the fence so she could get her self-indictment word for word. *No piety, no natural affection; they will be implacable in their hatreds, scandal-mongers.* Well, that fit her, all right. *Scandal-monger* fit her to a T.

She had no idea when she had turned to gaze down the hillside. The ground floor of the parsonage overflowed with light, heads and shoulders in silhouette. The sloping landscape sank from sight and resurfaced farther on, and the pallor of the chapel thrust it from the deepening dark. A door slammed. She saw someone hasten from the parsonage, and her hope that Reverend Tauke was rushing to look for her both appealed and shamed her. Was that what she expected? That he'd come running? Because he had—what? Read her mind? As if he was Jesus and she was what? His soul mate? One of his saints? Lord, she hoped she wasn't waiting for that—for an engraved invitation—because she'd be up here alone a long time if she was. Hadn't he already told her she belonged, they all belonged, or else they wouldn't be in his flock?

When the cow grunted, she whirled, wincing with pain deep in her hip. "Get away from me! Stop looking at me." She gestured as if swirling something scary to cows. She pantomimed cocking her arm to throw a rock. "I mean it. I don't want any more to do with you!" She bit back the urge to yelp as her leg clenched and burned to slow her start down the hill. It was up to her to go to Reverend Tauke and join the others. And the good news was she knew where to find them, and no one would tell her to get back where she'd come from. Because the only one who'd ordered her up here in the first place was Bernice Doorley.

The cow groaned behind her. A clattering of hooves on the hard dirt called to her. But she was picturing warmth up ahead. She saw herself joining in one of the little study groups organized by Alice Kuhn to learn the new song. All at once it washed over her, the comfort of no longer being herself in particular, but one of the flock. She would follow their lead. Their smiles would guide her. If some were quiet, others would talk, and she would listen and trust their sincerity. She would not let doubt poison her any longer. Other than whispering "Praise Jesus" and "Hallelujah," she would hold her tongue until she was cured of her bitter thoughts. Especially her spite about Hazel. Especially jealousy of Alice. Because they were her sisters in Reverend Tauke's congregation, all brothers and sisters, for whom she wanted to feel only love and duty.

And it seemed possible as she trudged along. Her mood had a shiny freshness, as if she'd been cleaned up inside and out. Her faith had never felt like this before. She was over the hump. The night would bear them away all together. It was going to happen. So many things she had struggled to believe as best she could were now real in a new, unquestionable way that was as clear as the nose on her face. Until this second, she had shrugged off the most important thing about a congregation, giving only lip service to the ties that joined the members, refusing to accept that they were a bunch of ordinary people turned into a body of faithful souls held together, as Reverend Tauke told them, by the same scriptures, the same love and grace, the same Jesus.

Her knee ached and her hip throbbed, her worn-out old eyesight troubled by the light fading, the uneven ground. The sun was low, the moon faint and waiting. Smoke from a wood fire perfumed the air, and she imagined the fireplace with everyone gathered, and they were a family—her new family, and she felt bound to them by something stronger than blood.

She sighed with gratitude for the firm hold her faith had on her at last. Better late than never, she thought, feeling followed and eyed, feeling haunted, and even before she looked, she knew no one was there. Because it was her old family tagging along, tracing her path at a ghostly distance, bidding for a last little bit of attention before she left them behind completely and went into the parsonage. Scattered memories scampered in the shadows. They approached shyly, like shame-faced strangers, like panhandlers wanting something, and she acknowledged them, considered them, nodding, remembering. But that wasn't what they wanted. They were insistent, asking for more, doubling in number, turning into a mob before she saw what was happening. They started jumping from one thing to another, making claims, telling stories, throwing up pictures, all kinds of silly, sweet yarns and tales, fuzzy notions, even facts and faces in a jumble, and some were bigger than life, almost legends. Where were they all going? Where were they coming from? It was as if having her new family had sent them all into a tizzy inside her, opening this sealed-up room locked tight as a fist, and out came her mom and dad, whom she'd been calling "Grandpa and Grandma" for years because that was what Irma called them. Wasn't that silly? Her own mom and dad called "Grandpa and Grandma." And Uncle Hank, seven years older and already dead over a decade. But there he was, her big brother jumping up and down in a straw cowboy hat and wearing Grandpa Thill's shiny black vest. Grandpa Thill was her mom's father and so her real grandpa and

Hank's, too. He'd surrendered the vest after Hank had badgered and begged, because it gave him the look of a western movie saloon gambler. With his finger in the air, Hank shouted at Bernice, "Deal the cards, missy, or you're a goner!" Were they all in heaven waiting, and would they give her a nice welcome? Even though she'd be arriving in this funny way, looking maybe uppity and full of herself sailing into heaven in her regular body like a saint. She saw a misty, foggy hallway tunneling off into smoke, her friends and relatives approaching through a clouded glow, just like they showed it on TV, which wasn't likely, though some said it was based on fact, and anyway, it was all she could come up with.

Wind curled around the chapel, rattling the hefty oaks hidden behind it. The longest branches crept over the roof like skinless hands reaching out through the gray beyond. Smoke was visible above the parsonage chimney. She smiled as if already inside and near the warmth of the flames.

The entrance to the church was edged in light. Though she was eager to join her new family waiting below, the chapel doorway slowed her with the invitation to enter and meet her dead relatives inside. She felt it strongly, that they waited just beyond those walls, and by going in, she could sit with them for a moment.

She was surprised to find a dozen or more people scattered about. She took a seat quietly, a few rows behind Carol Gunsolly and Thomas Hagg, who had been told he would die months ago from colon cancer, but there he was, skinny and pale and hanging on to Carol. They were both maybe fifty, and recently, Carol had quit her job as a manager at Target, sold her little house and then driven around to her kids, giving them all her money. Not long after that, the oldest and the youngest—she had four—started hanging around church, trying to figure things out, demanding an explanation, and then they called it all stupid and drove off. Bernice could remember the older one, a man of about thirty, yelling, "We'll just wait and see!" Claire Dotterweich, who was still good-looking, sat alone in an attractive gray cloth coat with some kind of fur trim. As a teenager, she had been such a knockout that every girl inside the city limits turned green with envy at the thought of her, Bernice included. Eban Scott had his own private little spot, too. His hair looked freshly cut, and he was nicely dressed in a dark blue sport jacket, and probably wore one of those bow ties he favored, though Bernice couldn't see. For a long time he'd argued with Reverend Tauke over the meaning of almost every scripture read in Bible study. Esther Huegel had an expression that could have been sad, and it worried Bernice, as she moved on to Edith Fritsch, who was with her first husband, Otto. Edith had divorced him way back and then remarried once they both turned up at Church of the Angel, where, as she put it, they could no longer avoid the fact that their reunion was in God's plan.

When her meandering gaze landed on Reverend Tauke just sitting in a pew like an ordinary person, she tried to conceal that she was the one who had gasped. It didn't seem possible he'd been there all along. But she would have noticed him walking in. His lanky frame was pushed into angles of bunched-up dark cloth by the narrowness of the pew. His features were commanding, his cheekbones bright beneath pale skin. Shaggy salt-and-pepper hair flowed over his dandruff-speckled coat, and his sideburns needed trimming. She wished she could see inside his head and hear his thoughts for just one second. Was he worried and waiting, like the rest of them? Was he praying for them all, as a good shepherd must, even for her and Marty Dolphin?

It seemed that something in his sermon had hinted at answers to these questions, and as she tried to recall the exact remark, her thoughts must have reached out and tapped him on the shoulder, for he looked directly at her. And she could not help but see how handsome he was. Yearning swept over her, and it was his, too, in those seconds, the wish that they could have met before all this. When they were young and could have gone walking to sit somewhere drinking sodas through straws.

Lord, she thought. Shame, like a hand in her hair, shoved her head low and shut her eyes. What in God's name was she doing throwing herself at Reverend Tauke? Was there no end to her foolishness? All of a sudden she was no better than some brazen hussy. But hadn't it only been drinking soda through straws? Maybe it wasn't so bad. Maybe the wild feeling that had come over her was like what Jesus had made her feel for

Esther Huegel, only this time the burst of love that Jesus put into her was for Reverend Tauke. Oh, sure, she thought, blame it all on Jesus.

She buried her face in her palms. What a joke. What a starry-eyed, schmaltzy joke. Romance, she thought, welcoming scorn and wanting more of it. She was an ignorant old bag who had better shut up, because she didn't have a clue about romance, since she'd lived her entire life without it. For an instant she worried she'd hurt poor Toby with that last thought, such an uncalled-for cruelty, and she wanted to take it back, but then the feeling came to her that he didn't mind and that he nodded wistfully, wherever he might be.

Reverend Tauke had left his pew. He went past the first row and up the step toward the pulpit, where she feared he might speak about the way she had just acted with him in her mind. A glance to her companions showed that they were studying his climb to the baptismal pool. Because winter wasn't far off, the water had been drained. Half in shadow, he stood motionless. Was he absorbed in the past, too, nostalgia returning him to the many times he'd mounted those stairs with souls to save? Born again, she thought. His departure felt violent, as if he had to rip himself free from all these invisible restraints. He moved swiftly to the stairs and down to the middle aisle, his eyes fixed straight ahead as he swept past them all and went out the door.

For a second, she had no recollection of why she'd come into the chapel. It was little more than reflex to open her Bible and read: *You are witness in your own cause; your testimony is not valid.* Her eyes scooted back along the line, until she saw it was the Pharisees speaking. Jesus replied, *My testimony is valid even though I do bear witness about myself; because I know where I come from, and where I am going. You do not know either where I come from or where I am going. You judge by worldly standards. I pass judgment on no man, but if I do judge, my judgment is valid because it is not I alone who judge, but I and he who sent me.*

Maybe she should just go on down to the parsonage like she'd started out doing. The impulse pushed her to her feet, where something stronger closed her eyes and shoved her back down. Instantly, her dad strode before her mind's eye, coming in the back door mad as hell. He slammed the door hard. Angry and dark as the inside of a fist.

The weight on her shoulder was so timid it almost asked her not to respond. But then it became tightening fingers, and the whisper seemed to belong to Janet Cawley. "I'm sorry to bother you, Bernice, but I thought you'd want to know. Admiral is dead."

Peering up as if from sleep, Bernice wondered what Janet Cawley was doing in the aisle of her church. What did she want that could have brought her all the way out here? And who was Admiral? "What's that, Janet?"

"I'm sorry. He's dead."

Her voice was so sad that Bernice wanted to avoid being unkind about whatever was troubling Janet by saying the wrong thing. She gazed into her remorse-filled eyes and said, "Oh."

"I didn't know what else to do."

The whites around the poor kid's pupils were bloodshot, and close up this way, she smelled of whiskey. "Okay."

"I did everything the way you wanted. I just found him. He seemed fine when I got there. I fell asleep in that recliner you have by the front door. I was worn out." She was speaking rapidly, but at least low and hushed, out of respect for their being in church. "I got his food ready just the way you told me, and when he stuck his nose up, I boiled him hot dogs."

Alarm, like distant thunder, came and went. "Wait a minute."

"And he got his pills. I put them in the cheese."

"Who are you talking about?"

"Admiral."

"Who?"

"Admiral."

Confusion raised their voices. Bernice stiffened against the annoyance of people around her who were demanding quiet. "Maybe we should go outside. I don't know who you're talking about."

"The old dog, the black one. He's out in the car."

"What's he doing out in the car?"

"I told you." Janet looked suddenly fearful that a trick was being played on her. "He's dead. Aren't you listening? The black dog."

Standing, Bernice thrust past Janet. "You're talking about General? General's dead? What are you saying?" Even as waves of panic left her weakening, she headed up the aisle. "How could you let that happen? What happened?" She banged open the door and searched the evening. "Where? Where?"

"Take it easy."

"Where is he?"

"Calm down. I'll show you. My car's in the lot."

"It's dark," Bernice said, hearing surprise in her own voice. She should have expected dusk to have passed, leaving night, yet she felt harried and rushed. Her aches and pains forced stiff-legged steps, and she grabbed on to Janet.

"There's nothing to be done," Janet was saying. "Just watch your step, okay? I don't want you tripping and falling."

"You're the one drunk," Bernice said.

"Just please watch your step."

"You're the one liable to fall on your face."

"I'm fine. You just please look where you're going."

"You smell like a distillery, let me tell you."

"Okay, you told me."

"I don't understand this at all. He even went to the vet's today, and they said he was fine, except he had this old-dog vesti-something-or-other."

"I don't know. He was sleeping. I was sleeping."

"What were you doing sleeping? Did you give him the right food?"

"Yes."

"Did you give him too many pills?"

"What? No."

"I don't understand why you were sleeping at my house!"

"I was tired."

"How many did you give him?"

"What?"

"Pills! Pills!"

"Two. In the cheese."

Bernice faltered as a shadow flew past. "What was that?"

"What?"

"That shadow."

"I don't know. The wind's blowing the trees around."

The patronizing expression that came with Janet's curt answer made Bernice indignant. "Why'd you call him that stupid name?"

"What?"

"When you said he was dead, I didn't even know who you were talking about."

"Sorry."

"A lot of good that does."

"I thought that was his name. You know, I got mixed up."

"You probably got some other things mixed up, too, didn't you?"

"I did what you told me, Bernice."

"How'm I supposed to believe that when you come up here calling him that stupid name?"

"Like what could I have done that killed him? Is that what you're suggesting?"

"You tell me."

"Don't you start blaming me, Bernice. Maybe you should have just stayed home instead of coming up here for this foolishness."

"So this is foolishness, is it?"

"I'd say so."

"Like you'd know foolishness if you saw it. Probably jump in and say, 'I'll take some of that.'"

"You know, you're probably right. And the fact that I'm here like this, going out of my way trying to be considerate of you, is proof enough."

"Everybody knows you drink too much."

"Shut up."

The moon was brazen, this round icy stare that, as Bernice got a good look at it, scared every trace of hope right out of her, so there was suddenly no way to see anything caring anywhere up there at all. Daylight hid the way it was all so big and dark and empty. Just blue, and that was that. But Janet whispering into her ear had unplugged something in her heart so emptiness and noise could take over the way it used to on TV when the programming came to an end at midnight and static ruled till dawn. Sometimes after the last show, they made a nice speech or played "The Star-Spangled Banner" over a picture of the flag. But sooner or later, this sign came on, the test-pattern insignia, and you could watch it if you wanted, until finally, the station signed off and the screen became static and hissing, spitting noise. Snow, they called it.

Janet said, "Mine's the red Honda up on the right."

They were picking their way down the last of the walkway. Bernice twisted around, wanting to see something she felt was behind her, but whatever it was, she didn't find it. "I just don't understand."

"I don't, either," Janet said. "I went to sleep, and he was okay. In fact, he even got all worked up at one point about something and ran across the room. I mean, he seemed lively."

"What do you mean, worked up?"

"Well, he had an accident in his bed."

"You mean he peed in his bed?"

"Actually, it was poop."

"He pooped in his bed? How did that happen? Did you walk him? Did you walk him, Janet?" When Janet let out a grumble like she really wanted to give herself a good kick, Bernice said, "Oh, Lord, you didn't walk him, did you?"

"I walked the other ones, and I was going to walk him, but he didn't act like he needed to go."

"You can't go by what he does. Sometimes I have to drag him out. He's old, you know."

"Nobody said anything about dragging him out."

"So then you fell asleep and left him on his own."

"I don't think that had anything to do with it, Bernice. I mean, he didn't have a heart attack. He ran across the room, and I cleaned things up, and then he went back and went to sleep. He seemed real peaceful, and that's where I found him. Like he was sleeping on his big pillow."

Moonlight smeared the rows of metal and glass to Bernice's left and right, the fragmentary cars giving the parking lot the feel of a junkyard. She wanted to turn away but managed only to turn inward, where she pictured a second sky, fantastic and yet oddly like the real one overhead, a big dark with tiny stars, but in this one she hurtled about in her clunky body, her outlandish arms, legs, bowels, guts, gore, shit streaming out of her, turds and piss. Everyone was there, all flying into this big inky hole. It was so stupid, suddenly and obviously. Where would they go? Claire Dotterweich. Carol Gunsolly and Thomas Hagg holding hands and zooming into outer space. Eban Scott in his bow tie. Edith Fritsch and Otto. Hazel and Alice. Esther Huegel, for heaven's sake. Naked or clothed, who knew which—she figured naked—rocketing into nothing, a bunch of naked lunatics spinning and caterwauling like fools on a carnival ride. Even Reverend Tauke. It made her feel silly. She could have laughed out loud, could have been in stitches.

When a door on the Honda opened and a lanky male figure emerged, Bernice was taken aback. "Is that your car?"

"That's a friend of mine. He can help."

"Help what?"

"Hello," said the figure in a thin, youthful voice.

25

WANTING TO MAKE HER ALLEGIANCE to Robbie absolutely clear, Janet crossed to him. He stood without a hint of concern or urgency, waiting politely until she got through the introductions, before he said, "Hello, Mrs. Doorley. Sorry about your dog."

"Thank you."

But his presence obviously flustered Bernice, whose attitude quickly became an annoyed demand for somebody to hurry up and tell her what he was doing there.

"I'm thinking maybe we could take a little walk, Bernice," Janet said. "Give you a little time with General to think about what you want. And then we can try to figure everything out. He's in the backseat."

The boy tugged the rear door open before Bernice had a chance to think about much at all, let alone decide what she wanted. In the ballooning light, a fragment of black surfaced, like a hunk of worn rug. "Okay," she said, and very slowly her eyes shut, only to open on her old friend partly covered by a yellow blanket. "Oh," she said. "Oh, General." Her entry to a place beside him was cautious, as if being dead made him frail and helpless. His posture did not look restful. His forepaws could have been midstride. Her hand moved toward his head only to hesitate above his shoulder before settling on his brow. Touch brought sad, undeniable certainty. "Oh," she said again. "Oh."

Janet and Robbie hadn't traveled far before she started worrying that his silence indicated he was feeling awkward. She rose on her tiptoes to locate her Honda in the field of saucerlike rooftops. With the door still open, Bernice's gray hair was visible in the overhead glow. She heard Robbie clear his throat behind her, as if he understood her concerns regarding him and wanted to put them to rest. He had eased over to the window of a nearby Cadillac to inspect the luxury of the fancy dashboard and leather seating. "Somebody's got some money," he said.

"What year is it?"

"I'm not up to speed on Caddies, but it's a year or two at most."

"And when whoever owns it goes flying off tonight, it'll just sit there."

"Right. You're serious about that, I guess." He straightened to show his grin, as if his tone might not have made his teasing clear.

"I'm not, but they are."

"Bunch of nuts." He pivoted with just enough exaggeration to turn the move into a performance meant to entertain her. In his light red jacket, he stared off, pretending to search the varied vehicles for symptoms of their owners' lunacy.

"Lots of luck," she said.

He closed his little skit with a shrug of surrender to the craziness everywhere. But when he faced her, his somber look was a surprise.

"Robbie." She smiled, offering pseudo-sympathy because she suspected he might still be fooling around. "What are you thinking?"

Smaller this time, his shrug was contrite. "It's not that I'm not a Christian, though."

"Oh, sure. Of course."

"Because I am. I found that out the hard way when things went the way they did with my dad, you know."

"Sure," she said.

He looked to the sky, and she watched him think about a question for which he had no answer. "The funeral and all. I found it out in spades." With his playfulness stripped away, he struck her as brave in his willingness just to stand there, wondering. She had to follow his lead, traveling upward, too, as if to join him, and the night had a depth that caught her unprepared. The black heavens revealed dimensions made visible by the disparity between the strength and faintness of far-flung stars.

"Up in the air," he murmured. His eyes passed over hers to let her see the mischievous glint resurfaced. "Everything, right? And everybody."

"Right. Pending and provisional. I sure am." When he blinked like a bewildered student in awe of her vocabulary, her stifled amusement caused her breath to throb happily. "What were you thinking of studying in college?"

"What?" He had a childlike indignation, as if bothered by her meddling.

"You heard me."

"I hadn't decided. Why?"

"Listen, Robbie. Don't take this wrong, okay? But would you like a drink?" She produced the half-pint from her purse. "I'm having one."

Tracking her gesture, his eyes narrowed as he playacted shock. "Miss Cawley."

"Yes, Mr. Oberhoffer."

"Is that what I think it is?"

"I told you what it was." She let him see her uncap the bottle and raise it slowly to her lips. She was unprepared for the unnerving effect of his interested glance.

"I wouldn't mind a taste," he said.

"Okay, but there's something I'm going to require first."

"I bet I know what it is."

"I doubt it."

"I think I do," he told her, his confidence boyish and charming.

"Okay. What?"

"You'd like me to stop calling you Miss Cawley. I've been feeling weird saying it anyway—'Miss Cawley.' I mean, you are Miss Cawley, but I know what you mean."

"What do I mean?" she said, handing over the bottle.

"You should keep in mind that I am not of drinking age."

"You know what? I know that. But you're not in the fourth grade anymore, either."

"You're right, there."

"It's like this," she said. "Time moves on."

"Jack Daniel's." He admired the bottle as if to store the memory. "The drinking going on at college was *Guinness Book of Records.*"

"I've heard that."

"It's true, and usually, it's very cheap stuff." The way he passed the bottle back congratulated her choice.

"We should probably get going. She's had long enough, don't you think?"

"I'm in no rush." He stretched to his full height in order to scout past her, then registered what he saw with an easygoing sigh. "She seems to be sitting real quiet." He sank back on his heels. "Must have pulled the door shut, because the light's off."

"We can take a roundabout way."

Movement intruded on Bernice, a shift in the light that wiped away her thoughts about General's last minutes. She searched for Janet and her friend, figuring they were behind whatever had changed, but she couldn't find hide or hair. The last she'd seen, they'd been bobbing amid hoods and fenders, giggling like they were playing a game. You had to wonder if they had a brain between them. Kids, she thought. Not that Janet wasn't half again his age. He was a kid, but that word didn't apply to Janet. Unless, of course, you were comparing her to an old bat like Bernice. Along those lines, Janet was about as fresh as a newborn just dropped off by the stork. And acting like it, too, she thought, while reaching for General and peeking at him out of the corner of her eyes, as if she didn't have the nerve to look right at him. Because she knew without a sliver of a doubt that he'd felt abandoned by her, that he'd felt alone as he died, believing she'd forgotten all about him. Which, if you got right down to it, she had. Why hadn't that bunch out at the vet's had some idea what was coming? They were supposed to be so smart. If only she'd been given some kind of warning! She wished she had that perky Dr. Manders with her right now, because she'd give her an earful. Where were those two young fools? she thought, shading the glass and searching the rows of darkened, motionless cars. Were they lost? Maybe she should open the door so the light came back on. Maybe they had no idea where they'd left her. She fiddled with the door handle but went no further. The dark was pleasant, the shadows bringing the walls in close like a cave that might keep her and General safe from everything and everybody. Except, of course, the silence that seemed to whisper about death and call for prayers. But if she was honest, she didn't have an ounce of prayerful feeling left in her right this second. Oh, what she wouldn't give for a chance to tell that bunch at the vet's a thing or two! Somebody needed to let them know they weren't the be-all and end-all they led everybody to think they were.

Janet was unable to decide whether Bernice had spied them or had simply turned in their direction. Whatever the case, her impulse to get back, her feeling that it was time to get going, brought with it the realization that once the dog was buried, the evening would end, and the instant of distress that followed made it impossible for her to avoid seeing how badly she didn't want that to happen. Robbie was straightening from where he had crouched. The fingers of one hand pinched a small object.

"Quarter," he said, showing her the coin.

Maybe if they planned to do something else, she could extend their time together. "Lucky you," she said, watching him flip the coin. They would arrive back at the Honda in seconds if they kept walking. Maybe they could go out to dinner afterward. Maybe if she said she needed to talk to him about something. Their shared past was a possibility, even the deaths of her mom and his dad. "Do you remember that story you wrote about a dog who was a bear?"

His quizzical expression made speech unnecessary, but he added, "Who? Me?"

"In my class."

"What a memory. I have to say I feel a little sorry for you, with your head full of that kind of gunk."

"Anyway, there's something I'd like to talk to you about if we get a chance."

"Not the story, I hope."

"No. Partly, I guess, but really what I'd like to talk about is all that back then."

"All what?"

"School. The classroom. What you remember." It was true, there were times when her loss of teaching felt excruciating, and yet she had done it to herself. "I'm trying to straighten out some things since my mom died and—well—I got divorced." It was important that he know, so she paused. For a split second, his gaze was veiled by a private thought. "I think it would help me to get some perspective," she said, and stopped. "Anyway." She waited. "I don't know what I mean, exactly." She felt at a loss, watching his uneven slouch set his hip in a roguish curve. His quiet expression said she should take all the time she needed to find her next remark. "Did you know I was divorced?" she asked.

"No."

"And I quit teaching."

"You did?"

She nodded, then waited while he looked into a nearby car, as though he knew someone inside who could shed light on his response, which had aspects he seemed reluctant to let her see. "Well, it's true. Both things."

"Sorry," he said.

"The divorce is good. Take my word for it."

"Okay."

"As for the teaching— Well, I'm not so sure. That's what I thought we might talk about—that it might be useful to have another point of view. Your point of view—an authentic eyewitness, right? If you'd be honest. Would you be honest?"

"About school? Sure. Why not?"

"But not now. Because I don't want to start and then have to stop. But let's see if we can find a little time later on."

"Okay. Sure."

He might have had more to say, but she crossed the last few yards to the car. A sense of rash, impulsive risk assailed her but showed little ability to make its nature clear, and she didn't feel like waiting. Her gentle knock brought Bernice around, moonlight glinting off her glasses behind the window in which Janet saw herself reflected. The door clicked open. The ceiling light raised Bernice from the gloom.

"How you doing?" said Janet.

"Okay. Except I was beginning to wonder if you'd run out on me."

"We took our time. We didn't figure there was a rush."

"Maybe not for you, but I'm just sittin' here, you know."

"We thought that's what you wanted."

"I don't know what I want. Where'd you get this blanket, anyway? It's mine, isn't it?"

"I didn't think you'd mind. I mean, it's falling apart." Janet was close to telling her that she was an old crank who should learn to mind her manners. "So that's the gratitude I get for coming out here, trying to do the right thing. I worried I'd be interrupting something important. But I thought you should know what happened."

"Fine. Thanks."

"That's why I'm here. I wanted to do the right thing. So do you know what you want?"

"I want a lot of things, but they're not looking likely."

"What I mean is, do you know what you want us to do? Are they expecting you back inside? Your friends? The reverend?"

Really in need of some good advice, Bernice studied the night, and failing there, she tried General, who seemed far more accepting and settled regarding his condition than she thought she'd ever be. His silence interested her, his stillness offering to tell her something soon, and while the seconds passed and she waited, she found she had less and less interest in talking to Janet, or anyone else, for that matter, and she closed her eyes. Doing anything at all, having a thought in her head, or answering anybody's questions, just lifting a finger or bothering to care seemed pointless and dumb.

Janet figured she better act fast, or they'd be stuck there for the next year. "Here's what I thought. If this sounds okay to you, Robbie has offered to help bury the dog and to even let us do it on his parents' property. They've got a beautiful little spot over in Homestead Development. You know it, right?"

"Sure."

"Somebody lives in there, right? I remember taking Mom over."

Bernice weighed the nonsensical part of Janet's remark and just couldn't pass it up. "A lot of people live there, I'd say. It's a big place."

"I mean somebody my mom knew, and you knew, too."

"Clara Shroeder."

"I don't know who."

"Well, that's who."

"So you're familiar with how beautiful some of it is over there."

The boy found an angle around Janet, sort of arching over her back. "We're right at the end of everything. My folks' property is right up against the countryside."

"Uh-huh." Bernice's mind was full of opinions and arguments, but none worth the breath it would take to say them. She was listening and thinking but ready to quit both.

"We've got some dogs of our own buried there," he said.

Bernice tilted in their direction, wanting a better sense of the boy. "What was your name again?"

"Robbie. Oberhoffer."

"Which Oberhoffers are yours?"

Janet blurted out, "Lawrence," right on top of him saying, "My dad was Lawrence." Then this foxy look shot between them, like jumping all over each other to spit out his dad's name was some special trick Bernice couldn't possibly appreciate.

"It's down the hill," Janet went on. "The spot he's talking about. I walked down real quick." She couldn't tell for sure whether Bernice was listening. "It was peaceful. Sun going down just then. It's a beautiful spot. There's pine trees and some rocks."

"Birch trees, too," he said, and Janet felt he was correcting her, not that she minded, because the way he was leaning close felt easy and nice. "A bunch of white birch."

Bernice kept rubbing General's ear in spite of its sickening texture. There was something funny going on with these two. "Birch are nice. Pretty," she said, while her halfhearted attempt to picture General gazing up white bark to limbs and maybe birds made her feel stupid.

"They are. And Robbie has tools and everything." Janet wasn't sure how much effort to expend trying to get through to Bernice, especially since her standoffish mood felt more manufactured than real. "I mean, it's not all that easy to dig a hole big enough. He works construction, and his dad worked on the roads for the city, so they have equipment."

"And lime," he said. "It keeps the critters away. Raccoons and fox. They'll dig things up if they get the smell. There's rocks we can put on top. This stone wall that's mostly fallen down. It was a pasture."

"How's that sound, Bernice?"

"Okay."

"So that's what we'll do."

Bernice thought, Well, why not? Since Janet was running the show, she figured the best course of action was to sit tight and await instructions. So she was confused, as nothing more was said. And she started getting downright aggravated when she saw how they were eyeing her and smirking, like she was too dumb to notice they were in cahoots and pretending she was the one dragging her feet, when all she wanted was to be told what to do next, if they could bother to stop fooling around. "I'm waiting," she snapped. With her knees and feet hurting and her dog dead, she had about all the license she needed to get testy.

"Well, see the thing is, you said okay, Bernice, but I don't think we know what to. Should we just go do it, Robbie and me? Because we can. We're fine with that if you have to stay here. Or do you want to come with us?"

"It won't take all that long," Robbie said. "Drive over, drive back. Maybe an hour and a half. Two at most."

The open car door separated them now, with the boy resting his chin on the frame. Janet straightened and grabbed the door inches from his mouth, like she couldn't manage the task any other way.

"It's up to you, Bernice, okay?" Janet said. "Whichever you want."

Bernice could feel a selfish streak running through the both of them. It was something she better keep an eye on, not just stupidly trust whatever lay behind their eager generosity. She moved her hand under General's throat, where she held on as if they were a couple of thieves. "I'll go."

"Okay. Good."

"You said you'd bring me back, right?"

"Sure. Absolutely."

"Okay, then."

Janet's cheek was inches from his. He offered the flicker of a smile, while his body exuded traces of turpentine that his shower had failed to wash away, an aroma of aftershave and the gusty shampoo that had left his sandy hair in thick waves. She liked the way they were about the same height. He must be a little over five-eleven, since she was about five-ten.

Bernice saw them towering into the gloom and thought how Janet was thin like Isabel but a tall drink of water like her dad. Gone with his grocery list. Pat on the head. Compliments, like bread crumbs.

"You drive, Robbie, okay?" Janet said, opening the passenger-side door.

The way he rubbed his hands, imitating a greedy miser, made no sense to Bernice except as foolishness. Of course Janet let him know how funny she thought he was, making the moment into another one of their special jokes Bernice was too dumb to enjoy.

Janet took a cold drink of the remnants of her spiked Dunkin' Donuts coffee just as the engine started. Robbie, with an eye on her every move, mimicked gagging. "We should stop somewhere quick and get you a fresh cup, don't you think?"

"This is fine."

"Really?"

"Yes."

"Okay. If you say so."

"I do. It's fine."

Bernice knew she was an old lady seated behind a couple of kids bantering away, but suddenly, as if her dad had dropped out of the sky, she was with him. He was at the wheel. He was the one spinning around to survey the dim world out the rear window behind their old Pontiac, and she ducked to get out of his line of fire while he scouted for the idiot who might have sneaked up to cause a fender-bender. Her mother was quiet beside him, and Bernice waited, her fingers consoling her Raggedy Ann doll in a faded dress and apron. Hank aimed his wooden rifle out the window. A get-together in Evans, Iowa, awaited them, or maybe Sampson, Illinois. Narrow houses on narrow streets where aunts and uncles lived, and the men drank beer, and went hunting in the day, and brought home squirrels or rabbits or ducks to butcher and eat. She could hear hide tearing, see feathers torn loose, fish flopping in the mud. At night they drank beer and played cards, bellowing like bears.

The driver startled her, dipping sideways, and she hoped he wouldn't look right at her. The last few seconds had made her want to hear her mother's voice, but it was Robbie, forcing her to meet his eyes, having caught her staring off into space.

"Mrs. Doorley. I'm glad to do this, okay? I love dogs."

"Well," she said, searching for General's ear. "It's real nice of you."

He was one pleasant guy, Janet noted, while wishing she'd laced her coffee with a smidge more booze. They were passing the parsonage, where the ground floor brimmed with light.

"Could we use a little music?" Robbie wondered.

"Let's wait till we're on the highway." Janet smiled at the thought. "How do you feel about a little music, Bernice? That okay with you?"

"I don't care."

It seemed for an instant that a blanket had blown loose from a laundry line to come flapping into their path. But then a lanky, angular man stood in front of them. Though they weren't going fast, the braking car jackknifed Janet out of her seat, and the impact of her palms against the dashboard made her yelp.

"Damn," said Robbie. "Sorry."

The figure in the middle of the road raised his right arm to shield himself against the force of the headlights. Janet didn't have to turn around to know the weight pressing from behind was Bernice, who then whispered loudly, "It's Reverend Tauke."

"What the heck does he think he's doing?" Robbie wanted to know.

"Does he want something, Bernice?"

"I don't know."

Stepping toward them, the figure freed the headlights, which hurtled on across a field strewn with stubble. Janet had the impression of something spooky hiding just past where the light petered out. The reverend loomed, his head bobbing, and his big hand took on the shape of a fist gently knocking on her window.

"Janet, what are you doing?" said Bernice.

"What?"

"He's knocking. Roll down the window and speak to the man, will you."

"It's you he probably wants to talk to."

"I can't get this contraption to open. You open yours and tell him."

He rapped again, then with both hands out of sight, he must have taken hold of the handle, because the vehicle rocked.

"Should I go talk to him?" Robbie asked.

"No, no. I'll do it." Janet found the button and watched the edge lower.

"Good evening," he said, pushing his head into the car. "May I help you? Do I know you?"

"What?" Janet said. "Me?"

"I do, don't I. Where have we met?"

"I don't think we have." Janet saw disagreement in his eyes along with confidence.

"Why are you leaving?"

"It's me," Bernice said.

"Who?"

"Bernice Doorley," she said timidly.

He swiveled, poking in so far that Janet had to make room. Still, she was grateful to be excused from his ferocity, which had been poised to crush any argument against his claimed knowledge of her. "Bernice, hello."

"Can you see me?"

"Now I can. I saw the car. I wondered who was leaving."

"I was just going to go take care of something."

"Now, I hope you're not going to say you don't know me, too. Like the young lady in the front seat here."

"Oh, no. I know you."

"And she does, too, I think."

"I don't think she's ever been here before, Reverend."

"Really?"

"I don't think so. Have you, Janet?"

"No."

"Janet," he said, shapeless in his retreat inches from her, his breath igniting a tingling in her cheek. "Do you want to join us, Janet?"

"I'm sorry, what?"

"I just think you should know that you cannot join up. We're not like that, you know. Not everyone is welcome."

Air escaped her with a sound that could have been "oh." She felt like informing him she would rather walk shoeless on broken glass than join his moronic church. But she said nothing, just sat smiling sweetly, settled in her decision to leave well enough alone, because she had to admit he sort of scared her.

His sly glance understood enough of the effect he was having to make him chuckle softly as he straightened, leaving her looking at his belt buckle.

"I hope you're coming back, Bernice."

"Oh, yes."

"And don't let it get too late. Please be here well before midnight."

"All right. I will."

"Do you promise?"

"We'll be sure to get her back on time, sir," said Robbie.

"Good. Midnight. Please," he said, and walked away. His thin legs pumping and long arms dangling, his outline fell onto his shadow in a combination that, flying across the silhouette of a tree, struck Janet as a spider skittering over his web.

"Shall we try it again?" Robbie asked, revving the engine, though they didn't move.

"Okay, Bernice?" Not the least surprised when there was no response, Janet didn't wait to try again. "Bernice?"

"He's such an impressive man, didn't you think? You can see why a person wants to put her faith in him."

Good Lord, thought Janet.

"I'm outta here," said Robbie, starting them forward. As the deserted old highway invited them aboard, he asked, "How about that music?"

Janet glanced at him, welcoming his carefree style, his ease behind the wheel of her car, so complete it was like he drove it every day, like they were old friends. At least back to the fourth grade. "All right, then." She smiled. "Let me check my CDs." She bent to the floor, where the zipped case must have fallen.

"We could try the radio," Robbie suggested.

"As a last resort." She bypassed several Styrofoam cups before finding what she wanted. "I'm taking requests."

"It's your car," he told her.

"Something real slow, okay?" said Bernice from the back. "Something that calms a person down. That's all I ask."

Janet was amused to see that in the last few seconds she'd lost all track of the fact that Bernice was still with them. Ahead, granules glittered in the pavement, the white divider climbing into the dark. She switched on the overhead light, flipping past Alanis Morissette and Liz Phair. Both unlikely, given Bernice, though Liz Phair might be fun once she and Robbie were on their own. Sheryl Crow was a maybe. There were a couple of Harry Connicks that would probably delight Bernice, but Janet wasn't in the mood. So maybe Sarah McLachlan was their best bet. She had both *Touch* and *Surfacing*. And of course she still hadn't picked up the CDs that were part of that weird errand, the one that had sent her to the hardware store for the duct tape and garden hose. As she had numerous times before, she wondered if Bernice was the person behind it. But wasn't that highly unlikely? On the other hand, since Bernice was right there, why not ask? Whoever it was, they were expecting a lot, which certainly sounded like Bernice. It would suit her just fine to send Janet on a wild-goose chase. Because that was what it was. How the hell could anybody expect Janet to do it? Bernice or whoever! To walk into a store and buy CDs without a clue? How about an album name? Or the artist, at least. It was such an insane job, she ought to just forget about it. It was too dumb. And yet even this momentary rebellion aroused guilt. She had to do it. She had no choice. Her obligation was single-minded and not so much the request of a pushy acquaintance as the tyrannical command of a mad-man, of madness itself, banging on her door. If she didn't watch her step, she'd end up out of her mind somewhere with the garden hose pumping fumes into her car.

In a crushing, slow-motion moment, she stared through a cloud of debris, the last particles of dust, and saw all the way to the fact that the errand belonged to her. She'd gone into that hardware store because of her own desires and demands. The duct tape and hose she'd purchased were for her to kill herself.

"How we doing there?" Robbie asked. "Any luck?"

She felt she was peering up from her grave. Bright-eyed, he had lifted the lid on her coffin to ask if she had found some music he might enjoy. "How about Sarah McLachlan?" she said. "I mean, everything considered."

"Yeah. She's good. And you're right that Mrs. Doorley might like her. I bet you like her, Mrs. Doorley."

Janet stared at him—at his fresh-faced, down-to-earth existence, which she was so overwhelmingly thankful to have in her car. Fitting *Surfacing* into the CD player, she knew to move it ahead to the second cut if she didn't want to hear Bernice complain. The apparatus whirred, decoding her intentions, and Janet leaned back with the keyboard's mournful cry, and then the voice joined in, almost whispering.

Just drive off into the countryside. She saw a meadow. Some thistles. Ragweed. Milkweed. Maybe a fallen tree. She pictured herself arriving. Or maybe some out-of-the-way spot out by the river. The CDs were suddenly no mystery at all—they were for her to die by. One was playing now. Ani DiFranco was another. No Doubt, that loose-limbed blonde. She would need to have some Morissette. She already owned them all. The garden hose was in the trunk, the duct tape, too. Cram in the hose, tape it tight. Feed it into the window with rags stuffed in to fill the gap. Have a big drink.

"She's good, huh?" Robbie said.

"Yeah. I'm surprised you like her."

"Why?"

"I don't know."

"What do you think, Mrs. Doorley?"

"She's okay."

"Kind of churchlike, don't you think?"

"Not really," said Bernice.

"There's a later one, you'll change your mind."

"I doubt it."

"But peaceful," said Robbie. "It's peaceful. You said you wanted peaceful, right?"

Janet could hear how earnest he was, so hopeful that Bernice would agree. The soaring keyboard was interlaced with the bold, brave singing voice, and it was as if Janet had just emerged from a long conversation with strangers who were plotting to take her life. And she felt oddly peaceful, oddly calm. It wasn't that she hadn't been shaken by the realization, or by the contact with her deeply secretive soul. But somehow to have made the discovery, to have brought the threat to light, consoled her as much as it scared her.

Robbie was taking them smoothly into a downward swerve. He used only one hand, his wrist casually guiding the wheel. And she felt, watching him, that the understanding reaching out to her was connected to him. Maybe even due to him. It had come to her because he was there. She could feel the truth of what she was trying to get at, and the idea was fighting to define itself as fiercely as she was struggling to give it shape. Robbie inhabited a plain way of being. His straightforward nature valued and responded to candor, and so his presence, forthright and sincere, had compelled the intrigue she had been devising against herself to rise into the light. It was as if his need to know had forced her to see. It had come to her because he was there.

The road stretched on straight now. Farmland flowed off to the right. Robbie swayed slightly as the keyboard and voice climbed. Janet turned from him to the window and saw distant lights in a collection that she believed was Homestead Development, their destination. The wavering voice tumbled, and the keyboard tried to cradle the fall.

26

J ANET AND ROBBIE SAT BERNICE down at the kitchen table
and left her with a green plastic tumbler of ice and a can of
Diet Pepsi. They said they had things to do and would be back in a jiffy.
So she took in the cozy sturdiness around her while getting a couple more
Tylenol from her purse and swallowing them with some Pepsi. The green
tile of the floor was dark enough that a person wouldn't have to think
about cleaning it every hour on the hour. It was a pleasant little spot, this
kitchen, all nicely laid out. Lots of overhead light, a plenty big sink with a
dishwasher close by. New-looking electric stove, Mr. Coffee all set up, nice
big microwave, and woodsy green doors on cabinets attached by brass
brackets to the paler green walls. Probably the shelves inside were jam-
packed with bowls and plates smartly tucked out of sight. Even the
rectangular farm table where she sat with her hands around her drink
pleased her. It was nice and long, and the stain was pretty. The fancy chairs
with spokes in the backrests could have struck her as fussy and impractical, but somehow they didn't. These Oberhoffers had to be good people,
the kind who cared, she thought, and she wished one of them was around,
Mr. or Mrs., so she could give them the high praise they deserved.

The living room had struck her as pretty nice, too, even though she
hadn't gotten a real good look, because of the rush they were in coming
through the front door. Janet had been whining about having to use the
ladies' room, and she'd scooted off like she owned the place. Robbie'd
kept on straight into the kitchen, with Bernice in tow, where all of a sudden he'd started acting shy. When he finally managed to ask if she needed

the use of a bathroom, too, she wondered if that was what had been going on—him trying to get up the nerve. And of course she did. There was a small one just off the hall leading to the kitchen. No tub or shower, just the essentials, a toilet and sink.

He'd been holding the Pepsi when she got back, so she'd made a little joke about how "first we gotta empty out, and then we gotta fill her up." He'd seemed to enjoy her kind of humor, smiling big and rocking back on his heels to tell her he had to go gather up some gear. The door he'd gone to and then held open revealed another, thicker, more solid-looking door that he'd explained led to the backyard. He'd told her she could step out there if she wanted, and look straight down from the back porch to the spot where they would be burying General. He told her he was sure she would see how pleasant it was, and then off he went.

And she would have to say that right about now, all that was starting to seem ages ago. She didn't know where Janet had disappeared to. Thinking she might take a peek in the cabinets to check out the dishware, she felt peculiar. Like a bus had dropped her off at the wrong stop. Or maybe a tornado had picked her up from the life she knew and put her down in this one. Some stranger's place with a nice icy drink in her hand and an ache in her guts. Not that she didn't know where she was and what had happened to get her there, but she couldn't shake the suspicion that what she knew left out everything important. And of course that led her to poor General alone out there in that dark backseat.

With the feeling that she was beginning a task that would let her help and console him, she got her feet under her and, carrying her Pepsi, went to the nearest window. The moment was somehow superstitious enough for her to believe General would feel her looking out at where he lay and would know she was thinking about him. Located near the sink, the window was faintly fogged over, a gray opening between pink curtains onto the driveway. The Honda was parked pretty close, and there was Janet bouncing around. Not really bouncing so much as bending and straightening. The steamy glass Bernice had to peer through made everything look like she was inside a cloud bank up high in an airplane. When she scrubbed a clear spot, Janet came out of the vapors carrying something shiny in one hand. Seated in the gap of the open driver's-side door, her legs spread and planted, she tilted the bright little object, which was shown now to be a bottle, to her lips. Her head flopped back long enough to establish beyond any doubt that she was having herself a pretty good snort from a booze bottle of some kind.

Good enough, thought Janet, adding a sip, then taking a deep, muscular swallow of night air. The half-pint lying in her palms was three quarters gone. Time to slow down. She still needed to make sense. Or at least appear to. She'd gone from the bathroom to the car, wanting a drink, and Robbie had surprised her coming around the corner just as she was about to pull the bottle from her purse. She'd gestured, as if to say the purse was what she'd come for, and he told her he was on his way to get some tools from a shed somewhere off in the direction he pointed. He'd focused on her then, almost shyly, before saying, "That's the tree," while his flashlight had flowed over a flat stretch until it hovered on a stump not far from a full-size tree. It was the site of his dad's mishap. By the time she'd looked back, he was on the move, and the edge of the garage eclipsed him.

Not much time had passed since then. Just enough for her to consider the tree and stump looking innocent enough as she sat down to have her big drink. He hadn't been gone very long, so her heart-to-heart with Mr. Jack Daniel's could stay secret, if she made sure it didn't go on too long. "You and me, buddy," she murmured, only to realize that she'd stupidly settled in the car with the wide-open door directly facing the house. She eyed the window, and fretted that Bernice might see her. Crazy old broad, she thought, staring into the light that flared from within.

Noise from an unexpected direction revealed Robbie approaching along a route different from the one he'd taken when he left. She had no idea where he was coming from, unless she'd gotten turned around. Several lengthy implements lay over one shoulder like the weapons of a marching soldier. On the other shoulder, he balanced a pillow-sized sack of some kind.

"Hey," he said, "all set?"

"You need a hand there?"

"Not so far."

Bernice watched them meet up. She was inching out of hiding, having ducked when Janet appeared to be trying to see if anybody inside had spotted her sneaking her drink. The boy was loaded down like a pack animal, but that didn't keep Janet from holding him up by just yakking at him on and on. Waving her hands this way, that way, like it was all so important if she said it. But all at once they were gone. Bernice scooted back to the table in case they were headed inside, which it turned out they were, and so she was seated, sipping her Pepsi, when the door slammed and they arrived empty-handed. She smiled like she was happy to see them, but the real source of her pleasure was the way she'd put one over on them both by keeping an eye on them without either one catching on.

"You okay?" Janet asked.

"I wouldn't mind something warm to drink," Bernice told her.

"How about cocoa? I could make some hot cocoa after we're done," Robbie offered.

"Is your mom around? I'd like to thank her for making me welcome this way."

"Oh, no. She's not," he said. "She's out. Sorry."

"Is she coming back? Because I just think that a person who keeps such a nice clean kitchen like this ought to be told."

"She'd appreciate hearing that, and I could pass it on."

"Well, that'd be second best."

"See, I'm afraid she won't be back tonight. My brother's still in high school—two of them, actually—brothers, I mean—and Edward had an away football game, so Mom and Denny drove down to Davenport, where they're playing and she has a sister living. My aunt Millie. Mom makes sure to go to the games since my dad passed away."

"Oh." She glared at him. There was no mistaking the irritation she felt, and she could hear it in her voice, like she was scolding him. "I didn't know that."

"Anyway, they're all staying over."

"Fine. Sure." Bernice wanted to backtrack, because she'd done something stupid and she was burned up about it. She felt like she should have known about the death of the father of such a nice boy. That every decent person should have known. Anybody worth their salt. "I'm sorry to hear that. About your dad."

"Thanks. Yeah, it's been rough. You know. I still expect the old pickup to pull in with him inside. Especially at a time like this, and him stomping in to ask us all, 'What the hell is going on now?' You know, acting rough. But the second he knew, he'd pitch in."

Janet was baffled by the way Bernice was scowling at Robbie. He'd crossed her, but who knew how. What more did she expect from the poor guy? "Sounds like he was a great dad, Robbie," she said.

"He was," he nodded.

Aiming to reassure him with her smile, she became aware of a hazy sort of secondary computation slipping into the forefront of her mind to point out its discovery that hidden within Robbie's explanation of his mother's whereabouts was the secret of the house being empty all through the night except for him. Excitement caught her, like a balloon in rapidly rising air, lifting her and leaving her aloft. She would have to wait for the ground to return. The hope was very old, and yet light and fresh-feeling, because she had put it away so long ago.

"Well," said Bernice, sounding halfway civilized at last, "if your mom's not coming back tonight, you just pass my appreciation along."

"I'll be sure to tell her," he said.

The house would be empty. Apprehension, too weak to keep Janet from seeing their flickering bodies, ignited instead a slow-rolling wave of longing. He was beautiful, so beautiful. "Anyway," she said, "we should get going, don't you think? We need to get Bernice back in time."

He nodded, then strode to the far side of the room, where he unveiled at least a dozen flashlights standing on end inside one of the cabinets. "This is the last of the stuff we need. It's maybe a hundred yards down." He flicked a yellow plastic flashlight on and off before presenting it to Bernice. "You take this one and watch your step. Then, Janet—" He smiled, admitting that he'd said her name for the first time. "If you carry the digging bar and shovel, I'll see to the lime and the pickax. Once we get settled down there, I'll hurry back and carry the dog down. What's his name again?"

"General."

"I'll carry General down."

The two of them had just come in, so their preparations didn't amount to much, but Bernice had to wrestle her way up, get used to standing, and then go through the trial of stuffing herself into her jacket, with every move hell to pay. Then her buttons decided to give her a hard time. After she'd secured the bottom two, one popped loose and the other was in the wrong hole. She was standing there peering down at the riddle of her ham-fisted effort, like some mad scientist lost in the trials of her big experiment, when she heard the door to the outside rattle open and slam shut. It would have been nice of them to wait for her or at least ask how she was doing. She was tempted to give up and just flop, but poor General wouldn't care for that. So she'd just go like she was, heading after them in an open coat, which was what she was doing when she saw that the button she'd thought naughty was right where it belonged and probably had been all along. Encouraged, she did up a few more.

Janet and Robbie were huddled a short way off as she came out. Several long tools leaned against Janet, a couple of them shovels. He was talking too softly to be overheard, but whatever he said to her caused the flashlight in her hand to search his face before lowering with him as he bent down to a big sack on the ground.

Look at her. Didn't she think she was something, Bernice thought, watching Janet follow Robbie moving off with the bag on his shoulder. Just the way she was glued to his every move, all sincere, almost starry-eyed. Like he was some kind of movie star, all glamour and muscles in the spotlight, and bending to pick up that sack made him bigger than life. Just had to help. Couldn't wait to help. Carrying the shovels, handing him the pickax when he reached out. What can she do for him next? What's he need? Like she didn't have a clue she amounted to nothing. Just another split-tail. That's all you are, little missy. Same as Irma. They were a pair to draw to. Bernice could hardly keep from letting the words out. They wanted out. She had to swallow hard to keep them back and snicker all to herself. Might as well be Irma, another useless daughter.

Robbie hesitated, appearing to shudder to rearrange the weight he carried. "Got it," he said to Janet, and he started back up and she went with him, keeping close, neither of them giving Bernice a second thought. She was as good as forgotten, trailing them into the sloping dark, the beam of light in her fist uncovering the huddled grass, the bent and parted weeds where they'd stepped. She felt just like that. Walked on morning, noon, and night. Everybody's doormat.

How'd that split-tail business get started, anyway? she wondered. It was a hoot, that was one thing for certain. They were all somewhere, and Grandpa Demming just up and called Irma a little split-tail. How'd he phrase it? "Well, there she is. Just another split-tail." What a riot. She wanted to laugh just thinking about it, and had to fight to keep it down, her bitter merriment, like a piece of bad food that needed out, her enjoyment a grumble concealed in a cough, while she carefully skirted a hunk of rotten log that could have tripped her.

That one remark was all it took, and they were off to the races. Didn't have to be, but Irma couldn't let it go. Oh no, not her. Not satisfied to let anything alone if it concerned her. Four or five years old and not half as clever as she thought she was. Such a little snot, so sure of herself. The stupidity made Bernice grin at the daffy, haywire memory of Irma pressuring her grandpa for more facts, more details, and repetitions, too, until he christened her "Grandpa's Little Split-tail." And then she wanted to know "Split-tail what, Grandpa?" So he told her, "Beaver." Irma squealed with delight while Grandpa Demming turned to Bernice, who'd happened into the doorway just in time to overhear them. His smirk brimmed with welcome as he invited Bernice to be his partner in this prank he couldn't believe he was lucky enough to get to pull on the stupid little girl.

And it was hilarious. More fun than a barrel full of monkeys. In fact, it was still darn funny all these years later to recall how Irma went about telling everyone she was "Grandpa's little split-tail beaver." No idea what she was saying. Five years old at most when it started. But so cocky, so full of herself, so bigheaded from the day she was born.

Robbie murmured up ahead, responding to something hushed from Janet. The light in Bernice's hand trembled with the recollected foolishness, and her feet along with the faded grass, the patches of dirt, weeds, and twigs, seemed to flutter. Janet wheeled, the eye of her flashlight racing to find Bernice, like a questioning look that Bernice waved away. She wasn't going to explain. Not for one second would she waste her time trying to describe how Irma kept the whole mess going for years. So if there was company parading in the door, or some family gathering with people arriving in bunches, or if they were all seated together at the long dinner table for Christmas or Thanksgiving, Irma could not be stopped from bragging how she was Grandpa Demming's favorite "little split-tail beaver," sometimes even dancing and singing about it. And of course every single adult would listen, nod, and congratulate her, and then once she ran off, they would bust a gut, laughing themselves silly behind her back. Bernice's brother, Hank, and Toby's kid sister, Lou, and her dimwit of a husband, Ronald, just tickled pink. Toby's brother, Andrew, and Toby, too. The bunch of them having a conniption. Sometimes sniggering and calling her "cute." Other times roaring helplessly about "the poor dope," until they were doubled up and just about rolling on the floor. One person would say, "The poor thing, she don't know shit from Shinola," while somebody else would hope and pray they were around when the light finally went on. Because they sure wanted to be there to see the look on Irma's face.

Noticing that Robbie and Janet had paused up ahead, Bernice stopped. Paired and linked by looping shadow, they faced her. Janet was smirking at Bernice for some unknown fault. "No, no, Bernice," Janet said. "Don't stop. Come on. We're waiting for you. You were falling back."

"I'm fine. I'm coming."

"We're about halfway," Robbie told her.

"Well, let's do the rest," Bernice announced, like she might start giving the orders. "Let's go if we're going."

Wide bands of purple and gray stretched side by side across the sky. It looked to Bernice almost like somebody had gone to the trouble of smearing paint on top of this smoke passing over the ragged edges of the big round moon. When her foot sank into a crevice, she lurched and had to hop, and she was glad once again to be wearing her sensible pantsuit and shoes. That'd put her in a fix, wouldn't it. Break her leg out here in the middle of nowhere. That'd give the two of them something to do. They could bury her with the dog.

On one or another morning way back—it had to be going on thirty-five years—Bernice had woken up thinking maybe this beaver thing had gone far enough, so she took Irma aside and asked her not to make such a fuss about being Grandpa's favorite anymore. She didn't have the nerve to explain why. Who would? Well, Irma stomped her foot, jammed her little fist against her hipbone, and declared she was not going to stop telling people Grandpa Demming loved her. She would shout it from the rooftops if she wanted! Where she got that one, who knew? But it did seem she had figured out what a hard man he was to please, and that like everybody else, she could see he didn't give a lick about Bernice. Irma sure wasn't going to take her advice about how to get along with him.

So, fine. If that was the way she wanted it, if she wanted to lay down with dogs, she could scratch her own fleas. That was the way it would be. She could just figure it out all by her lonesome. And, of course, she did. She caught on, or somebody told her. And who did she come to? Bernice, of course. Twelve, thirteen—almost scared to walk into the room and so mortified, her little face beet-red, eyes bulging, enough tears to fill a bucket. "Momma, is this what it is? Is it my peeing place, Momma?" Bernice felt like she'd been waiting a long time to tell Irma that if she really wanted to know the truth, all she had to do was take a gander at the way she looked down there, because that was pretty much it—Grandpa's little split-tail beaver. She nodded and said, "Yes, it is, Irma."

"You're laughing! Don't laugh!" Irma shouted.

"No, no." But she was, this unwanted, uncontainable, undeniable, irrepressible smirk.

Janet and Robbie had halted. With a grunting, bobbing gyration,

Robbie heaved the bag to the ground. He straightened and stretched, rolling his shoulder.

"That's a load, huh?" Janet said.

"Naw. I'm good," he grinned, turning to go.

Janet watched his buoyant body sail up the hill, his pace quickening. With the moon behind a dense island of clouds, he was visible solely through starlight.

The forlorn sound of Bernice exhaling came to Janet from a short way off behind her. She knew she ought to at least gesture with a friendly word or two in the old woman's direction, but she didn't really feel like it right this second and tried to refuse, while guilt nudged her around anyway. But Bernice wasn't even looking. An opaque statue, she faced downhill, her hands jammed into her coat pockets, a sullen air thickening her moody stillness, forbidding approach, and sealing her away in her thoughts.

It had been four, five, six years before the whole thing came back again. She could calculate the time exactly if she gave herself a chance to think. Because Irma was still in high school. So that meant she was seventeen or eighteen when one day out of the blue, she came swooping down so wild it was hard to hear a word at first, just screaming like a banshee that Bernice should have protected her. Bernice should have explained what was going on sooner. Bernice should have done this or done that— done something—anything except let her run around making a fool of herself all those years in front of the entire family. In front of everybody! Everybody!

Well, the funny thing was that Bernice blew her top. Calling Irma a crybaby. No slow burn. Just right straight through the roof. A little whiner crybaby! Because it was water under the bridge. It did not matter. Not a lick. All this fury bursting out of her, some of it needing words, some of it scorching and burning right through her skin. Because if anybody had a right to whine about her father, it was Bernice, who had been forced to put up with the miserable son of a bitch all her life. Irma backed away like she was staring into the face of a witch or some TV monster.

"Get back here!" But Irma kept going.

Janet was glad to see Robbie's silhouette, along with that of the dog he carried distinct against the sky. He sank in and out of view, given the dips and rises in the shadow-filled landscape, and then he vanished, melding into the embankment. He must have veered off.

The ground sighed, drawing Janet's attention to the dry crinkling of weeds underfoot as Bernice moved her weight from side to side. The wind had removed the thickest of the clouds, and the outline of her worn old face, if not her eyes, could be seen. She was staring up the hill. "How you holding up?" Janet wondered.

"I'll make it."

"It's a nice place here, don't you think?"

"It's okay." Bernice glanced around as if considering where they stood for the first time.

"You were thinking long and hard there for a bit."

"Who was?"

"Well," she said, and then hesitated as she felt how the underlying anger in Bernice's voice had declared that her demand for complete privacy was still in effect. "You were. Or I thought you were."

"You mean just now." She studied Janet, gathering the few particulars she needed to say, "I guess."

"You looked deep in thought. You know, lost in it."

"I suppose. It's been a long day."

Bernice removed her glasses, then fitted them back on and peered again toward the house. As if imitating, Janet followed along and saw Robbie bound for them, his figure increasingly detailed. "I was going to say something, but it felt like it'd be busting in, you know. Intruding."

"I don't know what I was thinking about, but I doubt it was all that much," Bernice said as the murmur of Robbie's footsteps in the weeds reached her. He was murky, the yellow and black heap of her dog and blanket floating across his chest. A paw drooped, and General's head swung free as Robbie strode up and squatted to settle the bundle down. He cleared his throat and moved hastily, needing neither rest nor instruction. With the flashlight drawn from Janet's hand, he indicated a low mound of rocks. "That's where we buried Arkansas two years ago. He was an Australian shepherd. And over there is where we buried Monk. He was a mongrel." The light presented a second set of mindfully placed stones. "So he'll be in good company." He reached for the pickax and took a long, exploratory stride with his head bowed. He then sidestepped to his left several yards and kicked his heel hard into the dirt. "I'll go right here, okay, Mrs. Doorley?"

"You mean dig there?"

"Yeah."

"Okay."

"What's that smell?" Janet wondered.

"Sage," he said, and the pickax arched and fell. "I went over where Mom has a little garden in the summer. I just thought we'd wrap it up in the blanket with him. You know, it's a nice smell." Having paused, he refocused with heightened commitment, the point of the pickax carving a loop overhead that sent it deep into the dirt. He hauled it free and swung again.

Bernice approached the blanket. General lay with a flap peeled back. Though she could easily imagine what she couldn't see, she leaned over, allowing a little give in her knees. The opening in his covers had widened, increasing the aroma, which had a nice sharp fullness, like on holidays, Thanksgiving, Christmas, a turkey in the oven, and everybody ready to eat. Chatty and hungry. The sage lay across his ribs with a sense, somehow, that it was a mark of respect, a blessing that would travel with him and make sure he was welcome somewhere. Her glance could not help but go to the sky.

Off behind her, Janet asked, "Robbie, should I dig, too?"

"No. At least not yet. Just keep the light there so I can see where I'm working."

Bernice plucked a sprig of sage and stood. The moon threw light past limbs and a few swaying leaves. The wind tugged at her, and she fiddled with a button as if considering closing her jacket farther. Her free hand held the fernlike keepsake away from her, like something sinful that she shouldn't be associated with, and yet she couldn't let it go. Robbie was lunging up and down with a long black spear kind of thing to pierce and pry open the dirt, and it scared her that he might stab into the other dogs he'd buried.

There'd been one more battle royal between her and Irma. A real donnybrook, it came along later when the whole thing ought to have been put away for good, or at least that was how it seemed to Bernice. Actually, it was only a couple of years back, and Bernice could recall being real confused for the first few minutes. Irma was fit to be tied, even though she must have seen that Bernice had no idea what she was carrying on about. But Irma wasn't buying in to that one, not for a second, clawing away as if her life depended on getting the both of them so hopping mad they were screeching and picking at the scab until it turned bloody again. Irma was having trouble with her husband, both of them in their forties, and she was trying to blame her problems on Bernice. She was crying, sobbing big-time, but chilly somehow, too, especially when she got around to warning Bernice that she didn't think she could ever forgive her for not helping her back when she was little. Grandpa Demming was still alive at the time, but in his nineties and sick with diabetes and the lung cancer that would kill him. He was in an old folks' home, Ambler Meadows, when he wasn't in the hospital getting radiation or cut apart. Irma's idea was that Bernice should go to him right then and there and tell him how terrible he was. Tell him that what he'd done was mean and wrong. She didn't care if he was sick or not. He was still alive, still able to hear and think and look a person in the eye, and so Bernice had to do it. She had to go over there right this second and stand up for Irma before it was too late. If she didn't have the gumption or understanding or motherly love to do the right thing when she should have, okay, there was no way to go back in time. But she could do it now, and she better. She had to.

Bernice let Irma rattle on, hoping she would run out of steam, though it didn't seem likely, and then, out of nowhere, Irma started scolding her about how Toby's idiot sister, Aunt Lou, had told her that even though everybody made fun of her behind her back, they all felt Bernice should have done something to stop it. Well, that was the last straw. Bernice's back went up. Having taken about all the abuse she cared to, she shouted she didn't give a damn what Aunt Lou thought. Not about that or anything else, for that matter, because Aunt Lou was an idiot. But if Irma wanted to take her side, fine. And if Irma wanted a knock-down, drag-out fight, that was fine, too. It could probably be arranged, though it sure wouldn't settle a thing. Because wanting her to go over and read the riot act to poor Grandpa Demming made no sense. He was old and foolish. He probably wouldn't even remember. Besides, if that was the worst thing Bernice had ever done to her, Irma was one lucky girl. And as far as for-giving Bernice, well, she really didn't need to trouble herself about that for one second longer. Because it wasn't something Bernice was losing any sleep over. She didn't need it. But what Irma should do, if she didn't mind a word of advice, was grow up. Act her age. Give that a try. And if she was hell-bent on having somebody give poor old half-dead, half-blind Grandpa Demming a piece of their mind, well, she could go on over and bawl him out herself. Bernice was not available. She was not on call to go scream at her dying father. Irma knew where to find him. Ambler Meadows in the hospice wing—or Koopman Hospital in postop, or intensive care—one or the other, because he was bouncing between them so fast and often, nobody could keep track. But if Irma needed the street address, Bernice knew them both by heart. And last time she checked, Irma had a car. Irma had a driver's license.

Of course, Irma didn't do it. She didn't go. Nobody did. And Grandpa Demming died not long after. Didn't last longer than another couple of weeks. Most everybody showed up for the funeral, and they all stood there at the grave site like a bunch of bystanders who'd come around a corner and bumped into a terrible car crash. That was how they all acted. Like they'd been surprised by something violent that not a single one of them had seen coming. Somehow Grandpa Demming's death at ninety-four after a long illness struck them as an accident, so unpredictable it left them dumbfounded. What they gazed at was wreckage, broken fend-ers and upside-down vehicles, dripping gasoline and sparks ready to start a fire at the heart of this eerie silence, in which the only sound was sirens getting closer. And then this sobbing. Middle forties and thick all the way around in her dark coat and dress, it was Irma, and she was shaking and gasping and, you'd have to say, convulsing, almost. She had reached her hands across her breasts so they could each grab high up on the opposite arm and squeeze, as if she would break into a million pieces if she didn't hold herself together. "Grandpa's little split-tail," said a hushed voice. Bernice knew instantly that it was Ronald, and she wanted to kill him, even though there was no way to mistake him for somebody wanting to be cruel. He was just hoping to help those around him understand, offering an explanation in case they'd forgotten. But he'd whispered too loud, and Irma heard him, and to Bernice's amazement, it started her crying all the harder. The way Irma looked at Ronald, she was lost at night in a neighborhood she knew nothing about. She seemed to wonder if he could show her the way out. Somebody nearby said, "Shhhhh." Ronald shrugged in their direction and then toward Irma. She looked from him to the faces on his left and then his right before she hurried off, as close to running as she could get. Her husband, John, said, "Oops," and gave everybody a friendly smile, hoping to smooth over the embarrassment she was causing. His shrug was different than Ronald's. Big and forceful and a lot more complicated, it wanted to shrink Irma's upset down to size, putting it into some kind of perspective by managing to remind them one and all that they'd be meeting soon at Loefler's Restaurant for a nice postfuneral luncheon. And he did it all without saying a word. Then he scurried away to catch up with her. A big man, he lumbered through the gravestones until he was even with her and she could lean on him for the rest of the climb to the road, where everyone's cars waited in a long line.

Robbie straightened with a sigh and stepped from the hole. He contemplated the depth as if to confirm he'd done enough, and then, glancing from Bernice to Janet, he bent slowly to lay the shovel down. Janet understood he was waiting for one of them to declare it was time for the next step. It seemed proper to defer to Bernice, who stood with one hand at her throat, the other extended awkwardly, as if hoping to surrender the spray of sage to an invisible visitor.

"Well, I guess it's time, okay?" Robbie said.

Janet interpreted Bernice's lack of response as sad reluctance and so tried for a soothing tone. "You ready, Bernice?"

"Yeah, okay."

"Do you want to pat him or anything?"

"What?" She sounded annoyed.

"You know. Do you want to pet him or anything?"

"Yeah." Bernice bowed a bit, stretching her arm down. Coming up short, she appeared leery of bending farther.

"I'll pick him up for you," Robbie said, and managed the feat quickly.

Bernice laid her hand along the dog's brow. While stroking, she surprised Janet by fixing on her in an attitude of startling smugness. She seemed to be making the final point in an argument that she wanted everyone to understand she had won. And her stare endured, leaving Janet stumped, until the harshness vanished entirely and the expression on her shadowy old face was one of unhappy distraction. Unready for whatever had come to her, she appeared nonplussed and seemed to realize she had missed something important. She searched the night air. "Is it getting colder?"

"Well, a little," said Robbie, looking around and then up.

Janet found the clouds varied, inky and dense in some spots and thinning in others. "We should probably get you inside, Bernice," she said.

Robbie stepped into the grave and lay the body down. The surrounding edges crumbled, trickling onto the blanket he folded over the quiet old face. The dark of one ear remained exposed, and Janet thought about pointing the problem out. But he moved so swiftly to the shovel, she didn't have a chance. He bent and lunged, heaving dirt. She watched for a moment, then picked up the spade. He smiled at her, and together they scooped up soil, which they balanced and transported, before spilling it from the tilting blades in streams. The ear vanished, and slowly, the yellow of the blanket dimmed under a mix of grime and discolored pebbles. They leaned and thrust. They drove the blades in with their heels. Steadily, they produced a soft barren knoll and the dog was gone. Robbie dropped the shovel and went after the stones. Janet guessed he was rushing because, like her, he was eager to move the evening along. She joined him by the rubble of the fallen fence. For the most part, the rocks were gray and

rough, though a few were white from sun and rain. Janet completed perhaps one trip to his three. She was crouched with her fingers squirming
under a rock when a startling bitter chuckle turned her to look.

Bernice could see Janet trying to find her in the dimness with a surprised, disapproving frown, which Bernice didn't mind at all. She understood that laughing the way she just had might be seen as a tad peculiar.
But she had watched the shovels, and she had watched the dirt. She had
seen the rocks begin in one place and end up in another. She had heard
Robbie breathe and Janet pant and the stones clink and clatter. Like little
Irma's fuss, her dog being dead was—she was sorry to say—comical. All
the trouble she'd put herself and these two through was hilarious. She
chortled again. Stupid was stupid, and that was that.

27

WITH HER CHEEK AGAINST THE glass, Janet watched Robbie tilt toward Bernice, his hand cupping her elbow as she chattered away and they sauntered toward her front door. When they'd come back up the hill, Robbie had offered soda if anybody was thirsty. Bernice had said a glass of plain water would do just fine and then announced she wanted to go home rather than back to church, and she needed to leave right away. As if they were trying to argue her out of the idea, she made a big show of drinking fast and all but slamming the glass down the second it was empty. Recalling that creepy laughter down by the grave, Janet couldn't wait to get rid of the crazy old thing. So they'd driven over, and then Bernice stumbled climbing out of the car, and Robbie, true to form, had scurried to her aid.

Impatiently, Janet turned the ignition on long enough to lower the window a few inches, but their voices remained indistinct. They were at the stoop, where Robbie appeared to respond happily to her babble. It made Janet squirm. But then she saw that even though his shoulders were aimed toward the house, he had one foot on the stoop, the other down a step, as if ready to bolt. As if he couldn't wait to get back. He'd be there soon, jumping in behind the wheel and racing to his house, where there would be no one home and no one coming back. It began with this thought, a phantom snaking away from her belly button into the tucked-away dark inside her, soundless and feathery, a feeling of opportunity and hope. A second shiver came, this one running cold and close to the surface, as she sought to fathom the way so many unexpected, unplanned events had put them together tonight, even emptied the house. People read horoscopes. They talked about fate. And not just foolishness but running all the way back in history. Because they felt it in their lives. They felt something like this.

But why was he taking so long? Why was he wasting their precious time standing there while Bernice yammered away? The dogs could be heard barking inside, but neither Bernice nor Robbie seemed to notice or care. Was he actually smiling now and gesturing in a way that led him, and Bernice with him, to wonder about something high overhead? Janet followed their gaze, and superimposed amid the stars, she saw the kitchen in Robbie's home, the door that had let them in, the hallways and stairways, the bedrooms that had to be on the floors above. So what if she'd been his teacher? She loved that about him. That she knew who he'd been and who he was now. Her heartbeat took such a leap that sense was left behind. She needed to slow her excitement and anticipation before they shredded into nothing but anxiety. Robbie and Bernice were tremulous figures she could barely see.

She shoved the door open. She waved in their direction but tramped around the car without bothering to take in their response. Popping the trunk, she had the liter unwrapped and open before it escaped the glow of the bulb. Her mouth closed on the nozzle as if someone might tear it from her hands. With the sting of the second hit, her eyes smarted. She felt lifted and improved, though she was wary of getting caught. Peering past the upraised trunk lid, she saw that Bernice had stepped inside, but Robbie still lingered, holding the door open, apparently listening. Janet took one more gulp and jerked the half-pint from her pocket. The task of matching the cumbersome liter to the smaller mouth made her feel like some mad scientist working against the clock. It was impossible not to spill. She licked her fingers, dried them against her thighs. With the liter standing uncapped, she closed the half-pint and stuffed it away in her jacket pocket while groping unsuccessfully for the larger top. She stuck her head deep into the trunk but, thinking she heard Robbie approaching, had to straighten and see where he was. Now it seemed good fortune that Bernice still had him trapped.

With both hands patting the trunk floor, she remembered that she had shoved the cap into her pocket. Stealing one more slug, she packed the liter away in its plastic bag with the blanket providing padding and disguise. Hearing Bernice's screen door clatter, she imagined Robbie hastening toward her. The booze coursed through her, swamping her insides with heat and consolation. Her body from head to toe, even her soul, was taking a gigantic breath and exhaling relief.

Robbie was right there, smiling, as she slammed the lid shut. "Problem?" he wondered.

"What?"

"I mean in the trunk."

"No, no. Everything's good. You all set?"

"You bet."

She sank into the car. "What did you and batty ole Bernice have to talk about so much?"

With a glance over his shoulder to make sure the road was clear, he got them going. "She was kind of rambling."

"What about you?"

"What do you mean?"

"What was your contribution?"

"To the rambling?"

"That's what I'm wondering."

"Want some music?" His hand was already on its way to the dial.

"Sure."

"CD? Same one?"

"Sure."

" 'Angel' is coming up," he said. "I think it's the last cut."

"My, my, my." She found him full of interesting surprises and wanted him to know it, the way she might if he was still that little boy. "So you really do know that album. I'm impressed." She was playacting without intending to, and without knowing exactly whom or what she meant to evoke. "You even have the cuts memorized."

"Not memorized."

"And it hasn't been out that long—pretty much hot off the presses. You must have rushed right out."

He answered with an ambivalent glance that ended in a smile, which she read as his admission that he was often helpless in the face of beautiful things.

"So I guess you are really crazy about that Sarah McLachlan." Her cocked head and penetrating eyes played at jealousy, as if he were her boyfriend and Sarah McLachlan was a rival for his heart.

"She's good," he said.

"I'm not sure I want to hear her anymore. If you like her so much." Her words had a lazy, sleepy rhythm, a slight intended exaggeration making her tone suggestive, so they both knew she was up to something.

"I thought you liked her," he said, sounding one hundred percent sincere.

His response was perfect, and she knew it, yet she missed some friction, a little sense of peril, so she said, "Don't be such a shit."

"What?" He laughed.

"You heard me."

"I guess I did." He definitely wanted to study her, but the demands of the road hauled him away. "But did I?"

"What do you mean, 'did I?' " She mocked him, caricaturing his question as small and cowardly. "What do you think I said?"

"You're awful frisky all of a sudden."

"Frisky?" She made it sound like a word so absurdly outmoded, it couldn't possibly apply. "Frisky?"

"Yeah."

"Anything wrong with that?"

"No."

"You're sure. Because tell me if you are."

"If I are what?"

"Excuse me," she said. "Pardon me." All lighthearted play, she enacted offended authority. "I beg your pardon. What?"

"If I are what?"

"No baby talk," she said, and was startled by her need to impose the ban forcefully. "No baby talk, okay?"

"Okay."

The car hit a bump and she sprawled, her body rippling with the sensations of a splash. "So are you troubled by my behavior or not, Robbie?"

"I said no."

"When?"

"Before."

"Because I am just glad to be free of that third wheel. That damn Bernice. Because I have been at her beck and call all day long, and I am not ashamed to say I'm glad to be done with her." She felt impish and capable of causing beguiling mischief in any number of ways.

"So do you want a different CD?"

"No," she told him. "Not at all. I think I can hold my own against this Sarah of yours. I think I can compete."

He chuckled. "I bet you can."

"You would win that bet."

"Anyway," he said, and the word poked at her, made her look. "As far as Mrs. Doorley, I was trying to get to the bottom of why she had us bring her to her house rather than back to the church." He was physically spanning much of the gap between them, as if needing proximity to make his point. "You asked what I was talking to her about, remember?"

"Sure." As he pulled away, she wriggled and stretched, searching for a little more comfort. "You mind if I close my eyes till we get there?"

"Tired?"

"Mmmmmmmm." He was looking at her as her lids lowered, and she wondered if he saw an intriguing older woman, an embarrassing former teacher, or just some totally trashed bitch. That last notion made her giggle, a pleasurable shiver she couldn't keep to herself.

"What?" He sounded as if he'd discovered her whispering to someone he didn't like.

Her headshake hoped to warn him not to expect an answer to every question, because she was often tickled by secrets that could not be shared. When she peeked, she found that he appeared willing to crash the car rather than look away from her. But then he changed his mind and, with a shrug, went back to the road.

"No problem," he said.

"Anyway. Where are we going?"

"You tell me."

"Okay." Her search for practical suggestions went straight to his house, which she was unwilling to say, so she sought an option that might work as a joke. "Except you're the one driving. You could go anywhere."

"But where? And why?"

"Okay, okay, too many questions. Okay?" Had she slurred? She didn't think so but worried that she'd heard a slothful sound or two stumbling around in spite of her careful concentration on the formation of every single one of her syllables. Not that it mattered. Boys liked drunk girls. Drunk was how they wanted them. Half in the bag, or in some imbecilic swoon, groaning and giving them credit.

"I'm hungry," he said.

"Yeah. Me, too." She prolonged the last word with a tiny growl.

"Are you?"

"Yes. Yes, I really am. I'm not sure when I ate last." Her brow furrowed as she ran through her day and, like an accountant finding disappointing numbers, was about to say that she hadn't had a bite since breakfast when she remembered. "Oh yeah. Lunch. But it wasn't much."

"What'd you have?"

"It was at the Olive Garden."

"You like it there?"

"It's okay."

"What are you hungry for? Anything in particular? I'm a pretty good cook."

"Stop it, just stop it. Now you're lying."

"What?" He appeared to doubt that he'd heard correctly, but then, realizing that he had, he seemed genuinely offended. "No, I am. Why would you say that?"

"Because you have to be."

"Why?"

"Because you do, that's all."

"I'm not saying I'm great. Or some kind of chef."

"Robbie. I don't believe you."

"I'm just saying I'm pretty good." Both his dismay and exasperation were endearingly sincere. "That's all I'm saying. I don't see how you can just rule it out."

"I know what you're saying, and I don't believe you, okay?"

"But you have no basis. I'll prove it to you."

"How?"

"I'll cook you dinner."

"Don't be ridiculous."

"No, I will. How do you feel about spaghetti? Or 'pasta' as the Italians call it. I've got two different sauces I made early in the week. Tomato and mushroom. There's some sausages in the freezer. I can thaw a couple and sauté them. Okay? And I can stir-fry some vegetables."

"You're serious."

"Yes, I'm serious."

She felt assailed by something sweet and beautiful out of the blue. A small, sorry bubble entered her throat, where it popped, and she was wistful to the point of tears. He was going to cook for her. It was so totally unexpected, so utterly unforeseen. The image of him scurrying amid pots and pans and boiling water, his effort characterized by concentration and sweat and the hope of pleasing her, seemed the fulfillment of an old, almost shameful yearning whose urgency she could no longer elude. "You're going to make me cry," she said.

"What?"

"I mean it. You're so nice."

"Nice. Me?"

"You are."

"I'm going to turn up the music. You are tired. You're so tired you're out of it."

"Where's that 'Angel'?" she said. "You promised 'Angel.' "

In the air between them, his hand glided to the dial near where her search for a restful position had lodged her knees, and he brushed them. "Coming up."

She was going to get away with murder. If she played her cards right. If he played his cards right. She was going to fuck that sweet little boy in the body of the big man playing music for her, cooking food for her, driving her car.

He kept his promise, and "Angel" delivered its first isolated note, distinct and absolute, though others followed. In the piano sequence, she heard a tantalizing promise simply made, and then the voice arrived with a sense of flying to the rescue. The words were about someone who had spent all her time waiting for a second chance. How about that, she thought. Lush and melancholy, the voice induced Janet to close her eyes. She hoped to blend the song with her thoughts and the humming of the tires. The voice tried to resist the summons of hope and yearning, and it cracked, full of hurt, but then found a different kind of strength. He was right there listening, she knew. She didn't have to look, didn't really want to, but then, stretched slantwise with her head against the glass, she was examining him from as far away as possible. He faced ahead, both hands on the wheel. A shadow muting his expression vanished and returned somehow darker, and she felt something crucial had changed, his posture tense and rigid. She worried that he was annoyed. She feared her teasing had gone too far.

"Robbie?"

"What?"

"How we doing?"

"Good. Almost there."

"I mean you."

"Me? What?" He didn't even glance at her.

The veiled, unreadable side of his head provided nothing to lessen her concern. "You look like you've got something on your mind."

"Well, yeah. Sure. I do."

"What?"

"What do you think? I'm planning the meal."

"Oh. Okay. Sure."

For a phrase or two, the piano ruled, but the voice reclaimed the foreground. As the keyboard pounded, the voice hurtled on, only to fall from some midway height. The lyric had to do with the angel and his enfolding wings, which was expected given the song's title, but the implications probed Janet with emotions and ironies. She was thinking of Bernice out in that old barn, imagining winged creatures roaring down like divebombers out of the clouds. She smiled, but sadly, feeling a faint, unwanted bond between Bernice—huddled with her pathetic friends, the old dog they had buried—and her and Robbie flying along in her car wherever they were at this exact second.

Janet was surprised to find that they were deep inside Homestead Development. She sat up. Like a child waking in the middle of a nighttime journey, she searched the passing world for identifying traits. He was already at the circle and slowing. In the next seconds, he'd turn onto his street. Her hand probed for the bottle. Just a little one. She'd been having fun, feeling wily and clever, but the invigorating rush was leaving, and she could feel encroaching timidity and doubt. Did she dare sneak a quick little pop before he parked? The interior of the car was dark. He wasn't looking. Or even if he was, he knew about the bottle.

Her hand was still in her pocket, the decision unmade, when she saw a lantern-like lamppost aglow with welcome near the end of his walkway. The kitchen and living room were illuminated. Someone had come back. Robbie's mom and brothers had returned, their plans having changed. It was over, she saw, and her eyes shut, her hopes dissolving. She could barely speak to ask, "That light? I don't remember it being on."

"Neat, huh?" Having slowed for the driveway, he guided them alongside the kitchen windows, stopping just about where they'd parked before, well short of the garage. "One of the last things Dad managed was to get all that working. It's on a timer."

"Oh," she said, and she felt pressures gathering against her to push her back, to hold her down. She had to get going. What she wanted was far more necessary than she had let herself understand, and it was vulnerable to all kinds of influences coming from every direction, and any one of them could ruin everything. She was hurrying to keep up with him as he led them toward the rear of the house.

"Nothing like a challenge," he told her. "I'm reconsidering the menu."

They flowed through the back porch into the kitchen, where he ripped off his jacket with an appetite for the coming task of ripping off her clothes. He had to know, didn't he? Depositing the jacket on one of several hooks by the door, he headed for the sink to wash his hands.

"Listen," she said, "I have to go to the bathroom, and then I'll help."

"No, you won't," he said. "I'm doing this on my own."

His steely eyes revealed an even harder element layered inside his stare. It caught her, then left her, as he looked away, reviving the memory of a nasty little incident in her classroom. She'd turned from the blackboard to find him whispering and smirking with one of his buddies. Having singled him out early in the year as bright and somehow special, she'd enjoyed those feelings without fully realizing that she expected him to reciprocate, if only in loyalty. She'd shouted both of their names, but the other boy didn't matter. She'd interrogated them, particularly Robbie, with questions intended not to get answers but to humiliate him. Some had been about the lesson of the day—had it been geography? She'd taunted them to share the remark that had made them grin so stupidly, and when neither would, she'd herded them to the back of the room, leaving them to face the pale wall for the remainder of the day.

Now he was lean and rangy, overseeing a faucet spewing noisily into a large stainless-steel pot, as he called to her over the rattling water, "You remember where the bathroom is?"

"Yep." Instead of going, she ambled close and looked coyly up. "I don't see why I can't help."

"Because I say so. It's my thing."

"Okay," she said. "You're the boss."

The bathroom wasn't far, just down the adjacent hall. Once inside, she hung her jacket on an empty towel hook, then sat and peed. Her elbow was on her knee, her chin propped up by her hand. Her thoughts went one way and then the other, sort of bumping into walls. The fingers that lay along her jawline tapped from first to last, as if to soothe her. She didn't expect to giggle when she took note of what she was doing, and yet it seemed okay that she did. Her fingertips caressed a tiny portion of her cheek. Bone lay inside and she could feel the pressure, the tenderness, of her own touch. She was in there somewhere, behind the layered meat. Behind the epidermis. The pelt, the fleece. This was what everybody wanted. It was what she wanted. To be touched. Caressed. To be handled. Found. But not like this. Not alone. Not by herself. She wiped and hissed, "Dammit," then stood and washed her hands.

From her dangling jacket, she lifted the half-pint, and gratefully, as if responding to an invitation from the dearest long-lost darling for a desperately desired, yearning-filled kiss, she closed her mouth and drank. Because it was good. Because she wanted to. Because she was there and the bottle was there. Because behind the epidermis, behind the pelt, behind the fleece, behind the skin, Janet Cawley waited. She tilted her head and guzzled, and when she finished, sadly, she saw how one more sip was all that remained. Because of the transparency of the glass in her hand, because of its gleam or its emptiness, the moment registered as one of such sweeping importance that she might never be able to understand it. When she took the last little gulp, the liquor plummeted to a previously undiscovered level, where it let loose an amazing, trustworthy band of sensations that climbed, like rescued riches, from some stupid, pointless, bitter, stingy darkness inside her.

She was already back at the kitchen doorway, through which she could see Robbie bowed over a counter with no idea she was there. His shirt sleeves were rolled up, and a book lay open before him. A cookbook, she was sure. Because his devotion to his task absorbed him completely, she was free to float backward unnoticed. She was free to wander off through the rooms and hallways of the house in search of something. In search of his room.

There were any number of corners and doorways, and two floors. There were other kinds of rooms, big and little, a linen closet, a storage closet, a bathroom, and a door that opened on stairs up to the attic and back down again. She walked into a bedroom that she recognized as his mother's by the pictures of Robbie and his brothers crowding the dresser and bedside tables. They adorned the vanity, hung on walls. Above the bed, a petite, freshly permed woman was posed happily with a graying, puffed-up version of Robbie against a background of forest and water. They wore bright vacation clothes, the man's big arm lightly curled around the woman's shoulders. He was rugged and tanned, the ball of his belly unmistakably taut. The neatness, the antiseptic, talcum-powdery smell filling the room, in which not a single piece of clothing had been haphazardly dropped and every item of makeup and hygiene was neatly placed, spoke of surprise and unfinished mourning.

Trudging on around a corner and up a rise of two more stairs, she was soon rewarded by a treasure trove of three bedrooms that left no doubt they belonged to boys. All three had desks with textbooks and shelves. But only in one did the shaft of hallway light dispelling the dimness show Robbie's work clothes strewn on his bed, his paint-spattered boots on the rug beside it.

"Robbie," she said when she'd returned. "I found your room."

"What?"

"I found your room."

"Where the heck have you been?" he said. He was swirling a big wooden spoon in a colorful smear of chopped vegetables and hissing oil.

"I just told you. I found your room."

"Whatta you mean?"

"I found your room. Your room. Where you sleep. Ohhh," she said. "Just a second, I'll be right back."

"Where you going now?"

Aiming for the back door, she shot forward as if the house were steeply pitched and she could only aim and hope. She fell right on through and landed in the night, huge and black except for the overwhelming moon. The liter was in the trunk just where it ought to be, and she tilted herself to the sky and had to scamper backward as the bulk of the bottle and the jolt and joy of the booze nearly tipped her over on her ass. Instead, she stood laughing happily, hugging her big-bellied, jovial buddy to her chest. But suddenly, she stopped, as it struck her unwise to loiter within the trunk light's spill. She slipped warily behind the car and crouched. The metal gleamed in the silvery waves raining down from the sky. Who was to say what it all was? It was something, okay. The planets and stars. The heavens. Majestic, okay. Fucking majestic. Who was she to think she understood anything? Who was she to think she had the right to all her demands, and that she could hope and beg for any one particular outcome? This was everything. This dark covered in clouds breaking into pieces like islands of ice in an arctic space to show the glitter of specks beyond, and they could be anything but were whatever they were. She had to gather her heft, and gauge her balance, and aim for the open trunk, where she nearly fell in.

When, after what seemed to her a completely ambiguous stretch of time, she arrived again in the kitchen, he was carefully arranging silverware as the final touch to a table set for two. He smiled at her and darted to the stove. She took a step or two after him but then stalled, fearing she was going to careen sideways with no end in sight except some wall. Even from afar, the coiled burners on the stove were scalding reminders of his buttons that she must pry open. The boiling water bubbled with his sighs. When he turned and said, "My mom loves this recipe," his wish for her to cross to him, to fit her fingers into that hair of his, and to take hold was so intense she looked away. The second hand on the wall clock displayed the details of time, broadcasting each lost instant with a jump forward she couldn't stop. When he lifted the empty pasta box to ask, "Do you know this brand?," he flashed with what they would do in bed. She felt a coaxing, tantalizing vibration. She did not want to end up with stranger after stranger, their groping and grabbing a mockery of what love could be. Sour sweat, heaving butts and cocks. As if she were fast asleep, an impulse searched for a way to surface and rouse her with the warning that she must not let this moment escape. Her eyes opened to an extravaganza of green, polish, and light—the kitchen. She was a romantic blur of hope for the dearest, deepest, pornographic happiness. She was auburn-haired and perfect, and she must kiss him with her lips and tongue, and then with the silk of her undies gone, with the silkier, silkiest kiss of all.

"Want to put on some music?" he asked.

"Sure. Where is it all?"

"Whatta you mean?"

"The player and you know. Stuff."

"CDs and all that?"

"Yeah."

"Living room. There's a whole stereo and everything along the wall to the right of the fireplace, as you go in. It's out in the open and everything. Want me to show you?"

"No, no." After a step, her willingness to do what he asked evaporated, and a burdensome, obscure idea furrowed her brow with a series of gloppy sensations. Finally, it came clear, and she was able to ask, "Could you make me some coffee?"

"Sure. You want some coffee?"

"What?"

"You want coffee?"

"Yeah. I'd like some coffee, if you could make it."

"I wouldn't mind some myself."

In her deep, lonely interior, the kiss waited. Oh, Robbie. "Okay, then." She was off again, only to glance back while still in the hall. He passed the frame of the kitchen entrance, and she waited, wanting to see him again. When he reappeared, he shot past with a red container in his hands.

In the living room, she scanned the layout methodically, finding first the fireplace and then the wall, which was to her right, just as he'd promised. Through the crack between partially open dark cherry doors, the black molded plastic of electronic equipment peeked out. Kneeling, she conducted a study of the control panel that grew confusing and dragged on, requiring backtracking and repetitions, as if the identity of the dials, buttons, and indicators were in flux. When he spoke behind her to ask, "How do you take your coffee?," she straightened slowly. Offering her wavering equilibrium some needed assistance, she planted a hand on a nearby flat surface. "Hi."

"Do you take cream and sugar in your coffee or just black?"

"Okay. Cream and sugar," she explained, just before a dizzy little swell raised the floor and changed her mind as she lost contact with the shelving. "No, black."

"Black?" he said. "So which is it? Black?"

"Yeah, black. Okay. Black."

"Got it."

Bent over and squinting, she pushed the open/close button, and the carousel wheeled out with all the visible slots occupied. Aside from being tiny, the print on the labels was fuzzy and wiggly and wavy, making it impossible to read. She kept trying and failing and decided that he'd probably like whatever had been last played. Since he was home alone, he'd probably played it.

The room had grown bigger somehow, the distance she needed to cross if she was to leave expanding, or else she was taking a more indirect route, because she hadn't gotten very far at all, when a mellow saxophone and whispering snare drums came on behind her.

He shouted from the kitchen, "Hey! Good! You decided to go with some of Mom's old-fashioned stuff. It's great, actually."

She shrugged. She hadn't decided anything. She'd just pushed something, the play function, or the indicator for the first CD. Now muted trumpets were preparing for a development that turned out to be clarinets and trombones blending with pulsing horns, the drums coaxing everybody along, until the whole extravaganza became a big band cresting in a wave whose fading made way for a young girl singing:

> I saw you last night
> and got that old feeling.

Janet slumped into an armchair and sat in a stupefied sprawl. It was too much. All of it. More than she could handle. She listened and knew that she should just give up. There was too much beauty in the world. She couldn't cope with the way it came at you when you least expected it, so you had no hope of being prepared. She shook her head, as if she had happened into the presence of something divine or at least close to earthly perfection. The woman sang of the accidental glance, the unbearable delight, and Janet's heart, like the heart in the song, stood still. Closing her eyes, the music zoomed her off into a dazzling, dreamy slow-motion vision that rendered a faraway impression in vivid detail. A kind of sepia-toned, moodily tender Bobby Crimmins embraced a nostalgically beautiful Isabel Cawley. They sailed and dipped, dancing through sunken dimness. Romance and foolishness again and again, filling her heart. Once Robbie arrived, she could dance with him. In his arms, she could share the music and the floor where her ex-husband swirled in and out of iridescent, shadowy spirals with her ex-mom.

She stood and started to go to find him. But he found her. She was surprised to see him, and he was surprised to find her. From the brightly lit hall, he gazed into his darkened bedroom, where she lay on her side in his bed. "What's going on?" he said.

"Did I fall asleep?"

"I don't know. What's going on?"

"I think I did."

"Dinner's ready," he told her.

"Good."

"Are you okay?"

"Great."

He inched in, smiling, amiable, a little puzzled. She could smell him, and it made her happy, a mix of sweat from his work burying the dog, a flavoring of rich tomato and basil, and something else, a scent that was becoming familiar, and it was purely Robbie. He wore an oven mitt on one hand. Was it here now, the long-awaited moment, the long-awaited love, with destiny opening its big, big heart for her at last? Sporadic illumination held him in a changing complexity with each little move he made. "What's going on?" he asked again.

"Could I have my coffee? I really would like it."

"Sure. It's ready. It's in the kitchen."

"No, I mean could you bring me a cup?"

"Here?"

"I really think I could use it. I've had a little too much to drink, and I could use it."

"Okay, but dinner's going to get cold."

"I'll just drink that cup and be good to go. Okay?"

"Okay. Sure." His departure left the door wide open so the music found her in smoky wisps leaking up the stairwell and through the vents, even piercing the thinness of the floor, to insist that she get out of her sweatshirt, that she wiggle free of her leggings, but not her bra or undies. No, no, not yet. She squirmed under the sheets and blanket, and something strung taut inside her let loose at the thought of him bringing her coffee in bed. For a moment she was sick and small and home from school, waiting. She fell back with a sense of having arrived finally, after so long, and though harried by nerves she couldn't distinguish from wild energy, she was on her way into that intoxicating world known to the music she had discovered accidentally, and played accidentally. But it was waiting for them now, and she would bring them both to it.

When he reappeared, he paused to absorb her pose, and when he crossed the room, she smiled and repositioned herself so she was semi-sitting, dragging the sheet with her, but in a way that left her shoulder exposed. He held out the coffee, and she imagined her coppery hair and pale skin against the white bedding curtained in the room's dusky mood. She could almost see him think about shutting the lights off, reaching for the wall switch and then the bedside lamp, but after a second he touched neither. Cradling the cup in both hands, she bowed to the lip, like someone outside in bitter cold.

"Looks like you're making yourself right at home."

"Yeah."

"I guess you're really not feeling so well."

"The coffee's going to fix me up."

"Yeah?"

"I think so." Modestly, she clamped the sheet to her ribs with her elbow and patted the bed for him to join her. When the contours sank in response to his weight, her pulse thudded. "Hi," she said, sipping again. She wondered why he didn't speak, but she found his thoughtful expression as compelling as a storm of words. She winced with the hot coffee she was drinking in a rush, but she needed it fast. Was he waiting for her to finish before taking hold of her? Should she incite him with a little more skin, a trace of bra, or should she just take hold of him? Trespass lingered in spite of their grade-school relationship being long past. Dipping her head, almost whistling as she tried to cool the coffee, she peeked at his thighs and the zipper between but wasn't sure she saw his cock. Which wasn't what she wanted to call it. Because he was Robbie. Sweet Robbie with his sweet penis. She felt like she was hurrying to a party somewhere, a little tipsy, but very excited about the approaching fun. "Set this on the table, will you?" she said, getting another gulp down. He had to turn to her and then away in order to obey, and a rightward bulge appeared in the rumpled folds of his crotch.

Touch was the way to go. Touch was electrifying. It was magic. Her hand moving across the vagueness that held them apart would goad the heady change, first with fingers on his arm and then his cheek and lips. Even when dizziness tipped her into seconds of nausea, she did not stop for long, blinking and calmly, repeatedly filling her lungs with air time after time. Where was he? Her thumb that had passed from his arm to his cheek was tracing his lips, and as his head fell toward hers, she saw, in the blur of his face, eyes that were young and expectant. His mouth was timid on hers, but she would help him. He conducted a pliable, pleasant little visit until she found his tongue with her own, and the effect shot into her brain while dropping down a thick, squirming ache to her groin. He muttered, and she felt him arguing, heard a melancholy sigh as tiny tremors swayed him to pull away, an impulse she canceled by clamping both hands around the back of his head. She drew on his tongue, sucking as if she would siphon him deep enough to touch her from within.

"Wait." He was struggling.

"What?"

"Wait, okay?"

"Okay," she said, gazing at him as if she were simple, as if she were honest, as if she was not ruthless and drunk, as if she was not ravenous, and so she would listen to whatever he had to say. But his fly was open, the zipper down, his chinos splayed and eager. His penis was in her grasp through the thin cotton of his boxers.

"Just hold on a second," he said. "There's— It's— I'm—"

He was too little to know what he wanted, or what he was doing, or trying to say. Little Robbie. How new it must all feel. Because it was new. Never before the two of them. Never. So sweet, her Robbie, but with a cock, it was a cock for sure flowing into her hand, not a penis at all but a smooth baby-skinned cock, and she was woozy again but defiant as she pushed back from the sickening plunge. "Okay, okay," she told him, trying to remember what he'd asked, while stroking with her thumb on a point near the tip so luxuriant and ample that it left him unable to speak, and his head sagged, his eyelids drooping. He shifted and appeared to suffer, and in his inability to escape her coaxing, he belonged to her more and more.

He said something that she knew was meant to be a word, and she thought the word was "Don't," but his slovenly mouth couldn't function. His eyes were closed, his expression tortured in contradictory, deeply satisfying ways. Why had she drunk so much? It was so dumb, when there was so much happiness here.

"C'mon, Robbie," she managed, her friendly enticement brushing aside his protests as pure fabrications whose futility she would prove. With a looping arm, she herded his head back down for her kiss, her thumb still twitching. He sounded bitter and hurt, clamping down on her as if to take her whole head in, first her lips, then the big hole of her mouth, then all of her, and in response her hand turned into a fluttering, whirling fist. He seemed to want to escape one last time, or maybe just felt that he ought to. She cherished his struggle, the impulse vibrating between them, but he was hopelessly responsive. He might want to retreat but could only advance, because leaving was unbearable. Like a baby, he could only yield and growl, grabbing her, his cock rising as if inhaling, as if taking a big breath. She enclosed him, mercilessly striving to hold back release as he rippled and jerked and foamed over her knuckles.

"There, there," she said, clinging to him; because only her embrace could keep him from breaking into pieces. She was glad she had found him, so glad, and she valiantly withstood another wave dragging her into the gyrating dark, where seasickness left her with no connection except to him. She reached and touched his cheek, found his hair. He had sunk onto his back, the powers that had consumed him draining away. She kept her hand on him, as if to hang on to the world and stay in the room, and though diminished, he remained enlarged. At eighteen he'd be ready again in seconds, she thought, anticipating him rolling to her. She tried to recall having ideas of this kind about him in class. No, not ideas. Maybe dreams. No, no, it wasn't that. He was a man. And she had him now in a big man's body. She wanted to devour him, she couldn't help herself, woozy or not, touching her lips to his cheek, his brow, his nose and mouth, neck and eyes in a downpour of scattered nips and tiny insatiable kisses.

Downstairs, the stereo endured, the music seeping back into her awareness. It must have been there all along, like the faint fumes that now reminded her of his efforts in the kitchen. She rested her head on his chest and smiled, noticing in the lighted hall an embroidered tree hanging in a gold metal frame, its roots stitched into grass. Nestled behind lowering eyelids, she experienced the woman's voice as meant for them alone, a memento, a keepsake she had misplaced for a while:

> . . . as time goes by.
> Moonlight and love songs . . .

Turning onto her side, she let her knees fold in a childish tuck. No longer was there any need to keep from falling away. He was motionless, maybe even asleep. He would wake her when he wanted her. Oh-oh, she thought, as if she saw something more, or felt it. She touched him, blindly now, a sleeper hoping to find that the world remained. He stirred, a shifting person, a hunk of flesh, a body. Was it slumber? It didn't matter. It must have been a dream in which they were two tiny people in a crib, and she settled her hand over her thigh, then, in a kindly way, over her cunt. She was waiting until he returned. Now she remembered, now she knew. She felt that she was sinking but peaceful in the depths. Forever and ever, until the mattress shifted and she saw he was standing, his belt unbuckled, his shirt disheveled.

She tried to sit up, but the bed was rolling, the walls in motion. "Okay, okay."

"Damn," he said. "Dammit."

"What? Robbie, what?"

"Goddamn son of a bitch! I shouldn't have done it. I'm sorry."

She pawed at his arm, finding his hand. "Okay, it's okay."

"No." He tugged gently to get away. "I shouldn't have let it happen."

She clung to him with tightening fists to lift herself up or maybe to simply hang on. Maybe just wanting the ground under her feet. "Wait."

"I screw up everything." He sounded enraged, he sounded miserable. "No matter what. I'm such a stupid screwup."

She thrashed until she stood, and there he was right next to her, buckling his belt for the third or fourth time, it seemed. But why? "What are you doing?"

"I'm going downstairs."

"What?"

"You have to go home. I'm going downstairs."

She wasn't sure exactly who was talking to her. He was angled away, and so, in crucial ways, he was obscured, leaving her somehow in the preposterous situation of trying to explain cataclysmic life-and-death matters to a distracted stranger. "Let me just . . ." She turned, searching. "I'll get my clothes." She climbed onto the bed.

"I'll drive you home."

"What?"

"I want to drive you home."

"What?" The repeated word had the overwhelming task of questioning not only what he'd said but the sudden excruciating failure of language, of sentences, of human speech to convey sense. Her stomach churned and she pivoted, fighting to find enough balance and stability to keep from puking all over his floor.

"I just couldn't stop. I have this amazing girlfriend. At college. When I was at college."

She felt like he was screaming, throwing things, punching her. "Can you wait a minute?"

"It was at school, okay? And we promised each other."

She started to sob. "Why are you doing this?" Her tears were like blood from a cut, and to that extent, because they were already shed, they didn't matter, but the cut had to be tended. "Wait a minute, okay?"

"I have this wonderful girlfriend. I'm sorry. At college."

Suddenly, he was incomprehensible. She'd heard and recognized what he'd said, and knew what he described, but was stunned that he could believe such things had any significance. Girlfriend? She was flailing around in fathomless black water. She was struggling to breathe, to somehow get from this second into the next alive. "Girlfriend?"

"At school. At college, okay? After my dad died, it was like we had to do it. I mean, we didn't have to do it, but it was like we did. And we promised each other."

Janet flopped down on the bed and looked around in horror. The world, and everything in it, was insane. Her leggings were somewhere, her sweatshirt somewhere else, and Robbie was talking gibberish, his every syllable so inappropriate and wrongheaded he seemed deluded, or oblivious, or worst of all, devious. And her shoes? Where were her fucking shoes?

"She's had this awful childhood. Really, it was unbelievable. From the very first day of her life."

Janet rolled to where she could peer down between the bed and the wall. Too dark to see into, the gap engulfed her arm as she probed for her clothes, while also struggling to come up with a way to help Robbie see how confused he was, how much he was missing, how completely distorted his understanding had become. "Dammit," she grumbled, raising his paint-stained pants from the shadows. So much flopping and bending had aggravated her throbbing head, and when the room was invaded by glare, she had to cover her eyes, as both the lamp and the ceiling bulb came on.

"You would never believe some of the stuff that happened to her, if I told you. And her parents did some of it. I can't tell you, but if I did. The worst childhood I ever heard of."

She had no idea where her leggings had come from but was glad to have them, even though her feet kept missing the openings and she had to stoop in spite of the pain trying to split her skull and the vertigo wanting to throw her down on her face, as she tried to somehow coordinate her limbs and this strangely complicated garment.

"So we promised—because I had to leave school after Dad died, and that scared her because we would have to be apart—we promised to be true to each other. And now I've screwed it all up."

She pulled violently. It was ridiculous that she couldn't put the stupid things on. She'd done this a million times. Her hand slipped and came leaping up to smack her in the face. "Oww," she said.

"You're drunk. Are you that drunk, really?"

Noticing the cup of cold coffee, she lunged for a lengthy swallow. The taste was dull and disagreeable, but she chugged it because Robbie was studying her closely, and she saw something in him that told her he knew somewhere in his heart how idiotic he was acting, and she became convinced that she could straighten him out if only she could get him to listen to her explanation of how his girlfriend didn't matter. College didn't matter. He didn't really matter. What he thought, what he said. Because she was disintegrating. In some lurking half-light where all the known laws of nature and science and psychology had been revoked, she had a twin who was ashen, truly ashen, and she was crumbling in an ashen room. And this heartbreaking end prophesied ruin for Janet unless she made Robbie see, unless she changed his perceptions, altered his point of view, so that he stopped looking at everything backward. So that he came to see it all in exactly the same way she did. He was above her, and she reached, not to touch him but to alert him. "Robbie. You don't know what you're talking about."

"What?"

"You don't know what you're—"

"I'm telling you I have a girlfriend and we—we—oh, I can't make any sense to you like this. When you're like this." He waved his hand with a shudder that threatened to become a fist smacking the wall but turned loose and pointless instead. "I had no idea we were going to end up like this."

"That's a lie. Don't lie."

"I'm going downstairs."

He disappeared, and she began to feel something she had never felt before. Cold black hands inside her like claws. He gutted her when he walked out, taking everything she needed with him, leaving her in a plummeting elevator, the room an uninhabitable hole. People talked about it. But this was it. She had talked about it. But this was what despair really was. And she was standing there alone with it. She refused to accept that everything she'd believed about tonight was in error. But unless he was lying, it was all mistaken. And why would he lie? Why would anybody lie? And everybody did. From as far back as she could remember, she had fought to safeguard the hope that what went on inside her was real and could be made real to other people. So that she could be known. To think that it was all nothing but this spinning in her head, this kind of movie she invented and looked at, always a mirror, never a window, so that the world was a dream, and in her case tonight, a drunken dream in which no matter what she hoped and believed, her body was not really who she was, but just something she was inside, like a specimen in a test tube sealed off from all the other specimens in their test tubes.

She was staring at the ceiling, his ceiling. He had to be lying. Because look where she was. Look what had happened. It wasn't all a drunken dream. Not all of it.

Okay, she thought, find him, follow him. But then for an elongated moment nothing happened except for her mind pondering, in slow motion, the odd immobility of her limbs, until she spied her feet padding over the rust-colored hallway rug. She clutched the coffee cup, believing that by getting it down to the kitchen, she would cancel some terrible liability. She lugged her bedraggled sweatshirt. Her nose still stung from when she'd punched herself, and then she spilled the coffee onto the rug, inflaming the liability she had hoped to heal. She knelt to scrub with her sweatshirt, and then she stood and pulled it on. People said things. They did things. With no grasp of the consequences, no grasp of what mattered.

In the kitchen, where every possible light had been brought to bear, Robbie was covering their dinner plates in Saran Wrap and moving them into the refrigerator. He'd already slipped his red jacket on, and zipping shut the front, he picked up her jacket from the back of a kitchen chair and held it out to her. "I found this on the bathroom floor. I want to go."

"We were having a good time. Weren't we?"

"You can't drive. I'm going to drive you."

"Just tell me. Weren't we having fun?"

"I didn't understand."

"Oh, don't do that. I will not let you do that. Don't lie. You're lying. When you came into the room, you did, you knew. You—"

"Okay, but—"

"You didn't have to stop. I didn't want it to stop. I didn't want you to stop."

She was near enough that the desire in her arms to flow around him was unbearable, and she released them in a blooming wish, a burgeoning outburst for which she had no words. He turned rigid, but she wrapped him close, and with her face against his ribs curving one by one into her cheek, her disintegrating twin saw that he was a cage and what she wanted was locked away inside the cage—but why should she be deprived again—locked away as she had been when she looked in through the wire at the beautiful old collie dog so long ago. Straining against what kept them apart, she whispered directly into his heart, "You and me. Just you and me. I want to be little again. You know—just little. That's all—that's not so hard. Let me be little again. Right now, okay. You, okay. And me. Little again, okay. Just now, okay? One more little."

"This is nuts," he grumbled into the top of her head.

"What?" The word was shrill and impoverished but all that she had. "What? What?"

"I don't want to do this anymore, okay?"

"Just pretend! Just fucking pretend! You stupid little shit!"

"You gotta stop. You are one of my favorite people. I mean, in my whole life, Miss Cawley."

She reared back, searching his treacherous face, and he looked befuddled when she hit him, offended, certainly, but without the slightest understanding, so she struck again, her fingers tingling and leaving the reddening imprint of her palm and the surprise of teardrops sparkling in his eyes. Belatedly, his arm rose in defense, and he stepped away, but the wall hemmed him in.

"You don't have a girlfriend. Stop lying."

"Her name is Amanda."

She sprang at him, but he snared her wrist in his big fingers, controlling her long enough to spin her away as if she were his to boss and twirl in a dance. "Just stop it!" he ordered.

Released and cast into the momentum he had started, she lurched until the wall became something she could use to keep from falling long enough to plant both hands on the countertop.

"I want you to drink this. Just sit down. You have to calm down." He stomped over to where he had brewed the coffee.

"I'm sorry, Robbie," she said. "Okay. I'm sorry."

"If you don't want me to drive you home, I'll call a cab. Should I do that?"

He put the coffee on the table as if laying down the law. His manner was so authoritative he needed no words, and she wanted to obey, wanted to go where he directed, wanted to sit and drink. But the crumbling twin was fleeing her ashen room. She was racing toward the kitchen, toward this very moment, while Janet dutifully closed her hands on the cup. "I don't want to have to go away, though, okay, Robbie? I want to stay."

"No."

"I'm sorry I slapped you."

"Look. I want you to go home. You have to go home."

The twin was steadily disintegrating, her dust whirling off. "I want to talk to you, that's all."

"No."

"How can you say no to talk?"

"Please," he said. "It's enough. That's all. That's all!"

"Just talk. Robbie. C'mon. What's wrong with talk? There's nothing wrong with talk."

"I can't."

"Of course you can."

"You just have to go. I'll call the cab, all right?"

"Robbie, no, no."

"I think that'd be best."

"Oh, you don't, really. We can talk. We have to. That's what—"

"No!"

"Just listen to me, listen to me. That's what people—"

"No!"

"Why won't you listen to me?"

"Because I can't."

"That's ridiculous. You could if you wanted to."

"Then I don't want to."

The twin screamed. Ragged and terrified by her onrushing dissolution, she toiled to exist and survive and, by these accomplishments, to appear in the room. "You're a child! You're acting like a spoiled little child!" she shouted. "You don't understand anything!"

"Okay, then, I don't."

"Am I attractive? Or don't you think so?"

"What?" He looked like he'd been warned the room was about to burst into flame and he wanted a way out.

"Am I attractive or not?"

"Of course."

"Don't say 'of course'! That's so fucking stupid. If the answer was 'of course,' would I ask?"

"C'mon." He sounded helpless and looked sad.

"C'mon, what? C'mon," she said, mocking the whining little baby he had become in her eyes. "C'mon. It's a simple enough question."

He strode toward the kitchen phone. It was almost over. Everything. "No, no, no, no. No, no, no, no." She watched him arrive and, before dialing, refer to an unfairly convenient magnet on the refrigerator door.

The twin was in a whirlwind of tears and screams. Layers spooled from her decaying shape. No, no, no, no. No, no, no, no. She was a cloud, and the winds were dispersing her in plumes and puffs and twirls.

"Hello," he said, and the twin, willful and fierce, fought against her extinction, and it was Janet who crumbled; it was Janet who disappeared. But the twin was there, the twin who understood the menace of this phone call, who saw the oncoming catastrophe that could not be allowed, the twin who was shrieking and wild.

The cup sailed through the air to explode in a black spray and clatter off the wall beside him. He sprang at her, shouting, "Goddammit!" She tried to run, but he leaped, his hands fierce and powerful, as her flailing feet left the floor and terror came over her, along with a sense of welcome, as if she were almost where she belonged. From the disorientation of the room, the rear entryway with the door propped open raced at her, because he was shoving her through it. He was trying to open the back door. She pounded his arms, then grabbed at emptiness until the tangle of her fingers snagged his hair. Yelping, he spun in a partial circle before she was loose and groundless, then thudding and skittering on her butt.

"Are you insane? Are you crazy?" he cried.

On her hands and knees, she said, "You want me to go? Is that what you want?"

"Yes."

"Is that what you really want?"

"Yes!"

He was knotted and twisted with loathing, with barely checked murder, his vicious heart on full display. "Okay," she said, and somehow she was in her car, where she managed to hit the little lock button in time to keep him from hauling her out. He banged the metal and slapped the glass, yelling something before he began striding in and out of the illumination pouring from the front of her car. She started the engine and the radio came on and she turned the volume loud, which prompted him to shout and gesture insanely. After slamming his hand on the hood, he disappeared, and she realized he was running to get behind her. Staring at the letter indicators on the gearshift until she was certain she was in reverse, she didn't bother to check before stomping on the gas. With a jolt, she shot backward, clattering onto the street. Straining mightily against the bizarrely cumbersome, unmanageable steering wheel, she forced the car to turn.

In the rearview mirror, he retreated through the red haze of her taillights. Loss came at her in a surge of resentment, bitterness, anger, all hungry for her, and she accepted them as the reckoning she was due. But she had to go, and transferring her focus in a slow blurry heave to the Honda's gears, she coughed up a great sob, just as the D for drive lit up, and she raced off.

28

I T PERPLEXED BERNICE TO STAND gazing out the window for as long as she did in the wake of Robbie and Janet's leaving. The road was empty, but there she was, the dogs emitting soft little moans, even raising a paw to her leg. She stroked them, said their names, and gradually came around to wondering if it was just the night that held her. But her mood had this big idea about itself, laying claim to a greater importance than the view of her neighborhood could cause, the industrial wasteland across the way, the streetlights shrinking in the distance. She felt like she was waiting for a visitor. A lot of her life had been spent like this, parting the curtains and looking for the first sign of a car rounding the corner to bring her company. Which would be about the last thing she wanted now. Good Lord, no, thank you. Maybe it was something about Janet and Robbie she was trying to figure out or reluctant to lose. Maybe they mattered more than she knew. They'd been there when she buried her dog, after all.

Finally, she turned, feeling kind of out of it. She flicked on the wall switch and stood, absorbing the mood of her little home, and it didn't take long to see that even though she knew better, she was thinking General might hobble into view, grumpy and grudging, the whole episode a bad dream. Every single item her eye fell on, every knickknack or photograph or piece of furniture, was something she had worked hard to get just so, and there it all sat, like it was willing to belong to anybody who came along. Even the TV had something odd and grim about it, and she was taken aback when she couldn't remember the last time she'd looked at the darn thing or even thought about one of her programs—not even her soap operas. Weariness flooded her, and there wasn't a thing she could do about it, except nod that she knew she was stupefied and darn near sleepwalking. Happy and Sappy gazed up at her, worried and considerate, understanding that she was almost out of gas.

From atop the backrest of the comfortable old cinnamon-colored couch, Ira sprang lightly to the floor. As Bernice moved, Elmira manifested, zigzagging between her ankles. General's empty plaid bed rubbed salt in the wound of his absence. She thought she should eat, but the idea of getting a meal together was more than she could manage, because she really had to be on her way. Like she'd told Robbie when he was so kind as to walk her to her door, she'd come home to look in on the animals, and then, as long as she was there, she couldn't see the point of them carting her back to church when her car was right at the curb. Still, she could take a minute to boil an egg, couldn't she? Maybe soft-boiled and toast would really hit the spot. It was a little after nine. Maybe put the radio on and get off her feet for a second. Reverend Tauke had been a bit peculiar, jumping in front of them on the road, marching around in the dark that way, and paying all that attention to Janet.

After freshening up the water bowls, she wondered if everybody'd been fed. With General passing away, it was easy to see Janet losing track. But empty cans in the garbage, which, judging by their smell, had been recently opened, convinced her dinner had been handled properly. Still, Bernice might throw them some kibble, so they'd feel loved when she left.

Bowl in hand, she was bent over the cat food bin when her heart disappeared. It had to be inside her, but she couldn't feel it. No whir or thumping. No beating in her ears. Not even a way-off tremor. She felt hung out in silence, and too scared to take her pulse because it might not be there. A glimpse of General's bed narrowed her eyes with the impulse to go lie down right there. She reached for the pantry shelving, and her heart seemed to slide out of hiding, beating crazily like a ticking clock uncertain of the correct time.

After five or six breaths, each one a little steadier, she went back to her chores, seeing to everybody's food, including her own two eggs in a saucepan of water, one thing after another, as if that scary little episode was nothing much to bother about. But the second she was finished, she made a beeline for her trusted recliner. With a creak and a tilt, the poor old cocoa-colored thing, which was about as close to being on its last legs as she was, rocked back in welcome. It made her chuckle, first with satisfaction at getting off her feet, and second with amusement at the way she got rid of her shoes, and then, picturing herself sprawled there all but drooling, it was as if she became somebody else, somebody who thought she looked ridiculous, and her laughter turned snide. The sound took her back to that field behind the Oberhoffers', where she'd acted like her dog dying was one heck of a good joke. Though what was funny about General getting left under all that dirt escaped her now. But then who knew what made a thing laughable, anyway? Half the time it was some poor sap gettin' punched, or left in the lurch, or stuck with a stupid-lookin' hat. Which was how she felt right now—like she had a stupid hat on. That had sure been the case often enough in her life. If you went by her dad, that was the key to every good gag—somebody gettin' kicked or tripped up or made to look foolish. At least they had that in common—seein' the saddest thing as a reason to yuk it up.

Faint at first, the ringing persisted until it reached her where she lay buried under layers of mud, her and poor old General, the both of them done for. Or was it fog they were under? Or could it be sleep? She flopped about, needing to know, alarmed that she was going to miss everything. She tried to find the old wall clock Toby had loved so much. Her glasses were crooked, and once righted, they brought into view the brass imitation of the sun with wooden rays sticking out. The big hands were blurry, but it was going on ten minutes to ten. Exhausted and annoyed, she was thankful nevertheless for whoever was on the other end of the line jangling away on the table beside her. "Hello."

"Bernice, thank God! What are you doing? I've been trying to find you."

"It's a good thing you did, Hazel."

"Where are you, anyway?"

"What? Where do you think I am? You just called me."

"I know you're not here, that's for sure. People saw you in a car. They said you went off with that Oberhoffer boy. What was all that about?"

"You gotta give me a minute. I'm all discombobulated. I just woke up. I must have nodded off."

"What are you doing at home, anyway? And nodding off, did you say? Did you say you were sleeping? You're supposed to be out here."

"I know."

"I don't understand why you left in the first place."

"It was Janet Cawley. She showed up. Something happened."

"But it was Oberhoffer behind the wheel is what I heard. People said so."

"Yes."

"When are you coming back? You gotta get back here."

Bernice didn't see how she could keep pretending Hazel cared about anybody but herself and maybe Alice Kuhn—if Alice was lucky. It was hard to accept that Hazel couldn't even be bothered to ask what had sent Bernice running off. Didn't it occur to her that it must have been impor- tant for Bernice to leave the way she had—that it must have been earth- shaking? Suddenly, their so-called friendship felt fake and shallow and terribly disappointing, and she said, "Do you mind if I call you back?"

"What for? Yes, I do. We just—"

"Because you woke me up. My feet hurt, my head hurts. I'm worn to a frazzle. I mean, everything is not a joke, Hazel. Everything is not one big joke!"

"Who said it was?"

Hints of Hazel's pompous, holier-than-thou attitude were creeping into her tone, and Bernice felt ready to start climbing the wall. "Where are you, Hazel? Are you still at church?"

"I'm at the parsonage. I gave Robbie Oberhoffer's folks' place a call on a long shot I might catch you. But he says, 'No, she's not here. She was here, but we took her home.'"

"That sounds about right."

"Because things are startin' to heat up over here, Bernice. So you better get a move on. Reverend Tauke says you need to get back."

With the phone occupying one hand, Bernice was having a dickens of a time getting her shoes back on, but she could still roll her eyes at Hazel's blathering. "Could you just put a lid on this nonsense, Hazel?"

"What nonsense?"

"I'm warning you, I'll hang up!"

"He sent me down here to call you. He said I had to make you promise."

"He did not!" It burst out, prompting bewilderment on the other end of the line.

"What has gotten into you?" Hazel wondered.

"There's no need to go around saying Reverend Tauke did things he didn't just to make yourself sound important."

"I don't know what you're getting so snippy about."

"I'm perfectly capable of finding my way back out there without you exaggerating everything."

"But why would you try to tell me the man didn't do what I know he did do?"

"Wait a minute. Just wait one minute." She wanted Hazel to quiet down, and when Hazel cooperated, the stillness was instantly scary. "What are you saying?"

"And you should know," Hazel told her, "that you need to be here before midnight."

"I do?"

"That's right. Because that's what Reverend Tauke says now. Midnight. That's when we're going."

She wanted to say, *What?* Or *Going where?* Or maybe *Wait a minute!* But all she got out was "We are?"

"Yes. Or do you think I'm making up some fib in my last hours? Is that what you think? You really have to be here by midnight."

"Okay."

"Because that's what it sounds like you think I'm doing and I'm not."

"That's what he says now? Midnight?"

"How many times do I have to say it, Bernice?"

"I don't know." She felt sad and pitiful and didn't think she could keep it all inside. "I just don't see him going to all that bother."

"What bother?"

"Thinkin' about me, Hazel. With all he's got to have on his mind. And then puttin' himself out by findin' you, and tellin' you to find me, and to—you know—whatever it is we're doin' in this conversation."

Sounding amused, affectionate, and mocking all at once, Hazel said, "You're a real oddball sometimes, Bernice. Why are you actin' so surprised? Of course he thinks about you. He thinks about all of us. I'd guess that's pretty much all he does."

"Oh, Lord. I don't know what to do." She felt like she could melt right into the sagging old recliner that she should have reupholstered long ago.

"About what?"

She nearly fumbled the little she got out. "It ain't right. I don't deserve it."

"What?" Hazel's curiosity was gentle and a touch sad. "You mean Reverend Tauke? That's what you're talkin' about."

"Yes, I am."

"That's somethin' most of us could say about ourselves, Bernice. I sure could. I don't think it's about if we deserve it."

"But I have these thoughts sometimes. Terrible thoughts."

"Oh, you do not."

"I'm being honest, Hazel."

"No worse than the next one."

"I don't care about the next one."

"And I'm tellin' you. You don't have terrible thoughts, Bernice. I know you."

"You don't know everything that goes on in my head. Sometimes they're bad—they're blasphemous. Take my word for it. Just give me a little credit, will you?"

"I don't know why you want to say that kind of crazy thing. I really don't."

Hazel's pigheadedness was maddening, driving Bernice into such a hot and bothered state that she started sweating and giving off this funny odor. "Because I think them. I have them, and you're saying I don't."

"There's no point to this way of talkin', Bernice."

She was so hot under the collar that her BO had a kind of scalding stink. "Well, stop being so thickheaded, and maybe we—" A rifle shot startled her. She could hear things breaking in the kitchen, and the metallic stench was coming from in there, too. "Oh, Lord," she said. She'd forgotten all about the eggs she was soft-boiling. "I left the burner on. I left the burner on."

"What?"

"I gotta hang up. I think my house might be on fire!"

"Just give me your word you're coming!"

"If my house don't burn down, Hazel!"

"Even if it does! I need to be able to tell him!"

"Okay, okay."

"So get a move on. It's almost ten twenty."

The clanging in the kitchen was the empty pot jumping around on the scarlet burner. Gore from exploded eggs coated the blackened sides, bits of shell and yolk thrown all over the place. Happy and Sappy were already nosing around at her feet like little vacuum cleaners. With an oven mitt, she moved the pot to the sink, where the hiss of the cold water startled the dogs and sent them scurrying. So now he was changing it again. It was going to be midnight. But he'd said that on the road, too, hadn't he? She wasn't sure. Something about midnight. She was turning the faucet to lessen the flow when the diminishing hiss made her need to pee. High-handed and fierce, the urge would not hear of a delay, and she was so sick of it all that she considered throwing off a lifetime of modesty and just peeing where she stood.

But she knew better than that, and off she went, feeling cowed and disgusted until she was done. Back in the living room, she stroked Ira and then let her palm rest against the hum in Elmira's belly. She had a lot to take care of, but she could hurry and, barring the unforeseen, get out there with time to spare. She sat on the edge of the recliner and bent to bring her eyes down to the level of the dogs. It was hard to keep from be-ing distracted by the smoky, sulfury smell that made her fearful the house was going to burn down, that it was just smoldering away somewhere in secret, getting ready to burst into flames. She lifted Happy's paw to shake hands, forcing her mind to take in the sensations of the sweetly padded foot. How could she leave them here to go up in smoke like poor Mrs. Tomlinson? Had the cause of that fire ever been known? Abruptly, she lunged, delving into the fur and muscle of Sappy's appreciative back.

When she straightened, the dogs both eyed the door, and she saw how hopeful they were that she intended to take them for a walk. She worried they were fidgety and nervous because the burned-egg stink concerned them. Or maybe they had to go to the bathroom. "Okay," she said, opening two windows to let in fresh air and reminding herself to close them before leaving. The screens were on so the cats couldn't es-cape. When she grabbed the dogs' leashes, they looked at her proudly, like they'd gotten an important point across. Out they went into the yard, where there was enough nip in the night air to remind her to bring along a heavier coat in case the weather didn't hold. The dogs wandered around with nothing much on their minds except to stroll and gawk. After a min-ute or two, she coaxed them. "C'mon, now, you know why we're out here." They seemed to get the idea and worked to come up with a few small turds. "Good," she said, deciding Janet must have walked them. "Good boy, good girl. Thank you."

Distracted and rushing around to close the windows, then double-check the stove and the water bowls, she was stopped in her tracks by the reminder that she needed to get her own Bible. Putting first things first, she made sure to slip it into her purse before another second went by. She then tucked the borrowed Bible under her arm, so she couldn't possibly forget to return it, made sure of the stove one last time, collected the win-ter coat she had thought a perfect steal when she got it marked down at a spring sale last year at Penney's, and turned off the ceiling light.

Why, after all that fuss, it seemed shocking to stand at the door ready to go, she would never know, but it did. In the glow of the living room lamp still burning, Happy lay on her belly, calmly resting. Sappy had wandered off to General's bed, where he stood thoughtfully contemplating the place that had belonged to General for so many years. It took him a while, but he stepped aboard. Turning in circles, sniffing and fretting, he found the winning spot, and there he settled. Head held high, he appeared pleased to have accomplished something so wonderful he could not understand why he hadn't done it before.

She called herself an idiot, driving away. The lump in her throat was stupid because they were just a bunch of animals in a stupid little house with a lawn of mainly crabgrass in the low-rent end of a stupid little Iowa town. What was she carryin' on about when she was on her way to heaven? She wouldn't have the good sense to pour piss out of a boot. Everybody'd said it when she was growing up. *Bernice, you wouldn't have the good sense to pour piss out of a boot, would you.* Her uncles and aunts. Her dad, too, from day one. She had more or less supposed they were right, gaping up and wondering, but afraid to ask how the piss got into the boot in the first place. Who was dumb enough or mean enough to piss in somebody's boot? And did grown-ups all go around checking their boots and shoes for piss before putting them on?

Worn out and, in spite of herself, emotional, she couldn't keep the road from fading almost to nothing behind a blurriness that came and went. She blinked and rubbed her eyes, fiddled with her glasses. But the traffic was light, so she made good time. Soon the familiar farmland rolled toward the horizon, where a huddle of lights seemed a big ocean liner far out at sea. As she started up the driveway, the moon edged free of the murk. Right before her eyes, the last few threads swept clear, magnifying the whiteness of the chapel on the hillside. She hated the irreverent noise of her tires crunching on the ruts and stones. It was close to eleven, and she felt misplaced and shy. Creeping along, she hoped to spot some other straggler, anyone at all. But the parking lot and the grounds were deserted. At the parsonage, every window was dark, even the porch light out.

Fearful that she had taken too long, or that her little Timex was wrong or the deadline altered yet again, she clambered out and stood in the stillness, clutching her purse with the Bible inside, like that was her ticket. When she heard music, or at least thought she did, she held her breath and listened. The chords of an organ were seeping through the walls shining above her. Alone and uneasy, she hastened up the long path, and as she toiled and panted, she heard singers, too. Arriving at last, she put her ear to the door, her bosom heaving, as she prayed that she be allowed to detect through the wood clues that would give her some idea what was going on inside. They were singing, that much was clear, and it was Reverend Tauke's new song, "All Rising to the Lord."

When she dared to peek in, the place was crammed. It looked like everybody was present but her, at least forty-some souls. The organ had been ghostly out in the parking lot, but it was booming now, that same karaoke recording they'd used before, that "A Whiter Whatever Whatever" piped over the loudspeakers. Of course, she hadn't found a minute to study the lyrics, not that it sounded like many people had. The music thumped sturdily along, but the hymn was ragged, the voices timid, except for a few strong souls carrying the load. But there was something else, too, something that she sensed, gradually, a kind of electricity in the air, this storm warning that promised thunder and lightning and tornado-like winds. She felt scared. She saw herself running away, getting out of there in her car, but instead, she pushed in, easing the door closed behind her.

The last pew on the right wasn't filled, so that was where she headed. With her eyes half-lowered and her head bowed, it struck her that, though the force inside these walls felt scary, it was probably something good, maybe joy, along with a strange wild energy. Curious about Hazel's whereabouts, she spied Bonnie and Raymond Frunke at the end of the front pew, Raymond's jittery leg stuck out in the aisle. Alice Kuhn was one row back, looking saintly, but no Hazel in sight. Edith Fritsch and that husband of hers, Otto, were next in line, and near them was that smart aleck in the silk or gabardine pants. But no Hazel, and no Esther, either. Not that Bernice saw. People were pretty dolled up, though, and it made her sad not to be wearing yesterday's outfit. Her pantsuit wasn't right, and she wasn't going to try to convince herself otherwise. Even the presence of several women in similarly inappropriate outfits, and a few who were far less presentable, was small comfort.

Out of nowhere, Hazel came toward her, beaming and gesturing for Bernice to make room. She couldn't wait to get seated before whispering excitedly, "Did he see you? Does he know you're here?"

"I don't think so. Where is he?"

"Down front, but he's walking around, so he'll find you." Passing over a printout of the lyrics to "All Rising to the Lord," she said, "In case you lost yours. Like I told you, we're goin' at midnight. See all the alarm clocks?"

"What?"

Somberly, raising her chin to point, Hazel directed Bernice to look up front where a number of alarm clocks had gone unnoticed. There was one on a windowsill, another on a chair. Others occupied the stairway to the baptismal font, a different chair, an opposing windowsill. A half dozen stood in a row along the edge of the first step up to the altar. Most were digital, though a few were the old-fashioned kind. When her questioning glance got back to Hazel, it was met with the grin of a child about to yell "surprise" at a birthday party. "They're all set for midnight. He wants us to pray and then sing. The one and then the other. Back and forth until they go off." Bernice couldn't help but gawk at her Timex, which read five or six minutes after eleven, so she was distracted when Hazel gave her hand a squeeze that might have been affection but was in fact farewell, because Hazel rose and walked away.

The music was ending. A certain amount of shifting went on, people standing and stretching, even changing seats. Bernice tracked Hazel, who had seemed tender in the seconds before she left. It was her worst nightmare coming true when Hazel's journey ended next to Alice Kuhn, the two of them whispering instantly, as thick as thieves. She should have known better than to expect anything else. After all, Alice Kuhn gave Hazel all those special feelings that Bernice Doorley lacked. Piety and inspiration and whatnot. So there they were—Hazel in her khaki and gold, all but hugging Alice, who looked like some daffy fairy princess. Lord, thought Bernice. It struck her that she better just close her eyes and pray and see if she couldn't find a way to lose some of her envious, jealous shortcomings before it was too late.

The jarring snort at her elbow came from a big ruddy-cheeked man, whose name she couldn't think of, blowing his nose. He swabbed under and around, pinching and wiping with a handkerchief and offering Bernice an apologetic nod. His eyes were red, and he kept sniffling. Bernice tried to show some sympathy, and the expression he gave back turned misery and rejoicing into the same thing, and she saw at that instant, as if he had whispered them to her, all the broken things in her own life. It was an urgent, pointless moment of realization, mostly about Irma, because even if there was something she could do to make things right between them, it was too late now. She was never going to get the chance.

A fluttering piece of paper, one of the xeroxed copies of the new lyrics that someone must have lost, sailed down onto the bloodred rug of the aisle. Unless she could do it from the other side, she thought, watching the white sheet settle. Unless maybe she could come back and fix things up the way those psychics on television talked about. Maybe be a presence nearby—come back to spread this warm glow all around people, around Irma and her family on a holiday or a birthday. Those psychics said that was when it tended to happen, when people went to the trouble to make the journey back for a visit. Not that anybody had ever done it for Bernice. So it probably wasn't the easiest thing to pull off. Not something she could hang her hopes on, or plan on, like she was trying to do. Her mom and dad were long gone, and if they'd ever come near, she didn't know it. Hank had been dead going on eleven years, and she'd seen him in dreams, of course—she'd seen them all in dreams, but not an inkling in any other way. Not even from Toby. You'da thought that if it could be done, he would have done it. On the other hand, if she was honest, she'd have to admit that Toby might not be the kind to see a whole lot of appeal in coming back as a warm glow. The way he went about things, he might not even think he had anything that needed saying or that he needed to make up for. Although Bernice could think of a couple things. Not that she was going to start taking digs at Toby. And the more she thought about it, the more she could see him up there, not wanting to tear himself away from whatever was going on in heaven, and who could blame him. So maybe it would just be up to her to be the first. Because she'd do it if she got the chance. Just to kind of let people know every-thing was okay, as far as she was concerned. Just kind of showing up out of the blue at Irma's house to cover them all in this warmth, like a big woolly blanket, burly old John, and little Alex John, and Irma most of all. Just fill them all up with this sweet tender feeling. Not something she'd ever been very good at. Spreading a warm glow around people. Especially Irma, especially the ones she really loved. But maybe she'd be better at it, coming back like that. Maybe she'd be able to find all that warmth she knew she had in her somewhere but just couldn't let out. Maybe she'd be able to do it once she was dead.

With a squawk and a scratch, the recorded karaoke came on, making her flinch. It seemed louder than before, as if Reverend Tauke or whoever was running the machine had raised the volume. Around her everybody scrambled for the lyrics, and when the part came for them to join in, peo-ple gave it a try, Bernice included, lifting her voice, as best she could.

> I trip and call to Jesus,
> fall hopeless to the floor,
> but then I feel him touch me.
> My soul calls out for more.
> The earth was spinning faster
> As the heavens flew away.
> And when I called out for another
> The heavens would not say.
> And so our struggling Angel
> Knew he must go higher
> And his face, at first just holy,
> Turned a blazing shade of fire.
> He said, "The Lord is coming
> And His law is plain to see.
> So look now, look above me
> His face in fire loves thee."
> For there the cross is turning
> For there the cross is blood.

And among the vestal virgins
Are those unwanted by the host
And though our eyes are closed,
I say—now make them open.
I say—go home my loved ones
To behold His holy face.
The blood that from the sky is falling,
The blood, the blood is grace.
And the cross is heaven's key
And the cross, the cross is turning,
To open Rapture's door!
And the Angel smiles so sweetly
That we must straightaway soar.
And soon we will be flying,
All rising to the Lord!

29

J ANET HADN'T GOTTEN VERY FAR when she started worrying
that Robbie was chasing her. Her rearview mirror showed
empty pavement bounded by quiet lawns, and houses floating off with
mostly darkened windows. The place might as well have been a ghost
town, and yet the impression remained that something was stalking her.
A second search presented a wake of different houses, lawns, and parked
cars. Though she warned herself repeatedly not to neglect the road, by
the time she looked back and got the mess in front of her into some kind
of order, she was about to slam into the curb. Overcorrecting, she shot
toward the opposite sidewalk, where a violent swerve let her escape but
sent her careening down a side street. A circle loomed, and while braking
had not occurred to her as a way out of either previous predicament, she
rocked to a halt.

The abrupt motionlessness felt imposed. Alone with the hum of the
engine, she heard the unsettling sound of her own breathing. No matter
what she felt, no matter how miserable she might become, her lungs
would keep pumping, dragging her on. A chill ran through her chest,
where her tears had clawed her open. That fucking Robbie and that bitch-
faced twat, little what's-her-name.

She marched to the trunk and stood under the streetlight having a
brazen rendezvous with her bottle, one long sweet swallow that she did
not want to end. The girlfriend would be young—probably a freshman,
like him. She saw them strolling side by side, lugging books and back-
packs down corridors. In the crowded lecture halls, amid the hubbub of

dining hall tables, they searched for each other. Amanda and Robbie. She was a stupid little blonde with a stupid fucking name and her belly bare between her T-shirt and low-cut spandex pants. Or maybe a redhead in a drawstring skirt, saying, "Untie me, Robbie." Whining about her pathetic childhood. Or maybe demure in a blouse and skirt. And they fucked for sure. Everything. Every dirty loving nasty thing, and in a flickering shadow show, she saw it all.

It was humiliating to feel left out, but she couldn't stop it, and even more alarming was the deep-down, raw, jealous ache warning of something far more perilous racing toward her. Because the really bad part was the way she'd ruined what she'd had. At least he'd been in her life. He'd been her friend. Excited when she called. Ready to drop everything at a moment's notice to do her a favor. Putting up with crazy Bernice. And bringing that sage to put into the grave. That was amazing. To make the poor thing sweet. Not that it would. But he'd thought of it.

With the effects of another small sip, sprigs of sage sprouted in her thoughts. Her hands were flexing and clenching. It was in him to do that—to think of such a thing—and now she'd fixed it so he'd never want to see her again. So he would never come anywhere near her. Wouldn't even want to talk to her.

She buckled at the waist in a bow that didn't end until the bottle, along with her hands, rested on the floor of the trunk, where she stayed, overcome by the weight of every stupid fucking bitchy thing she'd ever done. In the faint illumination of the little bulb, the duct tape lay with the hose. She picked them up, as if they were why she was back there in the first place and everything important regarding their transfer from the trunk to the front seat had been given all the consideration it needed. But arriving at the open door, she hesitated before the empty interior, the console reflecting the little dome light, and her sense for an instant was that she might intuit the future if she waited, if she concentrated, but instead, she snorted impatiently, cynically, and tossed her hose and duct tape in.

Her head tilting to take another small swallow brought the lettering on a street sign into view. Bentley Circle. That wasn't the one near Robbie's house. Had she gone farther than she thought? Missed a turn?

How the hell was she supposed to know? Her need to think had her slog-ging through a swamp, every step glop-encrusted. She wanted to go home but lacked the faintest idea where she was. Fixing on her watch, she wa-vered and focused. The little hand, the big hand—it was around ten thirty.

She fell into her car and took off. The bourbon bottle rode clamped between her thighs as she looped the circle, getting faster with each repe-tition, but she couldn't determine the way she'd come in. She didn't know, and with only a fraction of her fumbling brain working, and that part given over to incessantly reenacting her behavior with Robbie, she feared she would never know. She just wheeled down whatever lay in front of her. It was a road, so she took it, jealousy and hurt erupting in a jagged gash through which all of her faults wanted in, each determined to make sure she would never forget them. In came her college days with Kevin Garvey, who'd offended her by wanting to please her, and so she just had to bring in Byron Link with his vanity and narcissism to torture Kevin until he screamed, pinning her down in the street, his rage, as he slapped her, like Robbie's tonight. And Byron. She'd flipped his switch, too, so he turned vicious in his own special way by fucking those other girls.

An elderly man in a light spring jacket strode along near the curb, his pumping arms defining him as out for his nightly power walk. She cruised past, wondering if he might help her with directions, but Byron, overhearing her thoughts, jeered at her. He shook his head disgustedly while Kevin glared, and the truth of how she had provoked them both canceled everything she had ever believed with a brutal new insight. It was all her fault. She'd incited savagery in Kevin in order to win the re-ward of his desolation when she told him they were finished. And Byron's betrayal had been there from the start. Once she selected him, she had only to wait. And tonight she had done it again. If she wanted to refute that voice labeling her self-loathing excessive, all she had to do was look at Robbie. And there was no taking tonight back. Though it seemed she must. Because suddenly, Robbie, Kevin, and Byron were all wasted chances, and she needed forgiveness. At least from Robbie. But he was gone. They were all gone.

She took the next turn crazily and flew by another row of houses. Her weeping had broken something inside her, turning anxiety into a whirling blade increasing in rapidity and violence, and it wasn't going to stop. She didn't think she could stand it. She needed them to know, whoever they were, that she was sorry and it had to end. It had to stop. In spite of the absurdity of the notion, desperation commanded her to pound on some stranger's door and beg to use the telephone. She had to do it. And right now. Her misery was a crazy person arguing to convince her she could knock and they would let her in, and then she could call.

Oh my God, she hadn't even thought about Bobby. She hadn't even taken into account her super-bitch treatment of poor Bobby Crimmins. And Wayne, too. She acted like he was the treacherous one because he had a wife, but he'd never lied about it. Not to Janet or even to his wife. She missed him. She missed his beautiful dark hair. She was the liar, branding him selfish and fickle, accusing him of giving her nothing while she was the one making certain nothing was all they had. And what about his kids? Knocking over display racks so he'd run to them. Had she almost brought divorce down on their poor little heads? Had she almost done the worst possible thing? She wanted to apologize. To Wayne and to his wife, too. Call her and apologize. She wanted to promise with absolute certainty that any need to worry about that bitch Janet Cawley was over.

One day in the first weeks of her marriage, Bobby had come home from work early. She'd arrived from school only minutes before and was anticipating hours alone to correct papers when the front door chimed. Through the peephole, she saw him standing and waiting, ringing again. Had he forgotten his key? But then the opening door seemed an unveiling. His features were beautiful, his manner graceful. He was transformed by an innocence born from his surrender to the wonder he felt at the fact that she was there and she was his. The memory ran, like her first kiss of Robbie, from the root of her tongue into her groin with a physical sensation of wistfulness that drew tears to her eyes.

A mere thirty yards off, the power walker was crossing the street. He whirled with a frightened and then belligerent expression and hurried out of the way. She'd been turning corners at intersections and circles, all of them pointless, apparently, because she was back where she'd started. Past him only a short ways, she impulsively moved to the curb. She stuffed the whiskey into the gloom of the floor and hastened to roll down the window before he came alongside. Still pumping and stepping, he glanced at her with eyes set oddly close, his scrawny face a hatchet. She waved, and he stopped, not altogether happy to lower the earphones he wore, and stand there panting. Determined not to slur, she took a second to organize the muscles necessary for speech. "Hello," she said. "You're probably wondering what I'm doing. Well, sir . . ." The sloppy, shushing sound of her *s* made her smile, hoping to charm him. "I'm lost."

"Oh. I get it. I was wondering what the heck was going on."

"I hate to break up your walk, because you were looking good and strong, but can you tell me how to get out of here? I need to get to a phone."

She could see he welcomed her flattery. "You're lost, are you?"

"I was visiting a friend, and when I left, I must've mistaken a turn. I've been driving around ever since."

"Well, it's not the best layout in this joint, I'll grant you that. I dunno what they were thinking about, but it wasn't being helpful. But I have a cell phone," he said, "if you want."

"What?"

"For your call."

Call? she wondered. What was he talking about? "I just want to get out of here."

Something about her remark flustered him, even as he went about orienting himself to her request. He seemed to wrestle with a set of invisible markers meant to relate their present location to certain distant aspects of Belger. But when he turned back, he had a crafty glint. "I thought you said you had a call to make. You don't have a cell phone, I guess."

He was right, of course. She'd forgotten. All those regrets and apologies. Curiously, they did seem less crucial to her well-being at the moment, not exactly absent but diminished. Maybe she should keep talking to this old guy all night. Maybe if she stayed fixed on him, he would keep her distracted. "No, I don't," she said. "I guess I sort of like the fact that most of the time nobody can find me."

The guffaw that burst out of him left him looking resentful. "Well, that's the deal, all right. They find you. So you want to make that call?"

"It's not just one call. I have a lot of calls, and I could never make them in front of you."

"How many you talking about?"

"You mean exactly?"

"I can let you do one." His hand sprang to his pocket and emerged with the little folded apparatus.

"One would be pretty much useless."

"Well, one's what I had in mind."

"It'd be useless."

"Why'd you say it, then? It's what you said to begin with."

"I don't think I did."

"I'm here to tell you that you did."

"Then I was wrong, if I said that."

"Then you're wrong."

"I guess I am."

"Take my word for it."

"You know, I was thinking about that very thing, driving around. About how wrong I was—about what a screwed-up, messed-up, fucked-up piece of shit I am."

"Maybe you should just get on home."

"I'd like to, if I knew how to get out of here."

Suddenly, Janet saw that he really disliked her, and she loathed him, and it was clear that neither of them knew exactly what had provoked their hostility or when it had started, and both were perfectly untroubled by their ignorance.

"You and your smart mouth," he said.

"What about how I get out of here? Why don't you just tell me that?"

"Here's what you do," he said, fingering his earphones like he was tempted to clamp them back on and stalk off. "It's pretty damn simple if you get right down to it." He drew close. His eyes searched the interior of her car while he halfway ranted at her about how she should go straight for half a mile, then make a right-hand turn that would bring her to a circle. "Got it so far?"

"You bet." But either her concentration lapsed or his approach became perverse, because the next phase was a jumble. There were street names, one of which was Garfield, some further measurements in tenths of a mile, more street names.

"Who were you visiting? You said you were visiting somebody."

He straightened and stood waiting for her to answer, while she looked into his eyes and considered telling him absolutely everything. He wanted the truth, and her mood was hurtling toward devilish candor. But what would happen if she did that? Did anything ever come of the so-called truth, the much ballyhooed, overestimated bullshit of it all.

She cruised off. Refusing to glance back, she was preserved from even a second's worth of his indignant reaction to her rude departure, which left her free to execute the first part of his instruction flawlessly. But from then on, her ability to carry out what he'd told her vanished. Not that it mattered. Not that she really wanted to talk to anyone. She had nothing to say to any of them. Who had she been fretting about? Wayne's wife, for God's sake. She tried to sample the conversation. Ridiculous. But maybe Robbie. No, not him, either. Especially not him. She was sick of thinking about Robbie.

Wheeling left at one intersection and right at the next, she felt a sense of bitter anarchic accomplishment. She was lost in Homestead Development and never getting out. She took a drink and then another. She raised the bottle and hitched it twice, the glint of the glass obscuring the road but not her misery. While she'd screwed around with that old man, her poisons had receded, but now they were back, their lethal powers increased while in hiding, their appetites incensed at having been ignored. Though she knew she could not outrun them no matter how crazily she drove, she put the pedal to the metal. Tires squealing, knifing left at a corner, she intended to accelerate but then had the strangest intuition that her destination lay straight ahead, and she slowed to a crawl. Not the exit to the highway she had been trying to find, but the end of the development, its farthest extension, the outskirts.

The sweep of her high beams unveiled pavement ending in a dirt trail. Shapes hovered but all incomplete. The first unfinished house on the left concluded in skeletal rafters, while its neighbor went no farther than vertical struts and crossbeams outlining walls. A half dozen more were similar, their floors intact, their remainder sketched in timber without skins. She could look through the framing to the tilted landscape beyond. Hills carried off dark woodland clusters like small boats buoyed above the inky slashes of gullies.

Pausing beside the black pool of a freshly dug foundation, she thought how this pit would contain people living their lives someday. Families moving from other towns. Drawn by a new job, a transfer or promotion. Retirement. Newlyweds. Couples who had scrimped and saved to get out of an apartment. Everyone dreaming of the happiness a new home could bring.

She groaned because her torment, inspired by these sights, had become even more insidious, even more expert. Where once names and faces, misdeeds and accusations, were needed for it to flourish, now nothing was required. Like fumes from a buried fire, her heartache was opaque and without specifics, making it impossible to refute or understand. It was simply anguish—bone under a blade, skin on fire, the open nerve. It was almost monotonous.

The last of the staked-out lots ended at a ditch bordered by the start of a narrow, weedy track flowing into the countryside, which was where she wanted to go. With its steep slopes and bluffs, the rugged land had forced local farmers to come to terms with its skewed demands long ago. She figured she was following the remnants of a path formed over time by tractors and livestock. But now, because these fields were no longer tilled, it led nowhere. Suddenly leery of arousing suspicion by traveling over terrain that must go largely if not completely unused, she snuffed out her headlights. She could only hope she had not been spotted from one of the outlying homes. With the last of Homestead drifting away behind her, she prayed that no one would interrupt her.

Freed of her intruding headlights, the moon was drastic. The craggy sphere showered enough brilliance to cast shadows and create the impression of an overcast day. She felt directed even as the Honda lurched from pothole to pothole. She believed the black veil toward which she climbed would sort itself out once she got closer. Trunks and branches would emerge, some stalwart leaves, the first wave of a woods of some size. She sipped a little more and was capping the bottle when the car slammed into a hole. The struggle to exit nearly jerked the wheel from her grasp until the tires, spinning crazily, escaped. She strained and hunched forward in an attempt to see directly down onto the ground in front of her so she might skirt such dangers. But the awkward perch wore her out quickly. Dropping down to rest, she found the dense jumble some twenty yards in front of her turning into trees.

She crept under bare, angular branches. The moonlight dimmed in the thickening maze. Despair might sicken her, but she could leave it behind. Like a banished soul, she was going home. Like an exiled extraterrestrial, she had come to her launch site. That was a thought to bring her right to the brink of laughter, but it could not push her all the way over. Eyeing the tape and the hose, she wondered if she should review the necessary logistics. But what if she was too drunk? Too drunk to kill herself? Contempt eagerly added this failure to the long list of indictments already collected against her.

Outside the car, she stood concentrating and working the hose inside through the partly open window. Then she walked to the rear and crawled under, where the night was magnified. Her pale hands advanced, one with tape, the other aiming the hose to the exhaust, but a thumping noise startled her. Twisting to look back, she saw the hose she had just inserted had pulled loose and fallen to the ground. It lay in weeds. At that instant, intense heat nearly scorched her outstretched hand, and she retreated. After so much driving, the metal of the tailpipe must be scalding. Was nothing fucking simple?

Hands on knees, a push, a grunt, and she stood. For a moment she teetered, her gaze uplifted haphazardly, but then the planetary array spread out overhead captivated her and she concentrated, filling with wonder. What did people mean when they wished upon a star? Or when they sang "Over the Rainbow"? Let's be honest now, she thought. Everybody wanted out. Nobody liked it here. They loved it but didn't understand it. It hurt and made no fucking sense. That was the problem. She was going to find out. She would do it. Be everybody's hero. Or at least her own. "I'm going over the rainbow," she said. "The longest journey starts with a little step," she told no one and nothing, as if they were someone and were with her.

She flopped into the front seat, where heartbreak waited, arms open, ready to take hold of her and demonstrate its power and pitiless skill. It shook her and ground her up, until the little she had left to help her see and think understood that the only future awaiting her was this unbearable moment repeated without end. She nodded. *Hello.* She said, "Fuck you." She was done. She was leaving. But what if it went with her, the pain? What if its hold on her endured? What if it was entangled in her being and somehow integral? As deep inside her as her DNA, and so she died and transformed and it just went with her.

She took a quick sip in the hope of coming up with a meaningful approach to correcting her thinking, and then she took another. She was so drunk that her only chance at any kind of lucidity, any kind of orderly, sequential thought, was more booze.

She must have decided to get back to work, because she was standing outside, stuffing her rolled-up jacket into the inch-wide gap between the window and the frame. Molding the knotty folds, she forced the material to block all but a slit where she inserted the hose. Back in the car, she wound a ring of tape until the buildup was enough to keep the hose from popping out again.

She wondered if the tailpipe had cooled by now. She didn't want to crawl under and then have to crawl out again. Or just lie there if it hadn't. Her hands over her eyes failed to dim the hubbub in her head. She took another drink. Her arms, along with her hands, worked wearily, rubbing her brow, her eyes, her temple, while her sluggish thoughts staggered around in search of something to hang on to, an idea or something like an idea. It was oddly but undeniably soothing to recall the way she'd gone into that hardware store thinking she was on someone else's errand. And Robbie was there. The duct tape, the hose. All in the store. Big Baby Dog, too. And that other one. Not Jamal but the other one. It seemed guided, as if a farsighted friend had escorted her down that aisle and then made sure she got from there to here in order to fulfill a wish born somewhere unknown inside her, like maybe her soul.

Her anguish, as if boosted by this thought, was a flood now, yet the excruciating pain wasn't excruciating because of the booze. She was buffered by its fuddled, muzzy, muffling mud. Her hand waved in a gesture that left her gazing at its scrawny spread. No bracelets, no rings. Her fingers petted her barren throat. No necklace. Not even the one Bobby had given her. Labradorite, amethyst, and gray rice pearls. No, she'd sent it back. And that time he'd wanted to take her to a spa for her birthday, she'd scoffed at him, so she'd never been pampered and cared for, never bathed in some fanciful brew, never lain covered in purifying oils.

The unrolling tape produced noise after noise, one time a hiss, then a squeak. Debris fell from the underside of the car onto her face and arms. When she'd created a sizable bulge to serve as a stopper maybe a foot from the end, she inserted the hose into the pipe. Minutes of ripping and binding and panting and cinching fused the metal to the rubber with an airtight seal. She slid clear, wondering if she could really think that at last all that remained was for her to start the engine and sit there.

Sit where? Where was she? The door was closed, and she was fumbling through her CDs. She turned the key enough to gain electrical power and then to ignite the engine, waiting with nervous wonder, an intense, interested readiness. Her heart was hammering. On came Ani DiFranco, cranky and complaining and bragging that she could do a lot of things but sounding like she couldn't be bothered to do any of them.

What? What? What'd she say? Muttering. Muttering. Something something.

So fuck you and your untouchable face
And fuck you for existing in the first place.

But what had she said just before that? Janet shut the damn thing off, already overburdened with too much she didn't understand. The engine sputtered, and she flinched, but it pounded on. She checked to make sure the door was shut tight. Her heart was rattling like a child's toy drum. Poor thing, she thought, to soothe its sad little frenzy, while snatching the bottle for one more slug. One for the road. She gulped and sputtered, coughing, and felt a burning need to pee. "I don't think so," she said, and laughed. Wanting to speed things up, maybe even get them over and done with, she revved the gas, regretting that she didn't have a 'lude to knock herself out, as she brought the music back on. This wouldn't take long if she stayed put and hung on until she passed out. She could do that. So what if she pissed all over herself and that was how they found her. Not just dead and weird but sopping and stinking of urine. Oh man, she thought, hating the stupidity of it, just loathing the inconvenience of her idiotic body with its idiotic demands. Shoving the door open, she toppled out and scooted straight ahead to keep from going over on her face. She staggered, listing to her left, then weaved backward a few steps, her hands extended for any support. The empty air filled with bark, and she braced there, hanging on to a thin branch. She hauled her leggings and undies down in one fist and squatted, tilting back for a clear angle. But her balance was utterly, totally treacherous, and she was going to land on her ass, or pee all over her clothes, or probably do both, if she didn't pull at least one leg free, so she hopped and grunted until she lost a shoe but managed the job.

Because she'd left the door open, the dome light threw a faint glow from the interior out into the dark, while the engine grumbled and DiFranco nattered on. At last her bladder released, and the urine she had repressed gushed out. Weeds rattled, while her thighs and butt cheeks glazed over in goose bumps. Something spoke from the dark, where no one could be, and she wished that her piss would hurry up and end. She felt alone and scared, as if anything could happen. Wind muttered, and the undergrowth parted with something wanting to find her, and she felt observed and hunted. She tried to look around. The sharp sound of a breaking stick filled her with the belief that the dark was aroused and moving. She grabbed for her clothing and saw a figure sway and thought of a man and thought she saw him. Someone gangly and tall darting amid branches. Like that reverend jumping in front of their car. Could it be him? Bernice's reverend here? A ripple of movement between two tangles, a shuddering in a patch of light, then the shriek of a bird or something—she didn't know or care what—because when it came again, the cry was ravenous, and she ran for the car with the thing right behind her. It was close, it would catch her, this large gaunt phantom, this lunatic shape that wanted to fling her to the ground so it could stand over her roaring, and it was about to do it, the dread of its fingers reaching, except that she hurled herself into her car, slamming the door, and sat hoping she was safe as she threw the button to lock herself in.

Outside, nothing approached or retreated or hovered. Just the trees. The thing, if it had been there, was gone. She was alone. Just her and DiFranco singing her song. "I'm sorry, Ani," she murmured. It was true. She was sorry, and Ani seemed the person to tell the truth to—how Janet had bartered herself away bit by bit, her willingness to placate and comply betraying what she truly knew and honestly felt, and yet now at last she was free. It was no longer necessary to fulfill her obligations, nor did she have to avoid them, because she would soon be free. She was confessing her essential denial of everything, every moment, every breath. At each instant of surrender, she had smuggled a part of herself to a refuge of defiance deep in her heart. It was sad to have wasted every hour and breath, to have spent her days in deeds she did not accept as her own, to have merely gone through the motions of her life, but it had seemed the only way to escape total defeat.

Shadowy waves were coming out of the woods to enter the car and mix with the gas streaming in. He wanted it like this, whoever had chased her. She'd been running from him for years, just running and running every day of her life, but he'd caught her now. He was coming out of the trees and out of the hose. He was the darkness and he was the gas. *So fuck you and your untouchable face.*

It was as if the car slid off a bridge and struck nose-down into black water. *And fuck you for existing in the first place.* The figure that she need not see to know he was with her began his stifling caress, while the water crashed in through seams and cracks, and he was holding her under. He was pushing her down, but he wasn't alone. They were all with him. They all wanted it done. Wayne and Bobby and Byron and Kevin and some other ones, too, and even Robbie, especially Robbie—especially prudish Robbie—*So fuck you and your untouchable face, and fuck you*—judgmental, mean, selfish Robbie, who wouldn't embrace her and had thrown her aside. But not little Robbie. He still liked her. He was afraid for her. He was alarmed by her circumstances and worried about what was happening, because he didn't understand what was happening, but he didn't quite see how it could have come from her soul. What if it came from those others? The ones who hated her. Little-boy Robbie, gleaming and hopeful and gazing straight into her, and she could not help but stare into the shimmer inside him, and the next thing she knew, she was outside of the car. She lay in the grass, breathing.

30

Oh well, thought Bernice. She was finding it darn hard to sing the new words to the recorded tune. The music was powerful, she had to admit, the lyrics inspiring, but they didn't always make an easy fit, so she had to really put her thinking cap on. Some singers were better off than others, but for all the studying she'd imagined going on, the result at this point was still pretty slipshod. Everybody was too stuck in their ways. Deep down they wanted the hymns they knew by heart. Even the really good singers, the ones in the choir, hadn't figured things out. They were ahead of the game, and Bernice could only wish she sounded half as good. Not that they were satisfied. Not them. They were a bunch of perfectionists. Some even grumbled out loud about how embarrassed they were, because it wasn't right to sing so badly for God at such a moment. Three or four of them were in a clump off to her right, and first one would gripe, and then another would tell them not to be so vain, and then the whole bunch would pray for strength and go back to singing. Bernice could sympathize up to a point, but the truth was that for her, the job of thinking hard to match the words to the notes busied her mind in a way that was a blessing in disguise. It was when the music slowed and ended, as it was doing now, that she ran into trouble. Once things got quiet and all she had to go by was Reverend Tauke's instruction to close her eyes and prepare and pray, she simply couldn't do a thing to get her mind off Irma. Her thoughts might as well have been a bunch of circus clowns piling out with funny hair and horns to honk. Irma, Irma, Irma. Sometimes it was a lot of scolding and regret about the fight they'd had that afternoon. Or it might be some kind of tomfoolery from way back, but whenever or wherever, Irma showed up still a child. Oh, poor Irma!

The music was all but gone, the voices stilled, and she reached for her Bible on the seat beside her. There was a faint final hiss from the speakers and, after a little restlessness and murmuring, total silence. Oh, poor Irma! Oh, poor Irma! Good Lord. Her mind had a mind of its own, and try as she might, there wasn't much she could do about it. It was like this busybody shouting at her every five seconds, this nag dead set on making sure she didn't get a minute's peace. Some fool who couldn't see it was all water over the dam.

Not that actually finding a little calm, as she did now and then, wasn't a mixed blessing, because after a few peaceful seconds, she had one dickens of a time staying awake. Like right now, with her eyelids down and her brain in the dark, she was fighting off sleep. It was way past her bedtime, so she had that excuse, and she'd been through a lot. Nobody could blame her for finding the idea of a little catnap tempting. If somebody had poked her right that second and told her to "wake up" she wouldn't have been surprised, because a while ago when the music cranked up, she had to make a long swim back from somewhere, and she even caught sight of that Creature from the Black Lagoon, rising with her from the deep. She'd had to shake her head so hard to get rid of him that her teeth all but rattled.

Sudden sparking and crackling from the loudspeakers meant the karaoke music was ready to return. She blinked, feeling grateful, and saw Reverend Tauke advancing over the bloodred carpet. "Look at the clocks," he said, "and rejoice. Rejoice as you sing. Prepare as you rejoice."

On the old-fashioned alarm clocks, the hands were too far away for her to make out, and most of the digitals looked underwater, though two had numbers big enough for her to read 11:28 on one, and 11:29 on the other. The little old Timex on her wrist was about the same.

Reverend Tauke was turning in a circle as he approached, like a dark tall floodlight shining on the bunch of them. He was almost next to her, and she wondered if he'd noticed she was there. Some people had begun to sing shyly, while others stalled. Even though the organ and drums were building, it was hard not to worry that he might have more to say. The last thing anybody wanted was to drown him out. She lowered her head over the printed lyrics, thinking she'd give singing a try, but something grabbed at her. When she looked, it was into the dark dots of his eyes above her, flickering with a forceful idea she didn't get. Chills streamed through her as he sailed off, and she wanted to stay glued to him and maybe figure out what had just happened, but she knew better than to gawk.

Eleven twenty-eight, she thought. Or maybe eleven twenty-nine by now. The clocks she checked pretty much matched her guess. One half hour to midnight. The length of a TV sitcom. About the time it took for a quick shop at Eagle's Grocery. About as long as teenage Irma used to tie up the phone, yammering away until it drove Bernice up the wall. And then they'd be gone.

The music had reached full force, the vibrating beat hammering at the congregation. The voices were willing but jittery, while the speakers crackled, buzzing steadily, and the clumsily coordinated effort to harmonize disclosed a ragged desperate edge as everybody grew louder but not much better. Surrounded by this pure, simple striving, Bernice felt miserly, like a negligent bee at the center of a hardworking hive laboring to deliver Reverend Tauke's hymn. She ordered herself to pitch in—to do her duty and sing, and to pray, too, just in case. Just in case?

When the big man beside her groaned, she saw he had his hand over his mouth. His chin jerked to the left, as if he was denying something, but she could tell he had a bad case of nerves, and then he started panting. The scarlet in his cheeks was fever-bright, this overall wildness spreading through him.

"Are you okay?" she whispered.

"I'm . . . hyperventilating . . . sort of."

"You really are."

"I'm sort of . . . woozy . . . even." He plucked a silver pocket watch from inside his jacket.

"Can you stop?"

"I don't . . . want to . . . pass out." He gazed at the watch, like it had the most disappointing face. The two digital alarms that she could make out had moved on to 11:37 and 11:38. Her Timex made it more like 11:39. Ten minutes had flown by quick, she realized, and that pulled the rug out from under her, leaving her insides hollow except for the sensations of an enormous question. Did she really think that in the next minutes it could happen? Did it even matter what she thought? Only to her salvation! That's all it mattered to! Pray, she thought.

"Oh boy," the man said, straining to steady his voice. "I don't know about this. I really don't."

"It's okay," she told him. The windows framed the night, and she wondered what she hoped to see. Black clouds twisting in a sign. The funny green light that comes before a storm. "I bet it would help if you could sing with everybody," she told him. "Can you do that?"

He looked stricken, as if she'd asked him a really tough question that he must answer correctly, but before he found anything worth saying, someone hidden on the other side of him said, "Jesus is Lord, Bill. Jesus is Lord. C'mon, Bill."

"I know." He pivoted away from Bernice.

"So say it," ordered the raspy voice of a woman with the tattered throat of a longtime smoker.

"Jesus is Lord," said Bill.

"Won't be long now."

"Oh boy. Oh boy, Jesus is Lord!"

The makeshift assembly of voices was still a hodge-podge, nerves and uncertainty making everything harder for the singers staggering through the final few notes. But just as they got to the end, the recording, instead of shutting down, jumped back to the beginning, where it started over, drastically louder. With the last few repetitions, Bernice had wondered if the volume was going up, but now she was sure, and the result delivered this feeling of inspiration and momentum commanding the congregation to boost their output. The pews in front of her showed the backs of necks, shoulders, and haircuts in row after row of uplifted heads. She vowed to give it her best shot, warts and all, because once she started bellowing, any chance of her staying on key was headed out the window.

Across the aisle she was able to see faces, and she could honestly claim to have names for most, even if she couldn't bring each and every one to mind. They all sat erect with their eyes upraised like earnest children before a gigantic teacher. And when it struck her that they were starting to sing better, even halfway decent, she found it gratifying and consoling to conclude that all those repetitions were paying off. Maybe their skill was rough and a long way from perfect, but at least it allowed them to show their enthusiasm. Suddenly, Clarence Mulert was sitting there. She'd thought he was dead. But there he was. And just off his elbow, this girl who looked like Irma. Not a spitting image but enough to make Bernice feel somebody had sneaked up and punched her hard in the stomach.

She had to see Hazel before it was too late. We're friends! You hear me! she wanted to shout. Okay? All right? Alice Kuhn was hard to miss, all that floral silliness, like a bouquet in the brown of the pews, but where was Hazel? Khaki shouldn't be hard to find, when there wasn't that much of it. Just Hazel! The problem was a set of burly shoulders blocking Bernice's access to the spot she was sure Hazel occupied, right next to Alice. It was the oldest of the Theilin brothers, the one who was the fireman who fell off the back of the truck when they took that bad corner at Central and Birch on the way to the fire at Zee's Restaurant, and he'd had to retire and go on disability. For a second she saw him and Toby together, the two of them clear as day right in front of her and about to have a conniption arguing. Probably about baseball, or maybe politics. He was Curtis, that's who he was—Curtis Theilin. And then she saw Mrs. Tomlinson in that window and the fire truck in the street, and all the firemen, but not Theilin—he would have been too young, because Bernice was a child in her father's arms, looking up at Mrs. Tomlinson, screaming. Was she ever going to get that out of her head? Probably not if she lived to be a hundred. It was just like him, taking her into all that mess. Probably wanted to let her know how hard the world could be, sirens and fire and screaming. Scared the bejeezus out of her. On the other hand, they couldn't have left her home in her bed, now, could they, her mom and dad, if they wanted to get out to see the show like everybody else was doing. And how could they have ever known that, being so small, she'd remember?

The music cut out. Mid-thump, a mechanical clank eliminated the drums and organ. It felt violent, like an accident, somebody knocking a plug loose or the power failing and leaving nothing. Several singers staggered on but not for long. A high-pitched woman was the last to break off. "Jesus is Lord," said Bernice. "Jesus is Lord." People stirred, restless and jittery.

"What happened?" Bill whispered. "Did something happen?" He rose to his full height, and he was mountainous.

The best she could see, the two digitals were at 11:54 and 56. From somewhere behind them, Reverend Tauke said, "I did that. I turned it off. I'm sorry. I should have warned everyone. The singing was beautiful. It was beautiful, but it's done now."

Darkness fell over them. Night seemed to tumble from above and rise from below. Dense and overwhelming, it poured through the floor and ceiling and walls, dissolving the details of their faces, their bodies, and clothing.

"I've done that, too," said Reverend Tauke. "I've turned off the lights."

Looking around, Bernice saw that they were all becoming shadows. Without the overhead lamps, they had only the moon and stars funneled into shafts by the rectangles of glass. The digitals were eerie glow-in-the-dark smears.

"All right now," Reverend Tauke said, still behind them. "We must all close our eyes and pray."

She wished she didn't feel so alone, but those were her cards. With everyone dead, Toby and her mom and dad, her brother gone, with Hazel stuck on Alice Kuhn and Irma mad at her, who was left? Well, there was Jesus. Reminded of Bill by his hoarse muttering at her elbow, she figured she had him, too, as she took hold of one of his big fingers. "I don't mean to be pushy."

He gave her an anxious pat and then, speaking into the dark to their right, said, "Hang on, Ellie."

"Yep, yep," came the raspy reply.

"And I jumped out of planes," Bill said. "I was a paratrooper. I jumped out of airplanes."

Because she couldn't help herself, Bernice saw a big, winged apparatus zooming into the night. With her eyes pinched shut, she soared
through all kinds of outer-space stuff, galaxies and whatnot, the Milky
Way, other suns, all the stuff people talked about, other planets and me-
teors, until she came to this black that was the end. She could only wonder what went on behind it. Were the angels there, and were they getting
ready? Were their faces full of awe and grit because of the work they knew
they had to do? Did they have to prepare, loosening up with angel calis-
thenics? They reminded her of rough-and-tumble fliers in some old
World War II movie full of people like Bill getting ready to jump out into
the air, and the pilot was Dana Andrews, and they were all steeling their
hearts to do what was necessary, Bill and Dana and their buddies, the
ones who aimed the bombs, and the other ones who sat in those plastic
bubbles with guns sticking out. What was that movie?

At the buzz of the first alarm, Bill yelped and just about broke her
wrist, grabbing and hanging on. Then came a shrill beep and the squawk
of something stomped on over and over. A panicky bell jangled crazily,
and another, harsher clanging chimed in. Bernice opened her eyes and
saw dozens of people on their feet. A beep and a screech and a third bell
shoved their way into the thronging, earsplitting warnings. It was all
warning, warning, warning, filling the thunderous hollow of the old barn
until it quaked. She got to her feet. Everybody was doing it—standing
and groaning or sighing or praying. Bill stood beside her. Too short to
see, she begged him, "What's going on?"

"I don't know!"

He sounded angry but was probably just trying to make himself heard.
One woman kept asking if they'd been left behind. Did it go somewhere
else? Didn't Jesus want them? People were shushing her, while others told
her, "No, no," and one man shouted, "Have some patience, Esther!"

Was it Esther Huegel? Or was there some other Esther? It didn't
sound like Esther Huegel, but the woman was real upset, and maybe
Esther sounded like this other person when she was whining in a heartbroken voice that they were doomed to suffer the chastisement. "The

Antichrist," she sobbed. "The Antichrist." People soothed her like they would a suffering animal. "No, no. No, no."

Without waiting for the din of the clocks to lessen, a dozen other voices called to Reverend Tauke, like his name was a difficult question. Right across the aisle, Ross Houtakker wiped his face with the same gesture he'd used when he was about twelve and Bernice saw him step in front of a bus that stopped inches short of running him down. Some of the congregation had jammed into the aisle, bumping about like cows in a chute, and the more folks that did it, the more that wanted to do it. Everybody was trying to see better, all of them desperate for something, almost anything. With so much shouting and jostling added to the blood-curdling beeping and buzzing, the place was bedlam.

"What do you see? What's out there?"

A young boy stood on the windowsill, peering out through his hands circled against the glass.

"Jordy! Is anything out there?"

He was turning to answer when Reverend Tauke appeared. Maybe the light was too thin or the gloom distorting, the combination playing tricks with her eyes, so Bernice didn't know what she was seeing, or maybe Reverend Tauke actually looked as if something hurt really bad. His big hand shut on the boy's ankle. "You sit down, Jordy," he said, and then he shouted, "Everyone! Sit!"

As the congregation scurried back to the pews, Bernice became aware that a number of the alarms had gone silent. Others were running out of steam. By the time the crowd was seated and their scramble to obey had begun to slow and soften, only a couple of the bells, along with a weird lone beeping, still hung on. Everyone grew hushed. Reverend Tauke had his back to them. He studied the outside world through the haze of the window or, for all Bernice knew, stared right through the wall. The last bell stuttered. The beeping weakened so gradually, it was hard to be sure when it ended.

Silence poured in from above and below, as if the task begun by the dark minutes ago was to be finished by stillness. Bernice and everyone around her sat breathless and waiting, staying put, while doubt, worry, and fear prowled the aisles and the chapel transformed into a haunted house, ghostly and quiet. They were all just sitting there. All these lumps. Just all these lumps sitting there—Reverend Tauke and his flock. Like they were the vestal virgins not welcomed by the host. The door shut on them. The bridegroom locking them out. She felt bad for Reverend Tauke and bad for everyone around her. In fact, she felt bad for everybody on earth, everybody alive or who had ever lived in the whole history of the earth.

Reverend Tauke was pacing. He crossed the dais and came back through the dimness. He hovered at the pulpit, disappeared near the altar. He wandered into view once again, shoving the shadows around. She worried he was fighting back tears but then realized a man a few rows ahead was sobbing quietly. With a quick shift, he faced them, pointing a long arm and finger in anger, she felt, or disappointment, though she couldn't see his eyes. His spreading arms wanted to remind them that he was there, and that if he strode away in the next seconds, it would be because something important was calling to him. "Tell me what you're thinking," he said.

Surprise erupted around her. Confusion and shyness spread through the dark.

"What?" said one, and another one said, "What'd he say?"

"I want to know what you're thinking."

Shock was everywhere, gasps and sighs, at least some of it hers. Not in a million years would she have guessed those would be his words, and clearly, she was not the only one taken aback. She heard whispering and urgent hushed arguments, but no one spoke up to answer him, and as the minutes passed, she started thinking maybe no one would. But then a youthful voice asked from somewhere, "Should we turn the lights back on?"

"What for? What will we see? What would we see that we haven't already seen?" He leaned into movement that floated him all the way to the sacristy wall.

"Reverend Tauke?"

"Yes."

"Maybe we should listen to the radio."

"No." He found this question even more worthless. "No."

"I mean, just send a person out to one of the cars." The voice was familiar, but Bernice couldn't put a name to it. "That's all I mean. I'd volunteer to go. Just to see if it happened somewhere else."

"No."

"I mean, it didn't happen."

"I know."

"We're still here."

"Yes, we are."

"So shouldn't we find out what happened or didn't in other places? Wouldn't that help?"

"Help what? Our faith? Our need for faith? I don't see how knowing about strangers could help."

"Oh." The man sounded deflated and unfairly embarrassed as he sank from sight, his name on the tip of Bernice's tongue. "Thank you."

"Anyone else?" said Reverend Tauke. She wished she could see his expression. "Anything at all."

"I'm sorry! I'm checking my radio!" It was the same man, springing back up. "Because I have to say, we need to know. It's important to me to know what happened, and I think it might be to some others." He was a shadow pushing past neighboring shadows to get out of his pew. "Excuse me, excuse me," he said, and she recognized Curtis Theilin. "I just need to know what's going on. And if that's too much to ask, I'm sorry."

"You should be," someone scolded.

"Curtis, don't go," a woman called.

"Don't be scared—don't be a doubting Thomas," said a thin-voiced man clearly trying not to sound holier-than-thou.

"Curtis, please. Now, you just think twice." It was Esther Huegel, Curtis's half sister, and by the sound of things, she wasn't the one who'd been whining before.

"This has gone on long enough is what I know, Esther. That's what I know, and I'm glad to be saying it." He didn't sound all that glad or all that sure of himself. "And I have thought twice. More than twice—I'd hate to count how many times, Esther—but maybe it's time we face facts."

"How would you know?" said a man Bernice was ninety-nine percent sure was Edith Fritsch's husband, Otto. "Speak for yourself!"

"That's what I think I'm doing. Pretty darn sure of it."

"He doesn't speak for me, Reverend Tauke," said Otto.

"I'm not trying to. That's what I just said, I think. But if there's anybody feels the way I do, they are welcome to come along."

"Just go if you're going!"

"Fine by me, Otto. I don't know how I got mixed up in all this mess, anyway."

As he thumped to the door, Bernice searched lanes and angles through the crowd to keep an eye on him. She expected Reverend Tauke to put a stop to this ruckus the way he could any second now by stepping in and saying something meaningful, or by using that booming voice he could call on to send Curtis scurrying back to his seat. But the door separated from its framing, and moonlight dropped a white slash across Curtis as he stood alone at the edge of a moody strangeness waiting outside.

Bullying and mad as a hornet, Esther railed, "You just watch out you don't step out there into a whirlwind!" She was rumbling up the carpet straight at him, and there was little room to miss that she aimed to scare him into staying or chase him from the premises. "You better hope you're not walking into a Mixmaster out there!"

"You oughta come with me, Esther. That's what you ought to do."

"I'm talking about angels like a swarm of yellow jackets!"

"Fine by me!"

The door wheeled closed only to jiggle and bounce partway open. Something outside pushed it shut, securing it firmly this time.

Amid confusion, figures rose and fell, some fussing where they sat, while others paced. Esther covered her eyes with her hands, and several women guided her off, and Bernice turned her demand for answers on Bill, because the way Curtis had carried on was so half-baked and bullheaded, only another male of the species could make sense of it. However, Bill was facing forward with an intensity that turned her like a finger pointing, and there was Reverend Tauke, featureless in the dark, near the edge of the dais, but she could tell he was giving the whole bunch of them the once-over. Something in his posture marked him as ready to speak, and so the longer he stayed mute, the more nerve-racking it was to wait.

"Anyone else?" he asked, sounding relaxed, almost amused.

Another burst of freewheeling uncertainty raced from pew to pew, with everybody checking everybody else out, because the search was on for somebody fit and willing to speak up, or maybe just willing, fit or not.

"Here's what I'm thinking," said a man who took to his feet a couple rows up from Bernice. "Here's the way I'm going to look at this thing." It was Robert Turner, best known for running for mayor and losing way back. "I just think that to pinpoint such a thing like you've been trying to do has to be one of the hardest things ever for somebody to know exactly. And Reverend Tauke—I think we have to have faith in you no matter what. That's my honest opinion. I've weighed the pros and cons as well as the next man, and I'm no genius, but I've been around, and I've rubbed elbows with the best of them. Ongoing faith no matter what. That's the formula. And if Curtis Theilin wants to be a turncoat, well, there's not much anybody can do except shed a tear. What's there to say about him except he doesn't have faith, which is the thing you were saying we have to have a minute ago, and it's the thing I'm saying, too. We have to have faith in you, and you, Reverend Tauke— Well, you have to have faith in yourself most of all."

"Thank you."

"I second that, Reverend," said somebody from so far away that his few words didn't give Bernice time to locate him, let alone recognize him.

"Here's what we must do," said Reverend Tauke in a calm, steady whisper, and naturally enough, those words and the way he was unmoving and hard to see whetted the appetite of every soul listening. Like wheat in a field with the wind at their backs, they tilted toward him, and Bernice could all but hear their swarming, dithering thoughts, as if they were all one big head, and this head was full of questions no one dared ask. They were toeing the line, maybe gritting their teeth, maybe biting their nails, but hanging on, because he'd just announced he was going to tell them what to do.

"I appreciate what you are saying," Reverend Tauke went on, though still way too hushed and hesitant and, of all things, stopping again. More silence was the last thing anybody wanted from him. Bill was clicking his teeth and banging his fists against each other, bringing to mind little men fighting in front of his big chest.

"Guidance," said Reverend Tauke. "And so now I ask for quiet and prayers. And for guidance. If we deserve it. Prayers for instruction. We need instruction. And I feel that tonight, at this moment, it may not come to me. It may come to me, but it also may come to one of you." He paced to the side, long slow strides carrying him through vagueness and quiet.

Bernice didn't believe she'd heard correctly, or if she had, she just didn't have the smarts to know what he meant, and that was pretty much everybody's reaction, if she judged by the puzzled whispers, the stunned and confused comments and half-comments. Still calm and collected, he said, "If Jesus speaks to anyone here—anyone at all—then He speaks to all of us. Okay? Do you see? That's what I mean." He squared his mysterious outline to them. "We must all open our hearts and listen with our hearts. And pray that we hear the truth if it's offered." He sailed toward the pulpit but then passed on until, at the wall, he folded into the large wooden chair that he occupied whenever there were other speakers during a service.

Instantly, Robert Turner stood and asked, "Are you telling us to pray, Reverend, and be quiet and think that maybe Jesus might speak to one of us?"

"Yes."

"So you're saying that Jesus might speak to any one of us."

"To help us understand what we're to do." Reverend Tauke slumped like a bundle of old clothes, bowing into solitary prayer, and yet the authority he put into his voice let them know that though he was done with them for the moment, they must obey. "Quiet now. And pray."

Bernice's first thought was, Boy, am I in over my head. For the next few minutes, she tried to settle and get comfortable. The surrounding murk shook with sighs, some deep, others shallow, with throats clearing, bodies rearranging, a fit of coughing that went from this one to that one, the creak of some floorboards, the groan of a pew, all fading. Her wish for enough light to read her Bible was hopeless, she knew, but the feeling guided her to the idea of trying to recall the words of a psalm. Which would be best? She knew there was one she really wanted to summon up, and vowing to find it, she set about searching. But she remembered instead sitting on the curb in front of her childhood home, and the way other kids came along, wanting to play with her. Sometimes the game was hide-and-seek. Or sometimes hopscotch, if there was chalk and a place to draw the squares on the sidewalk. She saw the white lines scratched on the gray. She remembered throwing her marker. She remembered balancing on one foot and hopping.

"Reverend Tauke," someone said.

"Yes."

"I'm sorry. Nothing."

Waking to her distraction, she took up the Lord's Prayer, reciting it from start to finish and then repeating it a second time and a third, while drifting into a memory of all her dogs and cats in bed with her, like she was a doll surrounded by living toys.

"Reverend Tauke?"

"Yes."

"I think Jesus wants us to issue a worldwide warning that the scriptural predictions are coming. The burning cleansing of the earth with fire, unless mankind makes a change and changes his sinful ways." It was Raymond Frunke, taking a big breath in order to handle what came next. "I think—and I'm not sure here, but I think there's going to be a miracle, and we're supposed to point it out, and it will be right before the chastisement, but if it's seen—the miracle—if we point it out and recall God's children to a holy life, well then, that will be the warning, but if it isn't heeded, He will have to proceed with the chastisement."

"Do you have a sense of the miracle? Do you know what it is?"

"No. But somebody else might."

Reverend Tauke waited. Bernice could feel him holding the opportunity open, and when no one spoke, he said, "Anything else, Raymond?"

"No."

"All right, then. Let's return to the quiet."

Bernice thought of a cornfield. She looked from on high over acres of gigantic plants that surprised her with the memory of a magical kingdom she had made with her own hands as a child when she had been so jealous of Madge Stallman who lived down the street and had a Fisher-Price magic castle that Madge's parents, who liked to show off, had spent a ton of money on at Woolworth's. It wasn't that Bernice didn't know how to make do and get by on next to nothing, but Madge's trees were detailed and shiny, with perfect green leaves, and the castle walls were painted perfectly to look like real blocks of rough gray stone, while hers were from cardboard, the colors from crayons.

"I think what Jesus wants us to know is that the reason we didn't go tonight was our prayers. The way all of us prayed so hard and long, and together those prayers changed things in the world—or the universe, even—in a way we don't understand. Probably can't ever, really. I mean understand." It was a woman way up front, one of the real strong singers, and very tall. "But it was like in a balance where the weight on one side had us ready to go, and then our prayers changed it. Our prayers changed the balance of the light and the dark in the world and the good and the evil, and so— Well, the weight changed back to more, even. And it could still happen. That's still in the picture, like the Bible says. Not tonight but later. If the dark and evil come back bigger again, we might be taken off. 'For whatsoever is born of God overcometh the world: and this is the victory that overcometh the world, even our faith.'"

"Thank you," said Reverend Tauke.

"Do you think that's right, Reverend Tauke?"

She could feel expectation everywhere around her, the hopes of people on the rise and hanging by a thread, the puzzlement in their minds beating the air with longing for him to answer. It was like they were all one big body hungry for more, starving for more, but her gut feeling was that Reverend Tauke wasn't going to give anything further just now, so she closed her eyes and: Holy cow, she thought. Good Lord. There was somebody there. Who's that? And then she saw the slightly disappointed expression. What had she done now? Because it was Jesus. He was right there staring at her, and He wasn't movie-star handsome, like she might have expected. He was kind of scary and intense, with eyes you wanted to look into but at your own risk. And dark. Dark-complexioned. Dark hair, black beard, and these piercing eyes. That'd be the word for them. Fiery was the feeling He gave off, somebody full of gumption. Not a leading-man type, and yet He really made you want to look at Him.

Never more excited in her life, she wondered if everybody was seeing Him, and she was tempted to open her eyes. Would He still be there, hanging out in the air over the congregation, if she looked? But what if He wasn't and she lost him? What if trying to satisfy her curiosity made her miss out on learning the secret behind the powerful way He was studying her? She gazed at Him, and He was a sight for sore eyes, and she felt strongly, though not without some doubt, that He wanted her to wait just as she was, and so she did it. She waited.

And then he said, *Bernice.*

What?

His glance was stern but not harsh. Disappointed and fierce, as she'd first thought, but not unforgiving, and he said, *Really, Bernice. A split-tail beaver? What were you thinking?*

I know, I know.

To let it go on so long. Poisoning your beloved child. Poisoning her soul.

She opened her eyes and looked into the dark. *I know.*

A split-tail beaver, Bernice. How could you?

Oh, Lord.

"Reverend Tauke."

"Yes."

"Reverend Tauke."

"Yes."

"I have to go, Reverend Tauke. Jesus wants me to go. He wants me to go make things up with my daughter."

"Is that you, Bernice?"

"Yes. Yes, it is."

"Go where, Bernice? No, no. I think you must be quiet and pray. We need you here."

"That's what I was doing. And I'm supposed to try and make amends."

"In what way?"

"In the sense of bad blood between us. I should fix it up. I'm gonna go. All right? Is it all right?"

"Bernice, please. You must sit down. We need everyone here."

"But He told me." She had drifted into the aisle, where there was just enough moonlight on the bloodred carpet to make her look down at her feet. She was an old lady, that was all, and she knew it, with something churning in her broken old heart. "It's okay, Reverend Tauke. It's okay."

He stood, and the dark washed around him like smoke, a fragment of moonlight showing his somber expression. He gestured toward the baptismal fount. "Do you remember climbing those stairs, Bernice?" The area he indicated was so densely shadowed, it could have been anything. "Do you remember you were baptized?"

"Yes."

"Do you believe in Jesus, Bernice?"

Looking back to the way that, seconds ago, Jesus had known her so well, and the wisdom of what He had told her, she said, "Yes, I do."

"Well, that's the main thing. But I must warn you. Beware damnation."

She figured she was supposed to respond, and she wanted to, but there seemed to be way too many choices, and most of them liable to stir up trouble, so she held her tongue, until she realized that even though nothing was safe, she had to say something. "Okay."

"God bless you, Bernice."

Her backward step was hesitant. "God bless *you*, Reverend Tauke." She emphasized "you" to underscore how much more valuable he was than she could ever be, but aloud, the word made her cringe. It seemed to say she believed he needed her praise. "I'm sorry," she said.

"I just hope you understand what I'm telling you." He sounded worried, and she saw how she was adding to his burdens, piling on aggravation. "I hope you're telling the truth about why you're leaving us now."

"Oh, yes."

"I hope you're not lying, Bernice. Because the Rapture will come one day, and whether we know that day ahead of time or not, it will sweep us all away to terrible judgment. And then to heaven or to hell."

Her fingers found the door handle, and for the briefest instant, she anticipated stepping out into a ruined world, an apocalyptic vista with smoke in spirals above a blasted landscape, but instead she was under the bright moon, the star-sprinkled sky, the serene pasture above the tidy rows of cars bathed in shimmer.

She wanted to get a move on, but the stiffness in her knees kept her from picking up much speed. Her car looked miles off, and then her heart wobbled and seemed to twist sideways. She stopped, wondering what came next. One worried breath led to another, until her heart found a way to end its little bout of indecision, and she tottered on down the hill to the parking lot. Her poor old Chevy was too far behind the times to operate off one of those push-button gadgets, like Hazel's little beauty. She would have to get in the old-fashioned way, making sure to be careful on the uneven gravel and potholes, and then inserting the key, which was what she was doing when the chapel windows erupted with light. Dumbfounded as to what could be happening, she stared. Then the door sprang wide to release the crowd on a chute of light. She was so blurry-eyed and off her rocker, she thought she was staring at a mob bursting out to chase her down and drag her back. Or maybe it was a bolt of lightning fired from deep inside the church, dangerous and blinding, or maybe like heaven on TV, it was a blazing tunnel with her friends and relatives flowing toward her, body and soul. And was Isabel among them? Sailing over to reminisce about the hours they'd spent trying to pick out the right dress to wear to the dance, or when they were pregnant, or when they were each other's maids of honor, or that time they learned how to make fudge when they were just kids reading from a cookbook in Isabel's mother's kitchen.

But the figure coming toward her, having split from the ranks of the crowd, was Hazel. Bernice jumped in and started the engine. It was difficult backing up, because the slot was tight, and Hazel's voice found her, calling from somewhere she couldn't see, "Bernice, wait up! Wait up!"

She took off down the lane and was almost far enough that she could start thinking she was going to make it when Hazel all but fell in front of her. It was hit the brakes or run her down. Good Lord, she thought, almost bouncing off the steering wheel as she fought to stop. Hazel wobbled on quite a ways and seemed to have a lot of trouble slowing down.

Bernice cranked open the window. "Are you trying to get yourself killed, Hazel?"

"I'd just as soon you didn't yell at me first thing. I'm so tired I can't see straight."

Hazel's red leather jacket gaped crookedly, revealing her blazer undone from top to bottom over her rumpled gold blouse. She arrived at the door and sighed, her breath close to awful. Black splotchy skin under her bloodshot eyes gave her the look of somebody not long for this world. "You don't look all that well."

"Lemme in the car to sit down."

"I got to go."

"I need to sit down."

While Hazel staggered around to the passenger side, Bernice glanced at the wandering flock. Along the path, beams of flashlights had sprung up. Hazel had the door open when Bernice wondered, "What's going on, anyway? Did he call it a night?"

"Bathroom break. We're due back in fifteen minutes. How long till you get back?"

"I haven't even left yet, in case you haven't noticed."

Hazel flopped in beside her, and together they contemplated the knots of mostly women parading toward the parsonage. With the chapel lights ablaze, men could be seen roving in a widening circle to find enough darkness to let them pee in the grass.

"We're halfway sleep-deprived, the bunch of us," said Bernice.

"That's what I'd like to know. How do you think you're going to make that drive all the way to Sayersville at such an hour?"

"I don't feel that bad."

Hazel looked painfully uncomfortable, her stiff leather coat so askew that the right side of the collar jabbed into her cheek. "It's the middle of the night and a hard thirty miles any way you slice it. And you're going to have to cross over that crazy fool bridge with all those holes. You'll never make it."

"Hazel," she said. The bridge Hazel was thinking of had terrified them as kids. Daredevils, they'd stuck their heads out of car windows, scaring themselves silly by looking down through the thousands of quarter-size holes forged in the steel under their wheels and on to the gray shifting river far below. But it didn't exist anymore. A different bridge had been built at least twenty years ago. "You know that thing's long gone."

Hazel sat blinking and eyeing something she really didn't like. It disgusted her, and then she said, "Is that what you think you're going to do, though, drive that whole way to Sayersville?"

"Yes, I am."

Hazel's expression lost most of its sympathy. "Because Jesus said so."

"That's right."

All of a sudden Hazel was desperate to fasten her blazer, squinting and getting several holes and buttons quickly mismatched, and when she saw just how badly she'd started off, she shook her head at Bernice like the whole thing was her fault. "You'll fall asleep at the wheel, Bernice, then what? We're too old to be keepin' these kinda hours."

"Maybe that's why I'd like to get going."

"You'll end up in a ditch, you mark my words."

"I figure He'll keep an eye on me."

"Is that the thing? Jesus made it sound like there wasn't a second to waste, and you just had to jump right to it."

The way Hazel was tugging and jerking and lifting her fanny to fix the problem of her jacket before getting back to her blazer made absolutely clear that she was as pigheaded as ever.

"Hazel," Bernice said, "will you just get out of the car and let me be on my way?"

"Don't you start picking on me. You got to be nice to me, Bernice. I got to pee bad. I'm sitting here with you, so tired I can't see straight. You start giving me a hard time, I'll just go to pieces. I swear it. I'm giving you fair warning. I can't hardly stand it. I'm on my last legs. I'll pee my pants. I will."

"Well, go on to the bathroom and pee, if you have to so bad. Nobody's stopping you."

"I'd like to, believe me." She was in a struggle, all right, squirming and bouncing her legs.

"I hope you at least had the good sense to put on one of those Depends we got you."

"When would I have had a chance?"

"Don't you pee in my car, you hear me."

"I ain't makin' any promises."

"It's a junker, I admit, but it's not your pisspot."

"Just tell me what I want to know. I can't do all this without some help."

"All what?"

"If the angels show up, I'll tell 'em you're on the road to Sayersville. I'll tell them what you're driving and that you'll end up over at Irma's. What's her address?"

"Hazel."

"What?"

"I think you're sort of delirious."

"Sayersville, Wisconsin. I'm gonna make sure he hears me. Okay?"

Bernice weighed the merits of rolling with the punches against what might come from trying to clear things up. "Okay," she said.

"They'll have to stick a fistful of feathers in my mouth to shut me up. Did you tell me Irma's address?"

"Twenty-three MacDougal Street."

"It feels sort of military, doing this. All this organizing who's gonna be where when."

"You're dressed for it," she said, knowing she shouldn't have, but she just couldn't stop herself.

"What?"

"I had that thought myself earlier."

"Did you now?"

"It's not going to happen, Hazel."

Hazel's eyes were little slits stuffed away inside her sickly cheeks. Her distress had slowed to a gentle rocking, the urge lessening the way Bernice knew it could, just going away as sneakily as it had struck in the first place. Rubbing her fists in her puffy red eyes, Hazel looked like a four-year-old fighting against sleep. She seemed to have missed Bernice's last remark, which was probably just as well, since Bernice had startled herself, blurting it out like that.

"I can tell you one thing, Bernice Doorley. You caused quite a commotion back there, sayin' that stuff to Reverend Tauke."

"I suppose."

"Everybody heard."

"I guess they did."

"Let me assure you. They did." Bleary and brittle, Hazel tried to come up with a commanding tone. "So I guess you're just going to speak your mind from here on out, and let the chips fall where they may." She rested against the window, and her ragged sigh whispered meekly of a grim sort of notion she didn't much care for. "And it is, too, going to happen, Bernice. It is, too. It's gotta."

"Why."

"I don't know. It's just gotta."

Turned away, Hazel appeared to be mulling the night, unless her eyes were shut, which they well could be. Bernice had no way of knowing. And then Hazel twitched and started jiggling, the call of nature back with the force of a seizure. "I think that's why Reverend Tauke is keeping us here so late. He thinks so, too—that it's gonna happen for sure, but he's just shy to say it, and who could blame him?"

Bernice felt like she'd been holding her tongue for years. She wanted to wipe the slate clean. Maybe it was late in the game, but she could still break out a fresh deck. "Hazel, I have to tell you something. It just don't seem right not to. Now, this may not be the moment, and I hope you don't take it too much to heart and get all broken up about it, but I don't like you as much as you like me."

"That's all right."

"No, it's not."

"It is with me."

"How can it be all right? What's wrong with you?"

"Nothing's wrong with me."

"Are you so out of it you don't know what I'm telling you?"

"It's not that hard to follow, and it's not exactly the big news you seem to think it is. You just have to get used to it, Bernice. I like you. You got to put up with it."

"So you don't mind in the least."

"I guess I don't."

Bernice was surprised to find Hazel's unlikely reaction stirring a whole lot of something she didn't know she had much of, this sudden keen interest in puzzles and loose ends, an inclination that she guessed would have been philosophical in somebody else. "So, Hazel," she said, "if you like me so much, what's all this fuss about Alice Kuhn? She seems to be the one you can't stand being apart from for more than ten seconds."

"I like her, too. I have a big heart. I like the both of you. It's just my nature. You of all people ought to know that." She shouldered her way out of the car with a grunt. "I really gotta go pee."

She hobbled off. Watching for a second, and free to leave, Bernice slipped the old Chevy into gear. She nodded in Hazel's direction as she was about to pass by, but then Hazel waved frantically for Bernice to stop and roll down her window. Bernice had to laugh at herself for being fool enough to obey. "What now?"

"Don't take any wooden nickels."

"I'll try not to."

"Don't let the bedbugs bite."

Bernice chuckled and waved, on her way at last. But with the end of the driveway coming up fast, she felt called to slow down, and then she was parked, looking back. She saw the church on the hill, bits and pieces of people adrift, and then a kind of fantastic shape that could have been Hazel and was maybe looking out and signaling farewell. Without worrying whether she was right or not, she got back to business, heading off.

31

JANET WAS PUZZLED. IT WAS her, all right. She was standing naked in a narrow hallway with dim patches of wallpaper and furniture that were hard to place and yet not completely strange. In fact, they belonged to her apartment. She was naked, looking at her reflection in the hallway mirror. She was somewhere between her kitchen and bedroom. Her head ached. Her vision flickered, making everything wavy and trembling, but she was actually there. Her pale legs jutted out from dimly depicted hips in her glassy duplicate. One reason she was naked was because her clothing lay all over the floor. Bending to pick up her leggings, she needed several half-skipping adjustments to keep her balance, and her brain slammed against her skull. Accompanied by faint rattling, numerous pellets poked into the bare soles of her feet. Advil pills dotted the linoleum. A blue aluminum tumbler lay nearby. How long had she been back? She meandered in a slow circle, wondering and guessing and worrying without a clear idea what the issues were, or the uncertainties, until she fixed on the question of time. Circular and white-faced, the answer was a clock on the wall. She wanted to remember what had happened, and she did and didn't, glimpsing Robbie in his kitchen, in his bedroom, recalling being lost in Homestead Development, and seeing it all through a splintery window of cold regret and horror. It was 12:11, and she was home.

Sinking into the big armchair by the back window, she felt the forest fall jaggedly over her in a mix of shadow and enough moonlight for her to sort the leggings, her underwear, one sock. They seemed recently uncovered relics from a life lived in a dark age, clues to her lost history un-readable except in grass stains, dirt smears, tatters in the knees. She couldn't really see in the feeble light sneaking around the hallway corner where a single ceiling fixture burned, and she wished even that was off. She didn't know or care why, but she wanted the dark. Somehow she had managed to drive home, passing through disorder and dissonance, frac-tured events, abrupt starts and stops. But she had known to go slowly. Al-ways slowly. Everything slowly. Drive slowly. Think slowly. Speak with great care. Remember that the river of gray was in fact concrete—that the river of gray was in fact a road. At the drive-through window, she knew to try hard to speak as if each word were important, rather than cumber-some and awkward to use. "One . . . large . . . coffee . . . black . . . please." Every now and then the road lost its form, dissolving into currents she had to master as they swam left and swam right, and she had to cling hard to the wheel and hope she was really steering.

She remembered a wedge of Sunoco gas station in the spill of an anomalous streetlight, warning her to beware with a random jolt that was not random at all, for it had led her to spy the nose of the patrol car beside the shut-down convenience store. This cop and his lurking ambush had prompted her to swallow in a way that promised to aid focus. She'd gulped repeatedly, struggling for the dexterity to get by at a speed that would not attract his attention. Neither too fast nor too slow. She pictured him fol-lowing her, his blue-and-white vehicle whispering to a halt on the street outside her apartment. His hunt for her would have begun as an after-thought. Instinct, seeing to her core, would have dispatched him.

Even in her frazzled state, she did not fully believe he was walking to-ward her door. But she was finding it impossible to refute her fear with-out proof that he was not out there, was not going to knock. Along the way, she turned off the hall light and, raising the bedroom blinds, sur-veyed the neighborhood. The vista was one of moonlight, streetlight, resting vehicles, quiet houses. Only her Honda sat below, no red swirl on its roof, the slightly crooked angle at which it was parked the lone indica-tion of the bedlam she had passed through in order to return to her apartment and the window where she knelt peering out.

But how had she gotten out of Homestead? The details of her escape were a blank, and the work of trying to fill them in made her head hurt. Her pulses hammered on sheet-thin bone. She lay back on the floor and closed her eyes. She could not remember getting out, yet she could see other elements vividly, such as that old guy on his fucking power walk, and then a little road between unfinished houses. And Robbie. The duct tape, the hose. What she had almost done. Fucking DiFranco. The hard work of crawling under the car, the labor of stuffing the window. She had a semblance of everything, all of it jagged and exaggerated, surreal and excruciatingly intimate, except for why she was still alive. She had no idea what had moved her out of the car.

Awakening was a jolt, and she yelped as if shaken by what turned out to be the dark thrown together with heartsick sensations and terrible thirst. She hiccuped and started crying. It was a smattering of tears and a contorted noise without much emotion, other than what she felt in response to her view of herself as a piteous mess. At the sink, she drank and wondered whether she would be able to stomach anything if she tried to eat. And sleep. She needed sleep. But she should eat, even if only a bite or two. Her body craved something. Vitamins, maybe. She had some in the cabinet. And sleep. And more water. She gulped, taking in vitamins with a second big overflowing tumbler, and then, shuffling toward her bedroom, she broke into pointless sobs. She was hungry. Janet was hungry. Janet wanted to eat. Why couldn't she eat?

She felt conspicuous in the framing glow of the open refrigerator. The escaping cold made her shiver as she located a small strawberry yogurt and a loaf of bread. While waiting for two slices to brown in the toaster, she sat with oat bran in a bowl. Wary that milk might make her throw up, she used water and chomped away. A small spoonful of yogurt was followed by a larger portion, but her head was lowering onto the table's cool surface, where she settled, resting on her folded arms. Dissolution released a sigh that turned at the last second into a snore. Something emitted a click and a pop, and she was puzzled enough to stand and stare at the bread poking up from the toaster before staggering to her bedroom. She wrestled her way under the blanket and sank away with her knees tucked to her chest.

It was some time later that Wayne honked outside. She rose and followed him in her Honda, because she knew what he wanted. She had to make a U-turn on a cobblestone road and take several corners sharply, and she almost lost him, barely glimpsing the turn he made into the mall, and when she arrived, the vast parking lot was empty. Everyone was gone. Except for a hearse arriving and parking, and the men in black clothes who raised the coffin from the pavement and slid it through the gaping rear doors. But then one of them saw it was empty, and they showed it to her. The men carried Janet from her car to the coffin and put her inside. They drove off to bury her in Diana's grave, while a man and woman spoke somberly with British accents. But it made no sense. Because she was home in bed. Her car was parked out front. When she argued these points only to discover that they wouldn't listen, she decided she would explain everything to herself. They were heartless fucking monsters!

She opened her eyes. She felt inexplicably triumphant. She filled with pride. Because she had escaped them. She had defied them. She had beaten every fucking man who'd ever messed with her, Bobby and Wayne and Robbie. That cop lying in ambush. She'd fooled him. Fooled them all. And crazy Jamal. Her alarm clock read 4:42. A hand stroked her cheek and then rose, becoming a gentle patting sensation on the top of her head. But all around her, the room was empty. Hanging on her closet door was the pale stream of her nightgown, and she pulled it on before flopping back down, where her hope for more sleep was stymied by her busy mind, because she shouldn't have included Jamal. Even though he'd thrown that can at her. And Big Baby Dog didn't belong, either. But she didn't think she'd actually included him. And the way Jamal had waved his dick at her was almost cute. She had to laugh, her lips puckering up in pretend sympathy, as if she were playing with a baby who might cry. The memory of Big Baby Dog in the hardware store made her feel sad because he seemed like her friend. And maybe he was her friend. Along with Brenda. Even Jamal. Because if she was honest, the time spent at their house was pretty much the best part of her day. Wasn't that a joke? Her faint little smile was seasoned with irony, because they weren't her friends and she knew it, but whatever they were, they'd been open to her and welcoming and tolerant and accepting, letting her crash on their couch and then watch that tape of Lady Di. Making jokes and sharing what they had, no questions asked, offering kindness and generosity, even giving her that pipe and the crack. Which was out there in her car.

She sat up. She stood and walked to the window. Her Honda waited at the curb. She put on her robe and then had to endure an annoying, stupid search for her keys. They finally showed up on a kitchen chair, where she guessed they'd fallen after she'd probably dropped them on the table when she walked in. It was a moment she could almost recall. While placing a chair to prop open the door so it could not swing shut and lock her out the way it had before, she complimented herself on the care she was taking, the sensible way she was proceeding.

Quietly, she glided down the stairs and on through the ghostly pre-dawn to her car. She reached into the trash bag fastened to the headrest on the passenger seat. The folded cardboard cup was right where she'd hidden it. Big Baby Dog's gift waited inside. Oh yes, she thought, reminded that her escape from Homestead had been a matter of good luck, too. She'd ripped the hose loose, gotten the Honda moving, and returned to the streets, where she had simply chanced upon a car pulling out from a garage. Falling in behind it, the rest was easy. A few turns, and they were out of Homestead.

Seated at her kitchen table, she mimicked Brenda, reviewing her lesson, even hearing her words. The rock into the glass right below the screen. Then the touch of the match and the tilt. What had Big Baby Dog called Brenda? A Rockette? That was funny. Just a little rotation and the deep, deep breath. In spite of the scorch in her chest, she struck a second match to do it all again, but the boom of pleasure stopped her. Sweetness richer and more textured than anything she'd ever known transfixed her with the first of all wonders, a seed and flowering of delight let loose through a tiny, tucked-away trapdoor never before opened in the roof of her brain. Channels and circuitry carried her upward through interconnected gateways and membranes to bounty and goodness and love. And not just ordinary love but true love, so that everything she'd ever dreamed of and needed was waiting when she arrived, everything she adored. A long, blissful trance of paranormal warmth and paranormal serenity. And animals, too. Deer and bears. Cougars and rabbits and antelopes. Dogs and cats, all waiting, all watching. Even cattle safe in a field. She should have been a veterinarian. She really should have. Why hadn't she? Maybe she still could. They were visitors from a distant world, all these animals, emissaries of loss and migration and otherworldly translation. They were like angels, or maybe they were angels and it was happening to her. She was the one and they'd come for her. She thought of Bernice, and she wanted to telephone Bernice. She looked for the phone, wanting to call Bernice up so she knew that it was happening. They'd come for her, for Janet, and they'd taken her. "They're here, Bernice, listen to me. They're here. They're with me," she said. "I'm with them. I've been taken up. Just like you said. It's beautiful. Can you hear me?" She didn't really need Bernice to answer. She could answer for her. It didn't matter that she didn't have the phone in her hand, that she hadn't found it, had never dialed. Because she could answer, *Yes, yes, yes,* and she did answer, "Yes, yes, yes." She was lying by a window, peering up from the floor to the moon that she knew was out there somewhere—this enormous, far-reaching mercurial sheen. That's what it was, all of it, that's all that it was. A mist of fire and snow. It was a childish thing she said then, but she meant it, a childish breath leading to a child's sigh: "Heaven. Heaven. Heaven."

32

Bernice thought she was holding up okay. So far, so good. Intent on skirting town, she was on a road with houses few and far between, an outlying section of Belger she couldn't help but remember as the wide-open countryside from when she was a kid. Figuring a little company couldn't hurt, maybe even keep her sharp, she switched on the radio, landing on an oily-voiced adman and a flirt of a girl promoting cable television. No TV back then, she thought, still seeing the once-lush grassland that had been covered over by the pavement whispering under her wheels. Radio, if you were lucky. People on porches come evening. Porch swings, rocking chairs, the night air. Ice in iceboxes and coal clattering down chutes into dark basement bins where somebody had to feed it into the furnace if there was going to be heat in the house. Winter or summer, the iceman was some poor hunched-over fool with tongs clamped on a dripping block of ice drenching his back and trailing him up the stairs he labored to climb. It had been her dad in the basement. She could hear the scrape and crunch of the shovel digging into the heaped-up coal like it was yesterday. She could see the blade tipping through the unlatched furnace door, the dancing blue flames within. Might as well have been yesterday.

She had to get to the North End where the bridge crossed into Wisconsin and old 58 led to Sayersville. Heading straight through town would have been more direct, but she would have faced neighborhoods with stop signs and traffic lights holding her up, so she sat at deserted intersections, feeling as alone in the night as the last fool on earth.

Of course, going this way, she had to cope with a few red lights but no stop signs. And no horses, she thought. No wagons with harnessed horses clomping down the street. Not that she'd ever seen much of them. But when the sunfish weren't biting, Grandpa Thill could go on and on, glad on one day to be rid of the nags with their manure all over the road, then mourning their loss on the next, waxing poetic about their smell and their eyes, the sound of their hooves on the road. Ice wagons, junk wagons, the rich and uppity on parade in their fancy buggies, doctors deep in the night making house calls. Him and his brother, Silas, delivering groceries from their uncle's corner store with an old mare named Millie. Freight trains, too, were pretty much a thing of the past, though Bernice had seen more than her share of them. Used to be that coming up to a crossing at the wrong time, a person could get stuck watching cattle cars, boxcars, tankers, and flat cars, empty or loaded, bolting past until half a day felt lost, though it was exciting when the last of it flew by. There went the caboose, and the whole world that had been erased by that rattling blur returned. She could remember the feeling of being free to go, along with a sense of having witnessed something remarkable that was still visible way down the tracks, where the hugeness and booming clatter were fading. Her dad in the front seat would give the old Nash a tap on the gas with his toe to get them up and over the rail bed, while she thought how the train, coming from one far-off place and roaring on to another, proved there was more to the world than Belger.

Suddenly worried that she was lost, she got mad enough to spit. "You're the dumbest person alive, Bernice Doorley," she said, fretting about a turn she'd taken back a bit when she wasn't paying close attention. She'd known it was a mistake but had taken it anyway. Now she was searching for a driveway to get turned around so she could backtrack, and right as she spotted one, she heard the roar of interstate traffic. Straight ahead, faint but detectable, she saw the overpass she'd been hoping to find.

Five or six semi trucks and trailers hurtled under her in a bunched-up pack as she crossed over. Past them she spied Henry's Diner, a brightly lit truck stop next to an all-night service station on a feeder road. She figured

to get down by taking the first right. Now that she had a pretty good picture of where she was, she knew the bridge into Wisconsin was no farther
than a hop, skip, and a jump, with old 58, a beat-up two-lane, waiting on
the other side. Once she was on that, she'd be lucky to see another living
soul, let alone a gas station still open. So Henry's Diner would be her last
chance at coffee. And she ought to gas up.

She was on a flat stretch, passing a vacant lot surfaced in gravel next
to an abandoned warehouse. The big double doors sagged on their
hinges, and nearly every inch of glass was shattered. Probably kids throwing rocks. Or in this day and age, they were probably shooting guns. The
boys had made slingshots in her time, fixing a slice of worn-out inner
tube from their dad's tires onto tree forks whittled to size. Hank had
shown her how it was done, and once, along with Tommy Prescott, had
even let her shoot theirs. She'd strained to haul back on the rubber strap,
pinching tight on the little pouch with the stone inside, giggling and
blinking but determined to keep her eyes open. The dark flying dot went
out and up and then down, not far from the tin-can targets. Hank grinned
and punched his buddy in the arm, as if to say that Bernice was a pretty
good sister.

A few lightless houses, little more than oversize sheds, showed up. A
slow curve brought her to a large aluminum rectangle, which she put behind her before she realized it was Henry's Diner. The dark, closed-up
look of it made no sense until she understood she was on the back side.
Around front, the place was ablaze. She was eager for that coffee, and
since the OPEN ALL NIGHT sign was on full display at the station, she could
gas up later.

Needles and pins and downright pain, the one or the other, drilled
from her ankles into her knees and hips and on to a spasm in her lower
back the second her feet touched the ground. She grunted as the ache
went on to tie a knot in her neck. Her best bet was to just wait it out, so
she took a breath and then locked her car up safe and sound rather than
just standing there letting the time go to waste. Recovered enough to
move, she was bent a little, and every couple of steps brought a limp.

The overhead fluorescent tubes were fierce enough to darn near blind her once she hobbled inside. She had to squint to keep on course to the shiny black counter, where, as she sat, the stool spun, and she had to slap her hands down hard on the counter edge to keep from landing on the floor. That was when she felt a stab of fear and had to wonder if she was headed for trouble, trying to make this drive. For the first time she had to ask what on earth she thought she was doing.

"What can I get you, hon?" said a jaunty voice.

Running down the source, Bernice met the glossy, overly made-up face of a waitress coming toward her. She was so perky she was scary, like she was all set for a party that was going to break out any second.

"Up a little past your bedtime, aren't you?" the woman grinned.

Did everybody think they could pick on her? What with the blinding lights and the mean-spirited stool and now this woman giving her a dig, Bernice felt ganged up on past what she was willing to bear. "What business is it of yours, if I am?"

"Sorr-eeee," the woman said, like she thought she was a teenager.

"A cup of coffee, please."

"Anything else?"

"I'd like two coffees, as a matter of fact. One for here and one to go."

"Sure thing." Her smile was as fake as her eyelashes, and all part of the same half-baked act Bernice wasn't buying. But then the woman rolled her eyes, and Bernice realized that the entire show, every flounce and smirk, was for the benefit of an audience situated behind her somewhere.

Girlie giggles mixed with grumbles drew her around with a twinge that called her hand to her neck. Teenagers were stuffed in a booth, three boys and a couple of girls. Nervously rolling a pearl from her necklace between her thumb and forefinger, Bernice saw how they were sniggering and clutching at each other, as if they needed rescue from gaiety before it made them sick. She didn't have to think twice to gather that she was the butt of whatever stupid joke they thought made them so clever. The little peeks they stole at her gave it away, and then they checked with each other, like they didn't think they could stand how they were going to bust a gut if Bernice didn't cut it out, because she was just getting funnier and funnier by the second. Something about her. Probably the fact that she was alive—that she was there at all. In their world. Which was pretty much the whole wide world, the way they looked at things. Way too big for their britches, and you could say that for a fact. They kept eyeing her and conferring before throwing back their heads with their hands over their mouths, like they wanted more than anything to stuff their bratty guffaws back, but they couldn't because she was just too comical.

On the other hand, maybe they had her number, she thought, digging her billfold from her purse and laying down a five-dollar bill. She was an old fogey, and she probably did look like something the cat dragged in. She glanced up as both coffees were served, the one in a white china cup, the other in a Styrofoam container. The waitress nudged a metal pitcher of milk near, along with sugar and artificial sweeteners. Watching the tidy rearrangement, Bernice had to admit that the truth was, she could easily be as bad off as Hazel had been, or maybe worse, and not have a clue—bleary-eyed and smudged, puffed up and halfway green. Maybe if she got a gander at herself, she'd be yukking it up right along with them.

Tearing the bill from her pad, the waitress said, "Come again."

"I'm gonna apologize," Bernice told her. "For snapping at you that way. I probably do look a fright, and truth be told, I am so tired, I don't know if I'm coming or going. So I apologize."

"Don't you think twice about it, hon. I have to take a lot of shit." Her wink somehow substituted spite for friendliness. The same was true of her smile as she sashayed off.

Did the owner of this place—Henry, if that was his name—know what a nasty thing he had representing him to the public? She doubted it. But there was no doubting that the snot of a waitress thought she was in cahoots with the wiseacres in the booth. Thirty at least, the cheeky thing thought she could get away with acting sixteen. Bernice added milk and sugar and sat there with her coffee. It would take a minute to cool. When it came to her that she was fingering the earring in her sore right ear, she decided it was time to take them off. Round white porcelain the size of quarters rimmed in gold, they were beautiful but heavy. Deciding she was done with them for the night, she smiled fondly, hauling up her purse and placing them protectively inside.

The big clasp shut with a click that seemed to ignite a blast of sniggering and snorting, and she glanced around quick enough to find the whole sassy gang gawking at her as one of the girls, a redhead with bright spitfire eyes, pinched her nose shut, like something stank. Oh, she was feisty. They were all feisty. Knew how to show off, all right. Smart-alecky know-it-alls full of piss and vinegar, every one of them. Oh well, in another couple minutes she'd be done with the whole swellheaded bunch, so full of themselves. So sure they knew everything. In their heyday and going to be in it forever. Going to be young forever. Fat chance, she thought, enjoying a wicked little sense of superiority all her own, because she had the inside dope on that one. She knew just how they were all going to end up. And that was just like her. If they lived long enough. Maybe she should let them in on the big surprise. Because she knew what it was like to be young and sitting with Isabel Cawley—who wasn't Cawley then but Blanchard, just like Bernice wasn't Doorley yet but Demming, so they were Bernice Demming and Isabel Blanchard killing time at the soda fountain in Ohlson's Drugstore, the two of them swinging back and forth on stools pretty much like this one under her now, eating banana splits and finding old Mrs. Kloft just about the silliest thing they ever saw. The way she stood clutching that little beige coin purse and staring at the shelf full of aspirin bottles and then picking one up and counting her pennies and putting it back and picking it up—and her stockings droopy around her knees—well, she just had to be the biggest ninny to ever come down the pike, as far as they could see, and Bernice and Isabel were all but falling off their stools, laughing so hard they had tears in their eyes. Because the one thing they knew for sure was they were never going to be that old. The two of them swellheaded and just as stuck on themselves as that shiftless bunch in the booth behind her. She could tell them a thing or two, and maybe she would. The coffee was making her bold, and she emptied the cup and rattled it, asking for more. She'd give the pack of them a look when she left, just to let them know she was on to them. Stare them down. See how they liked it. Walk out with her head high. Because they didn't know the half of it, glued to their MTVs and Game Boys and whatnots. She ought to tell them about Donnie Holdridge hopping a freight train to run away from home and slipping under the wheels. Or Emma Weber trying to give herself an abortion with a coat hanger and tearing her insides up. Or her cousin Miriam, wanting to run away from home but going headfirst into that hole. Or poor Mary Madigan all alone after her twin, Carrie, drowned. Or Hank, her brother, coming back from the war nothing but skin and bones. He'd unfolded a red and white Japanese flag so big it covered the floor of the living room, where he wanted to leave it, but their dad made him settle for a wall in the garage. Sometimes he'd take it and put it up on the side of the house, and it would cover the whole of it, mostly. He had a bayonet, too, big as a sword, the way Bernice saw it, and when she told him it looked rusty, he told her it was bloodstained. And that scary Japanese pistol in a brown leather holster, stinking of sweat that had to be Japanese sweat from the Japanese man who never would have given that gun up unless somebody killed him to get it. Hank told about being close to dead himself so many times he'd lost count. He'd nearly died of tanks and bullets and bombs and cannons, nearly drowned three or four times, and in one big battle, it was so hot it was like they were being cooked alive in an oven, explosions and screams and blood running down from the higher ground to sink in the boiling sand, so none of them thought they would get out of there alive, and after a while there were some, and he was one of them, who thought maybe they didn't want to. Hank, she thought, wanting to remember something different, something nice, and then she did—that wonderful time when their living room needed painting, but she was useless because she had the flu. Hank came to help, and he brought cowboy hats for them all to wear, even her, as if they would paint better in cowboy hats, and Irma, who was no more than ten, and Toby and Hank did the whole job, with Bernice just lying on the couch watching.

The night gave her a lonesome feeling once she was back out in it, like it was a big hall she'd walked into where she wasn't expected and no one knew her. When she crossed over the wide part of the river, she wasn't on the scary long-gone bridge Hazel had worried about, but she felt like she was, and she heard the passage of her tires whistling through row after row of holes in that steel roadway that had disappeared years ago. Sneaking along so high up, she felt airborne above the water spread out in both directions with only a few lights ahead on the Wisconsin side. She didn't dare peek down for too long at the rippling waves glinting in patches like thousands of razor blades surrounded by blackness that looked choppy and cold. Her poor heart half expected every girder and weld and rivet to vanish right out from under her. Twinkling Belger lay off to her right, and she thought she could see all the way to where she had started, the farmland over there widening out around a spread of lights she was pretty sure could be Homestead. Not that long ago, Belger had been neighborhoods crowded around a business district. It haunted her, that old order. It seemed to still exist somewhere. Or it ought to, anyway, instead of all this newfangled sprawl where everywhere was the same as everywhere else. Back then there'd been a downtown with a street called Main Street, because that was what it was. It had all the important stores like JCPenney and Woolworth's and Sears and Kenning's Drugstore along with Billing's Hardware and Rhomberg's Department Store and Gustavson's Restaurant with old Mr. Gustavson, who had once been a chef in Europe, and the first of the Loefler's Restaurants had been down there, too. The movie theaters were the Strand, State, Grand, Orpheum, and the ice cream parlor had that big fat Mr. Schmidt running it and eating ice cream and smiling every time you went in. You could get dropped off and walk from one place to the next. Of course, you could do that at the mall, too, but downtown had been different and better somehow.

Ahead, things looked knotty and twisted, like the inside of a storm, but she was still glad the bridge was falling away behind her. Old 58 turned wild, the first strong descent pushing her into a tunnel of shadows tumbling out of clumps of forest. Soon she was gliding over long patches of highway between open fields.

With the radio on, she tasted music from the fifties, and then some longhaired stuff with fancy horns and unhappy violins that made her anxious, so she moved on. She heard a commercial for used cars with jingles and pitches, and then a White Sale was announced at Rhomberg's back in Belger. Specials were offered at Jane's Beauty Parlor, which she'd never heard of, even though the address given was right near where she lived. The road weaved past bluffs and dodged a creek, then used a stone bridge to span a gulley that she suspected was a section of the same creek, all dried up for some reason. The radio had gone on to sports, giving out baseball scores from the play-offs. Hearing the names—Marlins, Braves, Indians, Orioles—made her miss Toby, so she shut the darn thing off.

Entering Conway, a little one-horse town known far and wide as a speed trap, she slowed way down, because even in the wee hours, the local cop could be skulking around to pounce on some poor slob too tired to spot the twenty-five-mile-an-hour speed limit posted on a sign half hidden in the bushes. She sank to twenty and didn't pick back up until some miles on another signpost gave its official stamp of approval to fifty-five. Not that she went anywhere near that. She was barely comfortable at forty and backed off that if the curves got too sharp.

The moon surprised her, rising into view and waiting dead ahead at the end of a steep climb. It had been off to her right, and then, as the terrain shifted and rose and twined, she had seen it sinking from sight on her left. Suddenly, brown leaves were twirling and skittering in her headlights, and the moon hung directly ahead and weirdly low. Everything felt out of place, and she went searching the landscape to get her bearings, because she had the feeling something else might be amiss. When she looked back, she had no idea where she was. She recognized the fact of the road running away before her, but it seemed to have appeared out of nowhere—or she'd appeared on it—because she didn't have a clue where she was or where she wanted to go. A tree in a wide meadow drew her attention, something in its outline distinct and memorable. Studying the peculiar shape, she hoped to identify her surroundings as a place she had traveled through at some other time. But if she had ever been here before, she didn't know it. The pavement was battered, the white center line worn into frayed dashes. Turning and dipping and turning again, she held firm to the wheel. She was so tired and scared that her eyesight was dimming. Was she headed home? But why was she out so late? Maybe home was straight ahead. But if her mom and dad were waiting up and worrying, they'd be furious. She was going to catch hell and get herself a terrible whipping if she dared come traipsing in the front door this time of night. Her dad would tear his belt from its loops. He was going to tan her hide good. But where else could she go but home?

Oh Lord, she thought, help me out here. She searched the shoulder for a place to pull over and await rescue, or sit until daylight. The weeds and shrubs were threatening. They pressed out onto the roadway, and there were ridges and jagged rocky overhangs. She prayed a little more, and then, spotting a possible clearing on the right, she whispered, "Thank you, Lord. Thank you, Jesus." And her ignorance vanished. It all came sweeping back in an instant, even her clear vision. She sputtered in amazement at the memory of it all—Reverend Tauke and Hazel and General—that crazy bridge and Irma and how downright cute Jesus had been. How sly. Just showing up and saying the things He did. Oh, sure, He was laying down the law and leaving no doubt about what He wanted from her. But funny about it. Strong and forceful. But friendly and smiling. Sharp as a tack. And right on the nose. Because she should have known to give her little girl the helping hand she needed right at the start and not laughed like everybody else did just because laughing was what Grandpa wanted and most everybody was scared of him. But Jesus was right. It was like she'd been trying to protect her pa from his own cruelty by going along with him the way she did. Just going along with his idea that it was funny when it was just mean. You hear that, Dad? It was just mean. Nothing funny about poor Irma wanting you to love her and being so proud when she thought you did.

The first hint of Sayersville was the cemetery with that beautiful old iron gate, ten feet at least, and all those curls in the grille imitating flowers. The fence on both sides was tall black spikes that she really couldn't pick out in the dark. Details were hard to come by now that the moon was missing. She figured the cause was the road sinking down below the hillside that the grave markers flowed up. Ahead, a gas station under a lone streetlight told her that she had arrived in town. She passed quiet houses and then came to the stores that made up Main Street, where more dangling, swaying, lonely-looking streetlights came into view, but still stayed pretty scarce. She had to go all the way through to the end before turning at the firehouse onto MacDougal. Irma and John lived way out at the end where the road became dirt maybe fifty yards beyond their driveway. They had the last house built as the town expanded in that direction, though they hadn't been the builders and were, in fact, paying rent. It was a nice little ranch-style home with neat redbrick walls and white trim that faced across the road onto miles of cornfield. She could see it up ahead, the pickup in the driveway, the unlit windows, no sign of life at all as, slowing to a crawl, she sneaked past.

Feeling the change of the dirt under her tires, she parked, and with the engine off, the countryside threw up a towering quiet. It seemed to rise from the cornfield that had been chopped low but still ran in neat rows to its rim, where the moon was back now, though small, just a faintly purple shimmer like the head of a spoon bouncing twinkle and glimmer onto the tiny sketch of a way-off fence.

She rolled down the window and sat, looking out. The cool air felt nice, and she breathed some in. A while back she'd decided that marching up to Irma's front door the second she got there wasn't the smartest idea. Waking everybody up out of a sound sleep so they were scared half to death by her showing up out of nowhere, like there was some kind of emergency, she wouldn't exactly be putting her best foot forward. They'd be groggy and cranky and well within their rights. So she'd just have to wait till somebody woke up. She had that winter coat, should she need something more than her flannel jacket, but she doubted she would. Still, she reached and tugged it up into the front with her.

Last she'd heard, John still had that part-time job on Saturday mornings working as a janitor at the grade school, so he'd have to drag himself out of bed by seven, and Irma being Irma would crawl out ahead so the poor guy wouldn't have to cook his own breakfast. The kitchen lights going on would be her cue. She'd give them time enough for coffee and then head on over. It wasn't going to be easy, but she'd ask for a chance to get her apology said and hope to make sense. Picturing Irma listening intently, and then the both of them letting all those headstrong years disappear, felt like a prayer, and that got her thinking how maybe Jesus, wanting them to reconcile the way He did, might help out. Maybe He was already over there laying down some kind of groundwork in Irma's mind by visiting her in her sleep and giving her a little dream of the two of them free of everything but their heart-and-soul love.

A rustling in a nearby cluster of weeds showed her the outline of a rabbit standing as still as a statue. And watching him and the way he was so thoughtfully considering the night, as if he was the only rabbit in the world and the night and everything in it belonged to him, reminded her of how she used to sit with Toby, him in the one chair, her in the other, and they'd be doing the crossword puzzle together, and he'd be frowning, thinking so hard, and sometimes she'd know the answer but she would keep it to herself. Wouldn't come up with it so he could. And it made her feel so sad now to see that she missed that, of all things. How she'd hold her tongue and not speak, and more often than not, given half a chance, he'd come up with the answer and jot it down in that cocky manner of his, that self-satisfied way that somehow combined bragging with humility and this odd little sense of bravery. All because she'd waited and given him a chance.

A light was on in Irma's house, and she knew the layout well enough to be sure it was the bathroom. Then it went out. Bernice imagined whoever it was flushing the toilet and making their way back down the hall and then climbing back into bed, tugging the covers up, shifting around for a peaceful position. Or maybe they'd happened to glance out the window and had spotted her dark car stopped in that strange place, and so they were still there, staring out even now, secretly, trying to see well enough to figure out who it was at the end of the road, holding the curtain open just a slit so they could stay hidden the way Bernice used to kneel by her bedroom window, peering past the bottom edge of the blind onto Freddie Kane, who loved her and used to park his dad's car across from her house and just sit there. He was crazy for Bernice and seventeen, a full year older. Her dad would go charging out the door and chase him away sometimes, but there were nights when nobody knew he was out there except Bernice, and he sat in his car smoking cigarettes for hours. At school he couldn't even look at her if she tried to meet his eye.

The one or two times they talked, he mainly sighed and shifted and twisted, like he was full of this terrible ache he couldn't get away from. It made her feel strange, and everybody said he was spooky. A nutcase. Way too intense. No fun at all. She thought he did look sort of unhealthy, and he was a bookworm. Sometimes he struck her as looking a little like that snooty one from *Our Gang* movies. Alfalfa. But with beautiful hair. And he loved her in a way that made no sense. He was wild for her, dreaming outside her window, while she knelt inside, trying to fathom what it was he dreamed.

Her head was against the headrest, and she'd turned onto her side as much as she could, and she knew she'd be asleep in the next few seconds. She could feel it coming on, a gathering heaviness slowing down her thoughts that were, for the moment, full of Freddie Kane and the way he'd loved her. Where was he now? she wondered. And how had it all gone for him?

ACKNOWLEDGMENTS

First came the anecdote from a friend, Paula Gieseman, as I visited my mom some years ago in the town where I grew up, Dubuque, Iowa. Before anyone else, I have to thank her for telling me about the elderly woman who came knocking at her door asking for a favor. After that I was alone with the idea and what it might mean to me, and eventually alone with the writing until well into the story, perhaps four fifths of the way through, when I felt the need for some rudimentary feedback. I hired Rachel Berg to do a little copyediting. She gave the basic and enthusiastic response that I was hoping for at the time. And then she went on, as the months passed, to become an astute reader of the new material, re-reader of the old, a dogged researcher, and a source of sympathetic, valued prodding. Then came the crucial moment when my wife, Jill, went off with the manuscript. Though always supportive, she has not loved everything I've written. Her heartfelt exuberance was more than gratifying. Later on, the book benefited from the attention of Sheryl Kennedy, Davyne Verstandig, and Pat Toomay; my son Michael, who saw the spirit of the story in the moment-to-moment fluctuation of emotions; my son Jason, who responded to the intermingled fates of the humans and animals; my daughter Lily, who offered a key piece of advice. Late in the process, my sister, Marsha Rabe, became a regular, reliable sounding board as I polished and made final changes. Given our shared Midwestern roots, her insights, relish, and embrace of the book and characters had a special worth for me. Thanks to Dr. Jerry Clements and Dr. Gerald Fromm.

Thanks to Robin Sweeney for the sage, to Deborah Schneider for the promise she made, to David Rosenthal for his wonderful phone message, and to Sarah Hochman for steering the course from manuscript to book. And, finally, thanks to Okitty, Swinger, Mittens, and Mongo Jerry, the cats, and to Mickey, Midnight, Blueberry, Flash, Ruby, Tricks, Saz, and Tizja, the dogs.

ABOUT THE AUTHOR

David Rabe has been hailed as one of America's greatest living play-wrights. He is the author of many widely performed plays, including *The Basic Training of Pavlo Hummel, Sticks and Bones, In the Boom Boom Room, Streamers, Hurlyburly,* and *The Dog Problem.* Four of his plays have been nominated for Tony awards, including one win for Best Broadway Play. He is the recipient of an Obie Award, the American Academy of Arts and Letters Award, the Drama Desk Award, and the New York Drama Critics Circle Award, among others. His numerous screenwriting credits include *I'm Dancing as Fast as I Can, Casualties of War, Hurlyburly,* and *The Firm.*

Rabe is the critically acclaimed author of the novel *Recital of the Dog* and a collection of short stories, *A Primitive Heart.* Born in Dubuque, Iowa, Rabe lives with his family and two dogs in northwest Connecticut.